"Stella, I've got to ask you something. Something important." Mac removed the note from his pocket and laid it on the table.

"Regarding Aubrey?"

"Yes." He leaned forward and lowered his voice even though no one was within easy hearing. "Have you ever told anyone what happened?"

She blinked with surprise, but didn't seem to be upset by the question. "No, of course not."

"Are you sure?"

Stella glanced at the nearest table and, lowering her voice, said, "Certainly. Something like that doesn't slip out accidentally in conversation."

"What about with your therapist or masseuse or hairdresser?"

"Mac, I'm not an idiot. Don't you think I appreciate how sensitive that is? I scarcely allow myself to think about it, much less discuss it with anyone. Why?"

"I haven't said anything, either," he said. "Which means I'm hard-pressed to explain this note somebody left at my front door a couple of days ago." He slid the envelope across the table to her.

Stella picked it up, glancing at what had been written on the outside.

"Go ahead, read it."

She removed the slip of paper, her fingers trembling slightly. Mac watched her eyes. They rounded as she read, "I know what you did on Friday, October 13, 1978."

GLAMOURPUSS

R.J. KAISER

MIRA

ISBN 1-55166-614-6

GLAMOUR PUSS

Copyright © 2000 by Belles-Lettres, Inc.

Visit us at www.mirabooks.com

Printed in U.S.A.

To the memory of my mother,
Ruth E. Kaiser,
1913 to 1999.

The Past

Friday, October 13, 1978

West Los Angeles

Joseph McGowan was funny about some things. Adultery, for example. He never liked the word. Or what it stood for.

Of course, later, when Stella told him adultery was no longer a crime in California, he felt better about it. But only a little. "You don't have anything to worry about," she'd said. "I'm the one who committed adultery. You were a fornicator." Stella had a way of putting the most suggestive spin on things sometimes. But, considering he was only twenty-four, Joseph McGowan—known to the world as Mac McGowan—kind of liked that about her. It made her seem dangerous.

Standing in her backyard as Manny and Todd built the forms, Mac glanced up at the second-floor slider on the balcony outside Stella's bedroom. Sure enough, she was peeking from behind the drapes, smiling at him. Then she stuck out her bare leg for anybody to see. She could be a tease, that Stella. And she sure knew how to embarrass him.

Mac looked to see if the guys noticed, but they were busy doing their job. He shook his finger at her, giving her a disapproving look. But that only egged her on, because the next thing he knew, Stella had jumped out from behind the drapes in a little beach cover-up and flashed him. Then she closed the robe and blew him a kiss.

Mac about died, turning bright red. She must have known she'd embarrassed him because he could see her laugh. "You shouldn't do that," he'd told her a few days earlier when she'd done the same thing. "One of the guys might see."

"Where's your sense of adventure, Mac? You've got to loosen up."

"Hey, I'm making love to a married woman, practically under her husband's nose, and you're questioning my sense of adventure?"

"You're not doing that for the excitement," she'd said. "You're doing it for love."

And the funny thing was, he couldn't dispute that, even in his own mind.

"Hey, boss," Manny said, tossing down his shovel. "Any chance of me…" Having noticed Mac staring up at the house, he looked up, too. "Will you look at that," he said. "She's standing there in that little skimpy outfit again. You know, boss, she spends as much time looking at us as we do at her."

"I think she's lonely," Mac said innocently. "How'd you like to spend your days all by yourself in that big house?"

"With her, I wouldn't mind," Manny said, twisting his lip. "I think the woman's problem is she needs a good fuck."

Mac felt the color rising in his face again, but at least he knew Manny wasn't onto him, which was a good thing. Mac wasn't one to talk about his conquests, nor did he want to set a bad example. Hitting on the customers, especially customers' wives, was not the message he wanted to send to his crew.

"Never mind her," he said, reeling in his tape measure. "What were you saying?"

Manny gave a final glance up at Stella's window, but she'd already stepped away. "Uh...I was wondering if you'd mind if I took off a little early. I got to go by the DMV and straighten out a problem with my vehicle registration. Anyway, today's Friday the thirteenth. The less work done, the less you risk screwing up."

"Assuming you're superstitious," Mac said.

"You aren't?"

"No, but I was thinking we ought to knock off soon, anyway."

Manny, pleased to hear it, grinned.

"A short day today," Mac said, "but we make up for it tomorrow. We got to get this pool poured, which means showing up prepared to work. Todd," he called across the site, "let's knock off. We've got an early morning."

"And Monday we're off, too, right?"

"Right."

Mac moved to the other side of the huge hole in the ground where he could keep an eye on Stella's window without being obvious. He was already thinking about getting laid, which was fine, except he had to keep his wits about him enough to get this job done properly. They were at the stage where all the forms were pretty much in place and were ready for the first cement truck to come rolling in.

After a few minutes Manny and Todd had gathered their tools and were ready to go. "Don't forget, we've got an early start," he told them.

"Sure thing, boss," Todd said.

After glancing up at Stella's window, Manny nodded, then said goodbye. He and Todd lumbered off. Once they'd disappeared around the side of the house, Mac put his hands on his hips and gazed up at Stella's window once more. Sure enough, she appeared, smiling and posing in her little cover-up. She opened it again, but instead of a quick flash, she let it slide off her shoulders and drop to the floor. She was naked as a jaybird, and Mac, knowing what lay ahead, felt himself starting to get hard.

Stella held up a finger as if to say, "I'll be down in a minute," then she left the window. Mac went over to the pool house to wait for her. The place had a shower, but Stella told him she didn't want him to get cleaned up before they made love. "I want a raw man," she'd told him. "Just the way you are."

Mac knew he was living a fantasy, having sex daily with a beautiful starlet. And it was just as well he was close-mouthed about his personal life, because nobody would believe him.

There was a hitch, of course. Stella's husband. Aubrey St. George was not your average chump. He was a first-class, dyed-in-the-wool bastard. Pushy, condescending and downright mean. It was the mean part that got to Mac most.

He didn't want to use the fact that Aubrey was a prick to justify the fact that he was a fornicator. In fact, Mac felt terribly guilty. But he was able to live with himself because he was protecting Stella. Her vulnerability made it seem right that they should be together—almost destined.

Stella had a way of making a guy feel pretty good about himself, too. She made him feel like a stud. "God," she'd said after their first time. "Whatever made me think Glamour Puss was good? Compared to you, Mac, he's a piker."

That's the way everyone referred to Aubrey St. George—Glamour Puss. "When's Glamour Puss coming home?" he'd ask. "You sure he won't just show up unexpected?" And she'd say, "Don't worry about Glamour

Puss, he's off getting laid. And don't ask me who with. I've lost track."

In film circles, Aubrey St. George was called Glamour Puss because he was both handsome and self-possessed. But Mac and Stella used the term with derision. Mac didn't feel bad about that—just like he didn't feel too bad about laying the guy's wife in the first place—because Aubrey was a certified SOB. He was cruel to Stella, treating her worse than a dog. More than once, Mac had worried about her safety. When he'd told her that, she'd given him a kiss on the corner of the mouth and said, "You're a sweet man, Mac McGowan." The little quiver in her voice told him she meant it.

Maybe he was sweet, he didn't know. His mother used to tell him stuff like that when he was growing up and, yes, he was the type who'd dance with the wallflowers in high school, even if he was something of a stud. Not that he was a pretty boy like Aubrey St. George. Maybe not even truly handsome. Mac was "good-looking." At twenty-four, he was six-three, masculine, athletic, well built, fair. Stella called him a "big lug," but one who "sure knows his way around the bedroom." Mostly, though, she liked him because he made her feel safe. Mac liked that a lot because making her feel safe was exactly what he wanted to do. And with that as a starting point, love couldn't be far behind.

Mac was not one to hate people, but Aubrey St. George was someone he just couldn't abide. Actually, he'd formed a low opinion of the man the first time he laid eyes on him—the day Mac had first come to their house to bid on the new pool. He'd seen Stella for the first time that day, too, but they didn't speak. He had glimpses of her in the kitchen in this little yellow bikini, and later, when she'd come out on the deck. The image of her—blond and vulnerable—stuck in his brain and haunted him during the couple of weeks between that day and when they broke ground. It probably even induced him to trim some of the profit out of his bid to make sure he got the job.

St. George, much smaller than the man Mac had seen numerous times on the big silver screen, had greeted him at the door bare-chested, wearing shorts and with his Persian cat, G.P., in his arms. In naming his cat after himself, Glamour Puss not only showed how self-centered he was, but also that, after a fashion, he had a sense of humor. The actor, perfectly tanned, his blue eyes stunning against the backdrop of carefully coiffed dark hair and lashes, had said, "Mac McGowan? I didn't expect anybody so young."

"I've got plenty of experience, Mr. St. George. It's all on the info sheets I sent."

Aubrey looked at him critically as he stroked G.P. "Were you the one who did Jack Palance's pool?"

"Yes, sir."

"Well, come have a look at the site."

Mac had followed him through the house. Stella was at the kitchen table in her bikini, reading a magazine.

"Can you get off your butt long enough to get me a beer?" Aubrey snarled at her as they headed for the deck. "You want one, McGowan?"

"No thank you, sir."

"Just one!" he shouted back at Stella.

The two men had stood on the deck looking down the slope on which the house had been built, Aubrey stroking his cat, Mac evaluating the configuration of the land.

"The engineers were aware you were putting a pool in," Mac said.

"Yes. The big retaining wall down there was engineered precisely for that purpose."

Mac nodded, admiring the view for the first time. Brentwood lay in the smoggy haze around them. Most of the homes on the surrounding hillsides were newer, like the modern glass-and-wood marvel Aubrey St. George had built for himself and his twenty-eight-year-old wife. The star himself was pushing forty—Mac didn't know his exact age. He'd go to a movie now and then, but the gossip end of the Hollywood scene didn't interest him.

Not that he didn't hear things. The stewardess he'd dated off and on the past few months, Linda Maas, was really into the star gossip. When he'd told her he was bidding on a job for Aubrey St. George, she'd flipped. "Oh, how neat! You're so lucky, Mac. Boy, I'd sure love to meet him."

Besides Jack Palance, Mac had done a pool in Beverly Hills for a producer who Linda had never heard of, but that was pretty much the extent of his Hollywood jobs. His main interest was in the customer's ability to pay. "I'm a businessman," he told Linda, who found his nonchalance annoying. But, of course, Stella made *this* job more than just a business proposition.

When she'd come out onto the deck with Aubrey's beer, Stella had given Mac this embarrassed little smile, but there was pain in it, too. He was as aware of her torment as he was of her full breasts, her nipped-in waist and the sweet curve of her hips. Had he been Aubrey St. George, he'd have been stroking Stella, not the damn cat.

"So, how long you been in business?" Aubrey asked him.

"On my own, just over a year," Mac told him, "but I ran jobs for Stinski Pools for a year before that."

"They're bidding this job."

"Yeah, and I'll be under them by ten percent, plus you'll be getting the personal attention of the best foreman they ever had and haven't yet replaced."

Aubrey had grinned at the remark. "Pretty cocky for a kid, aren't you, McGowan?"

"In the business world, you've got to be sure of your-self, sir."

"Where you from? My guess is not L.A."

"No, sir. Toledo. When I got back from Nam, I decided to give California a shot. My mother died of cancer when I was still in-country and my father passed away when I was in high school. I didn't have a lot of reason to go back home."

"You picked the right business, kid. Everybody in California wants a pool."

"That's what I figure."

They'd walked the site. Mac took a good long look at the wall that had been reinforced with steel beams. With the heavy equipment he had to bring in, he didn't want the hillside giving way.

Aubrey showed him the pool house he'd had the con-tractor put in—the same pool house where Mac and Stella later made love on a daily basis, though, of course, at the time he couldn't have remotely conceived of that possi-bility. Mac was a straight shooter—not the type who ran around screwing other men's wives. At least, not until Stella St. George.

The week between the day he went to work for Glamour Puss and the day Stella first undressed him in the pool house seemed like a six-month courtship. It was amazing how quickly they'd gotten to know each other. But when she'd greeted him at the door his first day on the job, she'd struck him as shy, even self-conscious, which was odd, considering she was the wife of a big Hollywood star.

"If you need anything, a drink, a snack, just let me know," she'd said.

"That's very kind of you, Mrs. St. George, but my men and I bring our own provisions."

"Well, the offer's open."

She'd had on a little white summer dress and high-heel

sandals, the strappy kind that make a woman's feet look naked. But it was the sadness in her eyes that had gotten to him. The second morning on the job, he and Todd and Manny had been working about an hour when they heard a terrible din inside the house. There'd been yelling and glass breaking, cussing and the sound of Stella weeping. They could tell Aubrey was doing a number on her. A short time later they'd heard his Porsche go racing down the street. Then, at the end of the workday, after Todd and Manny had gone home, Mac was putting away his tools when Stella came out onto the deck.

"Mr. McGowan," she called to him. "How about a beer?"

She had two mugs in her hand and clearly wanted him to say, "Yeah, sure, why not?" Hell, the beer had already been poured. Mac was stripped to the waist, wearing jeans, boots and sunglasses, which made him feel self-conscious. But, recalling the row she'd had that morning with her husband and having worried about her all day, he decided it wouldn't hurt to be sociable. The sight of those long legs of hers didn't hurt, either.

By the time Mac had climbed up the steps to the big, sweeping deck, he could see the damage Aubrey had done. Her left eye was all puffed up, and she'd put a little Band-Aid in the corner where it had been cut. Somehow she managed not to look embarrassed.

"Did Mr. St. George do that to you, ma'am?"

She put the mug in his hand. "Aubrey has a temper." She motioned toward the big comfortable cushioned chairs and led the way across the redwood deck.

"It's wrong to do that to a pretty face like yours," he said, following her. "For that matter, it's wrong period. Nobody should have to go through that, least of all a woman."

"Aubrey says pretty faces are a dime a dozen. Thank

you for saying that, though, Mr. McGowan.'' She sat
down, crossing her shapely legs.

He dropped into the chair next to her, conscious of his
filthy pants and sweaty body. ''Call me Mac, ma'am.''

''I will if you stop calling me ma'am,'' she said with a
smile. ''My name's Stella.''

''Okay.'' He reached over and tapped his mug against
hers.

They each drank.

''I don't get a lot of sympathy,'' she said. ''Plenty of
women would change places with me in a minute, whether
it meant getting boxed around a little or not.''

''That is a real shame. No man has that right, I don't
care who he is.''

She studied him, her mug poised near her lips. ''You're
very protective, aren't you?''

Mac had colored, thinking perhaps he'd gone too far.
''Maybe I should keep my two cents' to myself.''

''I don't see why. You're right.''

Aubrey St. George's grayish-beige Persian, G.P., came
slithering along the deck just then, rubbing against Stella's
ankles. She gently nudged it away with her foot and then
crossed her legs, showing lots of thigh. Looking at her,
even with the banged-up eye, Mac's heart had kind of gone
ping. She was as pretty as any woman he'd ever seen. She
had a fabulous body. She was soulful…needy. She touched
him.

He took a long drink for courage, then said, ''I know
it's none of my business, but why do you put up with the
abuse?''

''I put up with it because I don't have a lot of choice,
unless I want to become a salesgirl at Frederick's of Hollywood. Aubrey has a lot of juice in this town. And he's
also got a very favorable prenup.''

''Favorable what?''

She'd smiled as though he'd said something funny. "Prenuptial agreement. Under the terms, if I divorce him, I get fifty thousand per year of marriage, regardless how much he makes. If he divorces me, it's double that. We've been married two and a half years. You figure it out."

"You wouldn't exactly be on the street."

Again she smiled. "I have to put up with some unpleasantness, but I live well. This life would be hard to walk away from," she said, waving vaguely at her big house. "Besides, I'm still hoping for my chance in films. Glamour Puss keeps telling me he'll talk to some people at the studio, but he doesn't want me hanging around like a hungry starlet who'll do anything for a role because he's afraid it will make him look bad. And that means I'm sort of stuck between a rock and a hard place. I'm totally at Aubrey's mercy."

Mac could see her dilemma, but he sure didn't like what she had to endure. Maybe he liked it even less than Stella herself.

After finishing his beer, Mac thanked her. But before he'd managed to get to his feet, she'd reached over and patted his hand. "You're a nice man, Mac. Not many guys are as concerned and thoughtful."

He hadn't known what to say because he didn't see himself as particularly special. In fact, he was just a "regular Joe," an epithet which got him some laughs whenever he used it.

That night Mac had lain awake for hours, thinking about Stella. It wasn't like him to get obsessed with a woman, but he had a terrible urge to drive over there, drag her out of that house and bring her home. Not that he expected she'd want that. In the end, he decided that if St. George ever whacked Stella in front of him, he'd knock the SOB on his ass.

The day after that, he'd hung around the job site after

the boys had gone home and, sure enough, Stella had come
out onto the deck again with a couple of mugs of beer.

Her eye looked a lot better after a night's rest. When he
told her that, she said, "Aubrey was in a better mood this
morning."

Mac wanted to say, "Well, hooray for him." But didn't.
He hated the guy.

Stella had on shorts and a little halter top and bare feet
the second time they had a beer together. She had her hair
piled up on her head, exposing her long neck. He kept
staring at her skin, thinking how he'd like to kiss it. For a
minute, the idea went through his head that she might be
a tease, but then he realized that the wife of a big-time
movie star wouldn't have any interest in a nobody swimming-pool contractor.

They'd joked around some, but mostly talked about serious things. Stella told him she was from Ames, Iowa,
that her real name was Judy Miller, and that after a year
of community college, she couldn't hack small-town life.
So, a week before the start of her second year of college,
she'd gotten on a bus and headed for sunny Southern California to find fame and fortune.

"Things seemed to have worked out," Mac said.

"Not without a struggle. I didn't have much money and
my parents weren't well off. My father worked at a grain
elevator until he got injured in a fall and went on disability.
They sent me a few thousand dollars, but the cost of living
being what it was in California, I was going through
money like it was water. I waitressed a little, hustled drinks
until I got fired for being too slow. Took as many acting
lessons as I could afford. Shared an apartment with four
girls and finally got so desperate I signed a contract to do
a nude photo spread for a men's magazine."

"Did you do it?"

"No, the next day I met Aubrey, and when I told him

about the photo spread, he said that if I was going to debauch myself, better I do it with him. He took me back to his place and seduced me. I became his mistress…I should say his live-in mistress. He was seeing other women on the side, even then."

"Forgive me, but this guy sounds like bad news. I don't care if he is a famous movie star."

"Mac, you're an idealist."

"Well, are you happy? Do you love him?"

"You're definitely an idealist."

"Seems to me that shouldn't be a hard question for a wife to answer."

"You know something, your innocence is really appealing."

Mac hadn't liked that comment, but he was in no position to complain. Stella St. George was giving him free beer and she thought enough of him to sit and talk. All he could figure was that she must be awfully lonely.

Still, Mac's instincts, which were usually pretty good, told him Stella wanted something, he just didn't know what. That afternoon she brought out a TV tray with some snacks, in addition to the beer.

"What would your husband say if he knew you were socializing with the help?" he asked.

"Oh, he'd be royally pissed."

"Then why do it?"

"Because I like you, Mac. And also because you make me feel safe."

He took that to mean she enjoyed friendly conversation without having to be afraid of getting hit on, which was both a compliment and cause for disappointment. Mac had really started getting the hots for Stella St. George, fantasized about her a lot, imagined her making a serious play for him, though other than showing him some tit and leg, she kept things proper. If she strayed, it was mostly in the way she talked to him.

The first major step in that direction was when she started asking questions about his love life. "Do you have a girlfriend, Mac?"

"No, I go out with one girl some, but it's not serious."

"What does she do?"

"Airline stewardess."

"Is she pretty?"

"Yeah, she is."

"What color hair?"

"Blond."

"Have you been intimate with her?"

He'd blinked. "Isn't that kind of a personal question?"

"Yes, very personal," she said.

"Then why'd you ask?"

"Because I was wondering if you think of me in sexual terms."

He fingered his beer mug. "What are you trying to say?"

"It's more a matter of what I'm trying to get you to say. I want to know what you think of me."

"I think you're beautiful."

"And what else?"

"I'm thinking some things your husband wouldn't like. And you probably shouldn't like them, either."

"Would it matter if I said I don't give a damn what Glamour Puss thinks?"

They'd heard Aubrey's Porsche out front just then, and Stella quickly gathered the tray of snacks and, giving Mac a naughty grin, went into the house. Mac went back down to the pool site, fiddled around for a while, mostly waiting to see if Aubrey St. George was going to beat the hell out of his wife.

As he put away his tools, Mac heard a meow behind

him. Spinning, he found G.P. glaring at him and baring his teeth. The Persian meowed again, then slinked off toward the house.

Mac listened hard for signs of a ruckus going on inside the house. But all was quiet. So he packed up his things and left.

The next day had been a Friday. Mac and his crew took off early. He hadn't seen Stella so he assumed she'd taken things as far as she dared. Either that, or Aubrey had put the fear of God in her. Saturday he took Linda Maas out to a movie, telling her she could pick whatever she wanted to see. She'd chosen Aubrey St. George's latest flick, thinking that would be neat for him. Mac hated every minute of it. That night he'd decided maybe he was in love with Stella St. George.

Mac had always thought love and sex ought to go together, not that he was a prude or anything, but intimacy, he believed, should mean something special. The whole time he'd been in Nam, he'd been with a prostitute only once. He didn't like it because it made him feel guilty—guilty for selfishly using another human being. He'd given the girl three times her price and apologized, a response that seemed to amuse her. Sure, what he'd done was easily rationalized, but he'd always cared more about what was right.

Which made the situation with Stella St. George a problem. Mac was in a quandary. He knew where things were headed and, for the first time in his life, he felt helpless to do anything but let it happen.

It was a Wednesday when they'd first made love. Stella had made it easy for him by taking the initiative, maybe sensing he needed to be seduced. She'd been very loving, and the sex had been incredible. Every time after had been great, too, but the desperation of that first time was best. Stella called him her "gentle lover." But they'd made love with abandon, too. "You make me feel free and fearless, Mac," she'd explained.

Afterward they were usually breathless and clinging to each other in a tangle of arms and legs. They'd lie on the rattan chaise longue in the pool house, their bodies spent, and he'd say things like, "Why don't you leave him?"

"Because there's more to life than sex, Mac," she'd replied. "I'm going to be a star," she'd say. "That's why I came to Hollywood, and that's why I stay. My time will come. I know it will."

"With Aubrey?"

"You got a better idea?"

That was the only thing about Stella that had given him pause. There was a part of her—her obsession with stardom—that existed separately, that he couldn't touch, no matter what. And that had bothered him.

Even so, they had drifted toward this day, this Friday the thirteenth, existing on the stolen hours they had together with no plan or goals or clear intentions. Mac was acutely aware that the job was coming to an end. He wasn't sure that Stella was capable of thinking that far ahead. For all he knew, once the pool was in, she'd let him walk away with nothing more than something like, "Thanks for the memories, you big lug. It's been fun."

Just then the sliding door off the deck opened and Stella stepped out. She had on her high-heel, strappy sandals and not another stitch. She came walking toward the pool house, caring not a lick about anybody who might happen to look her way from the nearby hill, walking along the huge hole in the ground where she could soon skinny-dip.

Mac got to his feet when she reached him. He took her in his arms, kissing her deeply. She kissed him back, biting his lips, moaning through her teeth. "I got wet just watching you work, Mac," she said. "Did seeing me in the window turn you on?"

"Me and the guys. I wish you wouldn't do that, sweetheart."

"You're as bad as Aubrey, Mac. Why do men want to control every move a woman makes?"

He couldn't say. Was it because he loved her?

"I don't want to talk," she said, taking him by the hand to the pool house. "Aubrey's going to spend the weekend at home, so I won't be able to be with you again until Tuesday."

"Are you going to have sex with him?" he asked her.

"That's none of your concern."

"Like this is none of his concern?"

"Just make love with me, Mac."

Stella was more assertive than usual, which in his experience meant she wanted to be taken forcefully—not hurt, but gently overpowered. She pulled him down on the floor and he took her there. They screwed long and hard until she was bathed in sweat—his and her own. Flushed by the time it was over and fighting for air, she said, "Damn, you're good."

That was when they heard him.

"Stella!"

He was outside. It sounded like he was coming toward the pool house.

"Oh my God!" she cried. "It's Aubrey." She practically threw Mac off her and rushed around, looking for something to wear. She found an old Hawaiian shirt and was slipping it on as Mac pulled on his shorts. Then the door flew open.

Aubrey St. George stood in the doorway, sunshine backlighting his body. Mac could make out his features well enough to see his eyes round and his nostrils flare.

"What the hell?" His voice was strong and resonant, making him seem a bigger man than usual. Mac could see the flash of gold in the thick rope chain at the open neck of his sport shirt. Aubrey stood akimbo, the crease in his tan slacks a perfect line, his dark blow-dried hair coiffed to perfection. His expression hardened and he bared his capped white teeth. "So," he said, "fucking the pool man, are you, Stella?" He laughed contemptuously. Then, "Goddamn slut!"

St. George slowly moved toward her, gliding with the cautious deliberateness of a gunslinger. Stella frantically worked the wooden buttons of her oversize Hawaiian shirt as though fastening it would somehow make a damning situation less disastrous.

"Please, Aubrey," she cried. "I...I can explain...I...Aubrey..."

"What's to explain, you cunt? You think I'm blind?"

Stella moved behind the chaise longue. Cowering, she backed against the wall, her head bumping on a basket hanging there. Aubrey unfastened his buckle and ripped the belt from his pants.

Stella began to whimper. "Please, Aubrey, please."

Mac, who'd been so shocked he hadn't moved, prompted himself to action. "Mr. St. George, this is not your wife's fault. It's mine."

The man whipped his head in Mac's direction, pointing his finger like a gun. "You shut up, you sonovabitch! In fact, get off my property and don't come back. I never want to see your worthless ass again! Get out!"

"Mr. St. George—"

"Listen, asshole, if I were you, I'd get in that truck of yours and I'd head back to Oklahoma or wherever it was you're from, because you'll never work again in this town. Now clear out of here before I get a gun and shoot your worthless ass!"

Mac, his anger building, picked up his jeans and quickly slipped them on, all the while watching Aubrey, who'd turned his attention back to Stella. She'd started crying.

"You despicable whore," he said, pulling his belt taut between his hands. "This is the thanks I get."

"Aubrey, you never pay any attention to me," Stella sobbed, her fists clutched at her throat. Black streaks of mascara ran down her cheeks. "Don't you know how hard it is for me, how lonely my life is with you always off with somebody? Don't you think I know what people are saying?"

"Oh, it's my fault you're fucking this hillbilly?"

"If you'd just show me a little kindness."

"I'm going to show you, all right." He struck the chaise longue with his belt, making a loud pop.

"Oh, please, Aubrey, please. I'm sorry. I swear I'll never do it again. Never."

"You've got that right."

St. George started around the chair. Stella covered her head and wailed. Mac, who'd gotten his pants on, knew he'd wronged the man and maybe deserved to be beaten, but he wasn't about to allow him to hurt Stella. He stepped over and grabbed hold of the belt as Aubrey swung it back to strike his wife.

"Don't do that, Mr. St. George. I told you, it's not her fault."

The man turned bright red. "And I told you to get your ass out of here!"

"I won't let you beat her, I don't care what you say."

"You aren't telling me what to do in my house!" he roared, spittle flying from his mouth. He was purple with rage.

St. George tried to jerk the belt free, but Mac wouldn't let go. He yanked harder, but Mac was unrelenting. For a moment they tugged on the belt, each on opposite sides of the chaise longue.

"Don't do it, I'm telling you," Mac warned.

Aubrey leaped across the chair and grabbed Mac by the

throat, cursing and shouting. Mac threw him back onto the
chair but Aubrey scrambled to his feet and snatched a teak-
wood figurine from the table next to the chair. Then he
charged, swinging the statue like a club, hitting Mac on
the wrist with his first swing, his shoulder with the second.

Enraged, Mac grabbed the bastard by the shoulders.
"Hit me again and I'll break your fucking neck," he
shouted.

St. George raised the figurine to strike again. Mac gave
him a violent shove, but at the same moment the actor
spun, his hand with the statue coming around and cracking
Mac on the side of the head. Everything went black and
Mac went down in a heap.

The next thing Mac knew, Stella was bent over him,
saying his name. He opened his eyes, seeing the horrified
expression on her face.

"What happened?" he mumbled.

"Oh, thank God," she said, pressing her cool fingers to
his face.

Mac, remembering Aubrey, lifted his head. Peering
over, he saw the man lying motionless a few feet away.
"Is he hurt?"

Stella's face was contorted with pain, in tears. "Oh,
God," she sobbed.

The anguish in her voice sent a stab of fear through him.
He again peered over at St. George's motionless body. "Is
he badly hurt?"

A spasm of sobs came from her. Mac sat up with some
difficulty and looked at Aubrey.

"Mac," Stella said, choking on her tears. "Aubrey's
dead."

Saturday, October 14, 1978

West Los Angeles

Mac McGowan listened to the rumble of the cement truck out front as he stared down at the mesh of rebar lining the hole. Looking closely, he could see the slight variation in the color of the soil where he'd dug the grave. Was it as obvious to anyone else? he wondered. He was grateful now for the web of steel masking the hole. But as he'd worked long into the night, first removing, then replacing a section of mesh so that he could get beneath it, he'd cursed the stuff.

It had taken him over three hours, working with nothing but a flashlight, an acetylene torch, a pick, shovel and welder. Fortunately the only house within hearing distance was still under construction. The big danger, as he saw it, was that somebody on the hill across from them had seen the welding flashes. But that was unlikely at three o'clock in the morning.

Stella hadn't been able to help, but she'd had plenty to do cleaning up the pool house. She'd mopped the floor five times, scrubbing the place "within an inch of its life," as she put it. Together they'd wrapped the body in a plastic sheet.

Stella told him that Aubrey had reeled backward from Mac's blow and hit his head on the large Chinese cheop

that was on the coffee table. The cheop broke and his head
was cracked open. When Mac came to, Aubrey was lying
in a pool of his own dark red blood. He seemed to have
died instantly. Stella told him Aubrey hadn't moved. Not
an inch.

The image sent a shiver through Mac even now, by the
light of day. He watched the pouring crew adjusting the
chute that would bring the river of cement into Aubrey St.
George's backyard, covering his body for all time—or so
Mac hoped. Glancing up at Stella's window, he saw her
watching him. She was covered from her neck to her shins
with a terry robe, her hair hanging limply, no longer the
coquette. Nor did she seem the innocent, childlike victim
of a brutal husband. Stella St. George had been transformed. She was now his partner in crime.

Mac McGowan knew deep in his bones that he was
making a terrible mistake. His soul cried out for him to
call a halt to this. It wasn't too late. The police, the prosecutors, would accept the fact that he'd thought better of
what he'd done. They'd give him credit for coming clean.
Maybe they wouldn't even charge him with homicide. It
was, after all, self-defense. But it would mean abandoning
Stella, ruining her life and, as she put it, her "chances for
a career." He couldn't do that.

With the chute in place, the signal was relayed to the
truck, and moments later the gray soup began sliding down
over Aubrey St. George's grave. Mac watched the cement
cover first the ground, then the rebar, sealing the tomb.
Glancing up at the house again, Mac saw Stella turn from
the window. He couldn't help wondering what was in her
heart.

It was amazing what a crisis did to people. Mac had
discovered he wasn't as clearheaded as he'd thought. What
should have been obvious, wasn't. And it was all because
of his uncertainty about Stella.

Not that he blamed her. In insisting that they cover things up rather than go to the police, she hadn't intended any harm. Sure, she was thinking of herself, but he couldn't bring himself to add to her misery, which was why he'd allowed her to convince him to do this.

Those first terrible, agonizing minutes after Aubrey died, they'd both been in shock. Mac didn't have to see the amount of blood on the tile floor, or to check the guy's pulse, to know he was dead. "Jesus," he'd muttered, staring at the lifeless face.

Stella sobbed uncontrollably.

Mac held her. "Maybe we should call an ambulance, anyway."

She hadn't responded, even after she stopped crying. All she did was stare at her husband's body, biting her lip as she sat hunched on the chaise longue like a terrified child.

"I'm calling the police then," he'd said.

Stella had her hands pressed together prayerfully, the tips of her fingers touching her mouth. "No," she said. "We have to think about this first."

"What do you mean?"

"The whole rest of our lives will depend on what we do. You understand that, don't you, Mac?"

"What's to think about?" he said. "It was self-defense."

"Maybe, but who will believe us? It's not like Aubrey had a gun. And look how much bigger you are than him. Who'd believe you had to kill him to save yourself? Plus, don't you think the police will wonder what was going on in the first place? We had every reason to want him dead. Both of us."

"We might have been having an affair, but that's no crime."

"It was to Aubrey. Mac, people kill their spouses because of things like this."

"Yeah, and that's exactly what he was trying to do."

"But don't you see? He's the one who's dead. They'll think we killed him so we could be together. And maybe get his money—who knows?"

"Will you be getting much?"

"I'm not sure, but I think the house and a little insurance money to live on. Most of his money went to his ex-wife when they divorced, which is why he made me sign a tough prenup. He was just beginning to build up his estate again."

"Stella, the police might be suspicious, but the truth is the truth. We both know what happened."

"We're lovers, Mac. There's no way they'll think this was innocent. Can't you image what the prosecutor will say?"

Mac had understood her words and he saw the logic, but his heart still told him the truth was the safest course. "I don't see that we have any choice but to call the police. I mean, he's lying here in a pool of blood."

Stella remained silent as Mac stared at her ghoulish face, badly streaked with mascara. He wondered what kind of nightmare he'd fallen into. He was obviously being punished for getting involved with a married woman.

"Maybe," she said finally, "Aubrey could disappear without a trace."

"What do you mean?"

"They're pouring the cement tomorrow, aren't they?"

"Yes."

"What if we bury the body in the bottom of the hole before the cement is poured?"

"Stella, we'll never get away with it. The police are smart. Anyway, people will notice he's missing. What are you going to tell them?"

"Maybe I'll be wondering where he is myself. What if Aubrey decides to go for a swim at the beach and disappears? He goes to Malibu all the time to swim. People know that. His first wife still has their Malibu house."

"It'll never work."

"Just let me make a few calls and see if anyone knew he was coming home. Aubrey had lunch with his agent. Jerry will know if he was headed here. I'll call around, acting like I'm trying to find him. Then, if in the morning they find his car parked at the beach, it'll be obvious what happened."

He shook his head. "It's too risky. I say we call the police and the quicker the better."

"Easy for you to say, Mac," she cried. "I'm the one whose career is in jeopardy."

"What about me? I'm the one who decked him."

"Yes, and if you do convince them it was self-defense, you'll be off scot-free. It won't ruin your life because who cares if a pool contractor got mixed up in something like this? But me, I lose no matter what. If this comes out, I'm through in this town. But if we have nothing to do with his death, I'm a tragic widow, an object of sympathy, not a woman under suspicion. Anyway, the police aren't going to believe you're innocent, Mac."

"But I am innocent!"

"There's no way you'll win."

"The truth is the truth."

She wiped her eyes. "Mac, you're too naive for your own good."

"If we try to cover this up and get caught, then we're dead for sure. Coming clean is our only chance, Stella."

"If we pull this off, then neither of us will be hurt," she said coolly. "I haven't come this far, put up with what I have all these years, to see my life flushed down the toilet." She got up from the chair and went to him. "Mac," she said, putting her open hand on his chest. "You've got to help me."

It was then they heard meowing. Mac looked over and saw Aubrey's cat, G.P., sitting in the open doorway. As they watched, the cat came slinking toward them. It went to Aubrey, stopping a few feet from the body and sniffing the air, perhaps smelling death. G.P. looked directly at Mac and let out a protracted, angry meow, baring his teeth. Then he scampered out the door.

Stella turned her attention back to Mac. "Please don't forsake me," she pleaded.

Against his better judgment, Mac had told her to make her calls, to see if a cover-up was possible. Nobody, it turned out, knew where Aubrey was. Everyone assumed, of course, that he was with another woman, though the words were never uttered. Mac had listened to her plaintive voice when she spoke on the phone. Stella was definitely an actress.

At midnight Stella had backed Aubrey's Porsche out of the garage and driven to Malibu with Mac following in his truck. On the drive home, he'd said, "What happens next?"

"We bury the body."

"No, I mean, what happens between you and me?"

"First, you act as if nothing has happened," Stella said. "Just go about your work like normal. How much longer will it take you to finish the job?"

"A couple of weeks, but I won't be here every day."

"Fine," she said. "I'm going to be grieving. People will expect me to be upset. Then, after the dust has settled, we'll be able to see each other."

"Do you want to see me, Stella, or are you just saying that?"

"Of course I want to see you," she said. "If I didn't care about you, Mac, if I didn't trust you, do you think I'd have done all this? Don't forget, I was an innocent bystander. You killed Aubrey. You don't see me turning against you, do you?''

Mac had gotten home at four-thirty that morning, had a shower, slept for an hour and a half, then drove back to the job site. And, with Aubrey St. George buried under tons of cement, he could only wonder if he'd ruined his life. He was a criminal now and, for a guy who'd never done anything worse than underage drinking, that wasn't easy to take. Nor was it just a matter of getting away with it. He would have to live with himself.

By midafternoon the pool was poured and Mac was numbly supervising the cleanup. After sending the crew home, he gathered his gear and put on his blue work shirt. Stella came out onto the deck before he'd trudged off to his truck.

"Mac," she called, her voice a half whisper even though there was nobody but him around to hear. "Come here."

He climbed the steps to the deck. Stella, looking fresher and more rested than she had that morning, wore a little blue cotton summer dress. She took his hand and led him inside. Then, after closing the slider, she put her arms around his neck and gave him a kiss. Mac held her, though not with the same enthusiasm as before.

"I've been wanting to do that all day," she said, pressing her face into his sweaty neck.

"Have you?"

"Mac, this experience has taught me how much I care for you, how much your love means."

He wondered about that. Maybe what she said was true. Or, maybe she was afraid she couldn't trust him. Stella read the uncertainty in his eyes.

"Don't you believe me?"

"It could be you're afraid to trust me," he said.

"We're in this together now," she said. "We have to trust each other." She ran her hand down his stomach and lightly touched his crotch.

Mac wondered how she could even think of sex at a time like this. He searched her eyes for her true feelings and discovered they weren't obvious. Had they ever been?

"I haven't yet reported Aubrey missing," she said. "You know what that means, don't you?"

"No, what?"

"That we can have this night together. One free night before the grand inquisition begins. Will you stay with me, Mac? You can put your truck in the garage and nobody will know you're here."

"Stella, I'm so tired I can barely walk."

"Then sleep in my arms. Please. I need you, Mac."

Her eyes got all glossy and he knew he couldn't say no. He understood then what she'd been saying. They really were in this together, probably forever.

The Present

Wednesday, August 23, 2000

Bel Air

It wasn't the first time in the last twenty or so years that Mac McGowan found himself looking over his shoulder. Exiting the San Diego Freeway at Sunset Boulevard, he had a feeling he was being followed. Again. He looked into the rearview mirror and saw nothing unusual. The car behind him didn't seem suspicious, especially not when it headed west on Sunset as Mac turned east. He checked his mirror again, thinking maybe it was the car behind that one, but it turned south on Sepulveda.

In his gut, Mac knew there was more than simple paranoia at play. Of late, cars seemed to be stopping outside his place at night or lingering in the road. His gardener had reported a few days earlier that somebody had sat parked in the drive of an empty house up the street for the better part of one afternoon. Finally, according to Tito, the Bel Air security patrol had run the vehicle off. Tito hadn't thought anything of it until Mac asked if he'd noted anybody unusual hanging around. Unfortunately, the gardener was unable to give much of a description of either the vehicle or its occupant, except to say it might have been an older Chevy, maybe blue or maybe green. Or black.

Mac wondered if the suspicious happenings might have something to do with the problems he'd been having in the Pool Maids division of his company. Art Conti, who ran the operation for Mac, had been telling him he was almost sure a couple of the pool maids were running drugs on company time.

"Being involved with drugs is bad enough," Mac had told him, "but dragging McGowan Enterprises into it by using our trucks is going way past the limit. Let's get to the bottom of it and, once we're sure, then we'll bring in the police."

"What do you want me to do, boss, hire an investigator?"

"Yeah, let's start there. And I'd like to talk to whoever you line up."

Pool Maids was not just another division of Mac's swimming pool-related conglomeration of companies. It was unique because all the actual pool-service personnel were women with criminal records.

Pool Maids was originally a separate company, founded by Arturo Conti, a longtime friend of Mac's. The operation had been successful in part because Art had a clever gimmick that had captured the imagination of the public. He put the girls in tight black shorts and a maid's apron and frilly hat to service swimming pools. In Toledo it would be lunacy, but in L.A. it was a reason to smile. And to sign a service contract with Pool Maids, Inc.

After Art had taken a bath following his fourth divorce, he decided he wanted a paycheck instead of the headaches of ownership. When he'd come knocking with an offer to sell, Mac was interested, not only because it made business sense, but because he saw it as a opportunity to make a contribution to society by helping women who needed a second chance. Art's motives weren't quite so altruistic— he liked having a bunch of women beholden to him. He'd hired his first girl after a chance occurrence. On the recommendation of a buddy in the Lions Club who was a muckety-muck with the State Parole Board, Art signed up an ex-felon with a good heart and great legs. She worked out well, so Art hired another. And another. Pretty soon he had a whole staff of pool maids who came to him with cleaning skills perfected in a nine-by-twelve prison cell at places like Chowchilla, Mule Creek and Corona.

The program had helped a number of women get their lives back on track, which appealed to Mac, who figured, "But for the grace of God..." Unlike Art, however, Mac hadn't any ulterior motives. He had no intention of paying Art to supervise a harem, so he'd made it a condition that Art keep his sexual conquests outside the company, explaining, "It's my ass they'll sue if you break somebody's heart."

Arturo Conti had agreed and, to the best of Mac's knowledge, he mostly stayed on the straight and narrow, though he may have had a quiet dalliance or two. But the drug thing was a different matter altogether. Art, who knew trouble when he saw it, was as concerned about the situation as Mac. They both realized they had to get a handle on it. And soon.

Before leaving the office that afternoon, Mac had asked Art for an update. "I've been interviewing detectives and I think I've got the right one. We're scheduled to meet one more time and, if everything goes well, I'll have her talk to you at the beginning of the week."

Mac would have preferred even sooner, but he could see Art was being methodical. "All right, I'll tell Bev to hold some time open on my calendar."

But as he made his way home, Mac wasn't so much worried about the detective or Pool Maids—or even the possibility that someone inside the operation was targeting him—as he was concerned about Bri.

Mac had been dating Sabrina Lovejoy for the better part of six months, and he knew they were rapidly approaching that point where things either progressed or ended. Women, he'd learned over the years, only had so much patience.

A couple of weeks earlier Bri had made the telltale comment. "Being with a married man is more of a pain than I expected, Mac," she'd said. "The liabilities do outweigh the benefits." Every woman got to that point eventually, regardless of their stated desires at the outset. When Bri had called him that morning and asked to come by so they could "talk," he figured their moment of truth had arrived.

Mac could hardly blame her. Most of the women he'd known, and there had been several, either accepted the fact that he wouldn't be getting a divorce from Stella, or ended things before they began. But every once in a while he got involved with one who kidded herself as well as him, hanging in there with the hope she could change his mind. It never happened. Mac had made his deal with Stella, and he would honor it to the bitter end. He had to.

He'd hoped, though, that he might be able to finesse things with Bri. She was among the more independent women he'd known. The lady was mature, levelheaded— a prominent businesswoman in her own right. She owned NetWork, the most successful independent public relations firm in Beverly Hills; she was smart, beautiful and she loved him. He didn't want to lose her, but he knew that's where things were headed. Why wasn't it enough that they were together? Why did the specter of marriage have to enter into it?

Mac turned off Sunset onto Copa de Oro and then onto Stone Canyon Road. He was about twenty minutes late, which meant Bri would be waiting. She was punctual to a fault.

Nearing his home, Mac saw Bri's BMW convertible on the circular drive at his door. He pulled up the Lexus behind her. Glancing in her rearview mirror, she got out.

"I'm sorry to be late, honey," he said. "I got stuck in a meeting."

"That's all right," she said, closing the car door. "At least you're here."

Bri, willowy in jeans and a pale yellow cotton sweater, put her hands on her hips as she watched him approach. There was dissatisfaction on her face. She impatiently brushed her light brown hair back off her shoulders. She did not appear interested in affection, so Mac made no attempt to kiss her. Why was it that when a woman seemed bent on ridding herself of a man, she was most desirable?

Mac stood there, savoring her, even knowing it could be for the last time. Bri had soft skin, lovely skin. He thought of her scent when they made love, her occasional impatience with him, the way she laughed at his awkward jokes. Her intelligence.

By her own account, Bri had brought class and culture to his life, transformed him from a "tradesman into gentry." He was Eliza to her Professor Higgins. He admired and respected her. Sabrina Lovejoy was about the classiest woman who'd ever been a part of his life. But knowing what was coming, Mac lost all desire for conversation.

"I hope you didn't have to leave anything important to meet with me," she said, turning to walk with him to the door.

"No, I pretty well finished what I had to get done."

As Mac pulled out his key, he noticed a white envelope peeking from under the corner of the welcome mat. Reaching down, he picked it up. The envelope was sealed. "McGowan" was written in block letters on the front, but there were no other markings. It was probably from a neighbor. Somebody was always trying to organize people to do something, to get the city to do this or that. But in Bel Air these things weren't done by carrying petitions door-to-door so much as by inviting people over for a drink and to hear a lawyer discuss the ins and outs of the environmental-impact report process.

After opening the door, he waited for Bri to enter, then followed her inside, tossing his car keys and the envelope on the entry table. "How about a drink?" he said, feeling the need for one himself.

"No thank you, Mac. I'm not going to stay long. There are some things I need to say and I want to do it sooner rather than later. I also want to say them to your face."

Mac had a sinking feeling. He peered at her, waiting. Bri looked determined, but for the moment, anyway, didn't speak. He decided to make it as easy for her as he could. "Let's go into the front room," he said.

"All right."

Bri led the way into the large sitting room, with its nubby beige sofas and leather armchairs. "Relaxed elegant" was the term she'd used when helping him redecorate a few months earlier. Was he imagining it, or did she glance around nostalgically, perhaps thinking of what might have been? She dropped into a leather wingback armchair, crossed her jean-clad legs and stared at him intently.

Mac sat on a nearby sofa, leaning forward with an expression of earnest concern. He always affected an innocent demeanor in these situations because he was innocent. He never lied—though a former lover had once told him that honesty wasn't enough if he knew the other party was deceiving herself. "You should've known I'd change my mind about marriage," one had said. He had come to realize that a guy unwilling to marry was always in a losing situation. Thinking it might be different with Bri had been naive of him.

"I suppose you know what I'm going to say," she began, breaking the momentary silence.

"I have an idea."

"I thought us being a couple would be enough for me, Mac," she said, "but I've come to realize I was mistaken. I know you're not going to divorce. And yes, I know, you made that clear up front. I honestly didn't set out to change your mind, but I can't help the way I feel now." She hesitated. "You should take that as a compliment, by the way."

"It's not the kind of compliment I'm looking for."

"I know, but there's nothing I can do about it. And I can't change my feelings."

"I understand."

"If I've been unfair," she said, "I'm sorry."

"Well, I'm sorry, too, Bri. I was hoping I could make you happy."

"You're your own worst enemy, Mac. You're too nice, too easy to like and to want to be with. And, well, having only a little piece of you just isn't enough."

She fell silent, giving him a chance to implore her not to go. He would have liked to because letting her walk away wasn't easy. But he had no choice.

She studied him. "I intend to go quietly, but I want to ask you something. Why do you cling to her, Mac? Or maybe I should say, why do you allow her to cling to you?"

Mac sighed. "There's no easy answer, Bri."

"It's not religion, surely. Is it financial?"

"No."

"Are you afraid of hurting her? Do you do it out of a sense of duty, some twisted feeling of loyalty? Is it because of your son?"

"There's no point in talking about it," he said sadly. "I'm not even sure I could explain it if I wanted to."

"No, I suppose you're right. What difference does it make, really? You're going to do what you're going to do, regardless."

"My feelings for you aren't any the less for it," he said.

He wanted to tell Bri that she was special, that his regret over losing her was greater than with anyone else, but he knew he wouldn't be doing her any favors. How could he possibly say that he was bound to Stella by crimes they'd committed together, by decades of lies and deceit? How could he say he was living in the skin of a man he couldn't respect? That he was stuck, with no way out?

"I wish things were different," he said. It was as honest, yet kind, a remark as he could make.

"Yeah, me, too."

Bri got to her feet. Mac did, as well. He had a terribly strong desire to take her into his arms. He hated these moments, but he'd also learned to endure them, to detach and accept his fate. That didn't make it any less painful, though.

When she wiped a tear from her eye, Mac felt his heart rise in his throat.

"Don't come to the door," she said. "I want to walk out by myself." The corner of her mouth twitched as she fought for control. Then Sabrina Lovejoy turned and strode from the room.

As always, Mac felt a ping in his heart—a ping that hurt, a dull pain of longing and regret. He told himself, as he had several times, that he wouldn't allow himself to do this again. Before Bri, he'd avoided a serious relationship for the better part of two years. But it was hard not to love and be loved, even knowing nothing more could come of it than an affair. Maybe he was just too damn softhearted for his own good.

He heard the engine of Bri's BMW come to life, and he heard her drive off, leaving him in the silence of his home. He dealt with his unhappiness for a while, then went upstairs to change.

* * *

Manuela Ordoñez felt better when the woman came out the door, got in her fancy BMW and drove off. For a while she thought it might be Mac McGowan's girlfriend, but he hadn't kissed her or anything. It probably had something to do with business. Which was a blessing because Manuela would just die if he had a girlfriend. It was bad enough that he had a wife.

Taking the gum from her mouth, she tossed it out the window of her dark blue Chevy and got a fresh piece from her purse. She'd been chomping like crazy as she'd sat there waiting and watching. Just thinking Mac might have somebody else was enough to make her sick. But she was determined not to blow it, because this was the opportunity of a lifetime. Maybe the best shot at a millionaire she'd ever have.

Manuela was so nervous her stomach hurt. Then, when she'd seen that woman waiting, she actually felt sick. But it was a false alarm. Now all she had to do was give Mac the chance to seduce her. She was sure he wanted her but was just too much of a gentleman to do anything about it. And, after talking to her best friend at Pool Maids, Ella Vanilla, Manuela knew why.

Ella's last name was Perkins, but the girls called her Ella Vanilla because she had really white skin that was always lathered up with so much sunblock that she was shades lighter than the rest of the crew. If you didn't start out dark, after six months cleaning pools you looked like a piece of toast. Except for Ella, who Manuela knew from Mule Creek where they'd done time together.

"Don't you know he's never going to do nothing, Manuela," Ella had said when Manuela confided that Mac liked her, but for some reason never came on to her.

"Why not?"

Ella rolled her eyes. "Why not?" she said. "Because of sexual harassment, dodo brain. That's why."

"Sexual harassment? He never put a hand on me."

"That's the point. He's afraid you're going to sue his ass. Don't you know guys are scared shitless about lawsuits nowadays? He don't want to take the chance, Manuela. That's why he ain't trying to get in your pants."

"You mean, even if I want him to come on to me, he won't?"

"It's risky. Look at it from his standpoint. It could cost him big bucks."

"But what if I tell him it's okay, that I want him to come on to me?"

Ella thought about that for a minute. "Maybe if he could prove it, he'd feel safe."

"How does that work?"

Ella thought again. "Well, if nothing happens at work, that probably would help. If you went to him, like at his house, for example, and said you know his hands are tied, but you want to make it easy for him, so you want him to know that you're available and that it's your idea—that might work."

"You think?"

"Tell him you're not expecting more pay or nothin' like that. Maybe if he knows you're coming on to him because you really like him and that it don't have anything to do with the job, then maybe he'd figure he's safe. But are you sure he's interested in you, Manuela?"

"Like he loaned me forty thousand dollars with no interest to pay off the loan on my mother's house. Duh. And he's always looking at my tits. All the time. What do you think, Ella? He's interested, believe me."

"Everybody looks at your tits. Even I look at your tits."

It was true. Manuela had the best set in the world. Lots of guys told her she had boobs to die for. Art Conti told her she had world-class tits. And was she not pretty? Maybe not Jennifer Lopez kind of beauty, but pretty.

At least Ella Vanilla had explained why Mac hadn't tried to fuck her. It was so obvious, she didn't know why she hadn't figured it out. Now it was up to her to give him the chance. And if she gave him a real good time and he really fell for her, maybe he'd dump his wife and marry her.

"Don't count on it, Manuela," her mother had said, mumbling the words as always since her stroke.

"Mama, if I want a man bad enough, I always get him."

"You always get sex, that's not the same."

"Plenty of guys have wanted to marry me. I could have gotten a ring ten times."

"But a gringo millionaire, Manuela?"

"He really likes me. He's so sweet and polite. He even hugged me when I cried."

"It would be nice," her mother said wistfully. "With your brother coming out of prison soon, God knows we could use a little money in the family. I always thought you could get a good man, a successful man, if you used your head."

Manuela had been using her head. After talking to Ella Vanilla, she'd talked to Debbie Smoltz in the personnel department. Debbie was Bev Wallace's niece and Bev was Mac's secretary, so Debbie knew a whole lot about Mac. Manuela learned that Mac hated smoking. So she'd quit. And she learned that he and his wife had been separated for ten years, which proved he didn't love the woman. He dated, but that's all.

Manuela figured what he needed was a better woman. She'd had a few problems, true, but Mac understood people made mistakes, and he wouldn't hold her troubles with the law against her—not considering he'd given her a job and loaned her money. She knew love in a man's eyes when she saw it.

Sitting there, looking at Mac McGowan's big house,

Manuela felt a shiver go through her. She could see herself living there, giving orders to the cooks and gardeners, making Mac happy, pampering him, giving him all the sex and blow jobs he could ever want. Looking pretty for him, buying things for both of them, being a good wife.

Manuela knew that everything depended on her handling him right, making it clear she was the one that wanted the sex, so he wouldn't have to worry about getting sued. She looked over at her plastic sack, a twinge of fear going through her. It was amazing how nervous she was, considering that before her troubles with the law she'd danced nude for a million guys at the Bottoms Up Club. But Mac McGowan was different. He was a millionaire.

Manuela drummed her fingers on the steering wheel of the Chevy, figuring she'd wait ten more minutes before she rang his bell. God, she wanted a cigarette. But she wouldn't give in to the temptation. She didn't want to give Mac any reason not to want her. Besides, she loved him. She truly did.

Having changed into chinos and a polo shirt, Mac went to the large bay window in his bedroom that overlooked the sweep of lawn in back, the huge pool and terraced garden that rose partway up the side of the canyon wall. The scene was bathed in afternoon sun.

Surveying his domain, it struck him as ironic that he should have so much and yet so little. He had a wonderful home, he was financially secure. As the biggest swimming pool and spa contractor in Southern California, he owned a chain of pool and garden shops, Pool Maids, a sporting goods outlet with six locations and was a cofounder and major investor of a bank in the San Fernando Valley. Yet he was permanently and irrevocably alone, married to a woman who held on even as she allowed him his separate, but empty life.

Aubrey's death, and the things he and Stella had been through, had sealed his fate. She would never let go. He knew that now. It wasn't her need for financial security because he'd assured her she'd be taken care of. For a while he thought it may have been Troy, but their son had turned twenty and was pretty much on his own, though Stella still gave him money. Maybe she simply wanted to know she hadn't lost control of the situation. "Glamour Puss might be dead, Mac," she'd said, "but he still has hold of us. I've been loyal to you and I expect you to be loyal to me."

He understood that to be a warning, if not a threat. Stella, in her subtle way, wouldn't let him forget who had killed Aubrey.

At times like this, Mac would think about that terrible dark day. It still seemed incredible that his youthful indiscretions should continue to haunt and rule his life. If only he'd insisted on going to the police, the whole thing would be long behind him now.

Those first few months after Aubrey's death had been the most difficult of his life. Once he'd finished the pool, he hadn't seen Stella again for weeks. Nor had they spoken on the phone, agreeing that any contact was dangerous.

Stella had gone through the public ordeal alone. She had been surprised when, instead of getting an outpouring of sympathy, Hollywood seemed to turn against her. Not even Glamour Puss's harshest critics had rallied to her side.

Without a body, there couldn't be a funeral, so Stella held a memorial service with the help of Aubrey's agent. It was not as well attended as Aubrey's stature would have suggested. His first wife boycotted the service. Though she made no public statements, she seemed to share the same suspicions as the rest of the town—that Stella was somehow behind Aubrey's disappearance.

The case was tried mostly in the papers as the police

never attempted to bring charges, though the detective conducting the investigation for the L.A.P.D., a guy named Jaime Caldron, did seem suspicious. But since what little evidence there was pointed to accidental drowning, the authorities had nothing to go on. Caldron questioned Stella four separate times, but was unable to trip her up.

Once, early in November, he'd dropped by to see Mac, as well. Caldron's questions were mostly about Stella. Mac had tried to be his usual earnest self. He'd told the detective he and his crew left the job early the afternoon Aubrey disappeared. He'd seen Stella inside the house that day, but had not spoken to her. Any further suspicion Caldron might have had was deflected when Manny mistakenly said Mac had driven away when he had, which was often the case. Or maybe Manny chose not to recall anything that could be damning, considering he hated cops. His ex-wife had divorced him and married one when Manny was in Nam.

For six weeks, Mac and Stella endured the ordeal, isolated from one another. Then, one day Stella called him from the pay phone at her supermarket. "I need to see you," she'd said, sounding terribly anxious. They met at a hotel near the Burbank airport. Stella gave him the news without wind-up or fanfare. "Mac," she said, "I'm pregnant." She told him she thought it had probably happened the night after the cement was poured, that last stolen night together. "I almost had an abortion," she'd said. "I even made an appointment, but I couldn't do it without talking to you."

That had been the moment when he realized that he and Stella were bound by more than their sins. They were also bound by their unborn child. "What do you want to do?" he'd asked her.

"I don't know. I don't know what's right."

They'd spent the night together, and he'd held her.

She'd cried, agonizing. In the morning, after a virtually sleepless night, he'd told her he thought they should get married.

"I don't want you to marry me because you feel sorry for me," she said.

"I wasn't with you all those times just for the sex." Then he'd said the most fateful thing of all. "I love you, Stella."

"Do you?"

"Yes, didn't you know? Couldn't you tell?"

Mac had meant what he'd said, but over the years he'd come to realize his feelings were based on all the wrong things—compassion, lust, fear, guilt, obligation, remorse. But Stella was pregnant, leaving him duty-bound to stand by her, just as she'd stood by him. They agreed to wait until it became impossible for her to hide her pregnancy. The delay gave Mac the opportunity to focus on his business, which was just beginning to take off. In fact, it was during those painful first weeks after Aubrey's death that Mac had gotten word that he'd won a major contract with a motel chain that was moving into the Southern California market. As it turned out, that was the critical break he'd needed. Within six months he'd become a relatively wealthy man.

What Mac didn't know at the time was that Stella had gotten word that she was through in Hollywood and that there would be little for her in Aubrey's estate. Equity in the house was about it. She'd never said it outright, but Mac was her only salvation.

Their love renewed, they saw each other secretly through the end of the year. Then, on Valentine's Day, when Stella was four months pregnant, they'd married at the Chapel of Perpetual Happiness in Las Vegas with first Nat King Cole's "Unforgettable," then Frank Sinatra's

"The Way You Look Tonight" playing softly in the background.

Troy was born in July. To Mac, the whole thing was incredible, leaving him in a daze. In a few months short of a year, he'd gone from a carefree bachelor to the married father of a child.

As he stood staring at his pool, his mind still on the central tragedy of his life, Mac heard the doorbell ring. Checking his watch, he couldn't imagine who it was, unless Bri was back. His heart lifted nicely at the thought. The prospect was unlikely, he knew, but he wanted to hope—he wanted to escape the gloom of yet another failed relationship. He hurried downstairs, but the woman standing on his porch wasn't Sabrina Lovejoy. The face was familiar, but he momentarily drew a blank.

"Hi, Mr. McGowan," she said. "Hope you don't mind me dropping by."

The twinge of an accent in her speech brought it all back. She was one of the pool maids, Manuela Ordoñez. Seeing her out of the context of work had thrown him. He remembered it clearly now. Her mother had had a stroke at the beginning of the year and the family was in danger of losing their home. Art Conti had told him the story.

"She's a fox," Art had said. "Sweet little Chicana. Bouncy as the dickens with big black eyes and the hugest hooters God ever put on a chick that small. Did three years in Mule Creek for involuntary manslaughter, but she's been a hell of a good worker."

"What man did she slaughter?" Mac had asked.

"Live-in boyfriend."

"I take it you've had the good sense to stay clear of her."

Art Conti grinned. "Not due to any virtue on my part, boss."

Mac hadn't cared about how hot Manuela was, considering he never got personally involved with his employees. But he did believe in looking out for his people. Taking compassion on Manuela, he had arranged for the company to make her an interest-free loan. Sometimes getting a little breathing room was all a person needed to get on their feet again. She'd been so touched by the gesture that she'd come to his office all teary, gushing her appreciation. She'd hugged him and thanked him and given him a big wet kiss. Then she'd sobbed like a little girl.

After that she'd come by his office every once in a while with little gifts for him, usually food her mother had made, but other things, as well—a CD or a video. Once a book of poems. Mac could tell she was taken by him, but he'd interpreted her attention as signs of gratitude and maybe admiration. Her gifts, he considered tokens of appreciation.

"What a surprise," he said in response to her appearance at his door. He noticed she had a small plastic sack in her hand. The prospect of another gift went through his mind. But he couldn't imagine why she was coming to his home, or even how she knew where he lived. Mac also noticed her miniskirt and low-cut blouse which revealed about as much cleavage as your average Bond girl. It would have been unkind to compare her to a hooker, but she was definitely dressed for that sort of allure.

"Yeah," Manuela said, beaming. "It was my day off and so I thought I'd maybe come by and say hello. It's been a while since I seen you."

"Yes, it has, hasn't it?"

Mac had the definite impression Manuela was waiting to be invited inside, which he hesitated doing.

"I got a little something for you," she said, indicating the sack in her hand.

"What sort of something?"

"A present."

"You don't have to give me presents, Manuela. You've already been very generous."

She laughed dismissively. "Not so generous like you, Mr. McGowan. Or, can I call you Mac? Since we're like friends already, you don't mind if I call you by your first name, do you?"

"No, I don't stand on ceremony," he said.

Manuela didn't understand the allusion, but seemed to get his meaning. She snapped the gum she was chewing. "So, can I come in?"

Mac didn't want to be impolite. "Yes, but I do have an appointment in a while, so I have to be leaving soon."

Manuela frowned. "That's too bad." Then she smiled. "Of course, maybe it's not so important as you think. You can always change your mind."

He'd figured a little white lie might help him get out of an awkward situation gracefully, but he wondered now if all he'd succeeded in doing was dig himself into a deeper hole.

Manuela seemed amused by his consternation and entered, moving past him into the entry. She was tiny standing beside him, five-one or -two at the most.

"Carumba! What a beautiful house, Mac," she enthused, looking around. "And so big!" She peered at the Waterford chandelier then went to the entrance to the dining room. Next she crossed to the other side of the entry and gazed at Mac's large front room where he'd sat with Bri earlier. "You have a really nice house. I love it."

"Thank you."

Manuela, facing him now, did a little shimmy that was blatantly sexual. "So, is anybody else here?"

"No."

"Don't you have somebody to cook and clean?"

"My housekeeper's on vacation. I've got a service coming in temporarily and I'm eating out a lot."

Manuela smacked her gum, then tapped her teeth with her long, red nails. "You like Mexican food?"

"Yes," Mac said, still wary, "I do."

"Maybe I'll come over and cook for you sometime. I'm not so good as my mother, but some people say my chicken molé is the best."

Mac didn't know what to say, but he could tell they were getting into an area where he didn't want to go. Manuela's confidence seemed to be building.

"Should we go in here?" she asked, tossing her thumb toward the front room.

Mac glanced at his watch, a gesture which Manuela ignored. Turning on her heel without waiting for a reply, she went into the front room, swinging her butt, the hem of her short skirt dancing against the backs of her shapely legs. Mac followed her as far as the doorway, where he stood watching her move in a big circle about the room, stopping now and then to touch a table or chair. At one point she picked up his ostrich egg, an artifact that his decorator had used to adorn an end table. She shook it.

"Some chicken."

Mac smiled.

Manuela put the egg back on its little stand. She eyed Mac. "So, how come you're just standing there?"

He wasn't sure if he should remind her he had to leave soon, or just accept the fact that he'd be wasting his breath. Manuela, growing more brazen by the moment, strode over to him and took his hand.

"Come on, Mac, it's your house."

She led him to a sitting group and they stopped in front of the wingback chair Bri had sat in. She still had hold of his hand.

"Mmm," she said, squeezing his fingers. "So big and warm."

Then, when she drew up his hand and pressed it to the

bare tops of her breasts, Mac was certain where she was headed. But he was so taken aback that he didn't know what to say.

"Does this feel cool?" she asked in a coquettish tone as she looked up at him through her lashes.

"Manuela...I don't think..."

She giggled, refusing to be discouraged. "Come on, it's time for you to see your present." With that she guided him to the chair, almost pushing him down. "Okay," she said coyly. "You ready?"

Manuela had opened the plastic bag and pulled out some sort of lacy undergarment. Tossing aside the bag, she held the frilly thing up in front of her. "It's a teddy," she announced. "I thought I'd model it for you. What do you think of that?"

Mac's mouth sagged as he watched her pose, twisting her body back and forth, putting first one leg in front of her, then the other as she pursed her lips. "I don't understand what you're doing. Are you under some sort of impression that—"

"Look, Mac," she said, putting her hands on her hips, just where her waist nipped in, "don't worry about it, okay? I know you're the boss, but I'm not going to make no big deal about it. I'm just trying to make things easy for both of us."

"Manuela, what are you thinking? That by giving you an interest-free loan I was trying to—"

"Mac, it's okay, really. I know you can't say nothing direct because you're the boss. So, I'm trying to let you know it's okay with me if you want to get it on. Nobody can blame you that way. No judge, nobody. You didn't tell me to come over here, right? I'm here because I want to be here. I think it's pretty obvious I like you as much as you like me, and there's nothing illegal about that. I mean, how can some lawyer get pushed out of shape if I'm the one who comes to you?''

"I'm not concerned about a lawsuit. You don't understand," he said.

Manuela began unbuttoning her blouse. "Yes, I do. You want it to come from me." She kicked off her shoes. "I'm going to give you a little treat. First because you've been so nice, and second because I want to be nice, too. I hope you know now how much I like you, Mac.''

"Manuela…''

"You know what? I think about you all the time. It's really true. I think you're the nicest man in the world.'' She pulled off her blouse, dropping it on the floor. Then she grasped the place on her bra between the cups.

"I bet you noticed my tits,'' she said with a grin. "Everybody does. Guys say I got the best set they ever seen.''

"Manuela…''

Mac started to get to his feet, but she stepped forward and gave him a gentle shove back into the chair. In practically the same motion she sat astride his knees, leaned forward and kissed him square on the mouth.

By now she'd unfastened her bra and lifted the cups off her melonous breasts, which she shook back and forth in front of his face. Mac knew he had to stop this and stop it now. Taking her by the waist, he lifted her off his knees and set her back on the floor.

"You misunderstand me, Manuela,'' he said emphatically. "This is not what I want.''

She stared up at him, her brow furrowed. "What's wrong?''

"Nothing's wrong. The things I did, the loan, weren't a play for your attention. I wasn't trying to buy any sexual favors. That's not what that was about.''

"Huh?''

"Manuela, I don't have a sexual interest in you.''

"You mean you don't think I'm pretty?"

"Of course I think you're pretty. You're a very attractive woman, but that doesn't mean I have romantic intentions."

"Are you saying you don't even want to screw?"

"I'm tempted, believe me...I mean, sure you're very appealing, but...well, who wouldn't want to...under normal circumstances, I mean. But that's not where I am, Manuela."

"Because of your wife? I thought you were separated."

"I am."

"You got somebody else, then?"

Mac saw an opportunity. "Yes, I do."

"Really?"

"Yes."

"Oh. Nobody said nothing about that." She actually looked shocked.

Mac was embarrassed for her. Surprisingly, having bared her breasts seemed not to faze her nearly so much as his disinterest. She casually leaned over and picked up her bra and put it on. Then she retrieved her blouse, a grimace of displeasure on her face as she buttoned it up.

"Is it serious?"

"Is what serious?"

"Your girlfriend."

The ploy seemed to be working. "Yes."

Manuela looked up at him. She bit her lip. "So, how come you were so nice to me, then?"

"Your family had problems, Manuela. You're my employee...I..."

Her eyes filled. "But I really liked you," she said, almost in tears. "And I thought you really liked me."

"I do. But not the way you think."

"I don't take off my shirt for just anybody," she said, tucking her blouse under the waistband of her skirt.

"I'm flattered you...well, think of me in those terms, Manuela," he said. "But it wouldn't be fair to take advantage of you just for...sex."

She shook her head, her eyes shimmering. "I was so sure you liked me. I told my mother, 'I really think he does.'"

"I'm truly sorry for the misunderstanding."

Her eyes brimmed. She stared up at him for a long moment, until finally tears overflowed and ran down her cheeks. "I hate you," she sobbed. Then, snatching up the teddy, she walked briskly from the room.

Mac heard the front door open then close. He pinched the bridge of his nose. "Christ," he said, shaking his head. First Bri, now this. Glancing toward the front window, he saw Manuela's car zip out the drive. It was a dark blue Chevy. "Christ," he said again.

Mac was unsure what had just happened. Had that been an innocent mistake, or did Manuela have something more sinister in mind? If she'd been trying to set him up, he couldn't imagine what she hoped to gain, unless she'd gotten pregnant by some penniless lout and decided to pin the wrap on somebody with a few bucks. No, that was unlikely, paranoia on his part. This business with Manuela had been building, and she did genuinely seem to have misread him. The woman was not the brightest thing to come down the pike.

He felt sorry for her, though. Maybe it was understandable she misconstrued his intentions. Not every employer was as generous. Mac knew he had a tendency to be overly compassionate. That had been his downfall with Stella— that and a propensity to take in strays. He'd been that way his whole life. "Believe it or not, Joseph, a man can have too big a heart," his mother once told him. His mama was right.

It was getting toward the dinner hour and he had no

desire to cook. As he so often did, he decided to run down to Westwood and grab a bite. When he got to the entry he snatched his car keys from the hall table, noticing the envelope that had been under the mat when he'd arrived. He picked it up and turned it over. There was nothing written on the back. He tore it open and removed the single sheet of notepaper. On it was a brief message, written in block letters. It said:

I KNOW WHAT YOU DID ON FRIDAY, OCTOBER 13, 1978.

It was unsigned.

West Hollywood

Jade Morro drove north on Fairfax Avenue and was maybe two miles from her bungalow—on which the rent was now past due a month—when the engine of her Ford Escort began to miss. It had been running well, so she wondered what could be wrong with the damn.... Then, glancing at the instrument panel, she gave the steering wheel a solid rap with her fist. "Shit!"

The engine sputtered, then died. Jade swung over and the car rolled to a stop at the curb. She was out of gas.

"Dammit," she said.

That morning as she'd arrived in Malibu she'd noticed the gas was low, and she'd made a mental note to fill up before heading home. And so, of course, she'd proceeded to forget. The clock on the dash confirmed she was already late. Ruthie was probably there at the house, waiting for her. Jade could picture her friend pacing on the sidewalk out front, her hands on her hips and saying something like, "Girlfriend, where the hell you been? Don't you know I took off work early just to help you find a dress for the ball?"

Jade sagged forward and let her forehead rest on the steering wheel as she tried to figure out what to do. She could look for a service station, buy some gas and lug it back, or she could hoof it home. Then it occurred to her, she had her bicycle on top of the damn car. She'd spent the morning and afternoon on a fifty-mile bike ride up the coast. What was another two miles or so? Of course. What was she thinking?

Jade hopped out of the car and went around to the passenger side where she could remove the bike from the roof without getting her butt knocked off by a passing vehicle. As she unfastened her bike from the rack, she wondered if she might have unconsciously wanted to run out of gas. Ruthie would undoubtedly agree with that theory—"Easy way of getting out of buying that dress, girl." Jade couldn't deny it. The fact was she'd had mixed feelings about going to this dance ever since Art Conti had asked her.

Thus far Art had taken her to lunch and to dinner—with the ostensible purpose of talking about her doing some investigative work for Pool Maids. And, even though he had gone over the problem with the company in some detail, Jade knew he had another agenda, as well. But when she'd complained to Ruthie about it, her friend had been adamant. "That so bad?" Ruthie had asked. "It is natural to get laid occasionally, you know."

"Laid? Listen, that's the very last thing I'm interested in," Jade told her. "The only reason I'm seeing the guy is because I got to deal with him to get to Mac McGowan, the owner. And believe me, Conti's not making it easy."

"He hitting on you?"

"Nothing too blatant yet, but that's where he's headed."

"He must know how bad you need that job."

"I think the guy has a nose for desperation, Ruthie."

When it came to men, Jade relied heavily on Ruthie

Gibbons, first because she was her best friend, and second because Jade had been away from the dating game so long she was practically the "recycled virgin" Ruthie accused her of being. They had known each other since they were rookies on the force. Ruthie, having become a community relations officer for the police, was confident she knew people. And as for men, "Honey," she'd said once, "I was born knowing all there is to know about the rascals." Then, in the ghetto rap she favored when she joked around, Ruthie said, "Shoot, girl, there ain't all that much to 'em if you think about it. You got what they want. They know it. You know it. Simple as that."

Jade had no problem fending off unwanted advances. In fact, when it came to that, she didn't have a timid bone in her body. Her problem was finessing a tricky situation, like the one she faced with Art Conti. But somehow, she'd find a way to make it work. She always did.

Jade got the front wheel of her bike out of the trunk and attached it to the frame. Then she got her riding helmet from the back seat, strapped her fanny pack on over her spandex riding togs, locked up the car, took a swig from her water bottle and took off up the street. Glancing at her watch, she estimated she would be half an hour late, enough to send Ruthie into a shit fit.

The plan was for Ruthie to help her find a dress in time to get any necessary alterations done. Actually, the dress had been all Ruthie had talked about the past week, ever since Art had issued the invitation. When Jade had called to tell her friend what was in the works, Ruthie had been stunned. A good five seconds had passed before she could even reply.

"You're going to a what?"

"A ball."

"You mean like Cinderella?"

"Everything but the glass slipper and the prince."

"Whoa, girl. And you're going with What's-his-name?"

"Yeah, Arturo Conti."

"How'd this happen?"

"It's a Chamber of Commerce Ball. Art said a lot of business and networking goes on, and it'll be a chance for me to meet lots of people, including Mac McGowan."

"So now lover boy is helping you with your career."

"He knows I'm just getting started and need contacts, Ruthie. And there will be hundreds of businesspeople there. I figure I'll stuff my purse with business cards."

"I guess things have been a little slow for you."

"Slow? It's been six weeks since I've had a case of any consequence. All I've done is piddling stuff, nickel-and-dime work. I still haven't paid this month's rent."

"But Mr. Art's ridin' to the rescue."

Jade thought about that a moment. "Think there's any chance he's doing it out of the kindness of his heart, Ruthie?"

Her friend laughed.

"Yeah," Jade groaned. "I was afraid you'd say that."

"It doesn't have to be a bad thing, girl. What's this dude like?"

"He's good-looking enough, I guess. And, of course, he knows it."

"That's not necessarily bad. Could be he'll show you a good time."

"Ruthie, I'm not interested in that. All I want is a chance to meet Mac McGowan and get the job."

"Honey, you can use him to get to McGowan just as much as he can use you. It's all about knowing the tricks of the trade. And fortunately you got yourself a world-class consultant."

So, Jade had accepted Art Conti's invitation to the Chamber of Commerce Ball with every intention of turning it to her advantage. She did face a few practical problems, however. First, she wasn't a dress-up kind of girl—she didn't even like to wear a skirt. And second, she wasn't much of a dancer. Naturally, Ruthie had a solution to that, too. But Jade had refused to go to any clubs with her. "The lessons I got in junior high will have to do." Ruthie, who wasn't easily denied, had come over Monday night to put on some music and demonstrate some steps and moves, anyway.

The third reason was the most important of all. Jade didn't want to get pressed for sexual favors in exchange for a job, and she knew Conti would at least make a stab at it. Ruthie seemed to think a guy like Art could be humored enough to keep him in her corner without giving away the store, but Jade herself wasn't sure how much she could stomach. A few years ago, it might not have been so tough, but ever since Ricky Santos, Jade had had a major problem with men.

Still a few blocks from home, she glanced at her watch. She was going to have to hurry to get cleaned up so they could make it to the charity shop. A charity shop seemed to Jade like a strange place to find a ball gown, but Ruthie assured her it was the place to buy an affordable dress. "Honey, we ain't talkin' Salvation Army. Society ladies run this place."

The whole thing still seemed like a bad idea, though. Here she was in her spandex shorts, sweating like a pig on her bike and supposedly trying on ball gowns in less than an hour.

As she rounded the corner and started down her street, she could see Ruthie's car. After several more yards she saw Ruthie, too, sitting on the front steps. Ruthie did not get up when Jade swung into the drive and screeched to a halt. In fact, she had a sober look on her face. Jade got off her bike and walked it across the little patch of lawn to where Ruthie sat.

"Sorry to be late, kid. Damn car ran out of gas over on Fairfax. Fortunately, I had backup transportation."

Her friend did not smile; she did not grunt or groan. She continued to look depressed.

"Ruthie, what's wrong? You pissed?"

Rubbing her bare arms, Ruthie got up. "Jade, I think I saw Ricky."

"Huh?"

"It was maybe ten minutes ago. This old Chevy came down the street kind of slow. I didn't pay much attention until it was right out there in front, then the guy gunned it and went flying up the street."

"And it was Ricky?"

"I couldn't swear to it, not a hundred percent. The guy had on shades and a baseball cap, but it sure looked like him. Definitely Latino."

"You must be mistaken," Jade told her. "Ricky's in Mexico."

"He could have come back."

"If so, he wouldn't be coming around here."

"Why not? Maybe he still loves you."

"Ruthie, he might have been desperate a couple of years ago—desperate enough to lurk around—but too much time has passed. And stalking, if that's what you're suggesting, isn't his style."

"Maybe he was just curious."

"And maybe it wasn't Ricky at all. He did reconcile with his wife, you know."

"Could have got a divorce."

"You almost sound like you want it to be Ricky," Jade said.

"No way. You know I hate the sonovabitch as much as you. I'm sayin' be careful, girl. That's what I'm saying."

"Careful of what?"

"Guys can get crazy over women."

"It wasn't Ricky," Jade told her. "Much as I hate the fact, I know the guy. Trust me. He's in Mexico with his wife and children."

Ruthie looked at her watch and sighed. "Well then, table that and let's get going. We're wasting perfectly good shopping time. You'd better get your butt in the shower."

Jade took her key out of her fanny pack and unlocked the door. Then she wheeled the bike up the steps and inside. Ruthie, who'd slung her bag over her shoulder, followed her into the house.

"I'll get something for you to wear to the shop," Ruthie said, "assuming I can find something that doesn't need ironing." She headed off to the bedroom.

When her friend was out of sight, Jade went over to the window and looked out at her peaceful tree-lined street. She remembered the day she'd pitched Ricky out the door. It had been one of the most emotionally wrenching days of her life. Shivering, Jade headed for the bathroom, thinking that whoever Ruthie saw, it couldn't have been Ricky Santos. Surely.

Bel Air

Mac tried for the fifth or sixth time to reach Stella, but all he got was her machine. After the second time, he stopped leaving messages. The urgency of his need to speak with her had already been made clear. But not being able to reach her only added to his anxiety. He still couldn't believe it. After all these years. The ten words kept going through his head like a commandment from God—"I know what you did on Friday, October 13, 1978."

Who? he wondered. Who could be behind this?

Manuela and Bri came to mind, if only because he'd just had encounters with them, but there was no way either of them could know he'd killed Aubrey St. George. Nor did either woman have a motive for harassing him. The writer of the note clearly intended to make him sweat. And he or she was doing a good job.

Mac paced about the house, as he had been for the better part of an hour, picking up a phone every so often to make sure it was working or to try to reach Stella yet again. He'd been so certain that their dirty little secret was safe. Obviously he was wrong. "I know what you did on Friday, October 13, 1978."

Who?

He didn't know who Stella had been talking to, but she'd definitely talked to somebody because Mac hadn't breathed a word to a living soul. That meant Stella had blabbed to someone. Unless it was Stella herself who'd sent the note. There was no other explanation.

Losing patience, Mac picked up the phone and again dialed his wife's number. Again he got the answering machine. He slammed down the receiver. If he didn't know better, he'd have thought Stella was doing this to torture him. Where the hell was she?

It actually was no surprise she wasn't home. Stella spent her time shopping, going to luncheons, teas, parties and—to her credit—she did a little charity work, as well. She kept busy.

It was surprising, though, that Bonny wasn't home. Bonny was Stella's French-speaking Caribbean house-keeper. She'd been with her since Troy was a year old. Originally from Martinique, Bonny was actually named Marie Boniface, but Troy had called her Bonny as a small child, and the name stuck. She'd been Mammy to Stella's Scarlet for nearly twenty years, though the two women were about the same age. Bonny understood Stella's needs and foibles about as well as anyone on the planet. During the negotiations for Stella's and Mac's separate maintenance agreement, Maury Levine, Mac's attorney, had jokingly referred to the pair as Don Quixote and Sancho Panza in drag. Not having been a college boy, Mac didn't exactly understand the reference, but he had a pretty good idea the implications were comical.

Mac went to the entry hall to have another look at the note. Naturally, Stella's absence—and for that matter, Bonny's—made him paranoid. What if something had happened? Could someone have kidnapped Stella and forced her to divulge their secret? No, that was ridiculous. He wouldn't have gotten a provocative note. It would have been a demand for ransom.

This thing was headed somewhere, he just didn't know where. But no question, his butt was hanging out. He could be ruined. And there was always the possibility he could be prosecuted for Aubrey's murder. Any claim of self-defense would ring hollow after all these years.

Mac had once asked Maury Levine if there was a statute of limitations for murder. It was while he was negotiating with Art to buy Pool Maids, Inc., which Maury knew involved personnel with criminal pasts.

"Nope," Maury had replied. "But that's not the only issue. What kind of time frame you talking?" he asked. "Is it something recent?"

"Twenty years or so."

"That's a hard case," Maury said. "The D.A. can legally prosecute, but getting a conviction is a whole different thing. When you get up around twenty years, it starts getting hard to come up with witnesses, physical evidence, you name it. A case that old, without a confession, isn't easy to make. What kind of citizen has she been since?"

"Exemplary."

"No criminal record?"

"No."

Maury looked puzzled. "I thought all these pool maids were ex-cons. You got one the law hasn't caught up with yet?"

"Yeah, but it's somebody with a very guilty conscience."

"You can probably forget it."

But Mac couldn't. Over the years his concern hadn't been about going to jail so much as protecting Stella and Troy. The only reason he'd agreed to the cover-up in the first place was to spare her the notoriety. From his present vantage point it hardly seemed a good reason, but he'd done it and had no choice now but to live with the consequences.

The way Mac looked at it, Glamour Puss had more than gotten his revenge. Mac and Stella had been locked in a twenty-year living hell of codependency. Their marriage had not had much of a chance, considering it was built on fear and guilt. Things had been uneasy between them from the moment they returned from Las Vegas. Stella had refused to move back into the house she'd shared with Aubrey, and Mac could hardly blame her, though he couldn't help worrying about strangers living in the house.

Still, in the end, he let her have her way. But the problem was, there was only minimal overlap between his budget and Stella's taste. Fortunately his business was growing, and yet another big contract came in as they were hunting for a place to buy. Using all the money she got out of the Brentwood house and a jumbo loan, they bought one of the grand old storied homes in Beverly Hills, moving in when Stella was eight months pregnant.

For a while Mac thought maybe their troubles were behind them. Even an unexpected visit from Detective Jaime Caldron on moving day hadn't put a damper on their joy. "Hey, congratulations!" Caldron had said as he stood with

Mac on the front lawn, watching the moving men carry Aubrey St. George's sofas into the new house. "Nice to see you two got together and are moving right up in the world."

"I've got a soft heart for widows," Mac told him brazenly.

"Pregnant ones at that," the detective noted.

They didn't hear from Caldron again, but Mac figured his appearance had been planned for effect—sewing seeds of doubt and fear. The unspoken message was, "I'm watching, folks."

If the L.A.P.D. hadn't been able to put a crimp in their married life, ironically, the birth of their son had. Stella developed a severe case of postpartum depression. All she could do was cry and talk about her failed film career. She was terribly bitter toward the people who'd refused to give her a chance. Nor had she liked it when Mac had tried to convince her it might all be for the good. "Now you don't have to worry about what might have been," he'd told her. The remark had made her livid. "I won't give up my dream," she'd screamed. "I didn't ask to have this baby. I was meant to be a film star. If I wanted this, I could have stayed in Iowa!"

But there was no arguing with the powers that be in Hollywood. Stella, even with the protection of a husband who was becoming progressively more wealthy, remained a pariah. Nobody would talk to her about being in a film. Once, a couple of years after they were married and Mac's net worth had moved well into the seven figure range, she'd tried to convince him to invest in a hot project, *Ordinary People*, theorizing that money talked and a part in the film could be found for her.

"Stella," he'd told her, "getting into stuff I know nothing about is a sure way to lose money. I'm a bricks-and-mortar kind of guy. I might as well flush my capital down

the toilet as buy into a film deal.'' She'd tried everything
to get him to open his wallet—everything but turn him in
to the police—but he'd held firm. ''Making the money and
investing it is my bailiwick,'' he'd said. ''You might call
the shots in other areas, but not this one. Besides, what
about Troy?''

''Women can both work and be mothers, Mac. Haven't
you heard that yet, or are you still living in the Stone
Age?''

Stella never forgave him. Whether their marriage had
been doomed even before their spat over *Ordinary People*
or not, things were definitely not the same thereafter. As
a gesture of defiance she began using her original stage
name, Stella Hampton, and she spent several months going
through the motions of pursuing a career in film. For a
while she even had an agent, but nothing of consequence
ever came of her efforts. Then she made yet another fateful
decision. She decided to transfer her dreams to their son.

Troy did his first commercial at age three and had his
first part in a TV movie at six. Stella had launched her
career as a stage mom, making Troy her alter ego in the
pursuit of fame and glory, much to Mac's chagrin. ''It's
one thing if you want to be in films or on TV, Stella,''
he'd told his wife. ''But your turning my son into a goddamn glamour puss, like—''

''Don't say it, Mac! Troy takes after me. He has the
soul of an artist. Is that so bad? There's nothing wrong
with wanting to be an actor. Nothing!''

If Stella was blinded by her obsession, Mac was left
feeling helpless. Not that Troy wasn't a willing victim. The
kid loved to ham it up, even as a toddler. The camera, the
lights, the glitz really appealed to him. Maybe Stella had
been right. Maybe Troy was born to it.

But that didn't keep Mac from being disappointed and
feeling shut out from his son's life. Nor had Stella done

anything to mitigate the circumstances, resisting Mac's attempts to broaden Troy's interests. Their fights became more and more bitter until finally she gave him an ultimatum. ''Either let us have our dream, Mac, or I'm leaving you.''

He'd suffered quietly for a few more years, devoting himself to his business, which continued to grow, making him a leading figure in the industry. But it was clear he'd become the odd man out in his own home. By the time he left, Mac was convinced his and Stella's differences were truly irreconcilable.

Hollywood and the ghost of Aubrey St. George may have driven them apart, but in a curious way, they also bound them together. If Stella had had relationships, they'd been discreet. Mac suspected her one true love could never be a man. She'd already given her heart to Hollywood and her dreams of stardom for Troy.

Whether Aubrey had gotten in the way of that, too, it was difficult to say, but Mac certainly felt the guy's presence, even in death. He hadn't been separated from Stella and in his new Bel Air home a month before Jaime Caldron was at his door. The detective hadn't said anything direct, but it was pretty obvious he'd wanted to drive a wedge between them. ''Showbiz marriages aren't easy,'' he'd said ironically.

Mac was determined not to give the man hope. He told Caldron he and Stella would always remain united in spirit, if not in fact. The detective had left, supposedly taking Mac at his word, but Mac sensed the bastard was smiling underneath.

Things had been tough for them all, but for Mac, losing Troy had been the most painful development. Try as he may, he'd never managed to get close to his son. Even as a child, he'd resisted Mac's overtures. And, like his mother, Troy's successes were, at best, mixed. His credits consisted of minor roles in half a dozen films. The biggest part was in a TV drama that was jerked from the schedule after two episodes. The pattern seemed to be one step forward, one step back.

Mac stayed out of it, hoping that Troy's celluloid dreams would eventually run their course. When the boy started high school, Mac asked him to consider college. And if college didn't interest him, a place in the family business. But Mac's pleas fell on deaf ears. Things got so bad that by the time Troy was sixteen, they hardly spoke. The last straw came when Troy turned eighteen and officially changed his name to Hampton in lieu of the less marketable and more plebeian McGowan. Mac was crushed.

Stella insisted that he shouldn't take it personally. "Actors change their names all the time. Troy didn't choose my name over yours, Mac. Hampton's my stage name. It works with 'Troy' beautifully." That may have been Stella's take, but Mac knew there was an underlying hostility toward him on Troy's part. The kid hated him and Mac didn't know why.

He'd tried to communicate with his son, even going so far as to do a mea culpa once. "I know we don't see eye-to-eye about your career, Troy," he'd said. "I realize that ultimately the decision is yours, and that maybe I should be more supportive of your choices. Maybe I've failed you in that regard, but is it wrong to point out alternatives?" The question hadn't gotten so much as a response. Troy had simply given him a dirty look and walked away. How did you communicate with someone who seemed to hate the sound of your voice, regardless of what you said?

Mostly Mac had endured his disappointment in silence. Whether out of guilt or habit he continued giving Stella money over and above his separate maintenance obligations, even knowing it was subsidizing Troy's failing acting career. Mac wasn't sure what to hope for—that one day his wife and son would wake up and realize they were wasting their time, or that they would slowly drift from his life, leaving him in peace.

The telephone rang, jolting him from his reverie. Mac went to the nearest extension.

"Hello?"

"Meester McGowan, I got your message on the telephone." It was Bonny, Stella's housekeeper. "She is not home, so I think I should call."

"Bonny, where is she? Do you expect her soon?"

"I don't know, *monsieur*. Yesterday, when I came home from the market, there was a leetle note. It said she is going out of town for a while. She would call me."

"And you haven't heard from her?"

"No, *monsieur*."

Mac had a sinking feeling. Was Stella's absence a coincidence, or could there be some connection to the mystery note? "She didn't say where she was going, or with whom?"

"No, *monsieur*."

"That's not like Stella, is it?"

"She usually says more to me. And not so suddenly, at the last minute."

"Has Stella been all right, Bonny? Have you noticed anything unusual?"

"She has been very excited about something the last week or more, Meester McGowan. I don't know what. She did not talk to me about it."

"Isn't that unusual?"

"Sometimes she does not talk to me. Sometimes she waits until she is very upset."

"She wasn't upset?"

"Not sad."

Mac didn't know whether to take heart or not. It was

possible Stella was completely oblivious to whatever was behind the note. But until he spoke with her, he'd have no way of knowing. "But you don't know when she'll be back?"

"She did not say."

"Listen, Bonny, it's very important that I talk to her. If she calls, tell her to get a hold of me, will you? It's very, very important."

"Yes, *monsieur*, of course."

Mac hung up, if anything, feeling worse than before. He slumped into an armchair. What a day. Bri had kissed him off. Manuela Ordoñez had kissed him. He'd found an anonymous note at his door and Stella had dropped from sight. Try as he may, he could find no explanation and no obvious connection. Of course, he could always blame Glamour Puss. Aubrey had been controlling Mac's life from the grave for twenty years now and was showing no signs of giving up.

As Mac sat brooding, another possibility occurred to him. Jaime Caldron. It had to be the better part of ten years since Mac had seen or heard from the police detective. If Caldron hadn't retired already, he had to be close to it. Was it possible he was taking a last stab at his unsolved cases? Shake the suspects up, get them nervous and talking in hopes they'd make a mistake. Would a cop go so far as to send anonymous notes? Or was that Mac's paranoia speaking again?

Burbank

Manuela Ordoñez lay on her bed, her eyes red and burning from crying. She felt like such a fool. God, she hated Mac McGowan, she truly did. In the blink of an eye he went from Prince Charming to just another rich gringo who thought Latinas were good for nothing but being cleaning ladies or hookers or pool maids. She rolled over onto her back, wiping her eyes with the backs of her hands as she stared at the dark ceiling. Donny had tried to use her, too, and he sure as hell got his. She shot his ass.

Manuela had been so sure Mac was a nice guy, that he respected her. Why did he do this to her? Couldn't he tell how much she liked him? What was wrong with her, anyway? Wasn't she good enough for him?

Just then she heard the front door open and close. And she heard Angel's voice. She wondered what he was doing home at ten o'clock. Usually he didn't show up until the early hours of the morning. He seemed to be grumbling to himself, cussing. There were more ''fucks'' and ''fucking A's'' coming from his mouth than usual. And he sounded mad. When she heard a chair go flying and crash against a wall, she knew something was wrong.

Manuela got up from the bed and went to the door. Her brother was slumped in a chair, looking like hell. Blood was running down the side of his face and over the front of his torn shirt. One eye was all puffed up.

''Angel,'' she said, ''what happened?''

''Nothing.''

''If it's nothing, why you got blood all over your face?''

He looked up at her. ''Fuck off, Manuela. Go give some gringo a blow job or something.''

''You've been fighting.''

''No, I've been playing tiddledywinks.''

''Why do you do this, Angel? They'll send you back to prison.''

''Because I got some blood on a barroom floor?''

''If you look like this I can only imagine what the other guy looks like. Did you kill him or what?''

Angel Ordoñez was not a big man. In fact, he was smaller than most, but he had a body like coiled steel and he was afraid of nothing and no one. In prison he'd killed three men, one of them a bodybuilder twice his size. Of course, the prison officials didn't know it was him who'd done it and none of the prisoners would rat on Angel Ordoñez. He was a fighter, a warrior, and the scars of war on his face, his neck, his arms, his torso and legs proved it. Since he was twelve Angel had gotten into fights—often with knives—about as frequently as most people went out to dinner.

"Not him—them," Angel said. "There were three of them. Two are in the hospital. The other one ran."

"What if somebody dies?"

"Then he ain't going to be sayin' nothing."

"The police will ask who did this."

"So? These muchachos won't say, because they know I will cut off their balls if they do."

"If you're in prison you're going to cut off their balls?"

"I could be in prison and still cut off their balls and they know it, Manuela. I myself was out only three days and I broke the arms of a man who was sleeping with the wife of an amigo in the slammer. The asshole is lucky I didn't cut off his dick. What I am saying is there are ways to do things even from prison."

"Well, I hope you had a good time fighting, Angel, because you look terrible. And you are bleeding all over the furniture. Why didn't you go to the hospital?"

"Because at the hospital they ask questions, what do you think?"

"You must do something."

"I will wash it, but for a minute I want to rest. And maybe have a *cerveza*. Bring me a Carta Blanca, will you, Manuela?"

"Maybe I should put a bandage on your face first."

"I want a beer."

"I will get you a beer if you will let me bandage your face."

"You think you are a mother just because you have big tits?"

"Fuck you, Angel."

"Fuck you, too."

"Okay," she said, "I am getting you a beer, but go into the bathroom and wash the blood off. I will put on a bandage."

"Fuck," Angel moaned. "Manuela, why don't you marry some *chico* and leave me alone?"

"Go," she commanded.

Manuela went to the kitchen and got Angel his beer. As she was opening it, she heard her mother snoring softly in the little room off the kitchen where she slept. After Manuela and Angel's father left them, their mother never again slept in the bedroom she'd shared with him, choosing instead the small room with a single bed. "It is my convent," she told Manuela. Until her stroke, their mother did all the cooking and cleaning. Now she could only do part of it. Manuela had to do the rest or pay Mrs. Gomez, who lived in the next house, to do it. Her mother told her that she was preparing to die. "But first, I am waiting for you to marry."

Manuela had made the mistake of telling her mother she would marry Mac McGowan. Now it would not happen. Their dreams had been killed, hacked up like one of Angel's victims.

She carried the bottle of beer to the bathroom where Angel was splashing water on the side of his face as he stood in a puddle of watery blood. Seeing her, he stopped, pressed a towel to his face and took the beer from her hand. Angel guzzled down half the bottle in one long gulp, the cords of his neck rippling.

"I can't tell you how many times when I was in my cell I would think of having a *cerveza*," he told her. "Sometimes, especially when it was hot, I would do anything for a beer, even kill, if that was the only way. A beer, when you cannot have one, is even more important in your mind than a woman.'' He took another long slug, the towel still pressed to his face. Angel scrutinized her. ''What is wrong with you?''

''What do you mean, what is wrong?''

''Your face. You've been crying.''

''So what?''

''Did somebody do something to you?''

''What difference does it make?'' she asked.

''You are my sister. I want to know.''

''I was your sister when we were little and that did not stop you from beating me up.''

''It was only play, Manuela.''

''Play that left bruises. Let me see your face.''

Angel lifted the towel from his cheek. Blood slowly oozed from the long, jagged cut.

''You should have a doctor sew this,'' she said, grimacing.

''It is not worth the trouble. Put on a bandage.''

Manuela opened the medicine cabinet and took out the bottle of Merthiolate, which she applied liberally to the gash. Angel winced but did not complain.

''Nobody raped you, did they?'' he asked, obviously obsessed. Angel was like that. He'd get something stuck in his mind and couldn't let go.

''No, of course not.''

''Why do you say of course not? When you were a topless dancer at O'Gill's club you were always having trouble with the customers.''

''That was different.''

''So, what happened?''

''Nothing.''

''Don't lie to me, Manuela. You are not crying for no reason.''

She tore off a long piece of tape. "If you squeeze the cut so that the skin is together, I will tape it shut. That way the scar will not be so bad."

"It was a man, wasn't it?" Angel said, his eyes growing hard as he began working his jaw. "What did he do?"

"Hold the cut closed."

Angel pushed the two sides of the cut together, but she knew his mind continued to turn, his protective impulse flaring like a fire out of control. When he was sixteen and their father had been gone for some months, Angel came home one afternoon and found Mr. Perez, the baker, kissing their mother. Angel flew into a rage and beat the man nearly senseless and slapped their mother, too. That was the reason for his first long stint in the juvenile facility.

Manuela pressed the tape onto her brother's skin. "There," she said. "Be careful and maybe it will stay closed."

Angel looked hard into her eyes. "Who was it, Manuela, and what did he do?"

"Will you shut up, Angel? It's none of your business."

His hand came up from nowhere, clasping her jaw, simultaneously driving her head back until it bumped against the door. "Answer me!" he shouted, his face only inches from hers.

When her brother lost his temper he was terrifying, like a rabid dog. Angel's fingers tightened, and for a moment she thought he might dislocate her jaw.

"You're hurting me!" she cried through her teeth.

"I asked you a question!"

"It was at work. My boss."

"The Italian? What did he do?" Angel reduced the pressure on her jaw, but he didn't let go.

"No, it wasn't him. It was the big boss, the owner."

Angel's eyes flashed. "What did the sonovabitch do to you?"

"He hurt my feelings."

"He didn't rape you or nothing like that?"

"No, I went to his house because I thought he liked me, but he made me leave."

"That's all?"

"Yes, Angel, that's all."

He let go of her and Manuela came down off her toes, not realizing until then that he had practically lifted her into the air. She worked her aching jaw, wishing she could smack him, but knowing she didn't dare.

Angel turned and gazed at his face in the mirror, glancing at her after a moment. "So, the guy wouldn't fuck you, huh? Or did he fuck you first, then throw you out?"

"I thought he liked me, but I was wrong."

Her brother turned to face her, giving her a quizzical look. "Is this the rich one, the one who helped us save the house?"

"Yes. I wanted to marry him."

"But he doesn't want to marry you?"

"No."

Angel thought for a minute. "You want me to kill him?"

"No, of course I don't want you to kill him. What do you think?"

"He made you cry. He offended your honor."

"No, he hurt my feelings."

Angel looked disgusted. "Then why are you crying? For nothing? No, you're trying to protect him, Manuela. If it's so bad what he did, then maybe somebody should teach him a lesson."

"Forget it," she said. "I didn't complain to you. You made me say it."

"But you are my sister. If the gringo sonovabitch offends you, he offends me. I have pride for my family. Don't you think he should know this?"

"Angel, Mac doesn't even know you, only that you were in prison."

"That's worse!" Angel cried, his anger mushrooming again.

She put her hand on her brother's arm. "Please, just forget I said anything. I will take care of this."

Angel kicked the wastebasket against the tub and stomped out of the bath, cursing as he went down the hall. Manuela leaned on the basin, dropping her head and closing her eyes. Her brother was crazy. Prison had turned him into a savage. She knew it was only a matter of time before he killed someone again. She was sure of it. And the sad thing was, he would give it no more thought than drinking a beer.

Thursday, August 24, 2000

Bel Air

Mac McGowan awoke at 5:00 a.m. At six he gave up trying to go back to sleep, went downstairs and made himself a pot of coffee. His calendar, as he recalled, was pretty clear for the day, though there were always reports to be reviewed and other paperwork to keep him busy. He considered staying home to make sure he wouldn't miss Stella's call…if she called. Maybe he should have told Bonny to have Stella phone him at the office if she wasn't able to reach him at home.

The note continued to haunt him. Thinking about it all evening and half the night hadn't gotten him any closer to understanding it. Stella, he decided, must hold the key. Which made her absence and her silence all the more difficult.

Mac considered calling her place again, if only to see if she might have checked in with Bonny. The housekeeper would have passed on his message for sure, but that didn't guarantee that Stella would call, because she did things at her own pace. "Yes, Mac," she'd say. "I fully intended to call, but one thing after another has come up." That was Stella.

Bonny was an early riser, but he waited until seven to phone, just the same.

"Yes, Meester McGowan, she telephoned late last night. I tell her what you say. She will call to you today. That's what she said to me."

Mac was relieved, but annoyed Stella hadn't already called. He should have said she should phone him regardless of the time. "Did she say where she was?"

"No, *monsieur*, we talk only for one minute. Only enough for me to give your message. Then she hang up."

"I hope she calls soon."

"I told to her your message, *monsieur*, that it is very important."

"Thanks, Bonny."

"Oui, monsieur."

Mac felt a little better. Stella was apparently alive and well. At least he didn't have to worry about that. But now, how long did he have to wait before she'd phone?

Subscribing to the theory that a watched pot never boiled, Mac decided to busy himself. Besides Stella and the damn note, he'd been worried about Bri and Manuela. There was nothing to be done about Bri—at least not for the moment—but the situation with Manuela could not be ignored. Lying in bed during the night, he'd decided benign neglect was the wrong approach. When there was a problem involving an employee, Mac had found the best policy was to address it immediately. Since Art was Manuela's supervisor, the place to start was with him.

On Thursdays Art normally was in the field, calling on the accounts, which meant he'd be likely heading out directly from home, and Mac wouldn't be able to talk to him until late afternoon. He didn't like bothering employees at home, but since the business with Manuela was rather sensitive, he figured an early-morning call would be justified.

Art sounded a bit groggy when he answered the phone.

"Hope I didn't wake you," Mac said.

"No, boss. I'm still in bed, but I wasn't sleeping."

"Ah, you're busy, in other words," Mac said, understanding Art was not alone. "I won't disturb you then. Give me a buzz when you're free."

"No, it's okay. Sherri just went to the kitchen to make us some coffee. I can talk."

"You sure?"

"Positive. What's up?"

"I had a little visit yesterday afternoon from one of your girls."

"Yeah? Who?"

"Manuela Ordoñez."

"She came to your house?"

"Yes."

"No kidding. What did she want?"

Mac told him what happened. Art listened, interjecting sympathetic groans from time to time. When Mac finished, Art said, "Jesus."

"You know the lady better than I do. What do you make of it?"

"Manuela's not the swiftest tart in the crew," Art said, "but I always considered her a pretty straight shooter. Sincere, I mean."

"I don't know if she's sincere about me or my money," Mac said.

"I guess that's always a problem for a guy in your shoes."

"You'd warned me the loan wasn't a good idea. I should have listened."

"These girls have a tendency to take what they can, considering they've spent most of their lives getting screwed. I always found the best approach is to be fair but firm."

"I can see my mistake."

"Want me to talk to her?"

"She was pretty upset when she left," Mac said. "I

don't know if she'll be able to put it behind her, or if there might be trouble ahead. But I do know you need to be aware what happened.''

"Definitely. Manuela's a little fireball, the kind who needs to be doused now and again. I'll talk to her, boss. Leave it in my hands.''

"I feel responsible for the misunderstanding.''

"Don't kid yourself. Manuela's no innocent lamb. She saw an opportunity and went for it. I know these girls.''

"I'm aware of that, Art. That's why you're in charge. But we can talk about this later. I'll let you get back to your coffee.''

Art laughed. "Which just arrived, as a matter of fact, and looking mighty savory.''

Mac imagined Art staring at a pair of bare breasts as he'd said it. There was something in his tone. "Well, bon appétit,'' Mac said, amused. He hung up.

There was only one Arturo Conti, God love him. Mac was grateful for the light moment. He needed a little relief.

Deciding to get cleaned up and dressed for work, but not wanting to miss Stella's call, Mac took the cordless phone into the bathroom, putting it on the vanity where he could easily reach it. As he showered, he thought about Jaime Caldron again. The note had brought the detective to mind, but over the years Caldron had popped into Mac's head without any special reason. Maybe it was because the guy was a symbol of the constant threat to Mac's freedom and peace of mind.

Drying himself after his shower, Mac had an idea. Taking the phone, he called information and asked to be put through to the administrative offices of the L.A.P.D. He asked for the personnel department. When a clerk came on the line, he told her he was a high-school classmate of Caldron's and was wondering if Jaime was still with the force. "Funny you should call,'' the girl said. "I saw some paperwork on Lieutenant Caldron the other day. He is due to retire soon, I know that. Would you like his extension?''

Mac said yes, but he didn't write it down, ending the call. For a minute he stood, looking in the mirror, trying to remember what Caldron looked like. He couldn't conjure up the man's features, but he could recall his steely image, shrewdness hidden under a facade of quietness and calm. But was he sneaky and underhanded? Mac didn't know him well enough to say.

After dressing, he went downstairs to pour himself another cup of coffee and try to decide whether to go into the office or sit and wait for Stella to contact him. Knowing he could hang around all day and never hear from her, he decided to go to the office. If he obsessed over her, he could drive himself nuts.

Mac was in the laundry room entering the alarm code into the pad when he heard the phone ring. He took the call on the kitchen phone.

''Mac, I'm glad I caught you at home.'' It was Stella.

''Where've you been?'' he said, trying not to sound as irritated as he was.

''I'm in Palm Springs,'' she said.

''Couldn't you have left a number or told Bonny or something?''

''Mac, since when do you care what I do and where I go?''

''I've got something important to discuss with you,'' he said.

''Well, I've got something important to discuss with you, too. Mac, it's incredible, absolutely fantastic. You won't believe it.''

''What?''

''I know you don't like to talk about Troy's career, but I have truly exciting news.''

Mac rolled his eyes, knowing he'd be hearing about it

in minute detail. He would have cut her off, but with Stella it was better letting her run out of steam. "Okay, what news?"

"We need to discuss it in person," she told him, "which is why I called. I've been working on this, planning it for a couple of days, and now everything's set up."

"What's set up?"

"I want you to come over to my place tomorrow evening, if you would."

"Just to talk?"

"No, I want you to meet some people, people who can make your son a star."

Unable to help himself, Mac groaned.

"Now before you get in a huff, listen to what I have to say," she admonished.

Mac bit his tongue. Talk of big career opportunities always evoked images of Glamour Puss and the whole awful business, which Mac hated. Why Stella wasn't sensitive to that, he'd never understood. Perhaps she was too focused on her own needs.

"These people have some wonderful ideas," she went on. "This is a golden opportunity for Troy and I want you to hear about it firsthand."

"Stella, you know I have no interest in getting into any of that Hollywood bullshit. I have nothing to contribute and I'd be in the way."

"No, you wouldn't. You must come," she pleaded. "It could be the most important day in Troy's life. If you never do another thing for me as long as you live, do this. I promise, you won't regret it. Tomorrow afternoon at my place. Say, four?"

"Stella, I've got news, too. And I'm afraid it's not very pleasant."

"For God's sake, Mac, not now, please."

"You've got to hear this."

"Can't it wait until tomorrow? I'm in a hurry. I can't concentrate when I'm rushed, you know that. I called because I want to tell the others you'll be there tomorrow for sure. Will you come, Mac?"

"All right, fine, but give me a couple minutes now. Yesterday afternoon somebody left—"

"Mac, I don't mean to be impolite, but I really have to go. I'll see you tomorrow." With that she hung up.

He slapped the receiver back into the cradle, pissed. It was vintage Stella—not giving a damn about anybody's desires but her own. But then, he ought to be used to it by now. It was the essence of their relationship and had always been.

Studio City

Manuela Ordoñez pulled into the McGowan Enterprises parking lot just as Ella Vanilla came walking out to her car. Ella, her face lathered up like usual, sauntered over to the Chevy.

"Where you been, Manuela? I hear Art's really pissed at you."

"Yeah, well, he can go fuck himself."

Ella's brows rose. "What happened?"

"I'm having a bad day, all right?"

"Well, excuse me."

"Hey, I'm sorry, Ella. I didn't mean nothing personal."

"Forget it. But you better have a pretty damn good excuse for showing up at work this late. You know how Art is about that shit."

"I know. He called and left a message on my machine."

"Well, good luck."

"Yeah, whatever. See you."

Manuela headed toward the warehouse, where Art had an office. The girls called it the whorehouse because Art was such a pussy hound—though nothing like he used to be when he owned the company. In those days he was screwing everybody, or at least a lot of the girls. The ones that put out got the best accounts, but Art never twisted anybody's arm or treated anybody bad. To hear him tell it, getting laid by Art Conti was a privilege. If a girl didn't appreciate that fact, she never got asked twice.

Word was he was a damn good lay. He liked his women and he treated them right. But there was a group of girls who just didn't get involved, for whatever reason. Manuela was one. Not that she wouldn't have considered a roll in the hay with Art Conti. It's just that the timing was never right. One or the other of them seemed to be involved with somebody. But sex was about the last thing she had to worry about now. Art was pissed.

Of course, Manuela was pretty pissed herself. She felt like she'd got the shaft from Mac McGowan, whether he intended it or not. And she was hurt as bad as she ever had been. Maybe he never laid a hand on her, but what he did—giving her hope when he didn't mean it—was a pretty shitty thing to do.

Once in the warehouse, Manuela headed for the corner where Art's office was located. She steeled herself, knowing this was going to be unpleasant. But fuck him, she told herself. She was the one who got screwed. She knocked on the door.

"Yeah?" came the voice from inside.

Manuela opened the door a crack and peeked in. She wasn't going to throw it open and charge in without making sure it was safe. Connie did that once and found Art with a chemical supplier sales rep. She was on his desk with her legs splayed open and Art in up to his ears. All the girls had a good laugh about it. "The Art Conti quick test for PH balance."

"Who is it?" came his voice from inside.

Manuela pushed the door open.

"Well, well, Ordoñez," Art said. "It's about time. Where have you been?"

He was sitting at his desk with his feet propped up, reading. Art was in his usual polo shirt with the Pool Maids logo on it. Manuela had to admit, Art wasn't hard to look at with his dark wavy hair and mustache. He worked out, so he had broad shoulders, muscular arms and a narrow waist.

"Sorry about being so late," she said, "but I had a problem today."

"No, I had a problem today. One of my girls—you—didn't show up. That meant I had to reassign your route to cover the accounts. I had to service one commercial account in Encino myself. I even got chlorine on my goddamn new loafers."

"So, I'm sorry. What do you want?"

"How about an explanation for starters?" he said, taking his feet down off the desk, looking real serious.

Manuela, who'd come partway into the office, took the last few steps to the guest chair across the desk from him and slipped into it. "I was depressed, all right?"

"Depressed?"

"Yeah, depressed. Ain't you ever been depressed, Art? Jesus Christ."

"Look, Manuela. I run a business here, not a psychiatric ward. And this sure as hell isn't the welfare office. You put in a day's work and you get a day's pay. Fuck up and you don't work here, it's as simple as that."

"So shoot me."

"Don't get smart," he said, wagging his finger at her. "You're already on thin ice. And what in the fuck are you doing going to the boss's place, trying to ball him? You got a death wish or something?"

"Give me a break. I was trying to be nice, is all."

"Nice, Manuela?"

"Yeah, you of all people ought to understand when a girl's trying to be nice."

"Don't be a smart-ass. You don't like it here, you know where the door is."

"And I bet you never heard of sexual harassment, either."

Art suddenly got very quiet, his eyes hardening. "Are you threatening me?"

"Hey, who got screwed? You or me?"

"Nobody screwed you."

"Yeah? Says who? Were you there?" Manuela didn't know why she said it. The words came out of nowhere. But why was she getting a hard time just because she thought Mac McGowan liked her, maybe loved her? What was so bad about telling a guy she liked him? It's okay for Art Conti to fuck every girl in the company, but she shows a little titty by mistake and suddenly everybody wants to send her back to the slammer. Well, fuck them!

Art's eyes got a little wider. "Are you saying Mac McGowan had sex with you, or that he tried to? Is that what you're saying?"

"I'm saying what I'm saying and I don't see what fucking business it is of yours, Conti."

Now his mouth dropped open. "I'll tell you what fucking business it is of mine. I run this goddamn operation, and no two-bit piece of ass is going to come waltzing into the office six hours late and tell me to go fuck myself."

Manuela was losing it, her anger rising right along with his. She got to her feet, glaring. "Oh, go to hell!"

Art leaped to his feet, pointing his finger at her. "You're one word from getting your ass fired. Now I suggest you get out of my office and tomorrow morning you'd better be here bright and early and ready to do your job. Either that or pack your bags."

"Not without an apology."

Art's chin almost landed on his chest. "What?" He was incredulous.

"You heard me. I want an apology. And not just from you. From Mr. McGowan, too. And I don't want missing work today deducted from my check."

"You're out of your fucking mind."

Manuela folded her arms under her breasts and glared as hard as she could. "Don't fuck with me, Art, or you'll be sorry. And I ain't kidding."

"Get out of here," he said under his breath. He was so pissed he was scarlet.

She leaned on his desk and, jutting out her chin, screamed, "Not without a goddamn apology."

"That's it! You're through. You're fired. You're canned. You're history, Ordoñez. Clean out your locker and don't set foot in here again. You'll get your final check in the mail."

"Fuck you."

"You just fucked yourself," he said, drawing himself up and puffing out his chest.

"Yeah, well, you ain't heard the last of me yet, asshole. Fucking count on it." With that, she turned and headed for the door, stopping only to grab a straight chair and hurl it across the room onto Art Conti's shiny desk. Then, flipping him off, she went out the door.

Manuela didn't cry until she was in her car. Even then, they were tears of anger. She hated the whole fucking bunch. They could take Pool Maids and shove it up their ass. Moments later, as she sat at the parking lot exit, waiting for a break in the traffic, she figured out what she'd do. She'd find Angel and tell him she'd been royally fucked. The assholes would be sorry then.

Friday, August 25, 2000

Beverly Hills

Mac McGowan guided the Lexus up the street where he'd once lived, glad that his interminable wait to talk to Stella was nearly over. Perhaps their problems were only beginning, but at least they'd have a better idea where they stood—assuming she could remember who she'd spilled her guts to about Aubrey.

When the large Mediterranean villa on upper Bedford Drive that he once shared with Stella came into view, Mac had that little wrench in his gut that came with proximity to the past. The place held many memories for him, few of them positive. But Stella just adored the house, more because of its Hollywood lineage than its amenities. No less than three marquee-caliber stars were in the chain of title—Jeanne Winslow from the thirties, Brandon Kirk from the forties and Loretta Thomas, the name star of the 1950s and 60s.

When they first saw the house it was as Loretta Thomas had redecorated it, in an art deco style. It truly looked like the set of a Jeanne Winslow movie. Mac sometimes thought these old places ought to have "papers" certifying their movie star authenticity, like a pedigree animal. With the old celluloid ghosts haunting the place, their casa, as

Stella called it, only needed a few wax statues to qualify as Madame Tussand's, Beverly Hills edition.

Driving through the gates of the casa, he followed the circular drive to the front door and stopped. Before he got out, he reached into his pocket, just to feel the envelope containing the anonymous note. Even after a couple of days it still seemed like a bad dream from which he ought to be able to awaken. But those ten chilling words had been hammering his brain like a mantra—"I know what you did on Friday, October 13, 1978."

Mac got out of the Lexus and went to the front door where he was greeted by Marie Boniface. "Hello, Bonny."

"Welcome, Meester McGowan," she said.

"So, how've you been?" he asked, entering the house. "You keeping Stella on the straight and narrow?"

"That's too much to ask even of the Virgin, *monsieur*," she replied. "But I do what I can, *n'est-ce pas?*"

"Good for you, Bonny. I know how tough a job that is."

Bonny, a long, angular woman with shoulders that would make a halfback proud, smiled appreciatively. "We do what we have to do, eh, Meester McGowan?"

"You've got that right." Mac fingered the envelope in the side pocket of his jacket.

He stood in the middle of the entry hall, looked toward the big sweeping staircase that could have come off a film set of, say, 1936. Stella had always adored the look. The place, he noted, had hardly changed since he'd been gone. Stella's color scheme was so muted that being in the house was practically like being in a black-and-white movie— elegance in shades of gray, silver, pearl, ivory, ebony, onyx, ad infinitum.

"Anybody else here?" he asked.

"No, *monsieur*. You are the first."

"Hmm."

Mac hadn't given a lot of thought to Stella's reason for
having him over, so obsessed was he by the note. But he
would have to contend with whatever she had planned,
regardless. Stella could remain remarkably oblivious, even
in the midst of a crisis, if she'd fastened onto something
she considered important.

If he had to guess what was in the wind, Stella was
planning a last-ditch effort to save Troy's career. She probably wanted Mac to pay for private lessons with an acting
coach or maybe fork over the money for a package deal
for aspiring talent—an agent, a publicist, an elocutionist,
an image consultant and a personal trainer, all for a cool
twenty-five grand, including a field trip to Hawaii for
R&R. And, knowing his wife, she'd have her pitch carefully rehearsed and prepared. She'd never given up acting,
she'd just given up expecting to get paid for it.

"Oh, Mac, you're here! Wonderful!"

It was Stella, descending the stairs, making her entrance.
She was in one of her Richard Tyler pantsuits, cool and
elegant as always. She looked good, fresh. What was it?
Her hair was lighter, he noted. More platinum streaks. But
there was something else…her skin. Then it hit him, she'd
had a face-lift…at least a partial one. Some eye work. And
her brow was smooth.

She came directly to him, smiling, upbeat, her eyes spar-
kling. A gracefully aging star. The woman was fifty, after
all. She pulled his face down and kissed him on the cheek.

"You look great, Stella."

"I feel good," she said, beaming. "And I've had a little
work done, in case you're wondering. My hairdresser said
it would do wonders for my morale and he was right."

Stella led him into the sitting room, sitting next to him
on one of the facing twin pale gray silk love seats. Her
eyes continued to sparkle. She seemed so happy. The

thought of having to tell her about the note put a sour knot in his gut. But there was no point in deflating her until he knew what this was about. He'd let her have her few minutes of joy.

"So, what's up?"

Stella continued to smile, her eyes shimmering with emotion as she gathered herself. It was at moments like this that Mac remembered the Stella of old, the battered starlet he'd rescued, the beautiful woman who'd lured him to the pool house and given him her body, asking only for his protection. This was the Stella who, even at age fifty, could still put a wrench in him.

"Mac, you won't believe this, but I've been given a second chance," she said, sounding almost giddy.

"A second chance at what?"

"Stardom." She gave his hands a heartfelt squeeze. "I am so excited."

Her obfuscation had him bewildered. He didn't know whether she was going to tell him she'd fallen in love with a studio exec and wanted her freedom, or that Troy had been offered a leading role in the next Steven Spielberg film.

"Stella, spit it out. What's going on?"

His wife again drew a deep breath, beaming, looking as though she wasn't quite sure whether to laugh or sob. "I've been given an opportunity to make a film, to play an important role!"

"You have?"

"Yes, isn't it incredible? For a week now, I've just been beside myself with glee. Every morning I wake up and pinch myself, asking if it can possibly be true."

"I thought this was about Troy, the most important development in his career."

"It is, but it's about me, too. We've both been given a golden—truly golden—opportunity, Mac."

"You'd better explain."

Stella drew a long, slow breath like an actress having been handed an Oscar, preparing to launch into her acceptance speech. "Troy met some people through his roommate, a film director by the name of Amal Kory and an actress named Venita Kumar."

"Never heard of them."

"No, of course you haven't. They're Indian, Mac. Very few Indian film personalities are known in this country."

"Indian? You mean like in India?"

Stella laughed. "Yes, of course. Did you know that more films are made there than practically the whole rest of the world combined? Not many are seen outside India, of course, but over there it's an incredibly important industry."

"And you're going to India to make a film?"

"No, silly. Amal and Venita are here to make a film for the American market. Amal is terribly talented. I've seen two or three of his films and they were fabulous. And Venita, well, in India, Venita is Julia Roberts, Michelle Pfeiffer and Gwyneth Paltrow all rolled into one. Mac, she's made literally hundreds of films! There are people who worship the ground she walks on. Men have killed themselves over her."

"And they want you and Troy in their film."

"Yes, that's not so startling, is it? I do have talent, you know. And now that I'm older, it's seasoned talent."

Mac didn't know what to think. He hated to say it, but his wife truly sounded delusional. She hadn't been in front of a camera in twenty years or more. And what credits she did have were less notable than their son's. He hoped to God she hadn't flipped her lid.

"Explain why they picked you," he said.

"Amal said he took one look at me and saw Hilda

Grimsley—you know the mother in John Warden's nine-teenth-century novel, *On Distant Shores.*"

Mac didn't know the book she was referring to, but gathered it was famous.

"Anyway," Stella went on, "when he heard I'd previously done work in films, he asked me to read for him from the script, informally. Mac, the man was enraptured. And so was Venita. She couldn't believe I hadn't had more credits. A woman who's made all those films was positively enthralled by my little reading, Mac!"

He didn't know thing one about Hollywood, but he was a businessman, he knew how the world worked, especially when money was involved. He smelled a rat. "What's the catch?"

"Oh, there's no catch. Troy's been all but cast in the role of Llewellyn, the best friend of the hero. It's a supporting role, as is mine. The starring roles have to go to name actors or the film won't get made, of course. They'd like Tom Cruise or Brad Pitt, and Gwyneth, she's magnificent in period pieces, but no decisions have been made yet." She beamed, tilting her head in that coquettish way he'd always found so endearing.

It had been almost twenty years since their brouhaha over *Ordinary People,* but Mac sensed they were about to do a remake. "Well, I don't know what to say, Stella. Congratulations, I guess."

"It's a dream come true."

"When do you begin shooting?"

"Oh, it's not a done deal yet. There's much to do before a movie can be made. Getting the right people on board is key. And it's an independent film, which means we'll want the backing of a studio, and there's always the distribution issue. But when things are still up in the air that means there are still opportunities for the right people."

Mac saw that he was right. His wife was about to hit

him up for investment money, just as she had all those years ago.

"Which brings me to my next point," Stella said. "Mac, there's an opportunity waiting here for you, too."

Out of respect he didn't laugh, though his foresight entitled him self-congratulations. "How so?"

"Amal and Venita are in the process of putting together their financing. There's no shortage of money around for the right projects, as I'm sure you know. To be blunt about it, I've asked them to give you a chance to get in on this on the ground floor."

"Stella," he said, trying to hide his annoyance, "I think we've been down this road before. I wasn't interested in getting involved in *Ordinary People* and I'm not about to get involved in a film deal now. Surely you know that."

Ignoring her crestfallen look, he got up and went to the French windows that overlooked the garden. The back lawn was green and lush. Mac recalled playing out there with Troy when he was just a little guy. Stella would bring him home from a day of auditions, and Mac would try to get him to kick a soccer ball. Troy always had the size and coordination for sports, but not the desire. He much preferred watching movies with Mommy.

Stella was soon at Mac's side. She took his arm, making him look at her. "This is different," she said, her voice plaintive, though not quite desperate. "We're talking about a project that might make Troy's career. These sorts of opportunities put young actors on the map. They only come along once in a lifetime. And it could fulfill a life-long dream of mine, too. But that's not important. What's important is that you have an opportunity to invest in your son's career. You have an opportunity to validate him, to do something with Troy, instead of always fighting him."

"I've offered to educate the boy, bring him into my

business, I've even offered to set him up in a business of his own. He's the one who won't listen, Stella."

"But this is what he wants. Isn't this a business?"

"No, it's egomania."

"I promise you, Mac, you'll be kicking yourself from now to kingdom come if you let it get away like you did *Ordinary People*. But, okay, you don't see this as a business opportunity. Forget making money. But don't you see it's something you can do for us?"

She put her hands on his chest, kitten-like, the way she always did when she was trying to soften him up. Mac really hated it when she did that because it reminded him of his weakness, his mistakes of the past. Even now, after all these years, he remembered the hold Stella had on him—the shared misery. It had taken years, but he'd finally learned that about their relationship, and it was one of the toughest lessons of his life.

Her eyes began to fill—he might have predicted that. He wanted to tell her not to bother. The tears started running down her cheeks. She angrily wiped them away. Mac started looking for a quick exit from the conversation.

"How much money are we talking?"

"One or two million."

"One or two million! Jesus and Mary, I thought you were going to say twenty or thirty thousand."

"Hollywood is big business, Mac."

"Stella, I think you've popped your cork. I'm serious. You don't know how crazy this is."

His wife looked hurt, positively, mortally wounded.

"I'm sorry," he said. "I shouldn't have said that. But I don't think you appreciate how bizarre this conversation is. At least to me."

"A million dollars is nothing to you," she said. "You have ten times that much in T-bills alone, and don't tell me you don't. My lawyer has all your financial data, as you well know.''

"The U.S. government and some movie people from India are very different kinds of investments,'' he replied. "I would have to be insane to give people like that my hard-earned money.''

"Investors will be lined up once the project gets rolling. Don't you see, it's the seed money, the first money in, that gets the biggest cut of the profit. The first million or two can get as much as twenty percent of a forty- or fifty-million-dollar film that makes seventy-five or a hundred. That's a tremendous return.''

"I'm no expert, God knows, but this I know about Hollywood—for every three movies that get made, one might make a profit for their investors. If I want to play those odds, I'll go to Las Vegas.''

Her expression turned stone cold. She stared at him, wiping away the last of her tears as she did. Mac McGowan knew that look well. He was about to get the climactic closing speech.

"You're a very smart man, Mac,'' she said, her voice modulated now. "You've been successful and you've been generous. I can't complain. But there's more to life than money. When you leave this world, what comfort will those T-bills bring you? None. But I can tell you what will give you satisfaction. Knowing your son has realized his dream. And believe me, I know all about dreams.

"You have the power to make Troy's and my dreams come true. And you don't have to risk your business, your home, your cars, your retirement to do it. Or would you rather spend your nights counting your T-bills? What's really in your heart, Mac?''

They stared at each other for a long time. Then he said, "One question. Did these Indian film folks make it a condition that before you and Troy get parts in the movie, I've got to put up a couple of million bucks?''

''No, but it wouldn't hurt.''

''You want me to put up that kind of money in hopes they'll pick you and Troy for the parts?''

''No, you could make it a condition,'' she said evenly.

Mac, who was never the quickest kid on the block, but had always been persistent enough to get to the finish line eventually, started getting the picture. ''All right, say, hypothetically, that I put some money into the deal. Are there any guarantees the movie will be made?''

''They would have to get enough to cover the cost of making the film, but once the seed money is there, the rest comes easily.''

''But what if it doesn't come and they've got to fold the project. Do I get my money back?''

''Whatever wasn't spent, I suppose.''

He nodded. ''Stella, there's this saying that I'm sure you've heard—'A fool and his money are soon parted.' Well, it sounds to me like this is a prime example. If these people are so good, they don't need me. In fact, I'm surprised they'd even want to talk to me.''

''They don't need you, or me, or Troy. And the only reason they're talking to you is because I asked them to. But they were impressed by our talent, and I wanted you to have the opportunity to help your son in a way that matters to him.''

Mac looked out at the garden, telling himself to stand his ground, even as his impulse was to placate her and dry up the tears. He drew a deep breath. ''I'll give you a check for fifty thousand dollars,'' he told her. ''You can give it to these people to reserve a role for yourself and Troy. I know you've got a little money stashed away, as well. If you want to sweeten the pot, that's up to you. But that's the best I can do.''

"Mac, I don't want your check. I want you to talk to Amal and Venita. I'll take your fifty thousand and give it right back to you, if you'll just talk to them. Please."

Mac McGowan drew a long breath. He hated this. He hated saying no to Stella, but he knew he was right. She had her head in the clouds, and as long as she chased pipe dreams, she'd never see the world for what it was. And she'd never see him. That was a foregone conclusion.

As far as Stella was concerned, he'd always been a means to an end. With him in the wings, she'd been able to deal with the pain of a gruesome marriage to an egocentric bully. His loyalty and devotion had enabled her to sweep a horrible, tragic accident under the rug. And now she had her hand out, yet again.

"All right. I'll meet with your friends. When are they going to be here?"

"Soon."

"Can we talk about my issue now?"

"How about after they leave? I promised you my undivided attention. I'm too keyed up now for something dreary. Surely you can sympathize with that, Mac. My future is literally hanging in the balance."

If you only knew, he thought to himself.

They were on Santa Monica Boulevard and had just passed the Los Angeles Country Club. It wouldn't be long before they arrived.

Venita Kumar, a dark beauty with large, ebony eyes and smooth latte-colored skin, sat in one corner of the rear seat of the limo. She wore a knit St. Johns suit rather than a sari, and only two of her favorite gold bracelets. She knew when to strive for a western look and when her native dress best served her interests. Her supple mind benefited her well, especially with Americans whose openness and naiveté were as convenient as they were pleasing.

She glanced over at Arjay Pantel, the con man she'd hired to play the role of Amal Kory. He sat in the other corner, as calm and stately as a maharajah. For a small man, he certainly had an imposing presence. It was his quiet charisma that had drawn her to him—that and his inimitable flair for the game. The man was fearless. He could do it all. Since they'd joined forces, Venita had congratulated herself on the wisdom of her choice. What she didn't know was the extent to which she could trust him. But that was true of every man. Arjay, though, bore special attention in that regard. He had a reputation for being as slippery as a snake.

Jugnu Singh, her devoted bodyguard and hand servant, sat in the front seat next to the driver. Jugnu was a Sikh, a huge man, bearded, always wearing the traditional turban, his hawkish face stunningly handsome. Jugnu glanced back at her every once in a while, his eyes never away from her for long. Without the guard's silent, soothing presence, Venita felt vulnerable. She borrowed his male strength. It gave her backbone when she operated in a man's world. Eternally silent, Jugnu was the body and she the brain—except in the feminine domain, where Venita was everything. Body, brain and soul. The arrangement worked extremely well.

The limo moved into the left-turn lane, indicating they didn't have far to go.

Venita was a bit nervous. Mac McGowan was the first halfway solid prospect they'd had since they'd begun their search for investors. The irony was the opportunity had come to them purely by chance. Had she not been introduced to Troy at that party, and had he not come on to her the way he had, there never would have been a conversation about money. Nor would they have met Stella. Venita could only hope that they would find a way to cash in on the chance encounter.

Arjay, who apparently had been thinking along the same lines said, "Tell me, Venita, what special challenges does our Mister McGowan pose?"

"From what I'm told, the chap knows nothing of the cinema."

"That's certainly convenient."

"Yes, but don't be complacent," she warned. "He's a successful businessman, which means he understands money perfectly well."

"And likes spending it, I trust."

"He won't be stuffing our pockets, at least not lightly. Those who have vast sums usually spend with the utmost reluctance. Profit, vanity and women are the reasons men of wealth spend, you know."

Her companion turned his silver-topped head in her direction, his heavy lids drooping. "You would know, love. But if I may be allowed to offer a suggestion..."

"Yes?"

"Do be careful not to upstage me. When you seem to order me about, the illusion of me being in charge is lost. Supposedly you are but the actress."

"I don't need to be told about acting, Arjay. That's the area where I reign supreme."

"Ah, but I act not for the cinema, but for life. There are similarities between the life of a charlatan and an actor, I grant you, but the object of my vocation is deception, yours is merely entertainment. Trust me in this, Venita."

"Don't worry, I will show *Amal* the proper deference," Venita assured him, "but I also know that in the end, it is *I* these people must trust and believe in. Amal is here to give me credibility and nothing more. He will fade away, but I shall become a fixture in Hollywood, a celebrated director in my own right. And nothing, absolutely nothing," she assured him, "shall deter me."

Arjay drew a long slow breath, raising his brows superciliously. "I take you at your word, and I shall do my utmost to make it so."

Considering what she was paying him—not to mention the cut of the project he was to receive—she certainly hoped so. He'd done a masterful job of seducing Stella Hampton, but their real prey was neither Stella nor Troy. It was Mac McGowan.

Venita tried not to worry about Arjay, though. Her immediate problem was to get from point A to point B without going into bankruptcy. Her funds were desperately low, with creditors already beginning to queue. Unless she got some "cash in the till," as the Americans say, and soon, it would be all over.

"I wouldn't have engaged you had I not believed in your capacities," she told her companion, judging a stroke was in order. The last thing she needed to do was offend him.

Arjay wore an amused but haughty look of disdain. "I was charming British aristocrats when you were still in nappies, my dear. I am the least of your worries. From what Stella tells me, our Mr. McGowan will be a tough nut to crack." His brow arched as he peered out the limousine window. "How rich is the gentleman, anyway? Stella wasn't certain, but she thought about thirty million, U.S."

"My sources indicate closer to fifty," Venita replied. "He has sufficient capital for our purposes, let me put it that way."

What she didn't tell Arjay was that she was rapidly coming to the conclusion that McGowan was their one best—perhaps only—hope. Every other lead she'd pursued had turned cold. Not that she had expected it to be easy, but she would have thought the other potential investors' curiosity value would be greater and that that would have led to interest in the project. But it hadn't worked out that way.

Still, if they got McGowan to put up the first money, the rest would surely come. People, she'd learned in her thirty-six years, were sheep. More so in Hollywood than anywhere else. So, having one fat sheep in the fold would almost certainly bring more. They badly needed Mac McGowan to show the way.

Venita couldn't help feeling a certain amount of resentment toward these damn, insular Americans, though. The Hollywood crowd knew nothing of the world beyond their studios. The name Venita Kumar meant nothing to them, despite the fact that more human beings on earth would recognize her face than Marilyn Monroe and Sophia Loren combined. And yet, here she could walk down Rodeo Drive and not a soul would turn a head, unless it was to look at her sari. Jugnu drew much more attention than she. How could she not feel bitter?

Still, America was her last hope. Her own country had little to recommend it, as far as she was concerned, not considering the disgrace and humiliation she'd suffered at the hands of her countrymen. After Ramda Bol there was no returning to India, not unless it was to be a glorified prostitute. Here she could use her fame and ignore her past. Americans allowed themselves to be used that way. Maurice Chevalier had done it. But she still had a mountain to climb. A huge mountain with Mac McGowan standing atop it.

Angel Ordoñez wasn't sure what was going on. First, McGowan goes to this big, fancy-assed place in Beverly Hills. Through the window Angel can see him with the blond lady, her acting all kissy-face. Then these Arabs show up in the limo and they're all talking and laughing. If this blonde is McGowan's broad, Angel thought, seems like he's planning on fucking her in front of the United Nations.

Angel returned to the Chevy he'd gotten in exchange for Manuela's, to wait and see what happened next.

If Angel had his way, he'd just put a shiv in McGowan's gut and let the fucker slowly bleed to death. But that wasn't what Manuela wanted. "You want to know the truth, Angel? I would marry him right now if he wanted to. He really is a nice man."

"I thought you said he was an asshole. Him and Conti both."

"Maybe he didn't mean to hurt me. The problem is the girlfriend. If he didn't have someone on the string already, I bet he'd have hopped right in the sack. I seen the way he stared at my boobs. I could tell what he was thinking."

"You're saying if he didn't have no girlfriend, he'd love you?"

"Could be."

"So what the fuck do you want? To get rid of her?"

"I don't know."

That was last night. Angel had been in no mood to fuck around. "When you figure it out let me know, okay?"

That morning, Manuela had made him coffee and sat with him at the little kitchen table. "Okay, this is what I want. Scare them, Angel, Mac and Art both. Don't kill nobody, just scare them. And I want to know who Mac's girlfriend is, too. I want to know what she's like."

"How the fuck am I supposed to find that out?"

"Can't you follow him or something?"

"That bullshit takes time, Manuela. You want me to put somebody in the hospital, now that's a no-brainer. Maybe an hour or two of my time. But, you're asking me to play fucking cop. I look like a cop to you?"

"If you don't do this for me, who will?"

"How you going to pay me and pay the bank when you don't got no job?"

"I'll think of something."

"Maybe I'd like to know, Manuela."

"So maybe I'll go back to the Bottoms Up Club."

"O'Gill will make you suck his cock."

"You think I never done that before, Angel? That's how you get the good jobs. Where you been?" Then she said, "Never mind, I know where you been."

"And you don't want to hear how you get the good jobs there."

The point was, Manuela didn't know what she wanted, but she was giving him a hundred dollars a day to do it. For that he'd fart around a while. But he'd much rather stick McGowan with a shiv and watch him squirm. Rich gringo bastard.

Pacific Palisades

The limousine wound its way up the curving street, passing the large homes terraced on the hillside with their magnificent views of the L.A. basin, Santa Monica, Venice, El Segundo and the Bay. Venita Kumar contemplated the check in her hand, repressing her delight. True, it was at best a consolation prize—fifty thousand dollars—but it would keep them going a few more months. God knew, the funds she had at home in India would be tied up in the courts for years, and the chances of getting more than a pittance out of the country were nominal at best.

Arjay looked over at her, watching her fondle the check. "It surprised me how little resistance he offered, considering the depth of his resentment."

"Our Mr. McGowan didn't give that money to me. It was a gift to his wife. He was buying her gratitude, assuring himself of her loyalty. He knew that we're using Stella."

"I quite agree. I think it proves she is the key."

"And you did remarkably well with her, Arjay, I must say. You have the woman eating from your hand."

"No small challenge with a husband present, if I do say so."

Arjay's diction was perfect, his accent practically non-existent. He exuded such confidence that half the time even Venita believed him. "Mac McGowan is protective," she said, "but I don't sense profound affection between them. If I were to hazard a wager, I'd say they are married in name only."

"And did you get any vibrations from our Mr. McGowan aimed in your direction?" Arjay asked.

"No, not really. He's a man and there are always certain marks of awareness—unless of course the person in question is homosexual—but I sensed more hostility than anything else. He did not like me. Or you. More even, he did not like what we do."

"Then Stella wasn't exaggerating when she said Hollywood has been a problem for him. Considering his attitudes, I should say the afternoon was something of a success."

"Thanks to Stella," Venita said.

"I wonder what McGowan was after."

"To be a hero would be my guess."

Arjay considered that. "You're probably right."

"But we weren't going to get another penny. He'd budgeted fifty thousand and Stella had her choice. She could have a new diamond, a car or us. That's why I took the money and ran."

"Could you have given up a trifle soon? In my experience a refusal to expect money will induce an offer of more."

"I think we're best advised to leave that to Stella. She has something up her sleeve. I don't know what, but she has a confidence that's more than simple whistling in the dark.''

''Perhaps you're right. I'm not used to taking a passive role. In any case, it's never wise to overplay one's hand,'' he said with an ironic smile. ''A lesson well learned, wouldn't you say?''

It was an oblique reference to the scandal that had caused her to flee India in disgrace. Venita did not appreciate the allusion. The mere thought of it set her blood to boiling. She could scarcely abide the mention of Ramda Bol's name. It pained her immensely even to think of him. The sod.

She often regretted not having killed the bloody bastard, though had she done, no question she'd be rotting in a stinking jail cell at this very moment. Fate and a bit of luck had given her a second chance. Nothing, absolutely nothing, would stop her this go-around. Not even Mac McGowan.

Reaching the crest of the hill, the limo entered the gate to the sprawling modern dwelling with its flat roof, its angular lines. It was where, for the past two months, they had lived. The vehicle continued along the drive lined with sago palms and cactus until they reached the portico of the house, stopping behind Troy Hampton's gimpy Mazda.

''Ah, and now the son,'' Venita said cheerily.

Troy Hampton, she'd decided, was the unknown piece of the puzzle. She knew the boy and his father were at odds but, as best she could tell, he was still the heir. Which made his role somewhat ambiguous. Stella seemed the key, but there was a great deal going on in Troy Hampton's head that left Venita wondering. He was very young, but he had a dark, mysterious quality that had caught her imagination. Of course, the real question was whether he had access to his father's wealth. Or was he just a pretty boy with pretensions? She sighed. One thing was certain, Troy

Hampton was a far cry from her last lover. Ramda Bol, the son-in-law of the prime minister, had been both the greatest conquest and the greatest disaster of her life, one that would surely torment her to her dying day.

Still, Troy Hampton did bring her pleasure. Just looking at him and watching him watch her was a source of joy. He was not so tall and imposing as his father, but he had his mother's refinement and beauty. A prettier young man she'd never seen in her life. A blond Adonis.

"I shall leave young Master Hampton to you, my dear," Arjay said, leaning toward her, his voice taking on a confidential tone. "It's safe to say he has little use for me apart from my cinematographic prowess."

"You can't take that personally, Arjay. He loves me, you know. In a young man there's nothing so potent as his sex drive."

"Everybody's in love with you," he replied diplomatically.

The remark brought another glance at her from Jugnu, who then got out of the limousine. Venita smiled modestly, though of course what Arjay had said was perfectly true.

"Still in all, you can't ignore him," she said to Arjay. "Troy's serious about his film career and we must cater to both his mind and his heart. The lad's more shrewd than you might think. He might adore me, but without the prospect of a role in our film, who knows how long I could keep his interest. Conquest, as you know, is ninety percent of it, especially in a young man. A woman must have skill to hold a man's interest if she has nothing to offer but her body. To be safe, we both must titillate him, Arjay. You with work, me with play. Don't forget, if we lose him, there's no hope of enticing the parents."

"Stella wants fame just as badly as her son."

"But Troy is the lever she uses with her husband. Can't

you see it? There is something profoundly emotional going on there. I'm not sure what."

"Yes, I sensed a ghost," Arjay said.

"Precisely. And we must make this ghost our friend."

Jugnu held the passenger door for her, but she ignored him. "Arjay, why don't you chat up young Master Hampton a bit?"

"What about you?"

"Oh, I shall warm him up for you, get his juices flowing. You can have a beer with him and tell him some stories about filmmaking. Tell him about your triumph, *The Night of the Tiger.*" She gave him one of her delighted laughs. "He'll be interested if only because I starred, if you'll recall."

"You've recounted it so often, how could I forget?"

Venita slid to the door and took Jugnu's proffered hand. He helped her out of the vehicle. She barely came to his armpit, he was so large. Glancing up at him, she said, "I think I should like a massage, Jugnu. Prepare everything."

He bowed slightly in acknowledgment. Venita moved past him, heading for the house. Even before she reached the double doors, one swung open. Cala, the shriveled, toothless maid Venita had brought from India, admitted her. Venita breezed past her, pausing on her way through the house at the entrance to the family room. Troy Hampton was seated on the floor cross-legged and watching a video of one of her films on the large-screen TV. That pleased her immensely.

Troy had a man's body, but his manner and image were more that of a boy—the jeans and white T-shirt, the Armani sunglasses pushed up into his bleached hair. His face was narrow and dominated by large blue eyes and dark lashes. His mouth, the slight fullness of his lips, gave him a pouty air. Though Venita had always been partial to men rather than boys, there was something about the lad she found quite stimulating. Perhaps it was because at thirty-six, she was getting to an age where younger men had their charms.

"Troy, my darling," she said, "how fortunate you're here."

He turned at the sound of her voice. "Hey, Venita."

"We've just come from your mother's home."

"Yeah?"

"Come with me for a walk in the garden and I'll tell you about it. Oh, you might wish to stop the tape there, my darling. You'll fancy the next scene. It's very sensuous."

Troy gave her a rakish smirk, apparently confident that she wanted him as badly as he wanted her. Venita found it odd how in some relationships one was as much the hunted as the hunter. The symmetry in that appealed to her. She, after all, had her needs. It was not always enough to be goddess to others.

Troy got to his feet, and she examined his body as he came toward her. He was a fine specimen. He had talent, as well, but only a modicum. The role of Llewellyn would be a stretch for him, and she might have to cast him in a lesser role before all was said and done, but for now, until they had his father's money, he was her star.

Troy savored the spicy richness of her perfume, the way she lightly bumped up against him as they walked toward the sunroom. Venita was exotic and she turned him on. Her mysterious nature appealed to him. What he wasn't sure of was whether she was coming on to him, or if she was just a flirt.

The thing was, he didn't want to misread her. Troy knew that actors nearly always wanted attention, to be worshiped even, and sex was often part of the mix. God knew, it was that way with him. But Venita and Amal had given him a

fantastic opportunity and he didn't want to blow it. The
thing to do, he'd decided, was to take his cue from her.

The only indication she might have romantic thoughts
was a remark she'd made about being closer to his
mother's age than to his. Why would she have said that
unless she was thinking of being with him? And she hadn't
been trying to discourage him, because her body language,
her looks, all said the opposite.

When they entered the sunroom, Venita stopped. "Oh
my, the sun's still quite bright out in the garden. I'll just
have Cala fetch a parasol. Cala!" she called.

The shriveled little servant, her skin dark as mahogany,
came running. Venita and Amal always spoke to her in
Hindu, or whatever the language was. Cala knew no English but "please" and "thank you," so everything else
she said was unintelligible to Troy. She couldn't have been
more than four foot ten and was so thin that she looked as
though she could be carried away by a good stiff breeze.
Venita had explained that Cala was a necessary member
of the household, if only to clean the toilets, for Cala was
an untouchable and no Indian of a higher class would
deign to clean a toilet. Certainly not a Brahman such as
Venita, who would die before she'd come in contact with
a toilet brush. "Why not hire a cleaning lady?" Troy had
asked.

"It's not just the cleaning of the toilet that's important,"
Venita explained. "It's also who in fact does it that matters. I want someone like Cala cleaning my toilet, changing
my bed linen, doing my wash. I know that sounds strange,
but some things simply can't be explained. But before you
look down your nose, there are things about your culture
that we find curious, as well."

"Like what?"

"Your rampant puritanism, for example. Your founding
fathers read too much Old and New Testament, in my

humble opinion. They would have been far better served to have read the *Kama Sutra* instead."

Cala returned with the parasol. Venita opened it as they stepped onto the patio. The sun was fairly low, but Venita acted as though she was allergic to it. She took Troy's arm and they began walking.

Venita hadn't been quite so familiar with him in the past, and though she'd touched him, brushing back a lock of hair from his face, this was the most womanlike she'd been with him.

"So, you and Amal met with my parents," he said as they strolled toward the pool. "Did you discuss me?"

"No, your name hardly came up," she replied. "Except that you were in our plans for the film. Were you expecting that it would?"

"I thought you might have felt them out about our friendship."

"Now, why would I do that?"

"You seem worried about the difference in our ages."

Venita stopped walking and turned to face him. "Don't waste your time with thoughts of me, my little duck," she said. "I'm much too old for you."

"Do you really feel that way, or are you just saying so because you think you have to?"

"My, but aren't you the brazen one?" They started walking again. "Be direct, love. Are you trying to tell me something, or just making conversation?"

"I'm trying to figure you out," he said.

"Don't you know it doesn't pay to try to figure out a woman? You never shall. The best you can hope for is her cooperation...and perhaps her love."

"In India aren't older women ever attracted to younger men?"

Venita arched a brow. "You don't lack for courage, do you?"

"Well?"

"It's been the custom in India for centuries, my love."

"My kind of custom," he said with a grin.

Troy saw her mouth bend into a smile, but she otherwise ignored his remark.

They'd come to the huge pool and Venita stopped there to gaze about "the garden," as she and Amal called it. It was a manicured acre of hilltop behind their rented palatial home. Troy and several of his friends had come at Amal's invitation to swim and enjoy the grounds. Twice they'd frolicked in the buff while Amal looked on approvingly with his bacchanal smile.

The director was a strange guy. Troy hadn't figured him out yet. Curiously, Venita had shown him less respect than Troy would have figured, considering he was the big-shot director. When he'd mentioned Amal's seeming deference toward Venita to his mother, Stella had said, "They probably do things very differently in India. Besides, no star is bigger in Indian cinema than Venita. But Amal has no need to put on airs. His body of work speaks for itself."

"So, what do you think of him?" he'd asked.

Stella told him she was most impressed. In fact, she'd said that she found Amal Kory "exceedingly stimulating, as both a man and an artist."

Troy had trouble understanding Amal's appeal, considering he was an old fart and three inches shorter than Stella. "What do you see in him, anyway? Besides his films, I mean?"

"It's not a physical thing," she said. "I don't mean I'm sexually attracted to him. It's his soul, that artistic spirit. When he talks to me I feel like he's looking right inside, that I can have no secrets from the man. That's a worthy quality in a director, don't you think?"

Troy wasn't so sure his mother wasn't playing it down.

He even wondered if she wasn't infatuated. Her love life was something they'd almost never discussed, but Troy had often wondered how she could live alone for so long, never getting involved with anybody. "You're never getting a divorce, are you?" he'd once said.

"No, and I'm not going to discuss why."

What Stella didn't realize was that he already knew why, and he had since he was fifteen. He'd overheard her and Mac arguing once when they weren't aware he was in the house. For five years now he'd known all about Aubrey St. George. But Troy was smart enough to save the dirt for a time when he could use it to his advantage. Maybe the time was now.

"Look at that sky," Venita said, noting the color beginning to gather off to the west. "Let's go out to the pavilion, shall we?"

As they made their way across the lawn, she moved closer to him, pressing her breast against his arm. Troy figured she was teasing him, or she had ideas. Either way he liked the attention.

The pavilion was circled by Greek columns. There was a hundred-and-eighty-degree view of the ocean, with Malibu at one end and Long Beach at the other. The edge of the garden was just beyond the pavilion and dropped a few hundred feet to the ravine below.

Going up the steps, he scanned the hazy Pacific. Santa Catalina Island lay on the horizon, a humped gray mass, seemingly floating on the sea. Venita squeezed his arm harder, allowing her hip to bump against his. Troy's heart jogged up a notch.

"Don't you want to know what happened when Amal and I met with your parents?" she asked, smoothing her skirt as she sat on the bench.

Troy dropped down beside her. "Sure, what happened?"

"Your father made a modest investment in the project. Nothing of consequence, but a nice gesture. It was mostly to please your mother, I think."

"He tries to buy people," Troy said. "That's the way he does things."

"He didn't seem very interested in the project."

"My old man has a problem with the whole Hollywood scene."

Venita lowered her parasol. Troy stared at the color in the sky where the sun was just dropping behind a bank of clouds. Venita seemed like she wanted to say something, but was having trouble finding a way. Troy decided to help her.

"Are you bummed about it?" he asked.

"Well, investors are a necessary evil in this business."

"Don't get down yet, Venita."

She studied him with curiosity. "Why? Do you know something I don't?"

"Yes," he said, giving her a quirky smile, "but I'm not quite ready to tell you just what."

"My, my, a man of mystery."

"I like having my ducks all lined up before I go public."

"And you're going to make me wait along with everyone else."

Troy grinned. "Let's just say I have a contingency plan."

Venita's brows rose slightly, but she withheld comment. For several minutes they stared out at the Pacific, neither of them speaking. Troy had been vague on purpose. He knew how to be a hero, but he also knew the importance of timing.

After a while, Venita surprised him by taking his hand. She toyed with his fingers. Troy breathed in her perfume again. Something about her got him right in the gut. Maybe it was because he'd never known a woman quite like her before. Not that he was inexperienced; he wasn't. He'd had his share of girls, but Venita was the first real woman to show this kind of interest in him, not counting his thirty-something drama coach, Irene, who'd seduced him when he was seventeen. In a way, that didn't count because she was going through a divorce at the time and ended up sleeping with virtually every guy in the class.

Troy liked the coolness of Venita's skin. And her touch. She'd managed to get him hard, scarcely doing a thing. The way she looked at him through her lashes was enough in itself to bring him off.

"Do you think we could be friends, Troy?" she asked.

"Friends? You mean, like intimate friends?"

"Yes."

"Sure, why not?"

"The better I get to know you, the more I'm convinced I should like that," she said, rubbing the back of his hand against her cheek. "You're a very special young man."

"I think you're pretty special, too."

"If this were India, instead of Puritan America, I would have no qualms whatsoever. It would be entirely natural to teach you the ways of the *Kama Sutra*."

Her words made his cock turn rock-hard. "Seriously?"

"Oh, very seriously. But I want to be proper and re-spectful. This is not my country."

"Everybody here's not a Puritan, you know. And besides, this is L.A., not Des Moines."

"Then you would be interested. You're not just being polite."

He gave a little laugh. "I wouldn't joke about something like that."

She ran her tongue over the edges of her teeth and pressed her bosom harder against him. "I don't frighten you, Troy?"

"Frighten? Why would you frighten me?"

"You are ahead of your years, aren't you?"

Troy touched her lip with his finger. "You know what your trouble is, Venita? You're too hung up on the age thing."

"Or, maybe I simply can't believe my luck."

The remark made him smile. She glanced toward the house. Troy did, too. He saw Jugnu standing in the window, peering toward them.

"Jugnu's ready, I see."

"Ready for what?"

"I'm going inside to have my massage now," Venita said.

"He gives you a massage?"

"Yes, and has done virtually nightly for years. Jugnu has the best hands in the world."

Troy could only blink.

"I know Amal would like to talk to you, but afterward perhaps you'd care to come visit me in my bath?"

"Really?"

"Yes, of course. We've decided to be friends, haven't we?" Venita pulled his face over to her and kissed him on the cheek. "Do try to forget your Puritan origins, my little duck. My way's so much easier and more enjoyable."

"You say it so casually. You aren't like this with just every guy, are you?"

Venita threw back her head and laughed. "Do you know how many people live in India, Troy?" she asked him.

He shook his head.

"A billion," she said. "That means about five hundred million of them are men. And you know what? Ninety percent of them would give an arm to be in Troy Hampton's shoes right now."

He grinned.

"How does that make you feel, love?" she asked.

Troy continued to grin.

She tweaked his nose. "I'll see you in an hour."

Beverly Hills

Mac had been waiting for Stella the better part of an hour, having ordered a second vodka tonic, his impatience growing more quickly than the relaxing effect of the alcohol. She'd talked him into having dinner with her at Dominick's, their favorite place to eat when they were still together, but he could see it had been a bad idea. He should have insisted on having their conversation as soon as the Indians had gotten out the door, as she'd promised.

"How long will this take?" she'd asked at her house when he pulled the note from his jacket pocket.

"That's hard to say. It's about Aubrey."

Stella's shoulders slumped. "In that case, let me freshen up and then, as a small token of appreciation, I want to take you to dinner. We can discuss whatever you want over cocktails. I still can't handle Aubrey without a good stiff belt."

"Stella…"

She'd pooched out her lip the way she did when she was unhappy and said, "Please, Mac."

"Oh, all right. But this can't be put off forever."

"It's not that. I just have to get myself in the right frame of mind. You know how I am."

He did, indeed.

"Why don't you run on down to the restaurant and get us a table?" she said. "I have a quick call to make and then I'll be right there." She started for the stairs, then stopped. "Oh, and order me a glass of chilled Chardonnay, would you, dear?"

The Chardonnay now sat at her empty place, no longer chilled. She hadn't come "right there," which shouldn't have been a surprise. The rhythms of Stella Hampton's life were unique unto her. Still, Mac was beginning to worry that she'd stood him up, that she'd run off to Palm Springs or someplace again. Maybe it was a mistake to have mentioned Aubrey's name.

Downing the last of his drink, Mac took out his cell phone to call her. If she did duck out on him, he'd never forgive her. Bonny had just answered when Mac glanced up and saw Stella making her way to the table. She had changed into a knit tank top and matching skirt. He hung up, then got to his feet.

"I'm sorry, Mac," Stella said as he helped her with her chair. "I spilled on myself. Two people called. It was one thing after another."

The glass of wine sitting before her was dewy with sweat. "That's probably warm," he said. "Let me order you another."

"No, this is fine." She picked it up. "Cheers." She took a healthy slug, put the glass down and glanced around the sparsely filled restaurant. Mac read her displeasure. She sighed. "It's lost some of its luster over the years, hasn't it?" she said wistfully.

"Yeah, it has."

"But then, so have we." Stella's eyes shone luminously, shimmering with regret.

The waiter came with menus, which they both ignored.

"Thank you for meeting with Amal and Venita," she said. "I didn't properly thank you for your time."

"It was important to you," he said, fiddling with his empty drink glass.

His wife looked at him wistfully. "You haven't lost your good heart, have you, Mac? I don't suppose you ever will."

The note in his jacket pocket felt as if it was going to burn right through his side. The guilt was suffocating. Even now, ten years removed from living with this woman, he felt her need like it was his own. Earlier, when she sat listening to Amal Kory, enraptured, he'd very nearly said, "All right, Stella, I'm giving you and Troy a million each to do with as you like." But he hadn't. He knew that giving them money to invest in a film would be like giving dope to an addict. As Mac saw it, a man did have a responsibility to do the right thing. Contributing to a person's misery did them no favors, regardless of how certain they were it was in their best interest.

Money was not the immediate concern, however. The note was. He removed it from his pocket and laid it on the table. "Stella, I've got to ask you something. Something important."

"Regarding Aubrey?"

"Yes." He leaned forward and lowered his voice even though no one was within easy hearing. "Have you ever told anyone what happened?"

She blinked with surprise, but didn't seem to be upset by the question. "No, of course not."

"Are you sure?"

Stella glanced at the nearest table and, lowering her voice, said, "Certainly. Something like that doesn't slip out accidentally in conversation."

"What about with your therapist or masseuse or hairdresser?"

"Mac, I'm no idiot. Don't you think I appreciate how sensitive that information is? I scarcely allow myself to think about it, much less discuss it with anyone. Why?"

"I haven't said anything, either," he said. "Which means I'm hard-pressed to explain this note somebody left at my front door a couple of days ago." He slid the envelope across the table to her.

Stella picked it up, glancing at what had been written on the outside.

"Go ahead, read it."

She removed the slip of paper, her fingers trembling slightly. Mac watched her eyes. They rounded as she read, her lower lip wilting. "Oh my God," she said, her voice barely a whisper. There was terror in her eyes. "Who..."

"I have no idea. I thought maybe you could clear up the mystery."

She read the note over and over. She chewed on her lip. Her hands shook more violently. She quickly folded the paper and put it in the envelope, then slid it back across the table as though she wanted nothing whatsoever to do with it.

"I swear to you, Mac, I haven't said a word to a soul. Not in twenty years. I have absolutely no idea who that could be from." She turned pale and looked as though she was going to be sick. "What are we going to do?"

"Figure out who's behind this and what they want. I have one theory, but nothing concrete to go on. I thought that detective, Jaime Caldron, might be behind it."

"A policeman? Why, Mac?"

"I checked and found out he's about to retire. Maybe this case has bugged him all these years and he wants to shake things up in hopes that something damning turns up."

Stella reached across the table and took his hand. "Then we must stick together more closely than ever," she said. "For Troy's sake, as well as for our own." She looked deep into his eyes. "Surely you agree. I mean...well, you were the one who..." Her voice trailed off.

He stared at the woman he'd married twenty years before, but oddly enough he didn't so much see his own wife as the woman who'd been married to Aubrey St. George. Just as all those years ago, Mac McGowan felt as though he was being sucked into something he knew deep in his heart to be wrong. "Yes," he said softly. "I know."

Pacific Palisades

Venita Kumar lay on the massage table as Jugnu Singh expertly worked her muscles with his large, strong hands. She was completely naked. They'd long since abandoned the false modesty of a sheet or towel. After fourteen years of the near-daily ritual—fourteen years that bridged her marriage to Ranjit Govind—Venita saw no point in pretense. While being massaged, her body was the clay and Jugnu the potter. He was to work and shape it as he wished.

Venita felt no modesty around Jugnu. She did not shrink from lying on her back and exposing herself. She had absolute faith in the man—certainly more faith in him than in her own brother, which said less than might be expected, considering the first man to take her was, in fact, her elder brother, Ram, who, for his trouble, was beaten to death by their father.

Jugnu, curiously enough, had been a gift from her father. When she'd disgraced her family by choosing to become a film star, a "celluloid prostitute," as he called it, rather than accept an arranged marriage—a modest one at that, as was befitting her impure condition—her father told her he would give her one gift and one gift only for life. What he gave was Jugnu, a man, her father told her, she could trust and rely on, a man who would stand by her through lovers and husbands, a man who would bend his life to her will, once and forever.

At the time, she was nineteen and Jugnu was twenty-five, a young Sikh warrior who, together with his father and brothers, owed her father their lives. The details of the story, she did not know, only that Jugnu's life was her father's to give and he had given it to her. Venita knew that Jugnu had spent some time in prison and that partially explained why he rarely spoke. During the seventeen years they had been together she'd heard his voice so seldom, it was a shock to her ears when she did hear it.

Nor had he ever touched her improperly or made any overture toward her she did not invite. Jugnu's sexuality was a complete mystery to her. He behaved like a eunuch, so complete was his control. They'd never had sex, for Venita was certain that would end her power over him, once and for all. She assumed he satisfied himself through masturbation and visits with prostitutes, but she really didn't know.

The massages did not begin until Jugnu had been in Venita's service for three years. For a long time they were completely chaste, and there was no intimate touching. Oddly, it was her husband, Ranjit, who'd encouraged an evolution in the massage ritual. A film director forty years her senior, Ranjit had taken great pleasure watching her receive her massage, which Jugnu would give her before the couple retired. Because he had a bad heart and found foreplay to be taxing, Ranjit suggested that sexual stimulation become a part of the massage ritual. Venita was reluctant but, considering the suggestion had come from her husband, she acceded to the request.

Venita would have thought that the introduction of sexuality into their master-servant relationship would have changed things, but they did not. Jugnu remained discreet to a fault. Never once did his own pleasure become a factor. When Ranjit died, the sexual massages ceased, though later, when Venita took a lover, she would sometimes instruct Jugnu, who was adept at arousing her, to prepare her for lovemaking.

It was, even by Indian standards, an unorthodox arrangement, but one that she had come strongly to rely on. The servant was, after all, hers to do with as she chose.

Jugnu had applied the last bit of oil to her feet and was, at the moment, working them with exquisite precision. It felt incredible, in some ways as good as sex. With the massage of her feet among the last steps in the ritual, Venita knew the time had come. When he paused, she turned over onto her back.

Jugnu took half a step back and waited, his eyes on hers.

"Take off your shirt," she said.

He knew she liked looking at his muscular shoulders and chest as he pleasured her. The command conveyed the required information as to what she expected. Jugnu obediently removed his shirt, laid it aside and began working her legs, but this time in a more sexual way, drawing his hands lightly up the insides of her knees and thighs. His face remained stoically calm. Venita sometimes wondered if that refusal to show passion or desire wasn't his way of maintaining control. In that way alone could he confound her, plus maintain his dignity. He refused nothing, demanded nothing. He gave everything but a glimpse inside his own soul. She would never ask him about that—what he was thinking or feeling—because that would be tanta-mount to surrender, and she would truly surrender to no man, certainly not one who served her.

"Yes," she said as he lightly stroked her clitoris, alter-nately rotating his thumb over her nub until the forces of orgasm began to build. "Continue," she said, her voice calm, but her insides already beginning to quiver. "A bit more firmly." She felt it starting to build like a thunder-storm on the Punjab plain. "And now your tongue," she said.

It took sixty seconds, perhaps a minute and a half, no more. He was that good. Venita arched her pelvis as her climax gripped her. She convulsed for several moments, then fell still on the table. The tingling continued though her muscles no longer contracted.

"Go," she said.

Jugnu took his shirt and left. Venita lay still, taking stock of the sensations coursing through her body. There could be no better physical experience. A second and a third orgasm would come easily now. It almost mattered not who was attached to the penis.

Venita knew there ought be power in that. And surely there was. When the emotional dimension was subsumed under the physical, everything became quantifiable. That was the way most men approached things. It was that way with her, as well. There was wisdom in it. Emotion was treacherous. Every time she allowed herself to be a slave to emotion, she got in trouble. In her experience with men, Venita found that sex had two dimensions—the mechani-cal and the emotional. Jugnu's expert manipulations rep-resented the mechanical side. The emotional dimension had to do with the effects of male power on her psyche—male physical power, the power of money, the power of passion, the power of amusement and delight.

The boy, Troy Hampton, potentially held the power of money. Perhaps, if she were lucky, he might also hold the power of amusement and delight. The secret of happiness, from her standpoint, was to find what pleasure she could in those things without losing control over them. And she would. For if not, they would devour her.

The maid, Cala, came for him when Amal was in the middle of a rather boring story about some picture he'd made in Madras. They had been sitting at the pavilion, watching the sunset. Troy hadn't really been listening because he was thinking about Venita and her bath. It was the clearest signal yet. Maybe an invitation to have sex.

He was ready.

Cala babbled something unintelligible at him, making a beckoning sign with her bony hand. Troy glanced at Amal.

"Venita wants to talk to you," Amal said. "Go ahead, my friend, run along. Her stories are, in any case, more amusing than mine."

Troy wasn't quite sure what Amal was implying, but he had no intention of waiting around for clarification. He went off, following the barefoot servant, who always seemed to move at a half run. She led him into the house, down the hall to the master suite where Venita slept on a huge heart-shaped bed. It was built-in and came, of course, with the house.

Cala only went partway into the room, where she stopped, pointed at the bath, then retreated, closing the bedroom door behind her. For a moment Troy stood there, aware that Venita was waiting for him. The mere thought of that brought his lingering erection to life.

"Troy? Is that you, love?"

"Yes," he replied.

"Come talk to me."

His chest swelling, he headed for the bath, where he found Venita in a large, raised tub, opposite the door. Her black hair was piled up on her head with tendrils dropping down over her ears and temples. She smiled with the same casual air as if they were meeting at the Hard Rock Café.

"So, did you have a nice chat with Amal?"

"Yeah."

"Come sit here and tell me what you learned," she said, putting her hand on the gleaming tiles.

Troy did not wait to be asked twice. He went to the tub, expecting to find the surface of the water covered with bubbles, but it wasn't. His mouth twisted into a grin. He checked out her body, liking what he saw. Her nipples were a dark chocolate. She had a very small waist and her thighs were full but well shaped. Finally, he was seeing what he'd only imagined under her sari.

"Do you like what you see?" she asked.

"Awesome," he said, his voice tempered with self-assurance. Troy sat on the edge of the tub.

"What bits of wisdom did Amal have for you, my darling?" she asked.

Troy continued to scope out her body. "We talked about his films."

"Which films?"

"Something about a tiger."

"That would be *The Night of the Tiger.*"

"Yes," he replied, "that's it."

Venita lifted the leg nearest him from the water and rested her heel on the edge of the tub, exposing her private parts. Troy's heart pounded harder.

"Did he tell you about the scene where the lover of the princess comes to her while she's in her bath?"

Troy shook his head. "No, he didn't."

"It was really quite a good scene, if I do say so. I was the princess, you see."

"Then it had to be good."

"Aren't you adorable." Venita put her hand between her legs and began stroking herself. "I don't believe we have a video of that one, but if you'd like to see how the scene went, we could act it out. Would you like that?"

"Now?"

"Why not?"

He shrugged. "Sure."

Venita smiled. "I thought perhaps you would. My lover in the film was a bandit and, of course, we both died a horrible death in the end. But before that, we had some pleasure. Let's do the pleasure part, shall we?"

"Fine by me."

"Raj, my lover, climbed in the window. You're Raj, of course, but you don't have to come in the window. We'll pretend you've already done that. The princess, Leela— that's me—is lying in the tub, her eyes closed. Raj silently undresses. So I'll close my eyes and you undress."

Chuckling, Troy took off his shirt. Venita was having her fun, but he didn't mind. In fact, he kind of liked it that she was making a game of it. He kicked off his shoes and peeled off his jeans and undershorts. His erection, fully unfurled, stood out from his body like a handle, so distended that it curved halfway up to his belly button. That was probably Venita's intent—to see if she could get him hard without so much as touching him. Well, she could, and it was cool with him. "Now what?" he said.

She put her finger to her lips and, her eyes tightly closed, said, "Raj stealthily climbs into the tub and sits opposite the princess."

Troy got into the water, his long legs sliding down the sides of the tub past her hips. Venita seemed so serious it made him laugh, but he was also getting hot. Her game was working.

"Now the princess, sensing that something is amiss, sits bolt upright." Venita sat up, her breasts glistening from the water. "But she keeps her eyes closed out of fear of what she will find. You must remember, the princess is a virgin and very innocent. She's never seen a male member, much less touched one. So what does she do? She feels around with her hand, thinking that she can never be blamed for communion with anything her eyes cannot see."

Venita reached around in the water until her hand touched his cock. Gently wrapping her fingers around it, she said, "Leela knows she has found something truly remarkable, but convinces herself she is safe if she keeps her eyes shut. This serpentlike creature is so very hard. She begins to caress it, hoping that if the beast has hostile intentions she can soothe it."

Venita began stroking him. Troy was afraid he'd come right then and there. His breathing stopped. When Venita began caressing his balls with her other hand, he was sure he was going to burst. Her eyes were still closed, but she had a little smile on her face. Troy knew he couldn't hold back much longer.

"Poor Raj couldn't help himself," Venita whispered. "He got up from the tub, dragged Leela off to her bed and had his way with her."

Troy didn't wait for further instruction. He got to his feet. Taking Venita's hands, he pulled her up, then he stepped from the tub, helping her out, as well. He took her to the heart-shaped bed, ripped back the spread and climbed onto the silk sheets. On his knees, he waited for her to position herself in front of him, her legs open.

Troy fell on her then and was barely in her before he

came, his body convulsing like it never had before and probably never would again. When he was finished, he lay spent, small tremors going through him. Venita rubbed his back, as a mother would a child.

"You got a bit ahead of the story, my darling," she whispered in his ear. "But that's okay. We can work on that last part and make you truly worthy of the princess and the role of leading man."

Troy let his body melt into the woman's soft breasts and stomach. He'd had sex many times before, but never with such urgency.

"You know what the first rule of acting is, my love?" she asked, stroking his head.

"What?"

"Mastering the use of imagination. I've given you a small demonstration. Once you have that sort of command, there is no limit to what you can do."

Troy drew a long, slow breath, savoring Venita's rich, womanly scent like a pothead savoring his toke. "Christ," he said.

"Did you like that?"

"Awesome."

She chuckled, but he didn't care. If the woman could bring him off like that, she could do anything she wanted. Troy lay in the mellow languor of his spent body. For several minutes Venita stroked his belly and his chest.

"Am I a better lover or a better actor?" he asked.

"You're putting me on the spot," she said. "Which Troy Hampton should I appeal to?"

"Just tell me straight."

"All right then, a better actor."

"Really?"

"Have I hurt your feelings?"

"No," he replied. "I'm surprised."

"Don't despair, my little duck. Lovemaking is much more easily taught."

"You mean there's hope for me?"

"Only if you have the wisdom to choose the right teacher."

He lightly stroked her nipple. "You've given me something to think about, haven't you, Venita?"

Beverly Hills

A warm wind blew over them as they came out of Dominick's. Stella, clearly tipsy, took Mac's arm with the ease of a woman confident of a man's love, the Sturm und Drang of the anonymous note seemingly forgotten. "I like a warm, night wind," she said. "It makes me think of the desert and Arab sheiks."

"Arab sheiks?"

"Anything associated with hot sensual nights. I suppose Bedouin horsemen with dark eyes and wrapped faces are a cliché, but it makes for a nice fantasy."

Mac didn't know what to say to that. Stella was definitely drunk.

"Are you secretly laughing at me?" she asked.

"No."

"Yes, you are. Don't lie, Joseph McGowan."

She put her head on his shoulder. Mac felt uncomfortable. He'd already decided he wasn't going to let her drive herself home. Not in her condition. But he wasn't going to let her misconstrue his intentions, either.

"Mac," she said as they strolled along Wilshire, the wind tossing her hair, "do you ever think of that first time we made love in the pool house?"

"I used to," he said honestly, "but not very often anymore."

Stella looked up at him and said, "Does a little part of you wish for that again?"

He was inclined not to tell her the truth and yet not lie, either. "That's well behind us, Stella."

"It doesn't have to be."

Mac couldn't find a diplomatic way to dispute the point.

"Will you come home with me?" she whispered.

"I'm driving you, but then I'm coming back here in a cab to get my car."

She looked wounded, but continued to walk alongside him, not holding his arm quite so tightly. Finally she said, "It's natural to slip every once in a while. I hope you won't hold it against me."

"Stella, I feel no ill will toward you. I'm having trouble with that note. Not knowing what's going on upsets me."

"If there'd been no note, you'd say the same."

He didn't reply.

"Have you always hated me, Mac?"

"I don't hate you."

"Let me change the question. Have you ever loved me?"

"Yes."

"But I ruined it. Is that what you think?"

"We married for the wrong reasons, Stella."

"I'm sure I made my share of mistakes. But I wasn't the one who killed Aubrey. Were it not for that…"

"You'd still be married to him."

"No," she said soberly. "I'd have learned. All he wanted was someone to slap around."

"Well, he still seems to be slapping people around. Or somebody is, in his name."

"I know you think it was a mistake faking his disappearance and burying him under that pool like we did," she said, "but I think we were very brave."

"What has it gotten us?"

"I still have hope. A chance. That's all I wanted."

They'd come to her car and stopped. She looked at him with glistening eyes. To Mac it seemed like 1978 all over again. The difference was he'd long since sold his soul, and his heart was empty now. She might still have hope, but he couldn't say he did. Nor had he any idea where to find it. Mac McGowan hadn't seen a future that counted for anything for a very long time.

"Let me have your keys," he said.

Stella obediently put her purse on the hood of her car and began digging through it. A stiff gust of wind came along and Mac glanced up. He saw an old Chevy coming up the street at an unnaturally slow speed. It was in the outside lane, nearest them. Mac noticed the window on the passenger side was down. Were it not for the deliberateness of the approach, he would have thought nothing of it. But he'd been more alert since the events of the past several days.

The Chevy slowed even more. With the reflection of the lights of all the vehicles in the street, Mac couldn't see the driver very well. But when the car nearly came to a stop beside Stella's Mercedes, Mac wondered if maybe somebody wanted directions. Until the driver lifted his hand and pointed a shiny object at them.

Mac grabbed Stella by the hips and pulled her down, the two of them landing in a heap on the sidewalk as a couple of loud bangs ensued and the plate-glass window on the shop behind them exploded and shards of glass rained down on them.

The Chevy roared away and Mac got to his feet, staring after it. Stella sat stunned on the concrete, looking positively terrified, a little girl about to burst into tears. He helped her to her feet.

"Dear God," she muttered. She was white as a sheet.

Cars meanwhile had stopped in the street, their occupants gawking. Other cars behind them, ignorant of what had happened, began honking. Amid the bedlam, Mac picked up Stella's purse, which had fallen on the sidewalk. Among some of the items that had spilled out were her car keys. He grabbed them, quickly put the other things in her bag, unlocked the door, shoved her inside, went around to the driver's side, got in and, after starting the engine, pulled out of the parking space.

Stella didn't say anything until they'd driven a block. "What happened?"

"I don't know, Stella. I don't know."

Saturday, August 26, 2000

Bel Air

Mac watched the sun come up from his bed, taking heart in the fact that he'd survived the night. He still didn't know what to make of the man who'd tried to kill them. He'd gotten a good enough look to determine it was a man driving, but little more. Young, dark, Hispanic probably. That was it. If there was anything that stood out in his mind, it was that gun pointed at them. What might have happened had he not looked up before the guy fired?

By the time he got her home, Stella had sufficiently come to her senses that she'd questioned why he hadn't called the police. Mac wasn't sure, except that he wanted as little to do with them as possible, especially with Stella involved and the note on both their minds. Maybe that was a mistake, though. Someone could have jotted down Stella's license-plate number. When the victims fled a crime scene, you knew something screwy was going on. He probably should have stayed until the cops arrived—or at least phoned them from Stella's place.

She hadn't argued the point, probably wanting to get the ordeal over with as much as he. She had wanted him to stay the night, though, using every weapon in her arsenal, from tears to subtle threats. "I don't know if I'll get

through the night alone," she'd beseeched him. "Please
stay, Mac."

"You'll be fine."

"But what about you? They could be waiting at your
car."

Mac was not eager to prove her wrong on the point, but
he wasn't going to spend the night with Stella, even in her
guest room. Still, he couldn't be insensitive to her needs.
He could ill afford her losing it and flipping out on him.
"I'll be fine," he told her. "It may not have been aimed
at us personally. It could have been a random act of violence."

"No, Mac, you know better than that."

He hadn't stayed around to debate the point. He'd given
Stella a pep talk, called a cab, retrieved his car and driven
home without incident. To the best of his knowledge he
hadn't even been followed.

Once home, he'd closed the blinds and shutters, feeling
like he was in Vietnam all over again, hunkered down in
his bunker and waiting for the nightly barrage of mortar
rounds and artillery shells. His life, it seemed, was going
from bad to worse. And he didn't know why.

In the safety of his bed, Mac had tried to figure out who
and why. The first possibility that came to mind was some
sort of connection to the note. A campaign of intimidation?
If he was right, his suspicions about the cop, Jaime Caldron, were wrong. A cop, even a desperate cop, would be
unlikely to resort to such extreme measures.

The other possibility was that it had nothing to do with
the note. Neither Bri nor Manuela Ordoñez were very
happy with him and could have hired the gunman. Of the
two, Manuela was the more likely candidate, considering
she already had a criminal record, though the passions of
love made everyone unpredictable. There was also a
chance that it was a simple random act of violence, as he'd

suggested to Stella. Two well-dressed people getting into an expensive car...if you were crazed on drugs or something, why not take a shot at them?

Mac hadn't explored with Stella the possibility that it had nothing to do with him, but rather that she was the target. But knowing her, she'd have volunteered the theory, if that was likely—God knows, she'd come up with every other possible excuse to show how vulnerable and needy she was. So really, it was anybody's guess as to why they'd been targeted. His gut, though, told him there was some connection to the note.

The phone on the bedside table rang. Mac picked up the receiver.

"Are you all right?" It was Stella.

"Yes, I'm fine."

"I'm sorry if I woke you, but I didn't sleep a wink, worrying. I had visions of..." Her voice trailed off.

"I was awake. Didn't sleep very well myself." He hesitated. "Stella..."

"Yes?"

"Is there any chance this is directed at you?"

It took a moment for her to reply. "You're asking if it was me they were trying to kill?"

"Is anybody mad at you?"

"Well, I was an hour late for my last hair appointment, which didn't win me any friends at the salon."

"It's a serious question."

"No, Mac, I don't have an enemy in the world that I'm aware of. Not a serious one, anyway. What about you?"

"Nobody likely to want to kill me, I don't think. But that was before I got the note and had a couple of bullets fired my way."

"Our way."

"Yes, our way."

There was a poignant pause and then Stella said, "This is our problem, Mac. We're in this together."

There was something about the way she said it that struck a chord. Maybe it was the feeling that she was somehow glad the attack had happened. He recalled the earnestness with which she'd implored him to stay with her. She'd had a bit too much to drink, true, but she'd also grabbed the opportunity zealously, which made him wonder. That didn't mean she was behind the incident, of course. Stella had a strong opportunistic streak. But she was also capable of the grand gesture. "And not for the first time," he said in response to her remark.

"What are we going to do?"

"We can't involve the police, obviously, at least not with respect to the note. Maybe I'll hire an investigator."

"Is that wise?"

"What else can I do?"

That was what was so difficult about the situation. They really were between a rock and a hard place. And Mac had a hunch that the writer of the note was well aware of that. He or she could pretty well do anything with impunity. And Stella was right. They were in this together.

"Be careful," he told her. "And, if anything strange happens, let me know right away."

"What can you do about it?" she asked.

Mac realized she had a point.

West Los Angeles

Percy Gaylord had taken a calculated risk in coming to America—having gone so far as to borrow two thousand pounds from his mum to make the trip—but he was certain he was onto the story of the century. At least the story of the century in Delhi. Dharam Awasthi of the *Times* had told him that if delivered the inside scoop of the Venita

Kumar/Ramda Bol affair, he'd not only pay him seventy thousand pounds, he'd have him canonized by the pope in Rome. Percy had gotten off the plane in Los Angeles with a chunk of his mother's retirement money in his pocket and no idea how to find Venita Kumar.

The manager of the motel on Santa Monica Boulevard where he'd set up residence, one Mrs. Irene Schlitz, had told him the Yellow Pages was as good a way to find a private detective as any. By "letting his fingers do the walking"—a curious catchphrase indeed—Percy had engaged the services of a gentleman by the name of Boots Conroy to locate Venita and her entourage.

Boots, a man of considerable girth and a full crop of graying hair, arrived at the motel as Percy was making his morning tea, blasphemous though it was to call the concoction "tea" when made with a bag on a string from water heated in a coffeemaker and combined with a powdered creamer derived largely from coconut oil. Only through the marvel of language was it tea.

Boots, carrying a manila envelope, was too large for the single, rather flimsy armchair in Percy's room, so he sat on the bed, sinking the corner halfway to the floor. Percy offered Boots tea, which the mountainous man declined.

"Well, my good man," Percy said, "what have you for me, then?"

"I've got the lady's current address, the name of her companion and the name and address of her boyfriend."

"Boyfriend, did you say?"

"That's right." Boots fished a large soiled handkerchief from his pocket and mopped the beads of perspiration from his brow.

"By what definition is he her boyfriend?"

"Last night he stayed over. Whether they fucked or not I can't tell you. Wasn't in the bedroom."

"I see."

"If you want the particulars, Mr. Gaylord, I'll need the rest of the money." He indicated the envelope. "I also got a couple of photos."

Percy's brows rose. "Indeed." He went to the dresser where he kept his wallet in a drawer. "Five hundred, is it?"

"Yeah, that's right. You already paid five hundred and the balance is five. Which is a deal, by the way. This took me half a day longer than I expected, and I had to pay the clerk at the rental agency a hundred for the names of the occupants."

Percy took five crisp one-hundred-dollar bills from his wallet and handed them to Boots, who folded them in half with his pudgy fingers and slipped them into the breast pocket of his somewhat threadbare jacket.

"Thanks," he said with a grunt. He opened the clasp of the envelope and took out a slip of paper, which he handed to Percy.

Percy examined the paper. "Amal Kory? Amal Kory is with Venita?"

"Yeah, older gray-headed guy, dark-skinned, short, dresses real snappy."

"There must be some mistake. Amal Kory is off on a retreat in Jammu and has been for some time. Besides, Amal Kory is rather tall and dresses plainly."

"I don't know about that, pal. All I can say is what was on the lease form. I also got a picture. See for yourself."

Boots pushed his fingers into the envelope and withdrew a glossy enlargement, which he handed to Percy. It was a telephoto shot of Venita and a man matching the description Boots had given. They appeared to be coming out of a restaurant or a shop. It was not the Amal Kory—the famous film director—that Percy knew by the photos he'd seen in the press.

"The rental agent described Kory as being just like the guy in the picture."

"I have no doubt," Percy said. "But the information comes as a surprise, to put it mildly." He studied the paper. "And this Troy Hampton in Van Nuys, he's the boyfriend?"

"Right. Young guy. I'd say early twenties. Didn't get any pictures of him. Actor, but must not have done much because he drives an old Mazda and shares a modest apartment with another kid. But his old man is a very wealthy businessman."

"Indeed."

"That's the story, then," Boots said. "Is there anything else?"

"No, this has been most helpful, Mr. Conroy."

"Well, if anything else comes up, you've got my card."

"Yes, thank you."

Boots got up from the bed, mopping his brow again as he waddled toward the door. He shook Percy's hand before stepping outside. "See you, then."

"Cheerio!"

Boots grinned and left. Percy closed the door and looked down at the paper in his hand. It seemed like Venita was up to something, all right. Whatever it was, she apparently felt she needed the cachet of a notable director. Amal Kory being incommunicado made him a logical choice. Percy Gaylord was pleased. He smelled desperation. That was good. Desperation in a subject made for an easier kill.

Bel Air

By early afternoon Mac had had it. He had to get out of his bunker. The world might be an unsafe place, but he couldn't spend his life with the covers pulled up over his head. Nor could he stand around waiting to see what would happen next. Engaging a detective was a step he could take immediately. Art was working on it, but the first of the week, when Art said he'd have candidates ready, was too long to wait. To Mac, it seemed an eternity.

He decided to get a status report. When he called Art's place, all he got was his machine. He tried Conti's cell phone and got Art on the golf course.

"I don't mean to make a habit of intruding in your private life," Mac told him, "but something's come up, an urgent personal matter, and I need an investigator. What's the status of your search?"

"As a matter of fact, I'm seeing the lady tonight, boss."

"When do you have her scheduled to see me?"

"I was going to discuss it with her this evening. I thought maybe early in the week."

"I don't suppose she works Sundays."

"I doubt it, Mac."

"Ask her if she could see her way to come by for a consultation, anyway, would you? Anytime tomorrow that's convenient for her. Offer her triple her normal rate for a full day."

"Sounds like it is urgent."

"I need some professional advice."

"I'll do my best to set it up, boss."

"Either of you can give me a call in the morning."

"You got it."

"Thanks, Art."

"Oh, boss. By the way, I had to can Manuela."

"You did?"

"Yeah, she didn't show up to work, and I had to call her to find out what was going on. When she finally showed up she got real belligerent. I gave her every chance, but she basically told me to go fuck myself. It was obvious she wanted to get fired."

"She must have been upset because of the incident at my place."

"Eh, she's just a hothead. I gave her flack and she didn't like it. She'd rather cuss me out than apologize. Believe me, I've seen it before."

"She didn't mention me?"

"Actually, I was the one that brought you up."

"Did she think that was why she was fired?"

"No, not at all. It was for being irresponsible and insubordinate. She knew she was in the wrong and didn't apologize, didn't even ask for another chance. Her time had come, boss. End of story."

"You don't think there's any reason to be concerned?"

"You mean will she sue us? I would be really surprised."

"All right. Let's hope it ends there."

"Trust me, it will."

"I'll look forward to hearing from you or…what's her name, by the way?"

"Jade Morro."

"She's good, is she?"

"From what I hear, the best."

"Great, I could use somebody with real expertise."

"Leave it to me."

Mac felt better knowing something was being done. But it still didn't make sitting around the house a pleasant prospect. He tried reading and watching golf on TV, but he found himself unable to concentrate. Finally, he decided he had to get out of the house. In the middle of the afternoon he grabbed his wallet and car keys and went for a drive up the coast. He kept an eye on his rearview mirror, but saw nothing suspicious.

It was a warm, hazy day, with not much breeze. Putting all the windows down, Mac drove along the Coast Highway as fast as traffic would allow. When he reached Oxnard, he turned around and headed back. On the way, he stopped in Malibu to walk on the beach. It was pretty crowded. The surf was apparently good, because there were dozens of surfers out on the water and even more girls in bikinis watching them.

Mac had on long pants, a polo shirt, athletic shoes and sunglasses—not typical beach attire, but not so extreme as to make people stare, either. It always struck him as odd how lonely a guy could feel in a crowd. Maybe it was the families that got to him. When Troy was little, they took him to the beach a few times, but it was mostly at Mac's insistence. Stella was not an outdoors person and she avoided the sun.

Actually, there was very little they'd done as a family. Stella and Troy were busy with their Hollywood thing and Mac had made his company his life, mostly because there wasn't anything else. Sometimes he thought of those early days after he'd first arrived in California, a Midwestern kid freshly back from Vietnam, with dreams of making something of himself, but little more.

He was a rich bastard now, a bit more worldly-wise maybe, but when he thought about it, he hadn't really changed all that much, just the circumstances in which he lived. The sad fact was, because of Aubrey and Stella, he couldn't be himself. That kid who'd pulled the movie starlet back from the brink became her puppet, and he was a man living for a woman he no longer loved. He was a prisoner of her need, just as she was a prisoner of his benevolence. But the events of the past few days had intensified things considerably. He'd been living with guilt and frustration for years, but now danger had been added to the mix. A danger he didn't fully understand.

On his way home Mac stopped in Santa Monica to have dinner. Many of Bri Lovejoy's favorite places were in the shopping district on Main, down by Ocean Park. He chose one of them, Florenza, maybe half hoping he would see her. Today his loneliness felt especially acute. Any port in a storm? Bri would hate him for the thought, but he dared not feel more.

He had a plate of pasta and a salad. He didn't see Bri. For her sake, he was glad.

While having his coffee, Mac pondered the puzzling events that had brought him to this point. It had been years since he'd given this much thought to Glamour Puss. Aubrey was haunting him.

As he contemplated returning home, it occurred to him that Brentwood wasn't all that much out of the way. Mac hadn't been back to the house where it had all begun since the day Stella moved out. There'd never been a reason to return, but with all the mysterious goings-on of late, he felt the place calling to him. It was almost as if he needed to confront Aubrey.

So, that's what he decided to do.

West Hollywood

"You look bad, girlfriend," Ruthie Gibbons said in her best ghettoese. "Really bad!"

"I feel like a two-bit hooker."

"No, you is hot, hot, hot!"

Jade Morro stood in front of the mirror on the outside of the bathroom door. She was in a strapless gold cocktail dress that came to midthigh. It was so tight, it appeared to be painted on. "I look like I'm asking for sex."

"*Look* being the operative word. Just because you look that way, it doesn't mean that's what you want."

"But why put on a 'fuck me' dress if my intentions are anything but that? It's degrading. Humiliating." She shook her head. "I should have just said I don't do dances."

"Jade, why're you so uptight? You should be thinking

you're going out to have yourself some fun. You're in charge, girl. Just keep that in mind.''

Jade looked at herself in the mirror, truly uncertain what to think. It was the first time she'd had on a skirt in months, the first dress she'd bought in years. She hadn't worn anything this short since she was seventeen. And to think it had cost her a month's worth of groceries—used! The woman at the charity shop said some starlet had worn it to the Academy Awards. Jade didn't remember who. She hadn't known the name.

The doorbell rang.

"Oh, shit," Jade said, looking at her watch. "He's not supposed to be here for another twenty minutes. Do I look all right, Ruthie?"

"Don't get all excited, girl. We're nowhere near finished. If the dude comes early, we'll just make him wait."

Ruthie went off and Jade contemplated her face in the mirror. She hadn't put on any makeup, as she normally didn't wear a speck. But it occurred to her the face and the dress didn't quite look like they went together. Makeup was probably what Ruthie had in mind when she said they weren't finished.

After a couple of minutes Ruthie returned. She had a slip of paper in her hand. "It wasn't Mr. Wonderful."

Jade looked at the paper. "What's that?"

"It's from Mr.…I don't remember his name. The little old skinny man who lives across the street."

"Mr. Mercer?"

"Yes, that's it. He came over to say some guy's been driving by all day long and that he seems to be checking out your place. Always slows up and gives this house a good long look before driving on. Mr. Mercer got a description of the car and driver, but didn't get the license number."

"And?"

Same general description of the dude I saw a couple of days ago. Same car, too." Ruthie frowned with consternation. "Guess you know what I'm thinking."

"That it's Ricky."

"I know men, honey, the good and the bad."

"Well, I bet you're wrong."

Ruthie indicated the slip of paper. "After you've gone to the ball, I'll call in and see if maybe Ricky's registered a vehicle matching the description. If so, we can have a little talk with him. But we don't have to worry about it now. Mr. Wonderful is going to be here before you know it and, honey, you ain't half done."

"Makeup?"

"You got it," Ruthie said. She dragged her into the bathroom and made her look into the medicine-cabinet mirror. "Look in there. What do you see?"

Jade looked at herself. "I see me."

"What about you?"

"My face."

"What's on your face, sister?"

Jade chuckled at Ruthie's ghettoese. "Skin."

"And what's on your skin?"

"Nothing."

"That's the point. When a man takes a girl out, especially to some fancy dance, he doesn't want to take her, he wants to take his fantasy. We're supposed to be prettier than we really are, and the men are supposed to be better than they really are. It's all a game, girl. I don't have to tell you that."

"Hey, I want this guy to use his influence with Mac McGowan and any other business owners out there—I'm not trying to seduce him."

"Oh yes you are. Same technique, different goal."

"Honestly, Ruthie…"

"I didn't make the rules, I just learned to use them to my advantage. Any girl who doesn't is a fool."

Jade thought of the past-due rent and sighed. "Okay, what's first?"

"I don't suppose you've got any liquid makeup."

"No."

"I didn't think so. Well, we'll ignore the freckles and go for color. Have any lip pencil and gloss?"

Jade got the shoe box in her closet where she kept what little makeup she owned. She brought it to the bathroom. Ruthie rummaged through the box.

"Lordy, Lordy. You been to a drugstore since high school?"

"Yes," Jade said indignantly. "As a matter of fact, I have."

"Maybe for tampons..."

Jade took the box from her, dug around and found a lip pencil. She handed it to Ruthie.

After examining it for a moment, her friend said, "Well, better than a crayon, I guess. Hold still now." Ruthie applied the lip pencil. The jar of gloss was so old she had trouble getting the lid off, but she finally managed. She spread it over Jade's lips using her little finger. "So far so good," she said, examining Jade's face in the mirror. "But we've got to put something on those eyes."

"I don't like eye makeup. It itches."

"Maybe in 1973. But, lucky for you, I've got a drugstore in my purse. You wait here." She got her purse. "Sharing makeup's about as bad as sharing needles, but this is an emergency," she said, taking liner and mascara from her purse.

"I don't need that."

"The hell you don't. Looking like a peeled grape you wouldn't bring twenty bucks on the street. Now hold still."

After Ruthie finished with her eyes, she pointed to the mirror. "So, what do you think?"

Jade looked at herself. The effect was rather surprising. She wouldn't use the word *glamorous,* especially out loud, because she wouldn't give Ruthie the satisfaction, but something about the face staring back at her was intriguing.

"Well?"

"Painted lady," Jade said.

"My ass. You know you hot."

Jade did smile. "Now that you've got me looking like a welcome mat, what's your advice when Art tries to put his hand up my skirt?"

"I think you're old enough to decide if you want his hand there or not. Just don't break his knuckles if you say no. But keep this in mind, Jade, you can have fun with a man even if you don't want to have his babies."

"I'll be polite," Jade said, "and I'll dance, but I'm not getting laid. By Art Conti or anybody else. I'll go to the poorhouse first."

Just then they heard a vehicle out front. A car door slammed.

"I think Mr. Wonderful has done arrived, girl."

Jade felt herself tense.

"You want me to go now or lock up after you're gone?" Ruthie asked.

"Stay until we go."

They heard steps on the porch, then the doorbell rang. Jade drew a deep breath, then went to the front room and opened the door. Arturo Conti stood there in the glow of the setting sun. He was in a powder blue dinner jacket with a white ruffled shirt and a black bow tie. His mustache was neatly trimmed, his dark hair was combed back, with enough gray in the temples to prove he was a man of experience. He wore a handsome, self-confident grin, which evolved from cocky self-assurance to awe as he took her in. He ran his eyes up and down her twice.

"Jesus, Jade," he said. "You look beautiful."

Brentwood

Darkness had fallen by the time Mac turned off Wilshire onto Bundy Drive. He felt a curious sense of morbid anticipation building. Glamour Puss might be dead, but who else was he going to stare down?

Ten minutes later he wound his way up the street where he'd built that pool for Aubrey and Stella. Mac had been twenty-four years old the last time he'd been here. Now he was trying to understand why and how, at forty-five, he was being dragged back into the same nightmare.

He followed the route he'd taken in that old pickup truck of his, the most valuable possession he'd owned when he met the St. Georges. During those critical weeks he'd made his daily trek up this hill, eager to see the beautiful blonde who'd anointed him her champion, Mac had been so obsessed with Stella's salvation that he'd blinded himself to reality, abandoning common sense. He wondered what tugged at him so relentlessly now. Was it Aubrey's ghost, his own demons or a faceless enemy lingering in the shadows?

The street had changed considerably. There were houses where before there was only vacant land. Saplings were now large trees shading gracefully aging homes. Rounding the last curve before reaching the old St. George residence, Mac slowed. The lights from a car coming down the hill flashed in his eyes, momentarily blinding him. Then, when it was past, Mac was suddenly at the house. He pulled over and stopped.

The first thing that caught his eye was a Realtor's For Sale sign in the front yard. The house was dark, though the place next door was brightly lit. The neighboring homes on either side hadn't yet been built in 1978.

Mac stared at the front door where Aubrey and his cat, G.P., had greeted him that day he'd come to inspect the site. Mac hadn't gone in the front door again until long after Aubrey was dead and the job complete, when he'd come to visit the grieving widow.

He got out of the car and stood looking at the house in the moonlight. He knew that just because it was dark didn't mean the place was unoccupied. Unable to resist, Mac crossed the street and went to the front door. Half a dozen rolled newspapers lay on the stoop, indicating the house was either unoccupied or the occupants had been away for some time. He rang the bell. There was no answer. Then he peeked through the shutters on both sides of the door. There was just enough light coming through the back windows that he could determine the place was in fact empty.

Feeling more bold, Mac went around to the side gate he and his crew had used back in 1978. As he undid the latch, the dog in the neighboring yard began to bark. But Mac wasn't going to be deterred. He followed the walk down the side of the house, past mature shrubs that hadn't even been planted the last time he was here. When he came around the corner of the house, he expected to see the moonlight shimmering on the water of the pool, but all he saw was a black hole. The pool had been drained.

Mac made his way over to the edge of the chasm. The moonlight was strong enough that he could see the muddy scum at the bottom of the pool. Apparently it had been drained for some time. There were predictable cracks in the plaster. The pool was in disrepair.

Turning, Mac looked up at the house, and especially the window where Stella had watched him as he worked. He could envision her there still—pretty and tragic-sad, looking down at him, waiting for the rest of the crew to leave so they could be together. The pool house, Mac saw, was intact, but also in need of work. He walked toward it, stepping around a broken lounge chair, a pool sweep and hose. The door was not locked. Mac pushed it open. He tried to turn on a light, but either the electricity had been turned off or the bulbs were burned out. He could see, though, that the place was empty. His eyes went to the spot where Aubrey St. George had lain dead, the spot where Stella had repeatedly scrubbed, scouring away her husband's blood.

Mac heard a sound behind him and spun around. But it was only a cat, looking up at him and meowing. Even so, his heart raced. G.P., he thought as it slinked off. Then he realized it couldn't be. After twenty years, Aubrey's cat was long since dead.

Mac went outside again and walked to the edge of the pool. He stared down at the spot where he'd dug the grave, thinking how inadequate their measures now seemed. The note proved their secret was not safe and secure. Glamour Puss had risen from the dead.

The emotions Mac felt were intense. Oddly, fear was not foremost among them. Mostly he felt guilt and a terrible gnawing emptiness, the need to do something. But he did not know what.

The dog next door had been quiet for a while, but again began to kick up a fuss, barking louder than ever. Mac heard the sound of a second dog, this one with a deeper voice. Then he saw a beam of light coming from along the side of the house. Knowing he was about to be discovered, he looked for a place to hide, but there was nowhere to go. The small yard was bare, without so much as a shrub to duck behind.

A man carrying a flashlight appeared. He had a large German shepherd on a leash. Seeing Mac, the dog began barking like crazy, straining on the leash. The flashlight swept across the yard, the beam of light coming to rest on Mac.

"Hold it there," the voice called. "Police. Don't move."

Mac's heart rose to his throat. The officer and police dog moved toward him, the light blinding Mac.

"What are you doing here, sir?" the cop demanded.

Before Mac could say anything, the police dog lunged, but the officer managed to restrain him, ordering him to quiet down.

"I saw the For Sale sign, Officer, and wanted to have a look at the yard and view. The house is empty."

"Maybe, but you shouldn't be here at night. The neighbors reported a prowler. Anyway, there's a Sold sign out there in front, too. Didn't you see it?"

"No, I didn't."

"You should be doing your house hunting in the daytime and with a real estate agent."

"You're right, Officer. I had an impulse to see the place and I followed it. It was a mistake."

"The Lexus across the street yours?"

"Yes."

"What's your name?"

"Joseph McGowan."

"You have some ID on you, Mr. McGowan?"

Mac got out his wallet. He removed his driver's license and handed it to the cop. As the police dog made a low rumbling growl, the cop checked out Mac's ID.

"All right, Mr. McGowan, you can go, but keep your house hunting to the daylight hours, okay?"

"Yes, Officer, thank you for your understanding."

"If you'd been driving an old Ford and were packing burglar tools, I wouldn't have been so understanding. Go on," he said, motioning with the flashlight. "Be careful not to fall into the pool, looks a bit dry."

"Thank you," Mac said.

He retreated the way he'd come, giving the empty pool a sideward glance. The cop and dog followed behind. When they reached the front of the house, a second patrol car pulled up. The first cop waved them off.

"Just a home buyer," he called to the two officers getting out of the vehicle.

Mac thanked the cop again and went to his car. He got in and started the engine. As he turned around in the drive, he noticed the Sold sign hanging beneath the For Sale sign. Suddenly, it occurred to him the new buyer would probably be repairing the pool, if not replacing it entirely—a routine development that could lead to catastrophe.

The ghost of Aubrey St. George, he knew, was not through with him yet.

Long Beach

Angel Ordoñez couldn't tell where the fuck they were going. He'd followed Conti west on the Santa Monica Freeway, south on the San Diego Freeway, then south on 710, the Long Beach Freeway. What was this? A tour of Los Angeles? If the cocksucker didn't stop soon Angel'd be out of gas. Finally, though, they exited when they got to the harbor, much to his relief. What the hell they were doing down here, he couldn't imagine.

The woman was an interesting twist. So much the better if he could make Conti shit in his pants in front of her. Manuela ought to like that. Of course, she didn't get all excited when he told her about McGowan. "I think that was his wife, Angel," she'd said. "Somebody told me she lived in Beverly Hills and that she was older than him."

"So, how'm I supposed to know? Wife, girlfriend, what difference does it make?"

"He doesn't care about his wife. It's the girlfriend I want to know about."

"So ask him."

Manuela hadn't liked that. Angel could tell she was jealous of somebody she didn't even know. When he pointed out how stupid that was, she told him to fuck himself. Angel thought that was funny because nothing women did made sense to him. But he went with it because she paid him to hassle McGowan and Conti. He still wanted to do this his way, though.

"I hope this is making you feel better," he said. "Because I think it's stupid."

"I'm happy, so don't worry about it, okay."

Angel thought it made more sense to bash heads. If somebody screws your sister over, or gives her a hard time, you do something about it. You show the fucker. Manuela didn't buy it, though.

"This is not about you, Angel. How many times do I have to tell you?"

He went along, biding his time. But the more he saw of McGowan and Conti, the madder he got. Especially seeing them with the broads. It was all he could do to shoot over McGowan's head. At least it was quick and simple.

This chasing Conti all over L.A. was a pain in the ass, though. Plus, Long Beach wasn't Angel's favorite part of town. It was here where he'd gotten busted for armed robbery. His first visit to Long Beach hadn't exactly been a barrel of laughs, either. It was back when he was a kid. He'd gone on a field trip with his seventh-grade class to see the big cruise ship, the *Queen Mary*. He'd actually gone to school a whole month before the trip just so he'd be allowed to participate. Angel figured he'd never have a chance to go on another cruise again, so he wasn't about to miss the opportunity. The ship was a big sucker and fancy as hell, but the thing wasn't going anywhere because they'd nailed it to the dock. When he found out they wouldn't be taking a ride out in the ocean he really got pissed off and started swearing at the teacher, Mrs. Lopez, for tricking him. She told him to shut up, but he wouldn't. He flipped her off instead, and she grabbed him by the collar and started dragging him to the bus. But Angel fixed her. He ripped her purse away and tossed it overboard into the harbor.

They suspended him from school for that, but he didn't care. The bastards cheated him out of his chance to go sailing in the ocean. What was so hot about walking around on some boat that wasn't going anywhere? False advertising, that's what it was. Angel could laugh about it now, but for a long time it made him hate school even more than he did before.

When Conti didn't cross Queensway Bay, staying on the north side of the harbor instead, Angel realized he wasn't taking his girl to the *Queen Mary*. But where were they going? All he knew for sure was it was someplace fancy, considering the way the two of them were dressed. Probably a ritzy restaurant.

Angel followed them into a parking garage and managed to park less than ten spots away, so as not to lose them. He trailed them at a distance, admiring the way Conti's woman looked, in her short shiny dress that was tight as hell. The bitch had damn good legs, even if she didn't have any tits.

Leaving the garage, they walked across the plaza area along with a bunch of other couples that were all dolled up, too—guys in monkey suits, broads in fancy party dresses, all looking like they were going to the prom, even if most of them were old and fat and gray. Angel was really confused, especially when he saw where everybody was headed—to the goddamn aquarium. The aquarium? What was this?

Conti and the broad went inside. Seeing that everybody had tickets, Angel knew that was as far as he was going. He wouldn't get in the way he was dressed, even if he did have a ticket. Not that he had any interest in any fancy-schmancy party. He just wanted to scare the bejesus out of Conti and be done with it. Manuela would like it if he pulled it off someplace public where he could make Conti look like a jackass, though Angel still had trouble understanding why Manuela got off on that.

"They won't even know it's coming from you," Angel told her, "so what's the big deal? Better you spit in their eye."

"I want to do it my way, Angel, all right?"

He just couldn't understand it. "Hell, half the pleasure of whacking some sonovabitch is seeing the look in their eye when you shove the blade between their ribs. The whole thing only takes a second, but you know exactly what they're thinking. 'Fuck, Angel Ordoñez got me. That little sonovabitch.'" He'd laughed. "There's nothing like knowing your face is the last one they'll ever see."

"Hey, amigo," one of the ticket-takers in the monkey suits called to him. "Service entrance is around the side." He pointed.

For a minute, Angel didn't understand, then he realized the guy thought he was a worker. He was about to tell the guy to go fuck himself, when it occurred to him they could be handing him an opportunity to get inside. So he went over to the guy and said, "Uh, yeah, but I wanted to make sure I had the right place. Which party is this?"

"Area Chamber of Commerce Ball." The guy pointed again. "Staff goes in the service entrance."

Angel nodded and wandered around the building. He found a catering truck at the gate and half a dozen guys unloading stuff from the back. Acting like he belonged, Angel walked past the truck, following one of the guys through the door. He wandered down the hall to the big kitchen where a whole mob of people were scurrying around, getting ready for the party. Then Angel saw a guy and a broad coming out of a little room to the side. The guy was buttoning up his white jacket and, for a second, Angel thought maybe they'd been screwing. But when somebody else came out, he realized that was where the workers were dressing.

Angel went in and, sure enough, it was a changing room with lockers. There were two guys talking while they put on their white jackets. Nobody paid much attention to him. Seeing a couple of piles of the jackets in different sizes, Angel went over and picked one out. All he had on was a T-shirt and black pants. His pants were pretty badly worn, but not all that different from what the others were wearing. He slipped on the jacket and buttoned it up.

The two guys gave him a funny look as they left, maybe because Angel hadn't shaved for several days and had a bandage on his face. Maybe he didn't look so sharp as everybody else, but what the fuck—what were they going to do, fire him? He followed the guys through the kitchen and out to where a fat woman with the attitude of a prison guard was giving assignments. Angel didn't wait for somebody to figure out he didn't belong.

Entering the main hall, he was amazed. The big room was filled with tables with white tablecloths and fancy dishes and glasses and flowers. The room was long and curved, with what seemed like hundreds of tables spread the length of it. Against one wall there were alcoves with dozens of huge fish tanks with all kinds of brightly colored, wildass-looking fish. Guests were milling about, standing, talking, drinking, staring at the fish. Halfway down there was a band playing, and a few couples were dancing in the empty area that had been made into a dance floor.

Angel wandered along, amazed. He'd seen stuff like this

on TV, in James Bond movies and shit like that, but he'd never actually been to this kind of party. Judging by all the gold watches and diamonds and pearls, not to mention all those expensive cars in the parking garage, there was a lot of dough—as well as fish—floating around this place.

Angel kept his eyes open for Conti and Jade, though he wondered if he'd find them in this mob. At the end of the hall there was a smaller darker passage, which people seemed to be entering and leaving. Angel followed the crowd, discovering it accessed dozens more tanks containing a jillion kinds of exotic fish and other creatures. In the relative closeness of the winding passageway, he could smell the perfume and cologne. The darkness reminded him of the Haunted House at Disneyland, except for the fact that the walls were fish tanks and everybody was talking and laughing.

Angel figured that if Conti was in here checking out the fish, he'd never find him, so he turned around and went back to the main hall. During his trip along the concourse, he realized there was an open-air terrace outside the hall where dozens more guests were having drinks in the balmy air. He made a quick circuit and was just about to give up when he spotted Conti and the woman by the railing, looking out at the moon shining on the bay.

Angel wondered if this might not be the opportunity he needed to humiliate him in front of a bunch of people, though he wasn't sure just what he could do. He'd left his gun in the car, but maybe something else would do.

Nearing them, Angel realized they weren't being all kissy-face, they were arguing. The broad was really giving it to him.

"You definitely gave me the impression Mac was going to be here, Art," she said, sounding real pissed.

"I thought he was. Honest, Jade."

"Did you?"

"Yeah. And he wants to see you, too. Badly. In fact, he said tomorrow, if you can do it. At his place."

"Seriously?"

"Swear to God. I'm being straight with you. The whole point of this was for you to be with Mac. He couldn't come at the last minute, that's all. Otherwise he'd be here."

Angel, who was at the railing, only a few feet away, felt somebody grab his arm.

"Hey, what are you doing?"

Angel turned. It was the fat broad from earlier who'd acted like a prison guard. She towered over him, the folds of fat forming a scowl on her face. He jerked his arm free.

"Back off, huh."

She drew herself up, all stiff and haughty like she had a broomstick up her ass. Her eyes narrowed. "Why are you just standing around? Haven't you been given an assignment?"

"I never did no assignment in school, why should I do one now?"

She looked astounded. "What's your name? I don't recognize you. Are you one of the contract workers?"

"No, I'm one of the rich SOB's who came to dance. So why don't you go back to your pigpen and leave me alone?"

Her eyes rounded. "Who are you?"

"Fuck off."

The woman turned and called to a couple of the barmen, beckoning them to come help her. Angel groaned, knowing there was going to be a confrontation. Glancing over his shoulder he saw that Conti and the broad, Jade, had wandered off. Now he wouldn't be able to find out what was up. He glared at the sow, whose pink skin had turned scarlet. The two barmen came up next to her.

"Escort this man to the kitchen and call security," she told them.

"What's your problem?" Angel said, getting really pissed.

"Come on, buddy," one of the guys said, taking Angel's arm. He was a head taller and outweighed him by fifty pounds.

Angel shoved him away. "Keep your hands off, asshole."

"Security!" the woman bellowed. "Security!"

The two men tried to grab him, but Angel, who was lightning quick, spun free, grabbing one man's wrist and, spinning, he snapped it like a twig. Screaming in agony, the guy dropped to his knees, cradling his dangling limb. The other guy and the woman both stepped back, amazed.

Angel, who was really pissed now, stabbed his finger at them, punctuating each word as he spoke. "Keep-your-goddamn-hands-off. Comprende?"

The man on the ground bellowed like a wounded moose. Everybody within fifty feet was staring.

Angel knew it was time to split. He threw a final hateful glare at the sow, muttered, "Fucking bitch," then he walked off, giving them all the middle-finger salute over his shoulder.

Santa Monica

The time difference in India was thirteen and a half hours, but Percy Gaylord could never figure out whether to add or subtract the extra hour and a half. Oh, sod it! he thought. The hour there was decent in any case, so he'd ring up Dharam at the *Times* and see if his fax had produced results.

As usual Dharam Awasthi was slow to come to the phone. His secretary said he was taking morning tea, but he could be bothered for a jingle coming halfway around the world.

"Awasthi here," he said over the crackle on the line.

"Dharam, it's Percy in America. Los Angeles."

"Yes, dear boy."

"Did you get my fax?"

"I did indeed. The photo was difficult to make out, but we think we may have made an identification."

"Smashing! Who is he?"

"Quite likely one Arjay Pantel, an inveterate impostor with half a dozen aliases of record, presently wanted in Britain, Canada and New Zealand."

"Virtually the whole bloody Commonwealth."

"Quite right."

"What's his game?"

"Fraud and theft, for the most part. Seems to ingratiate himself with the wealthy, influential classes, then, in the dead of night, makes off with the silver and jewels. His specialty seems to be impersonations. The gentleman's sufficiently urbane and cultured that he passes himself off as whatever the situation calls for—university professor, international banker, art dealer, even minor royalty on one occasion. The authorities tell us Pantel has been living abroad in semiretirement, but nobody seems to know just where."

"No longer true, old bean."

"Then you have him in your sights, do you?"

"I do indeed."

"Judging by the photo there's a connection with Miss Kumar."

"Yes, but too early to share details, Dharam. You shall have the whole bloody business in good time, I assure you."

"Keep in mind, I'm not interested in gossip, Percy. I want the Ramda Bol story."

"And you shall have it, I promise you. Have your checkbook ready."

"You have my word."

"Cheerio!"

Percy slipped the receiver back into the cradle and gave himself a spirited "Hurrah!"

For a few minutes he paced the room, considering strategy. He had the leverage he needed to force Venita's hand. That was key. Arjay Pantel was a godsend. Blimey! Percy couldn't have asked for more.

But if he were to do this right, he'd need more photographs. Lots of photographs. The more lurid the better. Perhaps that should be the first step, even before his interview with Venita, an interview she would have no choice now but to give him.

Giddy with joy, Percy went to the window and, pulling back the curtain, peered out at the avenue. Up the street he saw the blinking lights of a pub called Charlie's Joint. Normally he wasn't much of a drinker, but Percy Gaylord was in sufficiently high spirits that he reckoned he'd indulge himself a wee bit. Oh, happy day!

West Hollywood

As they turned onto her street, Art Conti glanced over at her. "You still pissed?"

Jade shifted uncomfortably. "I really hate being used."

"That wasn't my intention, honest. I really wanted to help you. And you did make some good contacts tonight, didn't you?"

"It was an afterthought, Art. You intended this as a social thing from the beginning, only you weren't straight with me."

"Look, I admit I was attracted to you and yes, I hoped you might see me as more than just a business associate, but the business part is serious, too."

Art pulled up to the curb and stopped in front of her

place. He turned off the engine and looked over at her like a wounded puppy. Jade tensed slightly, hoping he wouldn't make a play for her, adding insult to injury. During most of the evening he'd been respectful, cautious even. They had danced and he'd held her close, but Jade hadn't given him any encouragement whatsoever. If he was to be believed, things were under way with Mac McGowan. She hoped that wasn't bullshit, too.

"Were you being straight with me about Mac wanting to see me tomorrow?" she asked.

"Yes, he's got some sort of personal thing going and needs an investigator. I told him you were the best, Jade, so he asked me to line something up with you as quick as possible. He said he'd pay you triple your usual per diem since it's Sunday."

"You have any idea what it's about?"

"Nope. Mac didn't say. You need to call him in the morning and set up a time."

"And what about the Pool Maids investigation?"

"I guess he plans to talk to you about that, too."

A flutter of excitement went through her. Maybe playing Cinderella would end up paying, after all. God knew she needed the work. "I appreciate you arranging it, Art."

"I do have a lot of influence with Mac. And he trusts my judgment. A good word from me was essential."

Jade understood what he was getting at. What it amounted to was, "You owe me, baby." So, what did he think? That she'd put out for him out of gratitude? With men, you could never be sure. "I appreciate your confidence," she said.

Art gave her a long, suave—yes, seductive—look as if to say, "And now, with the niceties behind us, let's you and me get down to business." Jade knew she had to cut this one off before it got started.

"It was a nice evening, Art. I got to meet some people.

I'm pleased Mac's interested in talking to me. I had fun and I'd like to thank you.'' She extended her hand.

Art Conti blinked, but after a moment he took her hand. Rather than shake it, though, he gripped it firmly. ''I had a great time myself. You're quite a lady, Jade.''

She smiled, but it faded when he ran his other arm lightly over her forearm, all the while looking into her eyes with this ''Mr. Casanova'' expression on his face. Surely he couldn't be stupid enough to force himself on her, she thought.

''As a matter of fact, you're a refreshing change from what I have to deal with day to day. Dating a cop's a new angle and I like it. You're an amazing woman.''

Amazing woman? she thought. What was with this guy? Did he think she was an airhead? Didn't he know how transparent he was? ''Thanks,'' she said, ''but I don't really think of this as a date. Wouldn't you say we're more like colleagues at a business function?''

''The business part's over, Jade.'' Art put his hand on her knee, drawing it a ways up her bare thigh. Her whole body went stiff. Taking his wrist, she removed his hand from her leg. ''Art, I'm a serious person, and I'm not interested in you in that way,'' she insisted.

There was utter disbelief on his face. She reached for the door handle.

''I'm going in now.'' The door swung open and she climbed out awkwardly, feeling like she was all elbows and knees. Art quickly opened his door and got out, too. Jade looked at him over the roof of the car. ''Good night. And thanks.''

''Hang on, I'll walk you to the door.''

''Not necessary.'' She turned before he had a chance to argue and headed for her front door.

She hadn't gone ten feet before she heard a car come roaring up the street, tires squealing. Whirling around, she saw the vehicle flash past Art, who was smashed against his car, his eyes round as melons. The car, an old Chevy, couldn't have missed him by more than a foot. Jade looked after it, but its lights were off and she couldn't catch the plate. The Chevy careened around the corner and was gone.

Meanwhile, Art, with both arms sprawled over the top of his car, looked about as comfortable as a guy in the middle of a prostate exam. "Christ," he stammered.

Jade went around to the driver's side as Art unpeeled himself from the door. He was breathing hard, as though he'd just run around the block, his body slack as a wet towel.

"You all right?" she asked.

"Damned if I know. What was that?"

"I think somebody just tried to run you down. Or scare the shit out of you."

"They were successful." He looked down at himself, as if to make sure all his limbs were attached.

"Did you get a look at the driver?" she asked.

Art shook his head. "No, I didn't see a damn thing except the tank bearing down on me. How about you?"

"No, nothing."

He stared at her for a minute, still struggling to catch his breath. "You got a jealous boyfriend by any chance?"

"Me?" The suggestion seemed absurd, but then she recalled Ruthie's supposed sighting of Ricky a few days ago. "Well, no," she replied, "not really."

"Not really?"

"There's a remote possibility, Art, but I really don't think...no, it couldn't have been anybody I know. I'm sure."

"Well, *I* don't have any jealous boyfriends, that's for sure. The driver was a guy, wasn't he?"

"I think so, but I didn't get a very good look."

"My impression was a guy, too."

"You want to call the police?" she asked.

"I don't think I want the hassle, Jade. And except for losing a couple of years off my life, no harm was done."

She didn't want to invite him in for coffee or whatever, but she almost felt duty-bound after what had just happened. Art let her off the hook before she could issue the invitation, though.

"I think I'll go home and have a soak in my spa."

"You look like you could use it."

He nodded. Jade patted his arm sympathetically. As he climbed in his vehicle, she glanced up the street the direction the Chevy had gone. Ricky? No, she couldn't believe it. And yet...

She said good-night and went back around the car, jogging to the front door as fast as her tight skirt would allow. After fumbling with her key, she got the door open. When she glanced back, Art started his engine. She waved and went inside.

For a moment she stood in the dark living room, trying to sort out the currents of emotion going through her. Maybe she'd gotten a job. Maybe Ricky was back in town. And maybe neither was true. At least, for the most part, her dignity was intact. That in itself was a victory.

She went to the bathroom then, and looked at her face in the mirror. She didn't see the Jade Morro she knew. She saw a slut.

Taking the bar of soap, she began scrubbing her face. She didn't stop until she had all the makeup off. As she toweled her face dry, she saw a figure loom up behind her in the mirror.

Screaming, Jade spun around, her hands clenched into a fist, ready to fight. It took a couple of seconds before she realized that it wasn't Ricky or Art, nor was it a burglar or rapist. It was Ruthie Gibbons, sleepy-eyed, suddenly as frightened as Jade.

"Ruthie," she gasped. "You scared the shit out of me. What are you doing here?"

Ruthie rubbed her eyes. "I've been waiting for you, Jade. I laid down on your bed and I guess I fell asleep."

"Well, you damn near gave me a heart attack." She clasped her hands to her chest. "I thought you were going home."

"I was, but after you left I made some calls and decided I'd better stay and tell you about them."

Jade's heart still pounded from the adrenaline surge, but was slowly coming under control. "What calls?"

"I checked to see if a car fitting the description given by the old guy across the street is registered to Ricky."

"And?"

"Nothing's registered under his name. Which really doesn't mean anything because he could have borrowed it."

"You just don't want to give him the benefit of the doubt, Ruthie. He's probably in Mexico with the wife and kids."

Ruthie shook her head. "Nope. He's back in L.A. I called some friends who checked with some other friends. It's definitely confirmed."

Jade felt her stomach fall. "You sure? He's really back in town?"

"You got it, girlfriend."

Jade slumped against the basin. "Damn."

"What's wrong? Just because he's back, it doesn't mean you have to see him."

"Ruthie, a few minutes ago somebody in an old Chevy tried to run Art down when he got out of his car to walk me to the door."

"No shit?"

"No shit."

"Ricky?"

"I don't know. I didn't see either the driver or the plates."

"It was Ricky."

"You don't know that. And, personally, I still have trouble believing it."

"The man was crazy over you."

"I still don't buy it."

"Well, I couldn't go home without telling you what I found out. What you do with it is up to you."

The two of them exchanged a long look of mutual understanding.

Ruthie said, "So, how was the dance? Lose your glass slipper?"

"No, but I got a blister. And maybe a contract with McGowan Enterprises."

"You mean lover boy came through?" Ruthie exclaimed. "What did it cost you?"

"Surprisingly little. He only got about four inches above my knee."

"You're still a recycled virgin then."

"You better believe it."

"Oo-ee!" Ruthie exclaimed, laughing.

They exchanged high fives.

"Which reminds me," Ruthie said. "You had a call right after you left. From the man himself. Mr. McGowan. He wants you to phone him in the morning."

"Yeah, Art said Mac wanted to talk."

"Sounds like maybe you're flyin' high, girl."

"We'll see."

"Well, I'm pooped and ready for bed. I'm going home for some real sleep."

"Thanks for everything, Ruthie."

Her friend beamed. It was more than gratitude on her face.

"What are you smiling at?"

"For what it's worth, you really were hot tonight, Jade. I mean that. You looked beautiful."

Jade looked at her plain-Jade face in the mirror, knowing this was the real her, Ruthie's compliments and encouragement notwithstanding. Playing dress-up had served its purpose, though. She had her foot in the door at McGowan Enterprises.

And yet everything wasn't idyllic. Ruthie had brought troubling news, which sort of put a damper on things. Ricky Santos was back in town, meaning there could be trouble.

If there wasn't already.

Burbank

She was only half-asleep when she felt somebody sit on her bed. Manuela sat up abruptly. Then she saw who it was.

"Jesus, Angel, you scared the shit out of me. What are you doing?"

"I did my job, now I want to be paid."

"Now? In the middle of the night?"

"Yes, in the middle of the night. I got places to go, things I want to do. I need some bread. Get me my money."

Manuela straightened the top of her nightgown and rubbed her eyes. "So, what happened?"

"I got Conti to crap in his pants, just like McGowan. So your boys are taken care of."

"Aren't you going to tell me what you did?"

Angel briefly recounted the events of the evening. "And I found out the broad with Conti wasn't his date," he

added at the end. "She was there to see McGowan. I guess
Conti just picked her up for him. But McGowan didn't
show or something. All I know for sure is she was pissed."

"You mean the one tonight is Mac's girlfriend?"

"Yeah, I heard them talking about her going over to his
place tomorrow."

"Really?"

"Yeah, really. What do you think, that I'm making this
shit up?"

"But how…"

"I'm not a fucking detective, all right? Now quit farting
around, Manuela, and give me my money."

"First, what about this woman, Mac's girlfriend? Tell
me about her, Angel. Who is she? What's her name?"

"Let's see," Angel said, "I heard it. What was it?
Uh…Jade. Yeah, that's it. Her name's Jade."

"Jade?"

"Isn't that what I just said?"

"Jade. I wonder if it could be the same one."

"What same one?"

"I was talking to Ella Vanilla earlier. She called to see
how I was doing. And we talked about the company. Ella
said Art's been talking to this private investigator about
something to do with the Pool Maids."

"So?"

"Her name was Jade."

"She's an investigator?"

"More than that, she's a former cop. That's what Ella
said, anyway."

"That bitch tonight was a cop?"

"If it's the same one."

"How many Jades could he know?" Angel said.

"So it must be her."

"Shit, if I knew that, I'd have shoved her in the drink.
Or worse. Fucking bitch."

"What did she look like?"

"What difference does it make?"

"I want to know."

"She was a broad, what can I say?"

"Pretty?"

"Yeah."

"Well, is she blond or what?"

"No, dark hair. She had a good body, except she was flat." In the darkness Manuela could see her brother's frown. "She really a cop?" he asked, disbelieving.

"Used to be, according to Ella. And she's really Mac's girlfriend?"

"Isn't that what I said?" Angel, losing patience, stood up. "Okay, that's enough bullshit gossip. I'm through. Give me my money."

"Jesus, Angel, do you have to be so goddamn pushy?"

Her brother suddenly grabbed her by the arm and dragged her from her bed so brusquely she landed on her ass with a thud.

"Angel!"

He jerked her to her feet, practically ripping her arm from the socket.

"What are you doing?" she cried.

"My money, Manuela, get me my money."

She went to her chest of drawers and got the ten twenty-dollar bills she'd tucked away to pay her brother. Angel grabbed them out of her hand and left the room without a word. Manuela went and sat back down on her bed in the dark. Her arm hurt. Angel was crazy, there was no doubt about it. But she didn't think about him for long. It was Mac McGowan who was on her mind. So he did have a girlfriend. And of all things, a former cop.

Manuela put her head in her hands and thought of Mac's beautiful house. All that lovely furniture and the big rooms. And that big egg on the table. She'd thought about the house a lot. She'd imagined living there in Bel Air with Mac. Every day she'd pick up that egg and look at it and think how glad she was to be Mac McGowan's wife. She'd even thought of having babies with him. It didn't seem fair that it couldn't be. It was such a beautiful dream. And she'd been so sure that anybody that nice to her, that kind, loved her, too.

No, it wasn't fair. And who would be getting all that stuff? A former cop, that's who. The thought was enough to make her sick. And crazy mad. Same as Angel, who, when she stopped to think about it, wasn't all that different from her.

Sunday, August 27, 2000

Norwalk

Jaime Caldron finished watering the potted plants, then sat in his favorite chair under the aluminum patio cover to rest his slightly arthritic back. Sunday was his day off, but in another seven weeks gardening would be his full-time occupation. Hard as it was to believe, his career was nearly over. Though a cop's life wasn't easy, and most guys looked forward to a secure retirement, Caldron had mixed feelings. Lucia was eager to return to Arizona where she'd grown up, eager for the "easy life," far from the hustle and bustle, the pushing and shoving, the greed and the crime of L.A.

But all that had been an integral part of the fabric of his life—especially the crime. He'd been a soldier for justice so long that retirement, in a way, seemed like retreat. But of course there were other fighters, younger, healthier people ready to take his place. Still, it wasn't easy. "Don't worry," his wife had said. "I will keep you very busy. That's the key."

Caldron knew Lucia was right. The trouble was, his idea and her idea of busy were not the same. When he'd said maybe he'd start a security business in Arizona, she'd shook her head with grave disapproval. "Out of the frying pan and into the fire, Jaime. If you don't want to run the gift shop with me, then you must garden or something. You love to grow things. Do it for profit if you want.'' His dear wife had gotten him books on truck farming, new techniques for raising greenhouse vegetables. It struck him as more like school than retirement.

Caldron listened to the water splashing gently in Lucia's fountain in the back corner of their walled-in yard, her little sanctuary of peace and tranquillity. In the tree beyond the wall a bird twittered. But then out front a motorcycle roared past the house. It was the kid a few doors up who liked to announce his arrival and departure with a mechanical display of virility. The bike was new, along with the license to drive it. Caldron considered telling him to cool it, but the kid lived with his mother, a single parent who struggled mightily to hold things together. He decided not to add to her burdens, not considering his house was up for sale and he and Lucia would be gone in a matter of weeks.

The siren of an emergency vehicle sounded over on Rosecrans Avenue, bringing Caldron to attention before he relaxed again. That—out there in the streets, where the action was—had been his life. How would he exist without the challenge, the hot breath of danger, the fight?

Inside the house, he heard the phone ring. A moment later Lucia opened the sliding glass door.

"Jaime, it's your office calling."

He was a bit surprised. He had no hot cases going. He'd spent his time of late cleaning up old files, preparing for the end of his career. Under the circumstances, he couldn't imagine why he'd be getting a call on his day off, unless there had been a major incident, prompting an alert to all off-duty officers.

Caldron went into the kitchen where his wife had been baking, a smell that gave him a warm feeling about her—

second only to her favorite perfume. He picked up the phone. "Yes," he said. "Caldron."

"Lieutenant, this is Tory Fernandez in the documentation section, downtown. We talked about your old cases a few weeks ago."

Caldron remembered her, a little Filipino girl who couldn't have weighed ninety pounds. "Yes, what can I do for you?"

"I'm sorry to bother you on your day off, but I'm leaving tomorrow on vacation, and I didn't want some information I picked up to get lost along the way. Remember you asked me to run an update on the list of suspects on your open cases?"

"Yes, what about it?"

"Well, I put the names in the computer system to be flagged…at least everybody who wasn't dead or in prison. I thought, just in case something new came up, it would be a good idea. From all the files you gave me, there must have been thirty or forty names."

Caldron wanted to tell her to get to the point, but he recalled the girl was young and earnest. He didn't want to discourage initiative. So, he let her spin out her tale.

"I put in all the aliases and even the names of family members when I had them," she went on. "My supervisor gave me permission to run the names through the state and federal databases. I tried to be thorough."

"Sounds like you were very thorough," he said. "So what have you turned up? I assume you're calling because you found something."

"Yes, Lieutenant, I did. And funny thing is, the name turned up in a routine patrol report out of West L.A. Minor incident. Not even an arrest or anything."

"Who we talking about, Fernandez?"

"Joseph McGowan."

Caldron ran the name through his mind. "McGowan?"

"Yes, I guess he goes by Mac."

"Oh, my movie-star case. Aubrey St. George."

"Yes, sir. That's the one. 1978."

Caldron remembered the case well. Not because he couldn't solve it, so much as because he couldn't make a case against McGowan and St. George's wife, who, he was certain, were behind the actor's disappearance and probable death. "What do you have?"

"Last night a canine unit responded to a report of a prowler at a vacant home in Brentwood. It turned out to be your suspect, McGowan. Said he was checking out the property. No criminal activity or anything. The officer told him to leave. No big deal. I probably wouldn't even have made a note of it, except for one thing."

"What's that, Fernandez?"

"The location, sir. It was the address of your victim in 1978."

Caldron was surprised. "Really?"

"Yes, sir."

"That is interesting."

"I thought so, Lieutenant."

"You have the information there?" he asked.

"On my monitor."

"Why don't you give me that address."

She did and he jotted it down at the bottom of his wife's grocery list, thanking the clerk before hanging up the phone. Standing at the kitchen counter, Jaime Caldron ran the particulars of the case back through his mind. Over the years he recalled tweaking McGowan from time to time, but other than reading the file a couple of months ago, it had been a long time since he'd done anything with it. But this latest development—McGowan going to the St. George property some twenty years after the fact—struck him as very strange, something worth looking into.

"An emergency, Jaime?" his wife said.

"No," he replied. "Some interesting info on an old case, that's all."

Lucia looked at him as if she knew he was going to spend the rest of the day thinking about a dusty old file instead of focusing on her. And she was probably right.

"You getting hungry?" she asked. "I can have some chicken burritos ready in fifteen minutes."

"It's a nice day," Caldron said. "How about we go to the beach instead? Maybe get something to eat there?"

"You mean over to Manhattan Beach?"

"No, I was thinking more like Malibu."

"Why all the way up there?" his wife asked.

"Thought maybe we could swing by Brentwood on the way."

Lucia nodded with understanding. "Because that's where your case was, right?"

Jaime Caldron smiled. "*Cara mia,* you know me too well."

Bel Air

Manuela couldn't get Mac McGowan's girlfriend out of her mind. A former cop. The detective that arrested her after she'd wasted Donny was a woman, too, and the female guards at the prison were worse than some men. It made her blood boil to think of Mac with somebody like that. She really wanted to know what this Jade was like. Angel's description wasn't much help. But, since she knew the woman was visiting Mac today, she could see her for herself, though not up close, of course. Going to Mac's was risky, but she was so bummed out that she didn't care.

Manuela drove up the canyon above Mac's place, parked, then walked back, so nobody would spot her car nearby. With all the bushes and things, there were plenty of places to hide, and she camped out and waited, even knowing it might take all day. But what the hell, she didn't have anything else to do until that night when she was supposed to see Mike O'Gill.

She wasn't looking forward to that. When she'd called him, Mike was the same as always—wanting everything he could get for a favor. "Sure, you can come back and dance for me," he'd said. "I always got a place for you, Manuela. Why don't you come to my place Sunday night and we'll talk about it?" To Mike, "talking about it" really meant "Show me a good time and we'll see what I can do." It pissed her off to have to fuck somebody to get a job, but considering how good dancing at the Bottoms Up Club paid, Manuela would put up with a lot. Anyway, she'd had a lot worse than Mike O'Gill, even if he outweighed her by two hundred pounds. She had to pay Angel and keep food on the table somehow, didn't she? Could she let her old, sick mother starve?

That alone made her hate Mac for disappointing her. How wonderful it could have been. Brushing away a tear, Manuela stared at the beautiful house that could have—no should have—been hers. Damn Mac McGowan, anyway. And damn his girlfriend, the cop.

Mac, freshly showered and shaved, heard a car enter the drive as he entered the front room. He went to the window. A white Ford Escort with a couple of rusty dents blemishing the front fender sat at his door. The driver, a slender woman with short, dark hair got out. She had a notebook in her hand and pulled a large bag out after her, which she swung up on her shoulder. She was in jeans and a white, long-sleeve cotton T-shirt. The way she sort of swung around the car with long, athletic strides made him think of a jock, a soccer player or rock climber or something. Definitely the outdoors type. An environmentalist, maybe.

Someone who might champion the cause of an endangered frog.

He went to the door as the bell chimed. The girl on his doorstep had a large smile and exuded energy.

"Mac," she said, "I'm Jade Morro." She extended her hand, gripping his firmly. The hand he held was large, if slender, for a woman's. And strong.

"Come in, Jade."

She ran her fingers through her short-cropped hair—a boyish gesture that somehow was appealing, notwithstanding the fact she was a girl, though he suspected she would have taken umbrage at being referred to that way. Stepping past him, she moved into the entry and looked around.

"Nice place you've got here," she said as he closed the door.

For a moment they stood looking at each other, Jade a tomboyish ingenue crackling with energy and enthusiasm, Mac surprised by her. And intrigued.

Smiling, maybe to cover her nervousness, Jade went up and down on her toes a couple of times. She wasn't beautiful, nothing that would knock a guy's socks off, but rather attractive in a wholesome, real, unpretentious sort of way. Mac could see she wasn't as young as she first seemed. She was at least thirty, yet fresh-looking, honest, innocent. Not what you'd expect in a former cop. She was different.

His silence started making her uncomfortable. He could tell by the way she shifted her weight and furrowed her brow.

"Thanks for being so prompt," he said, knowing he had to say something. "And for agreeing to meet with me on a Sunday."

"Art said you had a pressing problem."

"Unfortunately, I do." He motioned toward the front room. "Let's go in there."

Jade swung her purse behind her and, locking it in place with her elbow, headed off. Mac checked her figure. The jeans were not super tight, but formfitting enough to reveal the nicely rounded, feminine curve of her hips. She was not bodacious by any means and certainly wouldn't be considered pinup material, but she was a sprite, a gamine and there was a distinct sexuality in that.

Jade sat in the middle of the largest sofa and put her notebook on the coffee table in front of her. As Mac sat in the armchair across from her, she dug into her purse, which was on the floor between her feet. Muttering, she started pulling the contents out onto the thick carpet. A calculator, a fat wallet, a cell phone, a small package of tampons and a shiny automatic pistol were among the items piled at her feet. Her insouciance surprised him. There was no pretense here.

Jade found a pen, which seemed to be what she was looking for. She slapped it between her teeth and proceeded to put her possessions back into her purse. Then she grabbed her notebook and leaned back, running her fingers through her hair again before taking the pen from between her teeth and crossing her legs.

"Hope you don't mind if I take notes," she said. "I've got a lousy memory for names and dates and phone numbers and stuff like that."

Mac was absolutely mesmerized. When he saw she expected an answer, he said, "No, whatever you want. That's fine."

She opened the notebook and rested it on her knee. "Let's recap where we are, just to make sure we're on the same page. You said on the phone you're eager to get an investigation started on this problem you've got, and our immediate objective is for me to determine if it's feasible and for you to determine if I'm the person to handle it. Sound right?"

Her earnestness and her syntax amused him. "Yes, that's about the size of it."

"Okay, well, how about if we start with you telling me the nature of the problem? Or, would you rather I give you a rundown on my professional qualifications first?" She gave him a self-deprecating smile. "I guess if you don't like what you hear there's no need to discuss your problem."

"Why don't you tell me about yourself first, Jade?" Mac said. "Not so much to see if I want to proceed, as to get acquainted. My situation is sensitive, and I'd have an easier time telling you about it if I knew you a little better."

"Fair enough." She got a pensive look, her tanned brow furrowing. "I got an A.A. in Administration of Justice from Pasadena City College about eight years ago. Since then I've been taking night classes at Long Beach State to get my bachelor's degree in Criminal Justice. I need eight more units, which, at the rate I'm going, will take me another three or four years," she said with a laugh.

"At least you're sticking with it."

"I need to send you to talk to my adviser, Mac. She considers me a flake."

"I assume you have to work to support yourself. That, to my mind, is commendable."

"A person does what they have to do. The last I checked, rent's not optional…unless you want to live in a cardboard box."

Mac smiled. He liked the woman. "You were with the L.A.P.D. for a while, weren't you?"

"I was a patrol officer for five years. Two commendations for bravery. One Purple Heart. Got knifed in the butt trying to break up a street fight in East L.A."

"Ouch."

"It was a superficial wound. Lots of blood but only a

couple dozen stitches. It was nothing compared to the time I got bit by a spider when I was crawling under an abandoned house chasing a car thief. My neck swelled up like a grapefruit. But none of that's relevant. I applied for detective, passed the exam and was on the list when I ran afoul the politicians in the department. The long and the short of it is, my boyfriend was on the force and we were living together. What I didn't know was he was married.''

"Ouch again."

"Yeah, that was a definite ouch. Nothing superficial about it. The only reason I mention it is because it messed up my career. When it became clear I wasn't going to make detective, I resigned. The two people I needed on my side were male chauvinist pigs and that cooked me.'' She hesitated. "If you're a chauvinist, Mac, forgive me. I tolerate it in clients, but not the people who supervise me."

"Don't worry, I'm liberated," he assured her.

"But a Republican, right?"

He shrugged. "I'm not very political."

"You vote your pocketbook. I can understand that. Personally, I'm pretty liberal, but I guess that's obvious, just looking at me."

Mac was bewitched.

"But we're getting off track," Jade said. "I normally don't talk about myself a lot, but I can see you're the type who wants to know who he's dealing with and expects the straight skinny. What you'll care about is that I apprenticed with Barry Cushman for almost a year before striking out on my own. Barry's one of the old-timers in the gumshoe game. Barry, I gotta say, knows his stuff. I learned a lot, as much as I'd learned all the years I was a cop. If you want to talk with Barry about me, you can. He'll probably give you a favorable report."

"Probably?"

"I hate to sound like a whiner, some kind of persecuted

feminist, but Barry and I had a falling-out over the fact that I'm a girl and he isn't.''

"He was prejudiced?"

"No, he hit on me. The guy's sixty-two, but he felt part of my training was proving his manhood. To be honest, I'm not sure which part of my experience working with him he'll remember.'' She paused. "Would you like to hear more?"

Mac thought for a moment. He was thoroughly enchanted. Maybe because she was so different. "I have a question, Jade. Did you go over all this with Art?"

"Not really. He wasn't very interested in the past. In most of our conversations he talked about Pool Maids and himself. Not that there's anything wrong with that, it's most guys' favorite topic, if you know what I mean."

"Hmm."

"So, that's pretty much my story, Mac. I'm sorry if you're disappointed, but I'd rather be honest than embellish. In the long run it doesn't pay to play games. It may not be the best marketing strategy, but it feels better to me than lying."

"That used to be my philosophy, too."

"Used to be?"

"Life has a way of corrupting people and, to be perfectly honest, it's corrupted me."

"Not too many people admit to that."

"Maybe we have a lot in common."

"Accepting who we are?"

"Yeah, without pretense."

"I hate playing games." She hesitated. "You mention being corrupted. Is that part of the problem we'll be discussing?"

"Yes."

She nodded. "Well, I'm definitely curious."

They stared at each other for a moment until she grew self-conscious.

"So that's my story," she repeated. "If you want to stop here, I'm cool with that. You won't hurt my feelings."

"No," he said. "Just the opposite. So far so good. I'm liking what I hear. But it won't do either of us any good unless you're up to the task. After I outline the problem, I'd like your honest opinion if you think you're the one to handle the investigation."

"Sure, but let me be certain I understand. Are we talking about your personal problem or the Pool Maids problem?"

"My personal problem. Art wants to hire you to investigate Pool Maid's personnel and that's fine with me. This is separate."

She brightened. "You mean I got the job?"

"Yes. But you'll be dealing with Art on that. My situation has nothing to do with the company and, of course, it's strictly confidential. It also takes priority, by the way."

"I understand, Mac. I'm also very discreet."

He could see that. They'd hardly spoken for more than a few minutes, but already he had the feeling he could trust her. The woman inspired confidence, and Mac liked her. He liked what he saw and he liked what he'd heard.

"Before we get started, would you like a cup of coffee or a soft drink or something?" he asked. "I'm not the best host, I'm afraid."

"I take it your wife's not home."

"My wife and I are separated, Jade. Have been for nearly ten years."

"Oh, I didn't know that."

"Stella lives in Beverly Hills, in the place we had together. We have a son who's twenty. Unfortunately, Troy and I don't get along. He's got his mother's acting bug.

Hollywood was more or less responsible for the breakup of my marriage and my falling-out with my son."

"I see."

"I'm not single," he said, "but it practically amounts to the same thing." Mac saw the wheels turning. "That doesn't make any difference, does it?"

"In what?"

He shrugged. "Your willingness to take the case."

A little smile formed at the corners of her mouth. "Not unless you're planning on hitting on me."

"I'm not."

"Then it's cool."

Mac was pleased. "Coffee, then?"

"Have any fruit juice?"

He thought. "There may be a can of V-8 in the cupboard somewhere."

"That would be fine."

Mac went to the kitchen, feeling hopeful. Maybe that was because Jade Morro was the first positive thing to happen along in a while. Or maybe he just needed someone he could trust and rely on. The truth was he'd been going it alone for a long time, confiding in no one. Not in Bri or any of the other women in his life. Not in his friends. But now he needed help, expertise, and Jade seemed the one. He certainly wanted her to be.

Mac found the V-8 juice and was putting some water on to boil for his instant coffee when Jade appeared at the kitchen door.

"Need some help?"

She was leaning against the doorframe, her legs crossed at the ankles, her slender jock body having just enough girlish curves to be alluring. Impish, cute. Mac found her fascinating.

"You can open the can of juice," he said. "Glasses are

in the cupboard to the right of the sink. Opener's in that middle top drawer, there.''

Jade got her juice while Mac leaned against the counter waiting for the water to boil. ''I'm thirsty,'' she said. ''Mind if I start without you?''

''Be my guest.''

She guzzled down a quarter of the glass, then wiped her mouth with the back of her hand. The woman disdained pretense and was as real as any person he'd known since grammar school. There was a tinge of ''in your face'' about her, but he suspected it came from the fact that she'd been hurt. She was genuine, but also wounded.

''This is a pretty big place for a single guy, or do you have a roommate?''

''I have had lady friends who've spent time here. Nobody's actually moved in. A housekeeper cleans the place and picks up after me, but she's on vacation at the moment.''

Jade glanced around. ''You don't appear to be a slob.''

''I try not to be.''

''You like knocking around a big empty house?''

''When I bought it, it seemed the thing to do.''

She nodded and drank more V-8 juice.

''Do you mind telling me about your family background?'' Mac said. ''I like knowing the person behind the business facade.''

For the first time she looked suspicious.

''If you'd rather not, that's okay,'' he said.

''Nobody's ever asked me about my family before.''

''Maybe I'm overly curious.''

''Why? What are you curious about?''

Mac could see she knew how to question people. ''If I'm going to be sharing some very personal stuff about myself, I'd like to know you better, that's all.''

''Okay, what do you want to know about me?''

He searched for some harmless way to get the conversation started. "Where're you from originally?"

"San Diego. Grew up in a broken home. My dad died when I was a little kid. My mother raised me as a single parent. She wasn't very good at it. She felt she needed a man and went through a series of abusive relationships, with me watching every beating. There were a couple of husbands and lots of live-ins. I had a ton of father figures to choose from, none very wholesome. My mother managed to put food on the table and keep her guys away from me, though when I was a teenager, it was touch-and-go. She died of breast cancer the summer after I graduated from high school. I've pretty much been on my own ever since."

Mac could see he was right about her. Jade Morro was a decent person who'd had a rough life. She had a bit of a chip on her shoulder, but she was doing the best she could.

"How about you, Mac? Where'd you grow up?"

Mac told her about childhood and youth in Toledo, Ohio, about the mother he adored and his mostly absent father. He told her about playing football in high school and going to Vietnam.

"And now you're a millionaire pool guy having troubles with your wife."

"Yes and no." The hot water was boiling. "It's sort of complicated. Let's go back in the living room to talk."

Mac made some instant coffee in a mug. Jade refilled her glass and they went back into the front room.

When they'd settled into their chairs, Mac said, "I think somebody's preparing to blackmail me, Jade, extort money from me over a situation in the past. It involves my wife and me. It's a very private matter, and I'd rather not share the details. I don't mean to be coy, but I'm not the only one concerned and I've got to respect that. Others could be hurt, so I have to be careful.''

"All right. So, what's happened?''

"I've received an anonymous note. There was no demand for money or threat to expose secrets, but that's where it's headed, I believe. What I'd like for you to do is track down whoever is responsible.''

"Can I see the note?''

"No.''

Jade seemed surprised, then slowly nodded. "I can't see the note and you can't tell me exactly what the potential blackmail is about, but you want me to find out who's responsible.''

"I know it sounds crazy.''

"It's a little like trying to play tennis blindfolded, Mac.''

"There was a damning—let's say embarrassing—incident twenty years ago involving my wife and myself, which is what this is all about. Stella and I thought we were the only ones who knew, but the blackmailer seems to have found out somehow. Stella swears she never told a soul. I know I haven't.''

"One of you is either mistaken or lying.''

"I suppose so.''

"Can you give me a hint about the sort of thing we're talking about?''

Mac shifted uncomfortably. His soul cried out to spill everything, to tell the whole story, but he couldn't. He opted to give Jade a sanitized version. "Stella and I had an affair while she was still married to her former husband. We thought we were the only ones who knew. We discover now that we aren't. There's more to the story, but I'm hoping that's sufficient for you to do what you have to do, which is find this person.''

Jade opened up her notebook, took the cap off her pen and jotted a note. "Who was her former husband?"

"Aubrey St. George."

"The movie star?"

"Yes."

"The one who died in a boating accident."

"He drowned while swimming in the ocean," Mac said. "And they never found the body. Do you remember the case? It was a long time ago. Back in 1978."

"I was eleven years old, Mac. I don't remember anything at the time, but I recall hearing about it later, reading about it. I've seen some of his old films."

"Then you have a pretty good idea who we're talking about. Aubrey was Stella's first husband."

"Interesting." She jotted something on her pad. "Can you tell me about the note, the circumstance in which you received it, and so forth?"

"It was left on my doorstep."

"You found it?"

"Yes. When I came home from work. I was meeting a friend here. She was in her car out front when I arrived. We came to the door together, the note was in an envelope under the welcome mat."

"Who's your friend?"

"Sabrina Lovejoy. She goes by Bri."

"When was this?"

"Wednesday afternoon."

"Did she see the note?"

"No, I didn't open it then. I put it on the table and didn't open it until later that evening."

"You don't think she could be involved?"

"No, I don't see how. And she certainly didn't act as though it was a factor. Actually, Bri and I had been dating, and the reason she came over was to end the relationship. She was preoccupied with that."

"I see."

"There's no connection between Bri and the note. I'm sure of it."

"Okay." She stared at her notebook, tapping her lower teeth with the end of the pen.

"There's another thing," Mac said. "I don't know if there's a connection between this and the note, but it's a definite cause for worry."

"Yes?"

"Friday night Stella and I went out to dinner, actually to discuss the business with the note. I thought maybe she could explain it. She claimed to have no idea, but there was an incident in the street after we left the restaurant. Basically, some guy came by and took a couple of shots at us. Neither of us was hurt, but it scared the hell out of us, needless to say."

"A drive-by?"

"Yes. We left without calling the police or anything."

"Why?"

"Frankly, I didn't want to get into the business with the note, open up that can of worms."

"You may have been wise. They wouldn't have been quite so understanding of your holding back information."

"That's why I wanted a private investigator."

"I don't suppose you could identify the assailant or the vehicle."

Mac told her what little he'd seen. "The violence concerns me," he said. "And frankly, I don't understand it, unless the intent was to unnerve us."

"Blackmail and drive-bys are an unusual combination," Jade said. "Is it possible they're unrelated or that the shooting was a random thing?"

"I thought about that. I don't know the answer. But, I figured you should be aware."

"There seems to be an epidemic of this sort of thing

going on. Art and I had a little near hit-and-run type incident ourselves last night.''

"Oh?"

"But that's another story."

He watched her pondering the situation. They were discussing something fairly momentous from his perspective, yet Mac found himself as interested in Jade as in the discussion itself. He liked watching her. He liked her manner, her directness, her looks, her innocence.

She tapped her teeth with the pen again. "The question is if I think I can help you."

"Yes."

"I don't claim to be Sam Spade," she said. "I think I can do as well as anybody, but I've got to be honest. You're asking me to do an investigation with one hand tied behind my back. I don't know if anybody could do a credible job under the circumstances. I could certainly poke around, though, and, who knows, I could be lucky. It's a question of whether you think it's worth the expense."

He was relieved she didn't say no. "In that case, I'd like you to do it, Jade."

"My fee's three-fifty a day, plus expenses."

"Let's make it five. How much of a retainer do you need? Is five thousand enough?"

He could tell she was pleasantly surprised and didn't try to hide it. "Sure."

"Let me get my checkbook."

"Mac, let's be clear about one thing. I can't promise you results, only my best effort."

"I understand. I just need to feel something is being done."

He went and got his checkbook. He also brought the envelope the note had come in, handing it to her. She examined it.

"Keep it if you want," he said.

"At what point are you going to bring in the police? If there's a demand for money?"

"I don't plan on bringing them in at all if I can help it."

"Regardless?"

"Yes."

Jade studied him. Mac wrote out the check and handed it to her. She took a simple one-page agreement from her purse and gave it to him. He signed it. She gave him a copy and wrote out a receipt for the retainer.

"Let me ask you something," he said. "Do you know Jaime Caldron?"

"I know of him. I've heard stories, but I don't know him personally. He's supposed to be a pretty hot detective. Why?"

"I have a hunch he's on the case and after me again."

"What case?"

"Aubrey St. George's death. For years Caldron's thought I was somehow involved or that I have information I haven't shared with the police. He's about to retire, and I'll bet dollars to donuts he's decided to nab another offender before he rides off into the sunset. It could be you'll cross paths with him while you're poking around. I thought you ought to know."

"I thought St. George's death was ruled accidental."

"That was the coroner's finding. Caldron doesn't buy it."

She nodded. "Anything else I should know?"

Mac told her about his visit to the vacant house and the cop finding him in the backyard.

"Why'd you go there, anyway?"

Mac took a moment to ponder his response. She seemed to realize it was a sensitive issue.

"Never mind," she said. "It doesn't matter."

"I know I'm not being very helpful, but it's not because I don't want to."

"You're in a tough spot. I understand. Will I be able to talk to your wife?"

"I'd prefer not, but if you think it's essential, then okay. I'd like to be there, though."

Jade thought about that one for a moment. "Why? Because you don't trust her?"

"That's not a very charitable way to put it, but I suppose that's what it amounts to. Stella has always regarded me as her protector. I consider it my duty to look out for her interests, even if it means saving her from herself. I know that sounds paternalistic and maybe it sticks in your craw, but that's been our relationship, Jade, and there's no point in pretending otherwise."

"I hear you."

"As far as your investigation is concerned... What happened twenty years ago is not the point. Finding out who's trying to take advantage of it is."

"They aren't unrelated."

"I know I'm not making it easy for you."

"But you're paying me either way. I will do my best."

"I'm sure you will."

She looked at her watch, gulped down the last of her juice and started to get up to take the glass to the kitchen.

"Leave it," Mac said.

She put the glass back down on the table. "Well, I should be going. Let me give you one of my cards." She started into her purse again.

"I've got one. Art gave it to me."

"Okay. If you hear from your mystery friend again, let me know right away."

She stood, slinging her purse over her shoulder. Mac got to his feet, as well. Jade reached across the table and gave him another firm handshake. And a smile.

"I'll be in touch," she said.

He nodded.

They went to the door. Jade stepped out onto the porch, then skipped down the steps and around her car. Lithe, quick, strong, yet somehow terribly feminine. She opened the door, then, stopping, stepped back. She looked at her tires. Mac did as well, only then seeing what she was looking at. All her tires were flat.

"Shit," she said, bending to examine the front tire on the driver's side. She looked over the fender at Mac, who'd come down off the porch. "Somebody cut off the valve stem." She stood up. "I'm going to have to get somebody up here. I don't have four spares."

"I can't imagine who'd do this in broad daylight. We almost never have a problem up here."

"I've been having a few problems with a former boyfriend," she said. "The near hit-and-run last night and now maybe this. If it was him, he could have followed me."

"Or it could be my mysterious friend," Mac said.

Jade shook her head. "How did we get to be so popular, Mac?"

He chuckled. "Yeah, two such nice people."

Van Nuys

Troy Hampton struggled with his tie as his roommate, Hernan Payro, stood watching at the bathroom door.

"The big end's got to be longer," Hernan said.

"Shit. The bastard who decided men should wear ties ought to be shot."

"If you're going to fuck older women you've got to learn how to do a Windsor knot, my friend."

Troy groaned, pulling the knot apart. He looked over at Hernan with helpless desperation. Hernan moved over behind him.

"Here, let me show you." Reaching around him, Hernan did the knot, step-by-step. Then he turned Troy around and slid the knot snugly up into the collar. "There," he said. "Now you look like a man of the world."

Troy's tabby cat, Oscar, came slinking into the bathroom, meowed, then rubbed against Troy's legs. Troy picked him up and gave him an affectionate hug. "What are you saying, old buddy? That I forgot to feed you?" Oscar meowed plaintively. "Well, you're right. I did."

Troy, with Oscar under his arm, examined himself in the mirror a final time. "I don't give a damn about looking like a man of the world," he said to Hernan. "I've just got to be irresistible to one particular woman."

"Well, remember what I told you, amigo. Focus on her. Make her feel like she's the center of the universe. Do that and you're halfway home."

"The first rule of being a gigolo?" Troy chided as he moved past Hernan on his way to the kitchen.

"Works for me," Hernan said, following him.

Troy put Oscar on the stool next to the counter so the cat could watch his meal being prepared. It was a ritual the two of them had. Hernan had found Troy's devotion to Oscar amusing. "You know what?" his friend had once said. "I think that cat is your one true love."

"He is. But it's not just Oscar. I love all cats."

"Why? Because you had one as a kid?"

"No, because I didn't have one as a kid. Mac wouldn't allow them in the house."

"Because he's allergic?"

"No, because he's an asshole. The prick tried to get me a dog."

"Tried?"

"When I was five my mother got me a cat without checking first with Mac. When we brought it home, he got all bent out of shape and made her take it back to the pet shop. Mom and I spent hours picking out that cat. I held him in my arms all the way home in the car. I called him Buttons. It was one of the few times in my childhood I was truly happy. Mom was so upset with Mac for breaking my heart that she refused to come to my room to take Buttons away from me, so Mac did. Later, he felt badly and tried to take me down to get a dog, but I refused to go. I hated the bastard.''

"And that's why you never got along? I thought it was because of his thing about Hollywood.''

"It was a lot of things. We clashed over everything, you name it. But that incident with Buttons stuck in my mind. Maybe he didn't like cats, and maybe my mother should have talked to him about it first, but he was still a prick. The sonovabitch never approved of me. That was the real problem. I felt it my whole life.''

After Troy had opened the can of cat food, he ran it past Oscar's nose. "That meet with your approval?''

Oscar meowed. Troy ran his hand over the cat's silky fur, then leaned down and kissed his nose. Hernan, who was sitting at the table, chuckled. "You show that kind of love to Venita and you'll have her eating out of your hand.''

"Hey, I hope so," Troy said, scraping the last of the cat food out of the can and into Oscar's bowl. "She's pretty great.''

"So much the better.''

Troy gave him a sly smile as he put Oscar's bowl on the floor. "But I like what she can do for me even better.''

"Therein lies the danger, my friend.''

"Well, it's a dangerous world, Hernan.'' Troy gave him a playful punch on the arm as he headed back to the bedroom to get his jacket. "I've got to get rolling. I still have to squeeze some money out of my old lady before I see Venita.''

Hernan followed him. "Does she know about you two?"

"Are you kidding? She'd have a shit-fit. Besides, basically, she'd rather not know. I never went out of my way to hide Ginger from her because I didn't have to. She didn't want to find out."

Ginger Lane was Troy's friend and occasional sex partner, though only when under the influence of drugs. She, Troy and Hernan had met in acting class. Ginger was only twenty-three, but a veteran of thirty-four porno movies. She'd retired from skin flicks at the age of twenty-one and was making a concerted effort to become a legitimate actor. Troy would be the first to say she had more talent than any of them, but thus far, mainstream Hollywood had turned a cold shoulder. The three of them hung together, but Ginger had made herself scarce the past several weeks—disappearing for stretches being normal behavior for her.

"A mother wouldn't find Ginger so threatening as Venita," Hernan told him. "My advice is to be discreet."

"Believe me, I will."

If there was one thing Troy had down pat, it was self-preservation. And the way he saw it, if there was any hope of getting to Mac, he'd need his mother's help. But the good news was, this film deal was just as important to her as it was to him.

Yet there were no givens. Troy was smart enough to know that he was essentially his mother's tool. But then, it worked both ways. He used her, too.

"So, where do things stand on the movie deal?" Hernan asked as he watched Troy slip on his suit coat.

"Sort of in limbo. And we don't have forever to get our act together. Sooner or later Amal and Venita will pick up their bags and move on."

"But you have a plan."

"In a word, yes."

There was a knock on their front door. They looked at one another.

"You expecting somebody?" Troy asked.

"No."

"Me neither."

They went to the front room and Hernan opened the door. Ginger Lane stood on their doorstep, her lovely face a halo of red curls. She had a shapely body and dressed to show it off, tank tops and short tight skirts being the staples of her wardrobe. She'd maintained the sex-kitten image not so much by design as because of the fact that it was, as she put it, "the real me."

"Well, long time no see," Hernan said.

"Yeah, been cruisin'." She stepped in, catching sight of Troy. "Look at the boy toy," she said. "Aren't you all dolled up? Got a hot date?"

"As a matter of fact."

"Our young star is moving up the ladder," Hernan said. "Dining and fucking his way to the top."

"Yeah?"

Ginger wanted to know the details and Troy filled her in. Which was, he decided, a good thing. Ginger might be very useful to his plan, and he'd been hoping she'd show up so he could get her on board—assuming plan A with his mother didn't work out.

After he brought Ginger up-to-date, she said, "Christ almighty, you are on your way, Troy."

"I'm not there yet. But you two could figure prominently into my plans."

"Really?"

"Yes."

"I need a beer," Ginger said.

The three of them went into the kitchen, where Oscar was finishing his meal. Troy picked him up and sat on the stool, petting him as Hernan got Ginger a Corona. She took a swig and sat on the table, letting her skirt ride up one thigh. She swung one leg, the big platform sandal on her foot moving like the pendulum of a clock.

"So, whatcha got?" she said.

"Okay, here's the deal," Troy said as he stroked Oscar. "If Mac finances *On Distant Shores*, I'm in the film for sure. There might be parts for my friends, but more importantly, I have juice in the production company, especially if I get myself in an influential position with Venita."

"Influential position, like between her legs?" Ginger said, drawing on her beer.

"To be crude about it, yes."

"When am I not crude? Besides, I know you, Troy."

He ignored that and went on. "Let's say I had a plan where enough money is raised to get the film going, plus the three of us each put, say, a hundred grand in our pockets."

"No way," Ginger said.

"Yeah way," Troy replied. "At least maybe. I still have some work to do on it."

Ginger frowned. "You serious, Troy, or are you bullshitting?"

"I'm dead serious."

"What's the plan?" Hernan asked.

Oscar had had enough affection and jumped down. Troy watched him slink away. "I'm not ready to lay it all out," he said, "but I've got to know you two would be willing to take a risk and then keep your mouths shut."

Ginger and Hernan looked at each other and grinned.

"He wants us to knock off his old man."

"I'm not bullshitting you," Troy said. "I'm talking serious business. No holds barred. Balls to the wall."

"Criminal stuff?" Hernan asked.

Troy shrugged. Again Hernan and Ginger looked at each other. This time they weren't smiling.

"Specifically what?" Hernan asked.

"I'm not ready to share specifics, but I will be soon."

After a pause, Ginger said, "Mind if I ask you something, Troy? How come you hate your old man so much?"

The question made him smile. How did you explain a lifelong hatred? To the world Mac McGowan might not be the asshole Troy knew, but the world didn't know what Troy knew. Nor was he about to share his knowledge—not until the right moment.

But that didn't keep him from thinking about it. The Mac McGowan he knew was a murdering sonovabitch. Of course, Troy wasn't supposed to know that. No one was. But one Saturday morning when he was fifteen he'd found out the true story.

It had happened by accident. Bonny was away and Mac planned to come over to talk to Stella about finances. Troy, who avoided seeing Mac whenever he could, planned to spend the day with a friend who only lived a few blocks away. At one point in the afternoon Troy returned home to get his joystick so he and his friend could play a new video game. He didn't want to see Mac, whose car was still in the drive, so he sneaked in the back. That's when he heard them arguing. His mother was crying and Troy heard her utter those fateful words, words that had haunted him ever since.

"I wasn't the one who killed Aubrey. It was you, Mac. And don't you ever forget it!"

Troy had borne that secret bitterly and with resentment, considering what else he knew about Aubrey St. George. The irony was that neither his mother nor Mac were aware he knew the truth. How could he hate Mac McGowan? How could he not?

"Ginger," he said calmly, "let's just say I have reasons." He checked his watch. "But I gotta get rolling. You guys give this thing some thought and we'll talk soon." He headed for the front door and Hernan followed.

Troy put his hand on the doorknob and stopped. In a low voice he said, "I know you're hot to get out of the gigolo business and I also know you're willing to take chances. Find out if Ginger would be willing to risk jail for a big break, will you?"

"You're not bullshitting about this, are you?"

"I'm tired of screwing around. I'm going for it, Hernan." Troy opened the door and went out. Hernan stepped out with him. The apartment manager, Mrs. Tuttle, was across the way, sweeping the walk.

Hernan said, "Oh, by the way, Troy, I just remembered. Mrs. Tuttle told me some guy was poking around this morning, asking about you."

"Who?"

"I don't know. She said he was English, or at least had a strong accent like Michael Caine."

"And he was asking about me?"

"That's what she said. The guy wanted to know who you were, what you did."

Troy shook his head. "God, I don't know who it could be. Did she say what he looked like?"

"Middle-aged. Sort of dark-complected. She said his accent didn't really go with his looks."

"I wonder if he could be Indian?"

"I don't know, but I wondered the same thing myself."

Troy pondered the news, looking for danger, but seeing nothing obvious. "I haven't the vaguest," Troy said.

"Well, keep your eyes open."

"You, too, sport."

Troy headed off to his car. Moments later he pulled out of the parking lot. By chance he glanced into his rearview mirror and saw a car that had been parked across from the complex make a U-turn and follow him down the street.

West Hollywood

I still don't think it's Ricky pulling this stuff," Jade told Ruthie on the phone, "but just in case it is, I'd better talk to him and straighten him out. Do you think you can get a message to him?"

"Probably. You want a phone number or do you want me to set up a meeting?"

"I guess face-to-face is best."

"I'm thinking like on neutral ground, not his turf," Ruthie said.

"Where do you suggest?"

"How about here at my place? Maybe I can have a brother or two just happen to be here."

Jade considered that. "I suppose that's better than at my place or the zoo."

"When you free?"

"Anytime. I'll make it a priority."

"If you don't, somebody might get hurt for real."

"This is so unlike him, Ruthie."

"If not him, who?"

"That's the point, I guess."

"I'll talk to Ricky," Ruthie said.

"You're a doll."

"So, except for getting your tires slashed, how'd it go with the big boss man?"

"Mac's really nice. He bought me four new tires when the tire guy said they were too worn to be repaired."

"He bought them for you, just like that?"

"It'll come out of my retainer fee, but it saved me advancing money I don't have."

"What's he like?"

"Nice."

"Nice ain't nothing, girl. Mr. Rogers is nice. Big Bird is nice."

"All men don't have to be dripping with gold chains, devilish smirks and sex appeal to be interesting, Ruthie. Been there, done that, don't forget. Do you have any idea how many assholes I've known?"

"Yeah. Tons, same as me."

"My mother decorated our house with them. And then there was Ricky. I'll never look twice at a pretty boy again. Mac is a refreshing change, that's all I'm saying."

"Right. He's 'nice,' your new favorite word."

"You'd have to meet him to know what I mean."

"Maybe you'll invite me to the wedding."

Jade laughed. "I'm just working for the man."

"So?"

"So, it's strictly business. I wouldn't want it any other way. I was just commenting on what a pleasant experience it was dealing with him. He's the kind of guy you feel you can trust…maybe it's some kind of quiet strength." She cleared her throat, kind of embarrassed. "Haven't you ever felt that way about someone?"

Ruthie laughed. "What you're saying, girlfriend, is that the dude is rich."

"Oh, Ruthie, it doesn't have anything to do with his money. He could be one of the guys who builds his pools and it would be the same."

"That I don't believe. Unless you're saying you got a crush on him."

"Absolutely not. I just met a man who's different, decent. And, considering all the shit in my life, I just thought my best friend would like to know I actually had a positive experience with a man."

"And I'm glad, Jade. Honest. I couldn't be more happy for you. But as you well know, I'm one of those show-me-the-money kind of girls. I mean, Big Bird is fine, but we both know every dude's got a bottom line and every sister better know what that bottom line is. Don't forget, it was me calling out warnings about Ricky.''

"This time you don't have to worry. Believe me, romance is the farthest thing from my mind.''

Beverly Hills

Stella sat at her little French antique writing desk, took her checkbook from her drawer and opened it. She glanced over at her son. Troy was in a navy blue suit and tie. She was absolutely amazed. She didn't even know he had a dark suit.

"Three hundred dollars,'' she said. "You must have quite an evening planned.''

"Yeah, I do.''

"A very special girl, obviously.''

"Yeah, I guess.''

"I don't suppose there's any chance you'll bring her by some time to meet your mother.''

"Mom, it's not like that.''

Stella looked up from her writing. "What do you mean, it's not like that? You're going to wait until after your second child is born before you introduce me?''

"Ma, give me a break. I'm not eloping. I'm going out to dinner, no big deal.''

"With a mystery woman.''

Her son gave her one of his quirky grins, handsome devil that he was. "You always said a man should be mysterious, didn't you? If I gotta keep the girls guessing, why not you?''

"Because I write the checks.''

"All right,'' Troy said, showing his annoyance. "Her name's Ashley and she's twenty-three. Satisfied?''

"Ashley? Is she in your acting class?"

"No, I met her at a party."

"You're serious about her?"

"Ma, we're just friends. Okay?"

Stella shook her head. "Mac and I have our differences, Lord knows, but I've got to say this about him, he was always honorable, he never lied to me."

"As far as you know."

She gave her son a look. But she wouldn't chastise him, even though she'd long thought Mac had deserved better from the boy. Some conflicts were just too elemental to overcome, apparently. Troy always responded to issues of his self-interest, however, and so she decided to take the conversation in that direction.

"It doesn't look like Mac is going to step up and help us with Amal and Venita," she said. "So perhaps it is time for us to go to him on bended knee."

"Don't you mean time for me to go to him on bended knee?"

"You are the stumbling block, Troy."

"No, Mom, you're the stumbling block. I'm the battle-ground. This has always been about you, not about me."

Troy, she realized, was no longer afraid to tell her what he thought. She laid her hand aside her cheek, realizing he was no longer a child. She couldn't patronize or manipulate him, and she wasn't finding it easy to be a mother to a headstrong young man. "Maybe Mac needs a victory."

"I'm not going to kiss his ass. All he wants is to ma-nipulate and control us."

"Troy, you've got to give something to get something."

"Not with him. He pays and expects to have his way. Sure, I could make the guy happy—by accepting a dog instead of a cat."

"You've never forgiven him for that, have you?"

"You sure did. Sorry to have to say this, but he owns you."

Stella shook her head. "You don't understand Mac's and my relationship, even if you think you do."

In response to that, Troy smiled.

"You don't," Stella insisted.

"What makes you so sure?"

"Did you know that somebody tried to kill Mac and me Friday night?"

"What?"

Stella studied her son long and hard. "It's true. Down on Wilshire. We were walking back to the car after having dinner and a man came by in an old car and fired shots at us. Fortunately he missed, but he was trying to kill us."

"You're shitting me."

"No, I'm not shitting you. It happened."

"Did you call the police?"

Again she studied him. "No, we didn't."

"Why?"

"Mac had his reasons."

Troy looked at her and she looked at him. She waited, watching him closely.

"What?" he said.

She said nothing.

"Mom?"

She still said nothing.

"What are you thinking? That I had something to do with it?"

"Neither of us can figure out who would have reason to see us dead."

Troy turned purple. "So naturally you assumed it was me! Is that what he said?" Troy stammered. "Did he say I was behind it?"

"No, of course not. Your name never once came up."

Troy paced back and forth. "Well, you just said it, didn't you?"

"I didn't accuse you, Troy, but I confess I was curious how you'd react when I brought it up."

"Thanks a lot, Mom. That's a real vote of confidence."

"You've said some terrible things about Mac. And you are his heir."

"Well, considering I'm not absolutely sure he hasn't written me out of his will, I'd be taking a hell of a risk for nothing, wouldn't I?"

"I'm sure he hasn't disowned you," Stella said. "He would have told me."

"So what are you saying? That I can go ahead and put out a contract on him because I am in the will?"

"Troy, what a terrible thing to say!"

"How does it feel, Ma?"

"You know that was not my intention. I just wanted to see how you felt. Not just about him, but about me."

"Well, I'm sorry somebody took a shot at you. Is that what you wanted to hear?"

"I didn't want it to be you, I didn't think it was you, but I wanted to be absolutely sure."

"I don't know whether that says more about you or me, Ma."

"I'm not a bad person," she said. "And for that matter your father is not the monster you make him out to be."

Troy flushed. "He's not my father, goddamn it. He only thinks he is, remember?"

"Troy!" Stella looked toward the door. "You promised never to mention that. And don't forget we are not alone."

"Bonny is not eavesdropping. She knows everything going on in this house, anyway. Without trying. I wouldn't be surprised if she doesn't know about this."

"Well, she doesn't!"

"Okay, fine."

"I never should have told you."

"You didn't. I guessed. Remember? I was what, twelve or thirteen?"

"I confirmed it."

"So big deal. I've never liked the bastard."

"If it weren't for him, you and I would be a lot hungrier, Troy."

"If it weren't for him, I'd have my real father. I'd be the son of a famous star. Doors would open that are closed to Mac McGowan's kid. Neither of us would have to beg for crumbs from a goddamn swimming-pool contractor who doesn't have an artistic bone in his body. Or, is getting your ten thou a month from Mac all you need to be happy, Mom?"

"You know I want this movie deal as much or more than you do. It would be nice if Mac solved the problem by investing with Amal and Venita, but he's certainly within his rights to refuse. We need to convince him, that's all."

"It won't happen by kissing his ass, I guarantee you."

"He needs to see it to be in his interest as well as ours."

"How you going to do that, Mom?"

"I haven't given up. I still have a few cards to play."

"Well, good luck."

Stella was getting annoyed with Troy's negativism. "Saying no to everything accomplishes nothing."

"I'm being realistic. Anyway, maybe I have a few cards of my own."

"What do you mean?"

"Never mind."

"I want to know," Stella insisted.

"You have your secrets and I have mine," he replied.

"I have no secrets from you."

"Oh?"

"That's right."

"Ma, give it a rest. You've already accused me of being a murderer, now you're taking me for a fool."

"I've done no such thing!"

"All right, fine. Truce. You do your thing and I'll do mine. The main thing is we've got to keep each other informed. We'll sink or swim together, you know."

Stella stared at him, as she had so often in the past, seeing so much of Aubrey in him. Sometimes it actually scared her. But Troy had his dreams, like her. He was also her son.

"So, are you going to give me the check, or aren't you?"

Stella sighed, signed the check and tore it out of the checkbook. She held it up between index and middle fingers. Troy came over and took it from her, gave her a peck on the cheek and said, "Thanks."

After he left, she sat at her desk, looking at her hands, hands that were no longer youthful. Oh, she'd had treatments to bleach the spots, and God knows how many other treatments to keep things in check. Age was not a battle she would win, though. She knew that. But neither did it mean she had to give up. She still had this opportunity with Amal that fate had given her—perhaps the final opportunity of her life. And if her time on this planet was to count for something, she couldn't let it slip away. She refused to let it slip away!

Drawing in a long slow breath to fortify herself, Stella reached over and picked up the phone, then dialed.

"I have another errand for you to run," she said when there was a response on the other end. "Can you come tonight?"

The answer was affirmative. She hung up the receiver. Then she opened the drawer and removed a sheet of notepaper. Her hand trembled as she picked up her pen. Closing her eyes, she thought of herself as Hilda Grimsley in

On Distant Shores. The image was as clear as it could be. It was clearer than the image of Judy Miller, clearer than that of Stella St. George or Stella McGowan, and it was every bit as clear as Stella Hampton. She understood destiny. Destiny spoke to her in a loud, clear voice.

Pacific Palisades

Troy hadn't noticed the car following him until he'd crossed the San Diego Freeway on Sunset Boulevard. Then it became obvious he had a tail. Because of the darkness, he couldn't get a good look at the vehicle or the driver, but the headlights stayed right with him. He wondered who the hell it could be, then remembered what Hernan had said about the dark-complected guy with the English accent. If that's who was behind him, it had to have something to do with Amal and Venita.

Just to be sure he was actually being followed, he made a couple of turns off Sunset, then came back on. The tail kept pace. Troy was baffled. And annoyed. Then he recalled his mother's story about somebody taking a shot at her and Mac, and he wondered if they all hadn't been sucked into something—something more than they'd bargained for.

At first he thought his mother had made up the story about the shooting, just to see how he'd react. But then he realized it was true. It did annoy him that she'd think he was behind it, even though it wasn't as far-fetched as he led her to believe. More than once he'd thought how, if Mac was dead, his life would dramatically change for the better. But that didn't make him a killer. Fantasies didn't count. The idea did have growing appeal, however.

The headlights behind him flashed in his mirror and Troy's attention was again drawn to the car following him. Whoever it was back there, it wasn't the person who'd taken a potshot at Mac. And the only person who might have an interest in him would be somebody connected with Venita and Amal. What else did he have going on in his life? Well, there was only one way to find out who it was. Before leaving Sunset to drive up the hill to Venita's place, Troy pulled over and stopped. The car followed suit, stopping maybe fifty feet back. The headlights of the vehicle went off.

Looking in the rearview mirror, Troy could see it was a Toyota. The driver appeared to be alone. Troy got out of the car and walked back. The window on the driver's side of the car slid down. Troy saw the smiling face of a man in his late thirties to early forties. He was dark-complected, but didn't appear to be Indian—more a person of mixed race.

"Evening, mate," he said cheerily.

Troy came up beside the car. "What are you following me for?"

"Actually, I'd like a word with you, if you don't mind, Mr. Hampton. You are Troy Hampton, are you not?"

"Yes, who are you?"

"The name's Gaylord. Percy Gaylord."

"So, what do you want?"

"I'm a journalist. A freelance journalist. Working on a story about your friends, Amal Kory and Venita Kumar. Thought perhaps I could ask a few questions. Buy you a cup of coffee?"

Troy shook his head. "Sorry, I'm in a hurry."

"It appears you're headed up to Venita's place now."

"What if I am?"

"My sources tell me that you and Miss Kumar are romantically involved, mate. Is that true?"

"I don't see how that's any business of yours."

"Perhaps it's not, quite right. But my readers do have a keen interest in the lady and all the people in her life."

"I don't have anything to say to you," Troy said, starting to turn away.

"You've been seen with one of the most famous women in India and you have nothing to say?" Gaylord called after him.

"That's right," Troy said over his shoulder.

"Would you have a comment on the rumors about Miss Kumar circulating back in India?"

Troy stopped. "What rumors?"

Gaylord seemed pleased to have piqued his interest.

"She hasn't mentioned Ramda Bol to you then?"

Troy wasn't sure whether to ask who Ramda Bol was. Judging by the man's tone, the association was nothing to be proud of. Troy opted for being vague. "No comment."

"No comment on one of the biggest scandals in modern Indian history?"

"That's right, no comment."

"Do you have a comment on Amal Kory, perhaps?"

"What kind of comment?"

"Out of curiosity, mate, have you ever seen this chap Kory's papers?"

"Papers?"

"His identification, passport, whatever."

"No, why would I?"

"Just curious, that's all. Mr. Kory's the reclusive sort. Seems odd he'd turn up in such a high-profile place as Hollywood."

Troy realized he best keep his mouth shut, at least until he'd had a chance to talk to Venita. "You'd have to talk to Amal about that."

"Right you are, governor. You are going up to see Mr. Kory and Miss Kumar now, aren't you?"

"Maybe."

"Capital. Perhaps you'd be so kind as to pass along a

message. Please tell them that Percy Gaylord is in town and that he'd fancy an interview.''

"Sure, I can tell them.''

"Thanks ever so, Mr. Hampton. And when you do speak to Amal, tell him his fans in India will be happy to hear he's alive and well and enjoying himself in America.''

Troy gave Gaylord a quizzical look, not understanding.

"I think he'll get my point,'' Gaylord explained. "And please tell Venita I'll give her a jingle.''

"Yeah, sure.''

"Oh, Mr. Hampton, since we're chatting, would you mind a photograph?''

"Huh?''

Before Troy knew what was happening, Percy Gaylord produced a camera and snapped a picture, the flash going off in his face. Troy recoiled.

"Cheerio!'' Gaylord said, and the window next to him slid up. He grinned through the glass and started the engine.

Troy went back to his car and Percy Gaylord drove off, giving him a little wave as he went by. Unsure of what the hell had just happened, Troy drove up the hill to Venita's.

"Don't worry about it, my dear,'' Venita told him after listening to his account of his meeting with Percy Gaylord. "You handled him perfectly. I'll take it from here.''

"Who is he, Venita?''

"Percy Gaylord is a major pain in the ass, if I may be blunt. He basically stirs up trouble in hopes of making news of it. Sells his garbage to the British tabloids and to the Indian papers as well. He's all charm on the surface, but in truth he's a snake, a dreadful man.''

"Is he English or Indian?''

"Both. English father who lived his entire life in India and a Scots great-grandfather on his mother's side. The rest of his ancestors are Indian. Got the worst of both races, to be frank. If he should approach you again, Troy, don't even speak with him."

"That's no problem."

She smiled appreciatively.

They were in the front room. Venita still had the roses Troy had brought her cradled in her arms. She smiled confidently, but Troy sensed she'd been shaken. He hadn't even mentioned the Ramda Bol scandal Gaylord had alluded to, thinking it was best to bring up one thing at a time. But it seemed like a good time to mention it now, so he did.

Venita looked at him with a sober, if not icy, expression. "What, exactly, did Percy say about Ramda?"

"Nothing much except that it was the biggest scandal in the modern history of India."

"That bloody sot. What a gasbag."

"I really have no idea what it's about," Troy told her in full innocence, "and it's none of my business."

"Maybe you should hear about it. With Percy scandalmongering, it's bound to come out. I'd rather tell you myself. The whole affair is of little consequence outside India, though I grant you it was a cause célèbre there. It was a political scandal, Troy, and I got sucked into it. Not completely blamelessly, I admit. You see, I had an affair with a man named Ramda Bol. That is not particularly newsworthy in itself, apart from gossip value, but there was one small problem. Ramda happens to be the son-in-law of the prime minister and a rising politician in his own right."

"Oh, I see."

"Actually, love, you probably don't, but I shall enlighten you. It's not particularly unusual for a man of power to take a celebrated film star for a lover. We did, after all, move in the same rarefied circles in Delhi. What was unusual was that the wife and her father's political henchmen chose to make a stink about it. Soon the whole bloody business became grist for the press's mill. Percy Gaylord was one of the most insistent and bloody dishonest of the lot. There was more fiction than fact in the stories that appeared in the papers. It was truly disgusting and, frankly, I soon had my fill of it. The timing was such that Amal and I, having laid our plans for America, decided to come straightaway. I was happy to take my leave of the lot and let them consume one another. I hate politics, Troy, and shall never get involved with another politician again, not so long as I live."

"What's Gaylord doing in L.A.?"

"I suspect he's come in hopes of getting a rejoinder to some charge or accusation leveled against me, but I shan't give them the satisfaction. I'm through with that bloody business."

"I'm sorry you have to put up with it."

"Oh," she said dismissively, "the price of fame requires a very strong stomach. But enough of that. I really can't be bothered." She smelled her roses. "Allow me a few minutes, Troy. I want to have Cala put these lovely flowers in a vase. And I shall need a word with Amal. He's no fan of Percy Gaylord and needs to be put on the alert. Why don't you fix yourself a drink. I should only be a few minutes."

"No problem."

Troy watched her go. Venita was cool as a cucumber, but his news had shaken her. Whether there was more to the story, he didn't know, but it was nice to know Venita had an Achilles heel. God knows, he had his own vulnerabilities. In his limited experience, he'd learned that it was best when neither partner had a decided advantage. He'd also learned it was good to have a little dirt on one's lover.

As he thought about it, maybe he'd been a bit too quick to send Percy Gaylord away.

Venita moved through the house with all the grace she could muster. The mere fact that Percy mentioned Amal proved he was onto her, and that meant she was dead—they both were. Her mind spinning, she found Cala and gave her the flowers. "And where is Arjay? In his room?"

Cala told her that he was in the pool.

Venita went to the sunroom, then out onto the terrace. A full moon illuminated the yard, and she was able to see Arjay doing slow, rhythmic strokes, leisurely moving from one end of the pool to the other. He liked to swim at night, then do his yoga and read. He rarely took much supper, taking his main meal in the afternoon, between lunch and tea.

"Arjay," Venita called, marching up to the edge of the pool, the fabric of her sari billowing in the breeze. "I need a word with you. Arjay!"

He stopped swimming and faced her, treading water, his gray hair scalloped bangs across his broad forehead. "Must it be now, my dear, in the middle of my training?"

"Yes, it must. We have a crisis and it must be dealt with promptly."

Arjay waded to the ladder and climbed from the pool. He was naked, his dark skin glistening in the moonlight. As he reached for his robe lying on a deck chair, Venita turned away out of respect, though she felt little true respect for the man—admiration for his acting ability and chutzpah, perhaps, but not genuine respect. In a minute, Arjay, swathed in terry, joined her.

"What urgent crisis has befallen us?" he asked, sounding somehow like a man forced to deal with tedium.

Venita motioned toward the umbrella table and they sat in the cushioned chairs. She crossed her legs and lay her arm on the table. She promptly began drumming her nails on the glass. "Percy Gaylord is in town," she said. "And he wants to talk."

His brows rose. "Bloody hell."

"Yes, bloody hell, indeed."

Holmby Hills

"You know what, Manuela?" Mike O'Gill said. "You fuck every bit as well as you dance."

"Thanks, Mike."

"That's a sincere compliment."

"And it was a sincere thanks."

Mike was lying on his "Olympic-size" water bed, which filled most of his large master bedroom. He was naked and looking like a beached whale. Not the prettiest sight she'd ever seen, but there was no denying the guy had a hell of a sex drive, even if he always looked like he was going to blow a gasket when he came.

"You're going to kill yourself someday, Mike," she'd told him. "You really got to lose weight."

"Did you have a good time, Manuela?"

"Yeah, I had a good time."

"Then don't worry about me, okay?"

Mike always let a girl be on top, which was a good thing because if he was on top, a girl could get killed. Actually he wasn't a bad guy, just oversexed. He was only thirty-seven and had a handsome face. Just fat. He did have pretty blue eyes and curly blond hair that, as one of the girls said, made him look like a Roman emperor, whatever that meant.

"I'm having a party Friday night," he told her. "After your shift, why don't you come over and join the fun?" Mike's parties were really orgies. She'd seen as many as seven or eight people on the water bed at one time. Mike loved it.

Manuela got up from the bed and went into the bathroom to wash herself off. When she came back, Mike was eating grapes from a bowl on the bed next to his huge pink-and-white body—that had something to do with emperors, too.

"You taking off, then?" Mike asked.

"Yeah, but let me ask you something," she said. "What would I have to do for you to get you to loan me ten thousand dollars?"

"Ten grand?"

"Yeah."

"Hell, be my sex slave for life."

"Seriously."

"What do you need ten thousand for, Manuela? A new car?"

"No, I want to pay to have somebody killed."

Mike O'Gill threw back his head and laughed. He popped a couple more grapes in his mouth and a couple of cookies from the bag on the other side of him. "That's rich," he said.

"What would I have to do?" she asked.

Mike got a half-serious look on his face. "I don't know. You obviously don't like the sex-slave idea."

"How about for three months?"

"You serious?"

"I need the money, Mike."

"Let me think about it and we'll talk, okay?"

Manuela beamed and started getting dressed. The whole time she was humping him, she'd been thinking about it. Getting the money was very important to her, especially after her conversation with Angel.

"Say, I want Mac and his girlfriend dead," she'd said to her brother. "What will it cost me?"

Angel, who'd been lying on the sofa cleaning his fingernails with his pocketknife, looked up at her and said, "Ten each."

"That's a lot of money."

"Killing somebody's not like washing a car."

"Promise you won't hit me, Angel?"

Her brother glanced up, his brow creasing with a deep furrow. "What?"

"Promise?"

"Okay, I promise. What?"

"That day I went to Mac's and he told me he didn't want me. You know when I mean?"

"Yeah…"

"Well, I lied to you. Mac fucked me first."

"He didn't."

"Yes, he did. Swear to God."

"How come you said he didn't?"

"Because I knew you'd kill him and I didn't want you to…then. But I changed my mind."

"Why?"

"Because I seen them together this morning."

Angel's face turned all red and, thinking he was about to explode, she took half a step backward. But he didn't get up and pop her. "This true?"

"Yes, it is."

Angel's face got still more red and the muscles in his jaw started to twitch. "I won't kill the sonovabitch for nothing," he said, "if that's what you're thinking, because I'd need enough money to go away for a while."

"How much?"

He thought for a minute. "Ten for the both of them."

"Can you do it so nobody will know who?"

"Do I look like some kind of idiot? What do you think? That I'd leave my name on the bodies?"

"No, I know you're a professional. When can you do it?"

"When can you have the money?"

"I'll tell you tonight."

"Don't wait too long," her brother said. "I like to do these things when I'm really pissed."

Manuela had finished dressing, and Mike, having finished off the cookies, crumpled the sack and tossed it toward the wastebasket across the room. He missed.

"So, when can you tell me when I can have the money?" she asked him.

He frowned. "Eager beaver, aren't you?"

"It's important, Mike."

"We're talking a loan?"

"How about fifty-fifty? I'll pay you back half and work off the rest."

"Like doing what?"

"Like I do you and your brother at the same time." That was something none of the girls ever wanted to do because Mike's brother, Arnold, was just as big as Mike and not as nice. Besides, a person could get killed doing both of them.

Mike's brows rose with delight. "We definitely have to talk, Manuela."

"What's the soonest for the money, Mike?"

He considered her question. "How about you stay late Tuesday night. Arnold will be here. If things go well, you can have it then."

"Okay, fine. Can you give me cash?"

"Ten thousand in green? That can be arranged, I guess."

Manuela blew him a kiss. "Bye, Mike." She headed for the door.

"Love your moves, babe."

She waved goodbye over her shoulder, only then aware

how sore she was. Screwing Mike was a chore, and she could see she would have a lot more of it to put up with. God, did she ever hate Mac McGowan. He'd taken her happiness and given her this.

Monday, August 28, 2000

Pacific Palisades

For the first time in months, Venita dreamed of her husband, Ranjit Govind. But she awoke next to her twenty-
year-old American lover, Troy Hampton. That was hardly
the story of the typical Indian woman, modern or otherwise. Ranjit was her past, the father-husband who had de-
fined her world and made her a queen—fashioned from his
own imagination and will. But then he'd died and Venita's
life had begun its gradual decent into infamy. Perhaps the
Hindu wives of old who'd practiced sati, climbing upon
their husbands' funeral pyres, knew what they were doing.
Perhaps the British, in abolishing the custom, had done the
Indian widows no favors. What, after all, was a few
minutes of agony in the flames compared to the water-
torture life of a woman struggling to make it alone in a
man's world?

Of course, Venita hadn't bowed to the will of the vengeful male gods. She'd bid Ranjit farewell, and then gone
on to pursue her dreams. Ramda Bol, unfortunately, had
proven to be a grave mistake, a dream become a nightmare—a nightmare presently in the guise of Percy Gaylord.

From the moment Troy had uttered Percy's name, Venita figured the game was over. All that remained was to

plan her exit. There was no way she could hold things together with Percy trumpeting her story. Once he'd gotten to the bottom of the Arjay-Amal business—if, indeed, he hadn't already—all of Hollywood would see her as a fraud.

What she couldn't absolutely be sure of, though, was what Percy was really up to. Like most journalists, he loved dirt—anything to feed the prurient minds of the reading public. And, like most journalists, Percy would gladly—cheerfully, even—provide the necessary corpses to feed the dogs.

If there was a sliver of hope, it was that Percy might be after something other than her scalp. Maybe it was Ramda Bol he wanted.

The whole story hadn't yet been told—nor would it ever, as far as she was concerned. But there were certain things that, were they to come out, would cause Ramda more harm than her. Was that where Percy had aimed his sights?

The irony was that Venita had brought much of her woe upon herself, allowing her ambition to carry her into the world of politics. She had been seduced not only by Ramda Bol, but by his dreams. At thirty-eight Ramda had been the darling of the Congress Party and roundly considered the likely successor to the prime minister. But being the mistress of such a man, while rewarding in some ways, had limitations. She'd have forever been Ramda Bol's whore—glorified whore, perhaps, but whore nonetheless.

Instead, Venita had aspired to hold the reins of political power in her own right. Looking back on it, she'd been terribly naive. Oh, but how tempting the dream had seemed at the time.

Arjay had asked her why it wasn't enough to be adored by millions of movie fans. And she'd told him the truth: "The adoration of the public can't be trusted." Oh, she

still had a few good years left, but Venita knew the road
ahead would inevitably take her from the heights to the
depths. Her beauty would soon begin to fade. She needed
a new course, a new career, a new strategy. Then, just
when the future looked bleakest, fate had offered her a
magnificent opportunity—marriage to a man who would
one day be the leader of the nation, the most powerful man
in the country! It meant, of course, first disposing of the
wife.

Venita had sorely underestimated the difficulty of that
task. Krishna was not just Ramda's wife, she was the
daughter of the sitting prime minister. Ramda had married
for political reasons. There was no doubt in Venita's mind
that it was she who he loved and adored, but that happy
fact also gave her false hope. It became clear that Ramda
would not leave his wife for her. As he put it, "I should
fall like a stone and it would be the end of me politically."

But one night while Ramda shared Venita's bed, he la-
mented the fact that Krishna stood between them. "I'm
trapped," he said. "She keeps us apart, but if I divorce
her I lose everything else. Damned if I do, damned if I
don't."

It was then Venita had asked the fateful question.
"What if you were to become a widower?"

Ramda had lain in silence in the dark room for a long
time. Then he said, "Krishna is young and in excellent
health."

"Tragedy befalls political figures, Ramda."

"Tragedy?"

"Assassination."

There was another long silence before Ramda said,
"Who besides you would have her dead?"

"There are crazy people everywhere."

"But the insanity would have to be shown and that
would require the culprit being apprehended. How does

one engineer that?'' He'd sighed, then added, ''On the other hand, mistakes do happen.''

''What do you mean?''

''It's not inconceivable that, say, I was the target and poor Krishna became the accidental victim.''

''You are saying there are many who would see you dead.''

''Precisely.''

''You have a devious mind, Ramda,'' she'd whispered.

''You as well, my love. There's a reason we are well suited.''

The conversation might have been dismissed as fanciful repartee. Ramda never mentioned the subject again, but the seed had been planted in Venita's mind. For weeks she'd obsessed over the notion, her frustration growing. Then she made the tactical error that proved her undoing. Through intermediaries, she began to explore the possibility of assassination.

Venita never quite got to the point of setting a plot in motion, but she'd come close enough that Delhi began whispering her name in connection with murder. Someone—she had no idea who—betrayed her. A firestorm was whipped up, and where the facts fell short, her enemies fabricated the case against her. She was soon isolated and found herself up against not only the first family, but the leadership of the Congress Party, the Ministry of Justice, the national police and eventually the powers-that-be of the film industry itself, people who were once her friends. All the while Ramda remained silent.

The adoration of a billion movie fans was not sufficient to hold back the tides of her destruction. Venita had one thing and one thing only going for her—the ability to take down Ramda Bol. When she communicated that fact to him, his answer was cryptic and not unexpected. ''It's your word against mine.''

"But can you afford even the suspicion, Ramda?" she'd asked. "Why would I have Krishna killed unless I was certain you would have me? Believe me, every detail of our affair will be made known. I may not be able to prove you conspired with me, but I can make the world wonder. What will that do for your political career?"

Her salvation, as it turned out, was that everybody wanted to spare him, including his wife. So rather than arrest her, they sought a more gentle means of removing Venita from the scene. The chairman of the Congress Party, Seetharamas Banerjee, was sent to negotiate with her—though pronouncing sentence was probably a more accurate way to describe what had gone on. They'd offered her exile.

The craggy old man, impeccable in a white Nehru jacket, had looked sadly into her eyes and said in a soft voice, "They will prove in court that you conspired to have Krishna Bol killed, Miss Kumar. They will imprison you and, as you might imagine, it should not be a pleasant existence."

Venita could see it mattered little that the evidence against her was flimsy at best. No, they were talking raw power. Her plotting justified their lies and deceit, though, of course, Banerjee didn't state it in such terms. Prison or exile. Ramda spared, in exchange for her freedom. Take it or leave it.

In the end Venita chose discretion over valor. Honor in death was a male notion. A woman typically chose to live and fight another day. What her enemies gave her was the opportunity to walk away, though with little more than the shirt on her back. What courtesy she got came as a result of Ramda's "generosity," or so she was told.

Venita was enough of a realist to accept that she'd overplayed her hand. Her vanity had blinded her to the fact that Ramda's love was...well, like the love of all men—

subject to overriding considerations. And so she'd lost her foray into the political realm, becoming a refugee not only from her native land, but also from the millions who adored her. Like the legendary unwashed masses who'd come before her, Venita Kumar had fled oppression and was now in the United States pursuing the American dream. The realization of that dream seemed to have fallen into the hands of Percy Gaylord.

But if Percy had followed her to the land of milk and honey, not to bring her head home on a platter, but rather to use her against Ramda Bol, then she was truly in a desperate situation. To betray Ramda, she would have to renege on the deal she'd made with Banerjee. That would mean permanent exile and never seeing a single rupee of the estate she'd left behind in India.

The young blond Adonis in her bed moaned. Venita, raising herself to her elbow, lightly stroked his stomach. His circumcised penis that couldn't get enough of her the night before now languished in sleep, like its master, though in the case of men and their sexual organs, it wasn't always clear who was master and who was slave. As a young girl she'd learned that a woman could tame the most ardent and virile man simply by opening her legs. She'd long suspected that was what made men fear women most—their ability to gain victory in submission. Gandhi understood the principle, which to Venita's way of thinking could only mean his feminine side was very well developed indeed.

Staring at the sleeping boy, Venita wondered if her dreams would be dashed before she was able to get her hands on Mac McGowan's millions. Would Percy Gaylord prove to be the Angel of Death?

The hour was early enough that no one in the house besides Cala would be stirring. Venita was not normally an early riser, but when she was awake at dawn, she liked being outside to watch the sunrise. Something about that gave her hope, and hope she needed above all else. As had been the case so often in the past, the world seemed to be conspiring against her.

Leaving her young lover, she washed herself in the bath, slipped on a pair of pink silk shantung lounging pajamas and went to the kitchen, where she found Cala scrubbing the floor. Venita asked for a glass of orange juice, which the maid dutifully brought. As she stood at the window sipping her juice and observing the break of dawn, Venita told Cala to go fetch her a shawl. When the wizened little woman returned, Venita took it and handed her the empty juice glass. Then she went outside.

There was no wind, but she could feel the coolness of the ocean in the air. Once the sun rose, it would begin to warm up, but for now she was glad for the shawl. Like most Indian women, she preferred to go barefoot, liking the cool, damp feel of the grass as she strolled toward the pavilion.

Sitting on the bench and staring at the gray Pacific, she hugged herself against the coolness of the air. Whenever she felt vulnerable, as she did now, she would think about her powers. Ranjit had taught her that. "Focus on your strengths," he'd said. "Only the weak are obsessed with their weaknesses." Following that advice, Venita had entered a new phase of her career, a phase where her films and the characters she played took on a more sensuous air. Sex, sensuality and feminine guile were her strengths. How did she use them in real life to secure victory and smite her foes?

Venita was deep in thought when she heard a grunting sound. She looked about, but saw no one. The sound, accompanied by gasps and labored breathing, grew louder, followed by muffled curses and epithets. She got to her feet, but could see nothing. Then it occurred to her that the noise—now clearly the sounds of someone struggling—was coming from over the ledge at the back of the garden. Stealing from the pavilion, Venita crept toward the low, foot-high wall that marked the boundary of the property. Beyond it, the hillside dropped precipitously into the ravine.

Cautiously peeking over the edge, she looked down. Ten feet below she saw the top of a man's head as he struggled to pull himself up the slope by grabbing shrubs. The rocky soil kept giving way and his feet slipped. Had he not clung to the shrubs, he surely would have slid down the steep hillside. The man's difficulties were made worse by the fact that he had a couple of cameras, lenses and what appeared to be a camera bag strapped about him.

From her vantage point, Venita was unable to see his face, though she was able to see lots of scalp through the thinning hair atop his head. The man was dark-complected, she could see that much.

"Bloody hell," he grumbled between gasps as once again the soil gave way beneath him.

Between the man's coloring, the camera equipment and the accent, Venita realized who it was.

"Percy Gaylord, what in the name of God are you doing climbing up my hill?"

Lifting his head suddenly in surprise, the man completely lost his footing, his legs went out from under him. One hand slipped from the bush it was gripping and he started to slide away. Were it not for his other hand, which clung desperately to a shrub, he would have been lost.

Gasping and wheezing, his face covered with dust, Percy Gaylord looked up at her with desperate, panicky eyes. "Throw me a line or something, for God's sake, woman! Can't you see I'm about to die?"

"If so, it's on my property, Percy. What are you doing trespassing?"

"Have a little compassion, for the sake of God," he cried.

"Why are you sneaking about?"

He managed to get his other hand on the shrub. And, after more struggle, pulled himself to his knees. Even so, he would have slid away but for the bush. "I wanted to talk to you," he said in answer to her question.

"Talk? Is this anyway to talk to a person? In most of the civilized world, people knock on one's front door, not sneak about, climbing over the garden wall. Even bloody journalists."

"Please, Venita. I've hurt my knee. Get that man of yours and have him pull me up."

"First, I want to know what you're up to. You weren't coming for an interview, Percy. You wanted to get some photographs. What's the matter, couldn't you get good enough pictures from that other hill? Want something closer? Is that it, Percy?"

"Dear God," he pleaded.

"The truth!" she shouted.

"All right. Yes, I was hoping for some photos."

"And you've been following my friends. Why?"

"Looking for a story, what else? I'm a bloody journalist, by God."

"Bloody journalist is right, you snake."

"Are you going to stand there cursing me or get help?" he implored. "This is not a joking matter. I'm about to lose my grip. My arms are tiring."

"It's your own fault," she shot back.

"For the love of God, Venita!"

"I want to know what you're up to, Percy. It's clearly no good. What's your angle?"

"How do you expect me to talk under these circumstances? I'm about to die."

"The world would be a better place for it, too."

"Please," he implored, virtually in tears.

"If I do get help, will you tell me precisely what you're up to?"

"Yes. Absolutely, Venita. I swear on my mother's head."

She turned then and peered back toward the house. As luck would have it, Jugnu, perhaps alerted by Cala, was headed in her direction. He was in shorts and a loose, unbuttoned shirt. He hadn't yet wound his turban, so his uncut hair flowed down to his waist. Venita had only seen him in that state of dishabille half a dozen times in all the years she'd known him.

With Percy Gaylord's cries becoming more urgent, she shouted to Jugnu to go to the garage and fetch a rope. "There's a man on the cliff," she called. "Quickly! He's about to fall!"

Taking off at a run, Jugnu disappeared back into the house, only to return in a few minutes with a length of rope. Percy was nearly sobbing by the time Jugnu lowered the rope to him. With his last bit of strength, Percy wrapped the rope around his wrists, and Jugnu, his powerful build and great strength a godsend, pulled the weeping journalist up the last bit of the hillside, then over the side of the wall, finally depositing him on the lawn, at Venita's feet. Percy stared up at her, his face covered with muddy sweat, his clothing dirty and torn, the tangle of camera straps coiled about his neck.

"So," she said, looking down at him with disgust, "the worm turns."

"Thanks for saving me," he said, "but if I may say so, you certainly took your bloody sweet time."

"You're lucky I didn't begin throwing rocks, Percy. You've caused me as much suffering as just about anybody I know."

Percy Gaylord sat up, taking the cameras from around

his neck and depositing them on the lawn next to him. "Your own ambition is your worst enemy, Venita, and you know it."

"Bugger off," she snapped.

Percy grinned but he didn't quite laugh. Venita glanced at Jugnu and tossed her head, indicating he should leave. Coiling up the rope, he obediently left. Percy, meanwhile, had dusted himself off and sat on the wall. He mopped the dusty sweat from his face and neck with his handkerchief.

"All right, then, my good man," she said, "now for your end of the bargain. What is it you want? Why are you harassing me?"

"I'd like the inside story on what happened with Ramda Bol. There is talk you spared him in exchange for your freedom, Venita. Is it true?"

"You aren't getting a thing from me about Ramda, I assure you. Anything else?"

Percy sighed, still mopping his brow. "Well, then, what are you doing in Los Angeles, seducing the son of a millionaire?"

"I beg your pardon?"

"I know all about your young friend, Venita. Didn't he tell you? I'll wager my last rupee that he's in your bed now, sleeping like a baby, unless, of course, he's already had his morning tea and said ta-ta. I do know with certainty he spent the night."

"In the guest room."

"With Amal Kory?" Percy gave her his most beguiling grin. "Come on, love, you're up to some sort of hijinks, it only remains to be seen just what."

"What difference does it make what I'm doing? It's of no consequence to you. I've never known you to write Hollywood gossip, Percy. That can't be your angle."

"Indeed," he said. "You're right about that."

"All right, then what?" she demanded. "You owe me, don't forget. I saved your ungrateful ass."

"And so you did, love. I shan't forget. I promise you that."

"You're playing games with me," she said angrily. "I'm not amused."

"All right then, I'll give it to you straight, Venita. I want the Ramda Bol story and I'll do whatever necessary to get it."

"You're barking up the wrong tree."

"No, I think before I'm through you'll be glad to cooperate. I mean, you're here in America, safely under the protection of the U.S. government, the CIA and the FBI. What harm can your enemies in India do you?"

"Perhaps I'd like to go back one day. I shouldn't want to fear arrest simply by setting foot in my own country."

"Rubbish," Percy Gaylord said. "You're through in India and you know it. This is your last chance and I know it. So why not cooperate? It'd be ever so much more pleasant for us both."

Venita studied him, sensing he was preparing to drop some sort of bombshell. "Percy, are you threatening me?"

"Threat? No, love, far be it from me to threaten the next Elizabeth Taylor. She was a foreigner, too, you know."

"Now you're mocking me."

"Not at all."

"Then spit it out, Percy, what is it you're intending?"

"I do hate to be blunt, Venita, but if it's what you want, then here it is. You've got a man in your party who you hold out to be an esteemed film director, Amal Kory. Now, these silly Americans may not know the difference between Kory and Arjay Pantel, but I assure you my readers do—at least the more sophisticated ones, not to mention the authorities in Britain, New Zealand and Canada. Nor,

I should think, shall your American millionaire friends be much amused when they learn the truth.''

Venita began to seethe. Percy Gaylord had her just where he wanted her. ''You're blackmailing me.''

''That's much too harsh, Venita. I simply want your cooperation.''

''It's blackmail.''

''Sod it,'' he said. ''Have it your way, then. Blackmail it is. Since we're being direct, here's my offer. You give me Ramda Bol, all the bloody details of your affair, his complicity in your schemes, and I shall keep the amusing little Hollywood game in total confidence. Arjay Pantel can go on being Amal Kory, and you can become queen of American cinema together with your adoring young man. I simply require Ramda Bol's head on a platter.'' Percy, having recovered now, got to his feet, smiling superciliously. ''What could be more reasonable and fair than that?''

''I'll tell you what I'd prefer. It's that you'd mind your own bloody business. You have no idea what you're asking.''

''Oh, but I do, love. And you're damn well going to give it to me.''

Venita's anger continued to build. ''Oh, but the joy you take in destroying lives. Anything for a story. I save your worthless, godforsaken life and what do you do but try to extort information from me!''

''Now don't get exercised, my dear. What harm will it do to disclose the truth about Ramda Bol? I mean, the buggers have already run you out of the country. I should think you'd welcome the opportunity for a little revenge.''

''I've made a deal with them,'' Venita said through her teeth, nearly beside herself with contempt. ''They've got my money tied up and if I ever hope to see one rupee of it, I must keep my mouth shut.''

"Gracious, you do have a problem, don't you?" Percy said. "One word from me and you'll never see a single Hollywood dollar, either. It appears you must choose between rupees and dollars. Keep in mind these American chaps are likely to run your sweet little ass out of the country once you're exposed. Then what will you do? Scrub toilets at a bed-and-breakfast in London?"

"You fucking bastard!" she shrieked. "I save your life and this is my reward?"

"Accept it, Venita. What little you have left I can snatch away with the blink of an eye. You're mine, and the sooner you recognize it the better."

Venita was absolutely livid. She would never in a million years take orders from a worm like Percy Gaylord. She'd rather die.

"I must say," he remarked, "it's rather amusing to see a queen on her knees. And gratifying to know I'm responsible. There was a time, you see, when I adored you, like the rest of India. Now, here you are, eating out of my hand."

"Enjoy it while you can, Percy, because it's about to end."

"Eh?"

With that, Venita gritted her teeth, moved forward and gave him a violent shove. Percy, whose heels were against the low wall, fell backward, crying out in terror as he toppled over, disappearing from view. Venita leaped forward and watched him tumbling head over heels down the slope, his arms and legs flailing like the broken limbs of a doll. Finally his body came to rest in a heap at the bottom of the ravine. He did not move.

Venita's heart raced as she stared at the crumpled body far below. Half the bones in his body had to have been broken. And she had done it! She'd killed him. Only then did the magnitude of what had happened begin to sink in.

She took a deep breath, trying to calm her raging heart. Percy Gaylord got what he deserved, she told herself. And besides, she never should have saved his pathetic carcass in the first place. All she'd done was undo her mistake.

Seeing his camera equipment, Venita realized she had to dispose of it. Using the corner of her shawl so as not to touch anything with her bare hands, she picked up each item and dropped it over the wall, watching to make sure everything tumbled down the slope.

Venita stared down at Percy's crumpled body, telling herself that the man was worse than a scoundrel, that she'd done what she'd done to preserve her life. Then, glancing toward the house, she saw Jugnu standing at the sliding glass door, staring at her. He'd probably witnessed her confrontation with Percy.

She started toward the house. Her servant waited for her, opening the door. She stepped inside and faced him.

"What you just saw did not happen, Jugnu. And earlier, we did not rescue Percy with the rope. I suspect what occurred was he lost his footing while trying to climb up to the property to spy on me. It'll look that way to the police, I'm certain. I want you to go and dispose of the rope. Burn it or something."

Her servant bowed his head, acknowledging the order. Then he left the room.

Venita turned and looked out across the garden, past the pavilion at the spot where she and the journalist had argued. She was not pleased he'd forced her to silence him, but he had given her no choice. If Percy had unmasked Arjay, Venita surely would have ended up cleaning toilets in London, as he'd suggested. As the daughter of a Brahman and a film goddess to hundreds of millions, she could not accept such a fate. It would be better to die. Or to kill.

* * *

Bel Air

Mac McGowan awoke early that morning, and though he had an appointment with his accountant at eight, he decided to take time for a swim. He tried to get in the pool for exercise at least a couple of times a week. The last several days had been tense and he needed to burn some energy. After putting on his suit, he grabbed his robe and headed outside to the huge pool he'd built when he bought the place.

As much as anything, swimming gave him time to think. Exercise before an important meeting or while contemplating a big decision helped clear his thoughts. Stella and Aubrey had been very much on his mind. Interestingly enough, Bri Lovejoy had not, though he had thought a lot about his new guardian angel, Jade Morro. He had felt good after their meeting, mostly due, he assumed, to relief at finally doing something about his problem. He hated feeling hamstrung.

But he also liked Jade. She was just a kid, compared to him. And she couldn't have been more different—not at all like Bri, who at just under forty was closer to his age and certainly more conversant with his way of life. Yet, something about the detective felt awfully comfortable. Even her quirkiness appealed to him. Maybe between his need for help and his need for a friend, she brought just the right touch.

The trouble was, his guilty past made even a professional relationship problematic. There were limits to how honest he could be, and that was hard. As usual, it wasn't safe to be himself. Even so, he liked having Jade involved, whether he could fully take her into his confidence or not.

Standing at the edge of the pool, Mac took a deep breath and plunged in the water. That brace of cold was what he hated most, though the actual temperature was high by most standards. It was a large pool and Mac swam a couple of laps at a vigorous pace, not slowing until he'd adjusted to the water temperature. Then he settled into a regular rhythm.

Thinking about his problems, he lost track of time. But then he felt his muscles begin to fatigue and knew it was time to quit. On his final lap, he slowed even more, bringing down his heartbeat. Then, touching the shallow end of the pool, he stood, wiped the water from his eyes and saw a pair of brown pant legs in front of him. He looked up into a face that was only slightly familiar.

"Mr. McGowan, I was out front and heard the splashing and came on back. Hope you don't mind."

The face was older, there was gray in the hair, the expression more world-weary than Mac recalled, but it was the same man. "Well, Sergeant Caldron," he said. "What a surprise."

"Is it a surprise, Mr. McGowan? Oh, and by the way, it's lieutenant now."

"Oh. My apologies. Congratulations, Lieutenant."

"You're really surprised to see me?"

Mac waded over to the ladder and climbed out of the pool. "No, actually it was a poor choice of words. It's not a surprise. You have a tendency to drop by from time to time."

"It must be ten years since we last spoke, Mr. Mc-Gowan."

"My, how time flies."

Caldron stood watching as Mac slipped on his robe. The sun had risen over the ridge on the far side of the canyon and the chilly morning air began to warm. Even so, Mac shivered as he did the tie of his robe.

"So, to what do we owe this visit?"

"I've been thinking about Aubrey St. George," Caldron said.

"Have you?"

"Yes, Mr. McGowan. Have you?"

"Why would I think about Aubrey St. George after all these years?"

Caldron's mouth twisted at the corner. It was the suggestion of a smile, but only a suggestion. "I understand you were roaming around his backyard Saturday night and, frankly, I found that sort of curious."

Mac was momentarily taken aback, but managed not to appear overly surprised. "My, Big Brother is here at last."

"The crooks aren't the only ones taking advantage of computers," Caldron said dryly. "The average citizen doesn't appreciate the fact, but mostly we're outgunned when it comes to professional criminals in both guns and technology. But that's another story. I am curious, though, what were you doing in St. George's backyard."

"I was in the neighborhood, saw the For Sale sign and was curious about the old place. That used to be my wife's home, you know, Lieutenant."

"Oh, then it was just a walk down memory lane, is that it, Mr. McGowan?"

"People actually do that kind of thing."

"Yeah, but you don't seem the type...with all due respect."

"Oh? Why do you think I was there, then?"

"That's the thing. I don't know. And unanswered questions bother me almost as much as unsolved crimes."

Water dripped from his hair onto his face and Mac dabbed at it with his towel. He was cold, but he didn't want to invite the detective into the house. Nor did he want to brush him off. "Unsolved crime, huh?"

"I never did feel real good about the theory that St. George went swimming in the ocean and never made it back to shore."

"The coroner did."

"Yes, true, but the coroner doesn't often look into the

eyes of people who've committed crimes. That's what I've done for a living the last twenty-five years.''

Mac stared at him intensely. "I look guilty, it that it?''

"My intuition tells me something's not quite right, and it's been telling me that for darn near twenty-one years. Look at it from my standpoint. A big shot vanishes and a few months later the wife marries a guy who happened to be putting a pool in the big shot's yard when he disappeared. Maybe that's a coincidence and maybe it's not.''

"Are you saying I drowned Aubrey St. George in the ocean?''

"No, I'm not saying that. Maybe it wasn't even you. But I have a feeling you know more than you're letting on.''

"How fortunate citizens aren't prosecuted for crimes based on some detective's gut instinct. A lot of innocent people could get hurt by somebody's wild imagination.''

Caldron gave him another of his pseudo smiles. "Very true, Mr. McGowan, but you know what happens a lot? Evidence starts to show up, proving the gut instinct was right all along.''

"Well, with all due respect, Lieutenant, this is one of those cases where the gut's wrong. If it was otherwise, somebody would be in jail and we wouldn't be having this conversation.''

"Yeah, well, the strongest structures can develop cracks. But maybe this is a conversation for another day. I can see you're cold. I'll be getting out of your hair.''

"Thanks for dropping by, Lieutenant. No offense, but I hope not to see you again for another ten years.''

"Don't count on that, Mr. McGowan. I think it will be a good deal sooner than that. My interest in the St. George case has been rekindled.''

"Seems like a terrible waste of the taxpayers' money.''

"Why do I have the feeling that you aren't worried

about the taxpayers so much as you're worried about your own neck, Mr. McGowan?''

"That sounds an awful lot like an accusation to me, Lieutenant.''

"Does that upset you?''

"I hope you don't have any ideas about harassing me and my family about a case that's closed.''

"And if I do?''

"If necessary I'll have my attorney bring it up with your superiors.''

Caldron gave him another pseudo smile. "That almost sounds like a threat.''

"It is,'' Mac said.

"You might as well know, Mr. McGowan, I'm not only tenacious, I'm not easily intimidated. And to be honest with you, I'm more convinced than ever that you're hiding something. The cracks are starting to show. So long.'' Caldron turned and headed back toward the side yard and the gate. He'd gone maybe five or six steps and stopped. "Speaking of cracks, the one in the St. George's pool is a beaut, isn't it?''

Lieutenant Jaime Caldron did not wait for an answer, he turned and walked away.

West Hollywood

Jade was in the shower when the phone rang, but she managed to get it before the machine came on. It was Ruthie.

"My place at four this afternoon.''

"You talked to Ricky, then.''

"Right.''

"What did he say?''

"He was surprised to hear my voice.''

"Did he say anything about me?''

"He didn't confess that he's been trying to run down your dates or slash your tires, if that's what you mean."

"No, but he must have been surprised to find out I wanted to talk to him. You didn't make it sound like this was me wanting to see him for...personal reasons, did you?"

"Stalking's pretty personal, Jade. But did I say you're still madly in love with him and are dying to see him? No. I said you have some business to discuss that has nothing to do with your past relationship."

"And he said?"

"He said, 'Sounds serious.' And I said, 'It is.'"

"Well, I guess that's safe enough."

"Don't worry, girl," Ruthie said. "If he's under any illusions, he won't be once you tell him how the cow ate the cabbage. And could be that he's scared enough that he won't even show."

"I guess that's okay, as long as he gets the message."

"I'd say."

"So, did he sound...guilty?"

"No, I can't exactly say he did. But Ricky was always pretty cocky."

Jade had to admit that was probably true, but when they were together she'd thought of it as exuberance, a guy who was full of life. What a difference a dose of reality made.

"I really appreciate you doing this, Ruthie," she said.

"Girl, that's what friends are for."

Bel Air

Mac slipped on his jacket and went downstairs for a quick cup of coffee before heading for his appointment. Jaime Caldron had succeeded in putting his stomach in a knot, which was probably exactly what the bastard intended. Mac knew now going to the Brentwood house had been a terrible mistake. It had taken twenty years, but he'd returned to the scene of the crime. And Caldron had pounced.

Mac reminded himself the detective didn't know any more now than before—that is, unless the mystery note writer was also sending missives to Caldron. That was unlikely, though, otherwise Caldron would have been more specific in his accusations. Even so, Mac knew if he ignored the visit, it would be at his own peril.

One thing was certain. If Caldron was harassing him, he'd likely be paying Stella a visit, as well. Mac knew he should forewarn her. His wife was pretty good in a crisis, particularly if she had time to prepare. Checking the time, he decided to call her, even though it was still early by Stella's standards.

Bonny answered. "She still in her bed, Meester McGowan."

"I hate to wake her," he said, "but it's very, very important."

"Okay, *monsieur*. One minute, please."

It was more like three or four before Stella finally came on the line.

"Mac, what's happened?" she said groggily.

"I know it's early and I'm sorry, but our problems are multiplying. Lieutenant Jaime Caldron of the L.A.P.D. was here bright and early this morning."

There was a stunned silence. "What did he want?"

"Essentially to tell me he's back on the case and suspicious about our involvement in Aubrey's death."

"Oh, Mac..." There was desperation in her tone. "What are we going to do?"

"There's no cause for panic. Just caution. Don't be surprised if Caldron comes by to see you, though. I'm calling to give you a heads-up."

"Thank you. If I'd opened the front door and found him there…well, I don't know what I'd have done."

"That's what I figured."

"God," she said, "after all these years."

"I don't suppose you've given any more thought to the note, like who might be behind it and how they found out?"

"I've thought about it, Mac, but I don't have any answers." She hesitated. "How about you?"

"I've hired an investigator to look into it."

Another pause. "Oh… Good."

"She—her name's Jade Morro—expressed an interest in talking to you, but I didn't give my approval. I wanted to check with you first."

"What does she want to talk to me for?"

"You're the other party in interest, Stella, supposedly the only other person besides me who's conversant with the facts."

"You didn't tell her about…you didn't tell her, did you?"

"Only that we had an affair while you were married to Aubrey and that the note concerned embarrassing information connected with that. That was as specific as I got. I told her I couldn't say more."

"That must have made her wonder."

"I'm sure it did."

"Mac, do you think bringing an investigator into it is a good idea? I mean, things seem to be going from bad to worse."

"What else can we do?"

Stella forced another dramatic pause, then said, "One thing I do know for sure, Mac. We've got to stick together."

"I agree."

Silence. Then, "Oh, God…"

Mac heard what sounded like a little sob. "Stella?"

She sniffled. "I'm all right. It's...it's just...so hard."

"Are you okay?"

"I'm...afraid."

"Everything will be fine," he said. "We've got to keep our heads."

"I know... It's just..."

"What?"

"Mac, I'm feeling shaky, vulnerable. Would...would you come over?"

Her words hit him and he felt their weight, the weight of her need, the burden of her helplessness. "Stella, I can't now. I'm late for an appointment with my accountant and then I've got to get to the office."

"I don't mean to be a bother... I just thought."

"Everything is going to be okay," he said. "I promise."

"Mac?"

"Yes."

"Maybe this is happening for a reason. Have you considered that?"

"What do you mean?"

"Well, maybe we've taken too much for granted. Maybe we need to take a fresh look at our lives. Sit down and have a real talk, heart-to-heart."

He still wasn't sure what she was getting at, but it was clearly a change in attitude from the past. Could she really think that her neediness would change things? Regardless of what she thought, she was vulnerable and he knew he had to be careful with her. "Yes, we probably do need to talk," he said. "Let me check how the next few days are shaping up and I'll get back to you."

"All right."

"Let me know if you hear from Caldron in the meantime."

"I will."

"Stella…"

"Yes?"

"You're right. We do have to stick together."

"It's the story of our lives, isn't it, Mac?"

He hung up then, feeling as low as he had in months. Was it his imagination or were things coming apart at the seams?

A few minutes later he backed the Lexus out of the garage and started around the circular drive. For some reason, he wasn't sure why, he glanced toward the front door and noticed what looked like an envelope taped to it.

Mac stopped, got out of the car and went to the front door. It was an envelope all right, with his name printed on it in block letters, just like the last note. For a moment he stared at it, almost afraid to touch it. But then he did, tearing it off the door.

The note inside was cryptic just like the first. It said:

AUBREY ST. GEORGE IS DEAD AND YOU'RE A MILLION-AIRE. THAT HARDLY SEEMS FAIR.

He read it over a couple of times, then stuffed the note back in the envelope and put it in his pocket.

No doubt about it. His world was crumbling fast.

Pacific Palisades

Troy stood in Venita's shower, letting the water pound on his head as he struggled to make sense of the bizarre turn of events. He'd been awakened a couple of hours earlier from a sound sleep by the maid's cries out in the hallway. Noticing that Venita was no longer in bed, he'd gotten up, put on a robe and went out to see what was going on. The commotion seemed to have shifted outside.

He'd gone to the small study across the hall from the master suite with a view of the back garden. From there he'd seen Jugnu, a rope in hand, rush out to where Venita stood by the low wall. Moments later the servant pulled Percy Gaylord up the cliff. Troy couldn't believe it. The whole thing had been bizarre, but not nearly so bizarre as when he'd watched Venita shove the journalist off the cliff. He'd seen it all. One moment Percy was there, the next he was gone. The sucker had to have fallen to his death. Just as surprising was Venita's reaction. No panic, no distress. The episode over, she'd calmly returned to the house. Unseen, Troy had quickly retreated to the bed they'd shared and feigned sleep. But his heart had pounded, mostly because he still couldn't believe it.

What Percy Gaylord was doing there to begin with Troy couldn't be sure, though the cameras were a pretty good clue he was after dirt. Venita had made no secret of the fact she hated the guy and considered him a snake. But now the question was, what did he do with his secret knowledge? His instinct was to wait and see. Having something on Venita could prove useful.

It was incredible, the things that fell into a person's lap, Troy thought. First his parents' dark secret. Now Venita's. And wouldn't it be ironic if he was able to use all three of them to his advantage? Maybe his time in the sun really had come.

Venita leaned toward the bathroom mirror, applying mascara as Troy Hampton sang lustily in the shower. She hoped he wouldn't emerge wanting sex because she wasn't in the mood. The image of Percy Gaylord's crumpled body lying at the base of the cliff haunted her. Plus she fretted over how best to handle the police when they arrived, as they assuredly would. She was confident Jugnu would not betray her. Cala had seen nothing—Venita had confirmed that with Jugnu—nor had Arjay, who hadn't come to breakfast until after Venita had had her coffee. Troy had been blissfully asleep.

There was always a chance someone in one of the homes on the hill opposite them had been looking out a window. However, the distance was considerable and, apart from being able to testify that a woman had done the deed, it was unlikely she could be identified as the culprit—unless, of course, they happened to be gazing through a telescope. But at that hour, it was unlikely. If she had been seen, surely she would have received a visit from the police by now. More likely the police wouldn't become involved until Percy's body was found.

Venita had her story ready. She would acknowledge having a less than amicable relationship with Percy Gaylord because of her celebrity. He was a tabloid journalist and everybody knew how unwanted that particular brand of vermin was. Percy, she'd say, had undoubtedly climbed the cliff to get pictures of her. She would admit she and her guests frequently did cavort about in the buff. Getting candid snaps of them was clearly his objective. The man obviously fell to his death before he'd succeeded. It was simple, clean, logical, entirely believable. Why would they think Percy had been given a shove?

The shower stopped and Troy stepped out. Venita tossed him a towel, but not until giving his ego a boost by observing his hard, lean, fat-free body. He had a big white-toothed grin on his pretty face.

"How's my goddess?" he asked.

"Struggling to become beautiful."

"With you, Venita, it comes naturally."

"My, but aren't you the quick learner?"

"You inspire me," he said as he finished drying himself.

She glanced down at his cock, already half-erect, smiled

and turned back to the mirror to complete her makeup. Moments later, Troy slipped up behind her, encircling her with his long, strong arms, cupping her breasts. She could feel the shaft of his penis rise hard against her backside.

"Aren't you the randy one this morning."

"You turn me on," he said, kissing her neck and running his thumbs over her nipples, the friction making them hard through the silk. "Must be your mysterious, dangerous nature."

"You think of me as dangerous?"

"Yes, and it's really a turn-on. Hasn't anybody described you that way before?"

"Not dangerous."

"Not even that politician, what was his name?"

"Ramda Bol?"

"Yeah, him."

"I believed Ramda considered me formidable, not dangerous."

"Then maybe I see something others don't," he said.

The comment gave her pause. "Whatever do you mean, Troy?" she asked, turning to face him.

"Nothing. Maybe I'm better tuned in to the real you, Venita."

His smile suggested he was simply mucking around. "Well, you certainly are in high spirits this morning. What's gotten into you?"

"I've been wondering. Remember when you said that in India women your age often take men my age for lovers?"

"Yes."

"Do they ever marry them?"

The question brought her up short. She looked into his eyes. "Why do you ask?"

"I was just curious if you see me as a lay, or if anything…let's say, more long-lasting has entered your mind.''

Venita turned back to the mirror and resumed applying her mascara. ''You're aware, Troy, that's a very dangerous question for a man to ask a woman.''

''A dangerous question for a dangerous woman.''

Venita wondered at all this talk of danger. The thought did cross her mind that he may have heard or seen something of her encounter with Percy, but she dismissed the notion. The boy couldn't be that cool. More likely he was trying to show he was man enough for even a formidable woman such as herself.

He leaned against the vanity, his arms folded over his chest, and watched until she was through with her makeup. When she was finished, she put down the mascara wand. ''Okay, why this sudden talk of a serious relationship?''

''I guess I know what I want, Venita. The question is, do you?''

''I'm interested in a good deal more than that blade you so urgently wish to shove between my legs. But I'm also understanding of the male mind,'' she told him. ''I know how quickly young men lose interest. When the day arrives that you find my head and heart as interesting as my Golden Lotus, then I may take you more seriously. Until that time, I shall regard you as a boy toy, thinking first and foremost of the pleasure you bring me. Does that answer your question?''

''Say I come into a couple of million soon. Would that change things?''

Again, his comment gave her pause. Was he posturing, or was he to be taken seriously? ''Do you plan on coming into a couple of million?''

''Yes,'' he said, ''as a matter of fact, I do.''

''How so?''

''Family money.''

"Your father is a young man, Troy. Surely you aren't expecting him to pass on and leave you his fortune."

"No, but it's possible he'll decide to share it with me."

"You're joking."

"No, I'm dead serious."

She looked at him skeptically, but he didn't waver.

"You've said a lot in the course of very few minutes," she said. "There's a lot to digest."

"I know, but I wanted to make sure we're thinking along the same lines." He grinned at her.

Venita was baffled by his sudden confidence. The boy didn't lack for gumption, but he'd certainly awoke full of himself. What was behind this? she wondered. A young man's bravado? Or, was he a man in the making—in every sense of the word? Talk was very cheap, indeed, but this was America where boys with computers became millionaires every day.

She would remain cautious because she had been burnt before, but how wonderful to think that there might be a basis for what he was saying. For a day that had begun abominably, perhaps this one would prove glorious, after all. How fantastic that would be.

But Venita was perfectly well aware that her young lover had to be handled carefully. After all, with Percy Gaylord lying in the bottom of the ravine, her situation was most delicate. If she could but weather the storm...

"So, what do you think?" he asked when she hadn't answered him.

"I'm cautious by nature, Troy," she told him, "especially in matters of the heart."

"That's cool."

"Anything's possible, though."

"True," he said. "You never know, do you, Venita?"

* * *

Studio City

Mac got out of his car and was headed for the entrance to the administration building when he saw a white Ford Escort enter the gate. It was Jade.

He'd intended to call her from the office and let her know that he'd received a second note, so her arrival was timely. When she jumped out of her car and headed for the warehouse, Mac figured she was probably on her way to see Art.

He called to her across the parking lot and she stopped. Seeing him, she ambled in his direction. She was in jeans and a pink T-shirt. She wore dark glasses. Her big purse was slung over her shoulder.

"Morning," he said.

"Hi."

"You have a meeting with Art?"

"Yeah. I'm getting a stack of personnel files from him. Wanted to do some preliminary work. But I'm not neglecting your situation, Mac. I've been thinking about it, trying to come up with a strategy. So far no brilliant ideas have occurred."

Unable to see her eyes because of the dark glasses, he became very aware of her mouth, which was more sensuous than he recalled. "There have been developments."

"Yeah? What?"

"Jaime Caldron came by at the crack of dawn."

"And?"

"Basically accused me of being implicated in Aubrey St. George's death."

"No kidding."

"I think it was intended as a shot across my bow. But more importantly still, I got another anonymous note. I found it taped to my door as I was leaving for work."

Jade's brows rose. "What did it say?"

Mac pulled the envelope from his pocket. "See for yourself."

"You want me to read it?" she asked, surprised.

"It doesn't say anything more than what Caldron said, so you might as well."

She took the note from the envelope and read it, then looked up at him with hidden eyes. He was sorry she had on the glasses because he would have liked to know what her eyes were saying.

"There's an oblique reference to money," she noted, handing back the note and envelope.

"Yes," he said, returning them to his pocket. "I've thought all along that's where this is headed. I expect the next one will ask that I share my wealth. The first note, by the way, alluded to my possible complicity in Aubrey's death."

Her jaw went a little slack and, again, Mac really hated it that he couldn't see her eyes.

"Why are you telling me now?"

He drew a slow breath. "With Caldron on the warpath, everything's out in the open, or will be soon. There's no point in being coy."

She didn't say anything. She just looked at him. Her sunglasses bothered him more than ever.

"You want to come to my office and talk?" he asked. "I can have my secretary let Art know you'll be late."

"That's all right, we don't have a definite appointment."

They began walking toward the admin building.

"I guess your secret admirer is convinced he...or she...has something on you," she said.

Mac was relieved her tone was analytical rather than accusatory. "I guess. The question is where they get their information, where this is coming from."

"It's pretty general, Mac. This note could have been written by anybody who had suspicions about you. Wasn't there gossip about your wife at the time it happened?"

"Yes, but these notes were directed at me."

"You're married to her and you're the one with the money."

They entered the building. Mac's office was in a large corner suite that occupied nearly a third of the ground floor. His secretary, Bev Wallace, greeted them. She was forty-two, had short brown hair and glasses, and was plainly dressed, with more the look of a den mother than an executive secretary. But she'd been with Mac for a dozen years and was the epitome of efficiency. She also knew the business backward and forward.

"Have one of the girls bring us coffee, would you, Bev?"

"Sure. Cream or sugar?" she asked Jade.

"You wouldn't have tea, by any chance?"

"I'm sure I can find something."

"Oh, sorry, forgot to introduce you two," Mac said. "Bev, this is Jade Morro. She'll be doing some investigative work for us, mostly the Pool Maids division. Jade, Bev Wallace."

"Welcome," Bev said.

"Thanks."

The two women exchanged smiles. Mac led the way into his private office. Jade went immediately to the leather sofa, dropping her purse at her feet with a thud. Mac closed the door, then took a quick look at the telephone messages on the corner of his desk before joining her. He sat in one of the leather armchairs. He was glad to see Jade had removed her sunglasses. She opened her purse and stuffed them inside, reminding him of the way she'd dealt with her purse in his living room. It was still odd to think of her with a gun.

"So, what do you think?" he asked.

She pondered his question, absently running her fingers

through her hair. "If you want to know the truth, something doesn't feel quite right to me."

"How so?"

"It doesn't seem like the work of a blackmailer. It's more like death by a thousand cuts. Somebody who wants money tends to hit hard and make demands up front. To me this is more like a campaign of intimidation, somebody wanting to annoy you."

"If it's annoy, they've succeeded. I've kind of thought the intent was to provoke. That's why, at first, I thought maybe Jaime Caldron was behind it. He, at least, has the knowledge and a motive."

Jade shook her head. "I don't know the guy, but that doesn't ring true. Besides, it seems a little heavy-handed to pay a visit and then leave a note."

"I suppose you're right."

Mac watched her. He wanted to ask what she thought of him. She had to wonder if there was anything to the accusations. And he wanted to tell her that it wasn't as bad as it seemed. But Jade, he gathered, wasn't evaluating guilt. She was trying to determine the origin of the notes.

There was a rap on his door and Bev stuck her head in. "Stella's here to see you, Mac."

"Stella?"

"Yes. Shall I get her a cup of coffee and have her wait?"

Mac glanced at Jade, who was looking at her hands. He wanted to tell Bev to send Stella away but, recalling how upset she'd been when they spoke, he realized he'd better see her. "Tell her to give me a minute, Bev."

Jade said, "You want me to go?"

"My wife's here because she's upset. I called her this morning and told her about Caldron's visit. I figured he'd be headed her way."

Jade got to her feet.

"No, don't go," he said. "At least not yet. This is a good opportunity for you to meet Stella, maybe even talk to her if she's in any condition to talk."

"Are you sure?"

"Yes."

Jade sat back down on the sofa and Mac went to the door, just as one of the girls from out front came with a mug of coffee for him and tea for Jade. He told her to bring another coffee for Stella. Then he stepped into the outer office.

His wife was seated on a sofa, perched on the edge of the cushion. She was in a lilac summer suit, well groomed as always, but struck him as overly made up. Seeing him, she stood.

"Mac, I have to talk to you."

"Maybe it's good you're here. Ms. Morro, the private investigator, is in my office. I'd like for you to meet her."

Stella looked distressed by the suggestion. "Is it necessary?"

"It won't hurt for you to meet her, maybe talk a little. Anyway, I've got more news."

"Lord, I don't know if I can take any more of your news, Mac."

"Come on in."

He escorted Stella into his office. Jade was instantly on her feet and shaking hands with Stella.

"Nice to meet you, Mrs. McGowan."

Stella mumbled something in return, looking bewildered. She dropped into the chair Mac had been in. He sat on the sofa next to Jade.

Mac didn't waste any time. "You might as well know, Stella, I got another anonymous note this morning. I found it on my front door after we spoke."

She blinked with surprise, her eyes going to Jade.

"I've shown it to Ms. Morro."

"Really?"

"No confidences have been breached," he said. "She's aware of the delicacy of the matter and is focusing on the origins of the notes, not the story behind them. Anyway, she can't do her job in a vacuum."

"Yes, Mac, but..."

"Part of my job is to be discreet, Mrs. McGowan," Jade said. "Embarrassing anyone is the last thing I want to do."

"That's good to know," Stella muttered.

One of the clerks brought in another mug of coffee, put it on the coffee table, then left the room. Jade sipped her tea. Mac drank some coffee. Stella ignored her cup, nervously wringing her hands.

Mac took the latest note from his pocket and handed it to her. She read it, briefly closed her eyes, then handed it back. She said nothing for a moment or two.

Then, "It's a sad commentary that people feel they can exploit anyone who's made a little money. We've become a society of vultures." The comment was clearly made for Jade's benefit.

Mac could tell this meeting probably wasn't a very good idea. He glanced at Jade, who was politely silent, perhaps uncomfortable for Stella as much as for herself. Looking at the two of them, he was struck by how different they were. First, there was enough difference in their ages that they could be mother and daughter, though that wasn't the essence of it. One was in a two-thousand-dollar suit, the other in jeans and a T-shirt. Stella was groomed and painted to a portrait-perfect standard of perfection; Jade was scrubbed and freckled, her hair slightly tousled, a young woman who appeared ready to romp on the beach. Just looking at her made him think of peanut butter and jelly sandwiches, something that probably hadn't entered his mind in thirty-five years.

"Mac, there are some private matters we need to discuss," his wife said to him.

"Yes, Stella, we can talk. But would you mind if Jade asked you a few questions while you're both here?"

"Must we? I'm really not in a very coherent state of mind."

"We can do it another time, Mac," Jade volunteered. "There's nothing urgent I need to ask."

"Bless you," Stella said.

"And I'll be better prepared later," Jade added.

"All right," Mac said.

Jade looked at the sports watch on her tanned wrist. "Art's expecting me, so maybe I should run."

Mac couldn't help feeling disappointed. He watched her take a big gulp of tea and put down the mug. She reached across the table and gave Stella's hand a shake.

"Nice meeting you, Mrs. McGowan. We'll talk another time."

Stella nodded, smiling faintly. Jade looked at Mac, running her fingers back through her hair, a mannerism he found terribly endearing. Reaching down, she lifted her purse, slinging it over her shoulder.

"Talk to you later then, Mac."

He went with her to the door and into the outer office. "Thanks," he said, though it wasn't entirely clear in his own mind what he was thanking her for.

"I'm sorry about what's happened," she said. "It's obviously bothering your wife a lot."

"Stella's prone to emotional extremes. She's an actress above all else. Which is not to say she isn't upset, but you get to know the symptoms pretty well when the patient's familiar."

Jade chewed on her lip and nodded.

"You know, I had an idea while we were sitting in there," Mac said.

"What's that?"

He glanced over at Bev, who worked at her desk, acting completely oblivious to their presence. He knew better, of course. Mac tossed his head toward the outer door. "Come on, I'll walk you out."

He didn't say anything until they were outside the building. Jade looked up at him with wholesome innocence, yet, at the same time, an air of plucky self-assurance.

"If you're going to help me," he said, "I think we'll need to have an in-depth discussion about the situation. Is there any chance you could come by my place this evening?"

"I've got a late afternoon appointment, Mac. I don't know how long it will take."

"The time doesn't matter. It can be late. In fact, I'm going to be tied up here for quite a while this evening."

She looked reluctant, and he wondered if he was pressing too hard, asking too much. She, after all, didn't share either his commitment or concern.

"If that's not convenient," he said, "don't worry about it. We can do it later."

"How about if I call you when I'm through? And if it's not too late, I'll come by."

"That would be fine."

"Okay, then," she said, "talk to you later."

He watched her head off toward the warehouse, her purse slung back over her shoulder. It wasn't what you'd call an ultrafeminine walk, because there was a touch of warrior in it. But Jade was plainly a woman. That came through strongly, as well.

He did not turn and go inside immediately, instead watching her until she was practically out of sight. Mac wondered if he had a crush on her or if he was so desperate to escape from the woman waiting in his office that any halfway pleasant fantasy was welcome, no matter how outlandish or unlikely.

Stella seemed a bit more relaxed when he returned to his office. She sat back in the chair, her legs crossed, the coffee mug cradled in her hands.

"What an unusual young woman," she said. "She's really a detective?"

"Yes, former cop. Decorated, as a matter of fact."

"She certainly has a casual air."

"Yeah," Mac said, dropping onto the sofa, "she does."

Stella, looking at him sadly and a touch wistfully said, "Mac, what's to become of us?"

"I wish I knew." He picked up his mug, then put it back down without drinking any coffee.

His wife let one of her long, dramatic pauses build, then said, "I've thought a lot about us the past several days."

She hesitated, waiting for a reaction, but Mac hardly heard her. He was still thinking of Jade.

"It's times like this I miss you most," she confessed.

The comment got his full attention, making him wonder where she was headed. Stella did not keep him wondering for long.

"Can I ask you a very direct question?"

"Sure."

"Do you think we'd be well served to try and improve our relationship?"

"What do you mean by that?"

Stella bit her lip, seemingly uncertain how to explain her thoughts. But then she plunged ahead. "Why don't you come over for dinner this evening? We haven't had a warm, friendly conversation in God knows how long. I'm feeling kindly toward you, Mac. And missing you. It occurs to me that maybe maintaining this isolation is foolish."

He wondered how she could come up with something

like that after all this time and after all the water that had passed under their marital bridge. Was she that desperate, that needy?

"I'm not opposed to good relations," he said, "but I'm not sure what you're getting at. A reconciliation?"

"I suppose it's foolish of me to think giving it another try would be worthwhile."

"Stella, you're frightened. That's not a very good reason to jump in bed with someone, even someone you know. That's how we got started in the first place, remember?"

"You certainly know how to let down a girl gently, Mac."

"I don't mean to hurt you. But I've got to be honest."

"Maybe I'm deluding myself. Maybe I deluded myself twenty years ago. But it would hurt me to think the sacrifices I made are unappreciated. We've both given and we've both received a lot in this marriage."

"And that's why we're sitting here now as man and wife."

"All I'm questioning is whether we've focused too much on the negative."

"The middle of a crisis is not the best time to evaluate things," he said.

"Mac, a crisis can open your eyes."

Pacific Palisades

To say it had been a day of ups and downs would be a gross understatement. Venita had gone from despair to joy and back again. Troy had left to "take care of some business," for which she was glad. She couldn't tell him what had happened with Percy, though her heart cried out to share her anxieties. But with who? Not Arjay. She could no more trust him than the snake charmer could trust the snake.

And so, she'd wandered about the house, hopelessly torn between euphoria and gloom. Cala scrubbed the tiles in the entry hall and Arjay lounged in the family room, watching videos of "his" films on the big-screen TV. He'd taken his role as Amal Kory very seriously. Arjay was actually quite remarkable in that he'd mastered so much of the jargon. In the beginning Venita had schooled him, but he'd taken to studying Amal's films on his own, some of his questions and insights striking her as astute.

Jugnu had made himself scarce, spending most of his time in his room, though that wasn't particularly unusual. She was never fully sure what he did with his time, except that he liked to read and listen to music. Over the years, Venita rarely entered his room.

But after the morning's events, she was sorely tempted to go to him so she could look into his eyes and gauge his mood. But Jugnu would sense her need for reassurance. When a master showed weakness—weakness of any sort— a servant lost his fear and his will to obedience. She could always find some excuse to summon him, whether to give her a massage or tend to some errand. But that would seem transparent, unless the need were real. No, she was much better off treating Jugnu as she would if nothing had happened.

But something dramatic *had* happened. She'd shoved Percy Gaylord to his death. And that was the source of her torment.

But where were the police? That, above all else, was driving her to distraction. Were they playing games with her? Surely not. She could only assume the body had not been found, which was odd, considering that people were always roaming about, even on a weekday—kids on their bikes, people walking their dogs. Plus, many of the homes had full views of the canyon. There was a little-used trail at the bottom of the ravine. When Venita had looked down, she'd noted that the journalist's body was right at the edge of it, in plain sight.

So, what was going on? The silence, the uncertainty, were unbearable.

"My, but you seem restless today," Arjay said as he passed her in the hallway on his way to the kitchen. "Worrying about Percy Gaylord, are you?"

Venita blinked with surprise until she recalled Arjay knew Percy was in town. What he didn't know was that the bloody sod was dead. Taking Arjay's arm, she walked with him toward the kitchen. "Should the bloke make trouble, I shall handle him, Arjay. You needn't fear that."

"Truly? Only last night you—"

"I confess I overreacted. Percy can be dealt with, though he has the ability to make things dicey, I admit. The important thing is that we not allow him to distract us from what we're doing."

"I admire your confidence."

They entered the kitchen and she watched him fetch a glass of juice from the fridge. Venita knew that Arjay would cut and run the moment it appeared the game was over. She also knew the importance of keeping him on the line, and that meant appearing very much in charge regardless of how desperate the situation truly was.

When Arjay turned, his glass of juice in hand, she said, "I shall deal with Percy if and when he shows his face. He's my concern, not yours. But I do have good news. It's quite possible we'll have our million, perhaps two, before very much longer."

Arjay's brow rose. "There've been developments, have there?"

"Troy seems to be a good deal more capable than I'd

first thought,'' she told him.

''The young man has ideas,'' Arjay allowed. ''And he's a schemer. But I've always been a chap who puts greater stock in deeds than words.''

''You're right, of course, Arjay. But we must show patience. And a steady hand. Most important of all we must stand together, you and I.''

''Indeed.''

''I chose you for this job, Arjay, because I knew there would be difficult moments, a need for patience and nerves of steel. That's also why the rewards are substantial.''

''You needn't be concerned about me, Venita. I'm very good at determining the best horse to ride. Get your two million and we're on our way.'' Smiling, he left the room.

Venita paced. She was frightened, perhaps more than she was willing to admit. Arjay Pantel, for all his gentle, reassuring words, was a concern. If the business with Percy were to blow up in her face, Arjay would turn tail. The key to keeping him in line was dangling those millions before his nose. Nonetheless, the man needed watching. Of that, Venita was thoroughly convinced.

Making her way to the window offering a perspective onto the garden, Venita looked out, her gaze going instantly to the low wall. In her mind's eye, she pictured Percy as he went flying over it backward. She visualized his corpse at the foot of the cliff. Where were the bloody police?

She drew a long, slow breath, trying to calm herself. She couldn't lose it now. This was her final chance. Wiping her eyes, she thought how incredible it was that her life, her future, were now totally dependent on a twenty-year-old boy and that corpse lying at the bottom of a ravine.

* * *

Beverly Hills

Stella had seen *It's a Wonderful Life* so many times that, five years ago, she'd bought her own copy. She always cried when she watched it, and not always at the expected places. She wasn't sure why. Maybe deep down she believed life truly could be that way, but wasn't. Who or what had failed? she wondered. She could not bear to think it was she.

Bad luck. That's what it was. Nobody could make it in this business alone. That was especially true if you were a woman. Twice she'd allied herself with a man who she thought could make a difference. Aubrey had failed her, and so had Mac. In a way, Mac was the greater disappointment, if only because he was a decent human being. And yet, he wouldn't budge when it came to what mattered to her most.

After talking with him that morning, she realized she was no closer to securing his cooperation than before. Nothing was working. She'd appealed to his self-interest only to discover the potential profits were of no interest to him. She'd appealed to his sense of duty, his obligations to her and his son, but that had fallen short, as well. She'd hoped to appeal to his heart, but Mac was unwilling to give her a chance. Any love he'd had for her was gone.

Stella quailed at the thought, but there was only one thing left. She could threaten to talk to the police. Either he put up the seed money for the film, or she would unburden herself of their dark secret. She dreaded doing that for there was danger in it for her, too. And Mac would hate her forever. But what, besides surrender, was left?

"Again, *madame?*" Bonny said, indicating the television set as she entered the room with Stella's tea.

"I can't bear not to see it at least once a month. Do you want to sit and watch with me?"

Stella, propped up on her bed, patted the mattress beside

her. Marie Boniface, who as a rule was not given to undue familiarity, though she could be outspoken at times, deigned to sit on the corner of the bed. She watched the TV with Stella for a minute or two.

Then, shaking her head, she said, "I am sorry, *madame,* but I don't understand. What is this saying?"

"It's saying that if people will just open their eyes, they will see what a difference they can make. Like my husband, for example. It's within his power to change my life and Troy's life, if he will."

"You are saying he could be an angel?"

"He could be, Bonny."

"And what about you, *madame?*"

But before Stella could consider the question, the door chimes sounded. Bonny left to answer the door.

"Unless it's terribly urgent, I'm indisposed," Stella called after her.

"Oui, madame."

Stella watched Jimmy Stewart and mouthed the dialogue along with him. Why, she wondered, hadn't she ever had a role and a script like this? Where were her angels? Bonny was soon back.

"It is the police, *madame.* Are you still indisposed?"

"The police?"

Stella fought back the niggle of panic. Gathering herself, she hurried off to the bathroom to check her makeup. Then she took a peek out the window to see if there were any news trucks or reporters out front. There were not. She wasn't sure if that was a good sign or a bad one.

The sad-eyed man waiting in the foyer was Jaime Caldron. Mac had warned her he might be calling, but she'd have recognized him, anyway—even after all these years. He was one of the characters in that terrible movie that always ran in her head.

"Inspector Caldron," she said upon reaching the last

step, her voice cautiously cheerful. "You at my door after all this time."

She extended her hand and smiled. Caldron took it, looking uncomfortable. "Yeah, good to see you, Mrs. McGowan," he mumbled, frowning. He glanced over at Bonny, who looked back at him for a moment or two, then withdrew. "Uh, could we talk in private?" he said to Stella.

"Sure. Let's go into the sitting room."

Stella led him into the front room, moving with studied grace. Her insides were in a knot, but fortunately she was prepared.

After returning from Mac's office, she'd changed into pale yellow silk pants and a white silk blouse. She sat on the padded bench, striking a demure but serious pose. Caldron sat in the wingback armchair closest to her. He did not lean back for a moment, then finally did, as if surrendering to his fatigue. Stella fought to sustain her pleasant, curious, yet completely innocent demeanor. She raised her brows slightly as if to say, "Well, what brings you here, my dear man?"

"I guess your husband told you we'd talked."

"Yes, Detective, he said he'd seen you."

"Did he explain what brings me back after all these years?"

"Something about you retiring, I believe."

Caldron grimaced. "Well, not exactly."

"Oh?"

"Look, Mrs. McGowan, can I be blunt?"

"If you wish."

"That house you had with your first husband, the one in Brentwood…"

"Yes, what about it?"

"I think it's about to give up a body."

"A body?"

"I talked to the real estate agent representing the new owners. They're going to put in a new pool. We plan to be there when the work is done. I expect to find Aubrey St. George."

She managed to hide her surprise. Mac had said nothing about this. Had he known? "Why would you expect that? Aubrey drowned out at Malibu while swimming."

"Yeah, I know that's the theory, but I think the facts are otherwise."

"Facts? What facts?" When he didn't respond, Stella added, "I'm certain you're mistaken, Inspector."

"Well, we could debate that all day long, I guess. When the time comes, we'll find out. But that's not really what I came here to discuss. I'm prepared to make you an offer that'll get you off the hook."

"What sort of offer?"

"I'll have to clear it with the D.A., of course, but I'm prepared to ask for reduced charges, no jail time, in exchange for testimony against your husband."

Stella was caught flat-footed. "Testimony about what?"

"That he killed Aubrey St. George and hid the body. If St. George's remains show evidence of a gunshot, then we'd want testimony that he shot the victim—or confirmation of whatever the evidence shows. You give us eyewitness testimony as to whatever you saw, and we overlook your participation in the crime. That's what I'm prepared to ask for. You cooperate and I'll sell it to the D.A."

She was incredulous. Caldron was handing her the perfect answer to her problem. She could go to her husband and use this as leverage. "They're making it easy for me, Mac. Give me a reason not to take their deal." Surely it would be worth a couple of million dollars to him. Surely.

But her immediate problem was not her husband, it was

Jaime Caldron. "But, Inspector," she said, "you don't expect me to lie, do you?"

He gave her a hard glare. There was no embarrassment in his eyes. He had the look of a tough, unrelenting cop. "Mrs. McGowan, you trying to tell me your husband didn't do it?"

"If by 'do it' you mean kill Aubrey, the answer is no, most definitely no."

"You understand that when the body shows evidence of death by foul play, and you're implicated, you won't be in such a good bargaining position as you are now."

"I won't lie."

"Maybe even though you and Mr. McGowan are separated you feel you've got to play the loyal wife. Maybe he's paying you a lot each month and you don't want to lose that. Or maybe you haven't had a chance to think this thing through. I don't know why you're protecting him. But remember this—I'm offering you a good deal, Mrs. McGowan, a real good deal. Why don't you give it some thought? You don't have to say yea or nay on the spot."

"The truth is the truth," she said.

Caldron smiled for the first time. "Yeah, that's definitely true. Well, you sleep on it. Let me give you my card."

He took a business card from his pocket and handed it to her. Stella studied it a moment. "Why are you so sure Mac killed Aubrey?"

"The way I see it, there's only one other possibility and that's you."

"Divide and conquer?"

He smiled faintly. "I sure hope you won't disappoint me, Mrs. McGowan."

"Thank you for stopping by, Inspector."

Caldron got to his feet. "Oh, and by the way, who was the young woman with your husband?"

"I beg your pardon?"

"At his office this morning. I came to see you earlier, but you were just leaving, so I followed you to Studio City, your husband's office. I see you go into the building, then he comes out with a young woman. Just curious what's going on."

"My, but you're eager."

"She have something to do with what's going on?"

"That was a private investigator who works for Mac. Her name's Jade Morro. They're having some sort of problem with a few of the employees. I don't know much about it."

"Oh, I see. Well, you give my offer some thought, Mrs. McGowan. Regardless of what you're saying now, I have a hunch you're going to do the right thing. And that's good because it'll make living the rest of your life a whole lot easier."

Stella smiled pleasantly. No, she thought, a couple of million dollars would make living her life a whole lot easier.

"Well, I'll be going. Don't get up," he said. "I can find my way out."

She did not move from her bench, nor did she let the shiver ripple though her until he'd left the room.

South Central Los Angeles

Jade had been feeling uneasy about having a showdown with Ricky Santos. It had been her fondest wish never to lay eyes on the man again. Probably what she feared most was that he would mistake her overture as interest, when in fact nothing could be further from the truth. She was going to nip this stalking business in the bud and, if that meant confronting an old lover she'd rather not think about, much less see, then that was what she'd do.

She turned onto Ruthie's street half an hour before the time of her scheduled meeting with Ricky. It was a neighborhood of simple, unpretentious bungalows, not that different than her own neighborhood, except the houses were newer by a decade or two and many had bars on the windows. But most of the homes were kept up, and a few of the lawns and flower beds were worthy of anything you'd find in West L.A.

She parked in front of a pleasant little bungalow, with beds of pansies in front and pots of fuchsias hanging from the roof of the porch. The bars on the windows had always seemed incongruous, but as Ruthie said, "I consider it cheap insurance." Jade went to the door and rang the bell.

Rundel Jones, Ruthie's cousin and longtime friend, answered the door. He was a two-hundred-fifty-pound pile of muscle in a black tank top and pair of basketball shorts that made his legs look like a pair of telephone poles in a skirt. A one-time linebacker in the L.A. Raiders development squad, Rundel's current occupation was bodyguard. He hired out to various celebrities and dignitaries, counting many among his friends.

"Hey, Señorita Morro," he said. "How's it goin'?"

Rundel had this idea Jade was Hispanic, probably because of her name, but it was only partially true. In fact, her father's father had been Puerto Rican, but her father's mother was Irish, her grandparents on her mother's side Cajun and Polish, Italian and Swedish. She'd gone over her genealogical data with Rundel before, but he liked to call her *señorita,* anyway.

"It's goin' okay," she replied as Rundel admitted her to Ruthie's tidy front room and closed the door.

"Ruthie!" he hollered toward the back of the house. "Jade's here."

Ruthie Gibbons came into the living room after a minute, giving Jade a hug. "You okay, sugar?"

"Sure, I'm fine. Why wouldn't I be?" She was being sincere, totally sincere, but she also knew Ruthie might know something she didn't, like maybe the fact that she was in denial. Which, when she thought about it, made her very uncomfortable. Maybe she ought to be a lot more upset about this. After all, Ricky had been the love of her life, the man who'd wounded her as badly as a woman could be wounded. Maybe she ought to be freaking out at the prospect of having to see him again. Or, at least nervous. Well, she was nervous, she wouldn't deny that. Wary, then? Afraid?

She was all of those things to one degree or another, but what bothered her most was the prospect that this whole thing was a dumb idea. Hell, she knew Ricky Santos, and she found it hard to believe he was behind this stalking business. She'd allowed Ruthie to talk her into believing it was Ricky. And she also knew exactly what he'd be thinking—that she was using the stalking as an excuse to see him again. Of course. If he was innocent, what else could he think?

"You don't look so fine to me," Ruthie said.

"I really am."

"You sure?"

Jade abruptly began to pace back and forth, finally blurting it out. "Ruthie, I don't think I want to do this."

"Why not, girl?"

"Because Ricky's going to think I'm making a play for him."

"What do you care what he thinks? The whole point is to find out what's going on, right?"

"Yes, but there's no need to make a fool of myself, is there?"

"Who's going to know but you and me and him? Screw the dude. And if he's doing what we think he's doing, then he's going to pay."

Jade could see there was no point in arguing. The more she denied her feelings, the more unsure she became. Ruthie was probably right. What did she care what Ricky Santos thought? About anything.

She shut up then and sat nervously waiting for Ricky, reminding herself how much she hated the bastard, how he'd screwed her over and how, if he was the moron behind these incidents, he'd get his due.

"So, how's Mr. McGowan?" Ruthie asked.

Jade was surprised by the question. "How'd you know I saw him this morning? I didn't tell you."

"I didn't know for sure. But you do have a glow on your cheeks."

Jade gave her a look. "I met with Mac and his wife."

"Wife? Yuck. Never did like that word. What she doing there?"

"I don't know. She came to see him about something."

"So, girl, don't keep me in the dark. What's she like?"

"Attractive, rich. She seemed well cared for, but I'd say older than Mac."

"Older wife? The man's ripe to be plucked, honey."

"I'm not in the plucking mood."

Ruthie put her hands on her hips. "What's it going to take to get you out of denial?"

"You're in denial, Ruthie. You can't accept that I'm happy the way I am."

Ruthie rolled her eyes. "Maybe I'll go make some coffee, just in case this little showdown at the OK Corral gets sociable."

"No chance of that."

"Then I'll make some for us chickens."

Poor Ruthie. She'd made Jade's love life her Holy Grail. The fact that it was a losing cause almost made Jade feel guilty. Funny thing, though, she had been thinking about Mac and his wife. Mostly she'd wondered how on earth

they could ever have gotten married. It had to have something to do with Aubrey St. George's death. She didn't
want to think Mac was mixed up in something illicit or
criminal, but her instincts told her he was. As a minimum
there was a dark secret, and it clearly had come back to
haunt him.

Jade found herself feeling sorry for him. Which didn't
mean she could forgive anything he did, but she wanted
to be on his side...and not just because he wrote the
checks. Mac was a nice guy—whether Ruthie appreciated
the word or not—and she liked him. There was something
soulful and caring about him. Yes, that was a good way
to describe him—Mac seemed to care. And not just about
himself.

She'd told Ruthie he was the cuddly type. Men, in her
experience, could be repulsive and they could be alluring,
but not many of them could be comfortable, and that was
a good way to describe Mac McGowan. He was a comfortable guy.

"So, you think this dude's going to show?" Rundel
asked as he kept an eye out front in fine bodyguard form.

"If he doesn't, that could be the story right there."

"If he been stalkin' you and he shows his ass, then he
got balls."

"Which means if he shows, he's probably innocent. To
tell you the truth, I'm not sure what to hope for."

"Well, you better make up your mind," Rundel said,
"because here's the dude now."

Jade's heart rose into her throat. Shit. She knew then
that she hadn't wanted him to show. But he was here, and
she'd have to deal with it. Was she ready? She knew she
wasn't. She hadn't figured out what to think, how to feel,
how to act, but she needed something. She frantically
searched for anger, indignation.

"And he got company," Rundel said, peering not too subtly out the curtains.

"How many?"

"Only one."

Jade relaxed a little at that. Two they'd be able to handle.

"Ruthie!" Rundel hollered. "Our boy's here."

Ruthie arrived from the kitchen, sassy with righteous energy. There was no sooner a knock and she opened the door. Jade stayed in her chair, struggling hard to be disdainful. From where she sat, she didn't have a clear view out the door. She heard Ricky's voice first.

"Hi, Ruthie," he said.

"Ricky…"

Jade heard surprise in her friend's voice. Just in the way she said his name. Then Ricky again.

"I'd like you to meet my wife," he said. "This is Luz."

Silence.

Wife? The word echoed in Jade's brain like a round fired into a bullet trap. Wife?

"Nice to meet you," Ruthie said. There was no enthusiasm in her tone, certainly no joy.

Wife?

Jade couldn't get rid of the word, nor could she conjure up the implications of its meaning. Not even when Ruthie stepped back to admit the visitors into the house. He brought his wife?

Luz Santos, the pretty *esposa* of Ricky Santos, stepped into Ruthie Gibbons's front room. Luz looked like the sort of person you'd expect to see in a milk commercial, south-of-the-border style. *Bonita, linda.* Not just pretty. Wholesome pretty. Pretty as in the young mother of two young children. Pretty as a contestant in the Mrs. Mexico contest. A little round of face and body, but only a little round, like a peach left on the tree a day too long.

Luz's hair was a black cloud, back-combed into a shiny, smooth, ebony corona. She was in a mostly white dress with black trim. Not virginal, but pure. She had large pretty eyes and a pretty mouth. A bit too much makeup, but maybe that was because she was in black heels and carried the sort of purse you'd take to see an expensive lawyer or to a family baptism. There was wifely pride in her carriage, fire in her rouged cheeks. Rectitude, Latin style.

Jade's former lover's wife glanced up at Rundel, towering above her like a redwood tree. Jade would have left right then and there if she could. Or she'd have melted into the chair like a stick of butter on a hot stone. But she was stuck, trapped there whether she liked it or not. Only then did Luz spot her, her eyes leveling on her with the impersonal hostility of a rattlesnake. Her pretty face seemed to say, "So, you, my husband's lover."

Ricky, the Ricky Santos Jade knew through the prism of hundreds of sexual encounters, appeared next to his wife, easing his body against her like an ocean liner kissing the dock. Jade knew it was the same man, but he was in disguise—the disguise of husband.

"Hello, Jade," he said, finding the happy balance between friendly and unfriendly. "This is Luz."

Jade got to her feet. She was in jeans and the long-sleeve pink T-shirt she'd worn all day, an outfit better suited to go one-on-one against Rundel on a basketball court than to meet Luz Santos at the baptismal font. She pushed her sleeves up her forearms, reminding herself that Luz was not the only aggrieved party here. Jade had slept with Ricky thinking he was single. The pretty wife was his secret. He was the villain in this melodrama.

Jade looked at him without clearly seeing him, mostly because she couldn't bring herself to see him. That vague cloud of masculine beauty across the room was a gigantic lie. An impostor. A joke. "This is Luz," he'd said, as if identifying a bloom of truth in a field of lies. Jade felt so sorry for herself, she wanted to cry. If he'd said he was sorry for all the suffering he'd caused, uttered a single word of remorse, she would have broken into sobs, bawled big salty tears right in front of the whole crowd. But he didn't. So, she didn't.

Ruthie, unwitting hostess of the farce, intervened. "Come sit down," she said, too solicitous by half.

Luz, a touch unpracticed in her heels, stepped over to the sofa and sat, arranging her ample skirts. Ricky, former pretty-boy cop, sat beside her. Jade could smell his cologne across the room, the cologne he'd put on after his shower and before they'd make love. He was close enough to his wife that their legs touched, but he did not lean back. Rather, he leaned forward, his elbows on his knees, the big, clunky watch on his wrist gleaming. Jade did not look into his eyes. She did, snake-to-snake, with Luz.

"I promised Luz that if I ever saw you again, she would be with me," he said, as if to explain the whole thing. His voice was soft, as though addressing a priest, his accent stronger than it had been when he was her unmarried lover and husband-to-be.

"That's very considerate, Ricky," Jade replied. "Too bad you didn't bring her with you on our first date. It might have saved everybody a lot of trouble."

Luz gave him a jab in the side with her elbow and said something under her breath to him in Spanish. Ricky replied in the same whispered tone. Jade realized then he was translating. Luz didn't speak English.

In a way, Jade was sorry. It was a pretty good bet the translations were going to be sanitized. But it did eliminate the need for diplomacy on her part. Ricky could add whatever was needed.

"Ruthie said you're having a problem and you need to talk to me face-to-face," he said.

The utter innocence in his voice made her want to scream obscenities. Still, his credulity seemed beyond reproach. He was not the author of these incidents, the attempt to run down Art Conti, the slashed tires. Impossible. That face? Yet, this was the same guy who in full innocence asked her to marry him, not bothering to mention he already had a wife. Jade decided to plunge ahead according to plan, ignoring the rouged, virgin bride at Ricky Santos's elbow.

"I've been harassed and stalked," she said, "people slashing my tires, trying to run down my friends, generally cruising the neighborhood, watching my place. There have been descriptions. An Hispanic guy."

She stopped there. Ricky waited for her to go on, only then realizing she'd made her point.

"You think it was me?" he said, disbelief registering clearly in his voice.

A flurry of jabs from Luz. Ricky explained. Luz flashed her eyes at Jade as if to say, "Carumba! Are you out of your mind? I've had my hand on his cock every minute the past year. He can't pee unless I loosen my grip!"

Ricky shook his head, his eyes husband-sad rather than lover-proud. "Jade, if somebody's bothering you, it's not me. I swear it. Why would I do this?"

She only half heard his denial, remembering his lover-lips and lover-eyes, remembering he was the bastard who had deceived her, scorning her love with betrayal. Ricky and his Luz. Ricky and his lie.

"Why wouldn't you, dude?" Ruthie interjected, lapsing into ghettoese. "You the only enemy she got. You done worse already!"

Ricky was clearly annoyed by the accusation, so annoyed that he ignored his wife's insistent elbow. He focused on Jade. "Look, I know what I did to you was wrong, and I've been paying for it. I'll continue paying for it. Which doesn't do you any good, I know. But stalk you, Jade? Slash your tires? Why? The only reason I came here was because I thought you needed help. I owed you that, but I had to be honest with my wife. I had to tell her. That's why we're both here. I've promised never to make the same mistake again."

His tone was plaintive. Jade believed him. She knew what he was saying was true even before he came. If Ruthie had manufactured a motive, Luz's presence belied it. This, to put it simply, was a wild-goose chase. "We haven't been able to figure out who would be doing this to me and why," she said, sounding apologetic. "We're grasping at straws."

"How long has it been going on? Have you reported it?"

Luz had given up her nonverbal imploration and was now in a sulk, giving her elbow a rest. She folded her arms under her breasts defiantly, probably aware it was unlikely that her husband and Jade were plotting a secret rendezvous, but she was miffed, nonetheless.

"It's been the last several days," Jade said. "We thought if it was because of some bad blood between me and you that it would be best to get to the bottom of it now, rather than drag in the police."

Ricky shook his head. "I'm innocent, Jade. I swear."

Luz snapped something at him in Spanish and Ricky accommodated her with several mumbled sentences, enough to satisfy her, evidently. But Jade hardly noticed. She was replaying his last words: "I'm innocent, Jade. I swear."

Innocent? That was Ricky, and it was not Ricky. Innocent and guilty, guilty and innocent. He was the bastard she'd once loved, but no longer did because it was impossible to love what was not true. But it was also impossible to forget what you'd once so desperately wanted to believe. The funny thing was, he no longer seemed like the man she'd known. He was only the shell of Ricky Santos, lover par excellence. He was but the puff of smoke left after the magic trick, a suggestion of what had once existed, if only in her mind. That former Ricky was dead, and the corpse was tied to the apron strings of this pretty Mrs. Mexico with her fiery cheeks and the black high heels.

"That being the case, we're wasting our time," Jade said. "I'm sorry to have brought you here unnecessarily." She wanted him to leave very badly and take the mother of his children with him. She wanted him gone, out of her life for good. She wanted no more of his innocence or guilt, his charm or his betrayal.

Ricky Santos who, after all, knew her more than a little bit, got the message. He took his wife by the hand and stood up. His last offering was a parting glance, a brief look into her eyes that sort of said, "I'm sorry."

None of them bothered with goodbye. Rundel held the door open for them. Ruthie managed to look both confounded and suspicious. Jade considered crying, but decided against it.

"Well, shit," Ruthie said when Ricky and Luz were gone.

That pretty well summed it up.

Pacific Palisades

Venita was surprised and upset when Arjay said he wanted to take the limo and go out for dinner. It also scared her. She wanted everybody in the household where she could see them, where she could be sure what they were doing, so she could be certain no one betrayed her.

Venita still hadn't seen Jugnu, though she'd confirmed he'd been in his room all day. Cala had napped, as she often did in the afternoon. So, with evening approaching, Venita found herself alone, battling her fears in solitude. Hours and hours—nearly a day—had passed since she'd shoved Percy Gaylord over the cliff, and there was still no sign of the police. She'd rehearsed her lines regarding Percy so many times that soon they would no longer sound spontaneous and natural. It was like being onstage and in costume at the theater, but the curtain refused to go up.

Troy had called her earlier, shortly after she'd had her bowl of soup in her room. He'd been chipper, enthusiastic, upbeat. His mood was in such contrast to her own that she'd welcomed it.

"How about if I pick up a pizza and we have a quiet little romantic dinner tonight, just the two of us?" he'd said.

"That would be lovely," she'd told him, craving company.

"And maybe if you've got some champagne around, you can put it on ice."

"Why's that?"

"Maybe we've got reason to celebrate."

"You have news?"

"Let's just say things are moving ahead. But I'll tell you about it later."

Venita wondered if he was referring to the possibility of his father investing in the film. But she was afraid to hope, especially with Percy Gaylord hanging over her like a sword on a thread.

Actually, Troy concerned her, if only because she felt control of the situation was passing from her hands to his. The boy was up to something, and he was being secretive about it. Her husband, Ranjit, had successfully manipulated her the same way, keeping her off balance, agonizing. Was Troy that astute, or was this a chance thing? Or perhaps it wasn't so much his skill as her desperation over the circumstances.

When Troy had left that morning, she'd been sure the police would have paid their visit and been gone long before his return. She'd even hoped they'd ask their questions and quietly go their way without him ever finding out they'd been here. But the bastards hadn't shown. Now she found herself craving Troy's youthful energy, his enthusiasm, his adoration, but above all, his father's money. She wanted badly to be queen again—loved and admired and desired, not tormented by the bloody police. She wanted this uncertainty over with!

By late afternoon she paced so much that she figured she'd easily covered five miles. Her feet were tired and she was spent. Several times she had to restrain herself from rousing Jugnu and sending him off to see what had become of Percy. Was it possible the body hadn't yet been discovered?

Arjay had been gone half an hour when Venita decided she couldn't bear the suspense any longer. It was not inconceivable that she should walk in her own garden. And wasn't it possible that she might stand by the wall, enjoying the view? Supposing even that the police were on a nearby hilltop watching her every move, surely a casual glance into the ravine wouldn't be seen as damning proof of anything untoward. She'd simply have to be nonchalant. The probable explanation for this horrible silence was that Percy's body had not yet been discovered. Undoubtedly it lay there where it had come to rest after the tragic fall. Once she'd confirmed that, she would at least know where things stood.

Taking her parasol, Venita went out onto the terrace, at first sitting at the table under the huge umbrella. For several minutes she stared off in the direction of the sea, though it was in fact the wall that held her attention. What if Percy hadn't died in his fall? What if he'd spent the day crawling back up the hill, inch by bloody inch? What if at any moment his gory face appeared above the wall, his eyes filled with rage? The image was so vivid. Try as she may, Venita couldn't banish it from her mind.

When she was a child afraid of the specters and goblins that haunted the dark corners of her room, her father had given her a torch to keep under her pillow, and when the fear consumed her, he told her to flash the light there to satisfy herself she was safe. Ever since, Venita had tended to attack her problems head-on. And so it was with Percy now. She realized if she were to master this threat, whether imagined or real, she must engage it full-on.

Rising from the table, she opened her parasol and casually strolled around the pool, making a full circle of it as though examining the condition of the water. Before heading for the pavilion, she stopped at a bed of roses and sniffed several of the blossoms, all the while hearing Percy Gaylord calling to her like a siren: "Come see my bloody corpse, so you'll know what you have done, murderess!"

"Oh, I'll be there in good time, my man," she bravely replied. "Never you fear."

At last Venita reached the pavilion where she made herself sit for a full five minutes, occupying herself by staring at the ocean, following the progress of an oil tanker crawling south along the horizon. Then, with the deliberateness of a holy man on his way to his meditation, she stepped from the pavilion and moved to the wall. For at least a minute she did not look down, staring instead at the neighboring hill and the homes pressed into its side, like nuts in a cake. Finally she lowered her eyes.

Though the bottom of the ravine was now in heavy shadow, the open area on the fire trail where Percy's body had come to rest was clearly visible. But there was no sign of Percy. He was gone!

Though it was what she should have expected, Venita was nonetheless shocked, just as she'd been as a child, the first time she'd shone the torch into the dark corner of her room only to find it empty. Composing herself, she drew her eyes from the canyon floor and gazed at the opposing hillside and the homes that, though remote, were in plain view. It was clearly paranoia, yet she had the feeling that some number of eyes were gauging her every move.

Drawing a fortifying breath, Venita again peered down the slope, but with the same result—no sign of a body, whatsoever. Spinning her parasol, she strolled a short distance in one direction, thinking perhaps the line of sight she'd had wasn't quite right. She lowered her eyes and studied the scene from a slightly altered perspective. Still nothing. She moved along the wall in the other direction. Nothing at all. So, if the body had been found, then where were the police? Surely they would investigate!

Venita peered up at the cloudless sky, imploring the gods for an explanation. Had Percy's remains been found? Or, had the unlikely occurred? Had he survived the fall? Venita couldn't see how that was possible, but even if it were, Percy surely would have lodged a complaint. And if he had, the police would have reacted by now. Dear God, was she going mad?

"Ah-ha! Here you are!"

Venita gasped. Spinning, she caught the heel of her sandal in the grass and lost her balance. As she went reeling toward the wall, she screamed; the parasol flew from her hand. She was sure she was doomed. But someone grabbed her by the arm just in time, jerking her back from the precipice.

"Oh my God, oh my God!" she cried as she lay against him, her face pressed to his chest. It was only when she pulled her head back and looked up at him that she was absolutely sure it was Troy.

"Hey, sorry," he said. "Didn't mean to scare you. You almost fell down the cliff."

"My God," she gasped, her heart racing so fast it felt like it was choking. "I was certain I was going over."

"That wouldn't be too cool," he said. "You fall down a slope like that and you could end up dead."

Still holding her, he leaned out and looked down. Venita gasped, clinging to him. Her body began to tremble. "Oh, please…"

Troy grinned. "What's the matter? I won't let you fall."

"Please, Troy, this isn't amusing. Set me down."

He eased back from the precipice and deposited her on the grass, a few feet from the wall. He gave her a big grin.

"You are a monster, Troy Hampton!"

The accusation made him laugh. "Yeah, that's me." Then his expression became quite sober. "How's your day been, Venita?"

He said it as if he knew. She heard it in his voice. He could just as easily have said, "The cops been here yet?"

But, it wasn't possible. Troy had been asleep, dreaming his libidinous young man's dreams.

"It's been quiet," she replied calmly, despite the wild rhythms of her heart.

She pressed her body close to his. Troy gestured toward the parasol.

"Want me to get that for you?"

"Good heavens, no!"

"Why not? It's just right there."

"No, absolutely not. Don't mind the parasol. Let's go inside."

Taking him firmly by the arm, she pulled him toward the house. True, the parasol, bright red and hanging on the bush, would be like a flag, drawing attention to the fateful spot from whence Percy Gaylord had fallen to his doom, but at this juncture Venita hardly cared. She wanted to go in the house and get as far away from the bloody wall as she possibly could.

Her head cleared and her heart finding a more normal rhythm, she said, "What then is your news, the cause for celebration?"

"It's not yet a done deal because there's still work that I have to do, but everything's in place."

"For what?"

"Bringing in a couple of mil for our movie."

"Troy, you can't be serious."

"I won't jinx it by saying more, but the first shot in the battle is about to be fired, Venita." He laughed and added, "So to speak."

Beverly Hills

Ever since Amal had called, asking if he could come by, Stella had been on pins and needles. "I want to discuss the project," he'd said. "I've been sparring with my muse the last few days and I thought your insights might be helpful."

He couldn't have any idea how much those words had thrilled her. She was being wooed by a famous movie director, and not for her body—Amal Kory was in love with her persona, her talent, her mind. Finally someone had seen what she truly had to offer.

Pacing about her room, she pondered the development. Of course, Mac's money was a factor in this, an important factor. But she also knew Amal wanted his film to be successful. The man was not just a businessman, he was an artist. He spoke not so much from the mind as the soul.

And yet, without capital, there would be no film. And unless Mac could be convinced to put in seed money her position was not secure, no matter how much Amal admired her talents. She just couldn't allow this final opportunity of a lifetime to pass her by. Mac would have to be brought around, whatever the cost.

The door chimes sounded and Stella's heart gave a little hop. That would be Amal. He either had something to tell her or there was something he needed to find out. And he undoubtedly had questions about Mac's intentions. Unfortunately she had no definitive answer. But, if she could just keep him on board until she got Mac straightened around, she might still realize her dream.

Since Bonny had the evening off, Stella answered the door herself.

Amal, suave, even dashing in an exotic, eccentric way, stood on her doorstep, his limousine sitting in the drive. "Stella, my dear, how lovely you look." He took her hand and kissed it.

"Come in, Amal."

They went into the sitting room. Stella offered him an aperitif, but he declined. They made small talk for several minutes, then he said, "May I discuss the project with you?"

"Certainly, Amal."

He looked terribly thoughtful and serious. She waited, not knowing what to expect.

"As you know, I'm totally consumed by *On Distant Shores*," he said. "Once my muse gets a hold of something, she won't let go until it becomes a work of art."

She was so relieved he didn't wish to discuss finances. "I know exactly what you mean!"

"I was going over the screenplay again last evening and, well, frankly, Stella, I think Hilda Grimsley needs tweaking."

"How so?"

"In my view, she's the most stock of Warden's characters, which is unfortunate because I think she has so much potential, opportunities for complexity. And I think the part could be expanded, as well.''

"Oh, I'm so glad you say that," she enthused. "I've been thinking the very same thing!"

"There you are then," he'd said. "We both can't be wrong about this."

For a while they discussed the different possibilities. Amal said he felt something more had to be done in Hilda's relationship with Llewellyn. "It's not enough she suffer a mother's fate," he said. "I need to see more vulnerability in her, an unfulfilled passion or longing."

"Yes," she said. "I couldn't agree more!"

They talked for another half hour and, though it was still early, Stella convinced him to have a light supper with her. They sat side by side at one end of the long dining-room table, a candle flickering between them, and ate and talked of film.

Amal refilled her wineglass as her cheeks burned with excitement. For once, someone who mattered actually cared what she thought. Amal had such wonderful stories. It almost made her wish she could make films in India, where the entire industry was at his beck and call. But taking on the American market was the challenge he'd chosen. And with friends like her, as he'd put it, he'd "subdue the tiger."

Stella knew she'd gotten herself into a thrilling and dangerous adventure. But she'd always been a risk-taker. She believed that if a person was to do anything meaningful in life it was necessary to take chances, be daring, go the extra mile. She did not want to grow old thinking of what might have been.

Amal leaned back in his chair and sighed contentedly, turning the stem of his crystal wineglass between his fingers. "You have a lovely home, Stella," he said. "And you are a delightful hostess. This has been a most pleasant evening.''

"I can't remember when I've had such a fascinating conversation," she told him.

"Considering we'll be working together, it's terribly important that our artistic vision is congruent. I'm encouraged by the fact we see Hilda in much the same way. I believe in letting my actors discover their character with minimal input from me. My role is to make the parts fit. That is the secret of directing a film, in my view."

Amal looked at her with those black, penetrating eyes. The passion in the man, the artistic verve, were incredible. Stella hadn't felt this much in tune with her destiny since Aubrey St. George had asked to marry her. And though that experiment had ended tragically, she'd refused to let it ruin her life. How sad Amal Kory hadn't come along sooner to justify her faith. He was not only a genius but, because he was somewhat of an outsider himself, he had needs, as well—needs she could help him with.

Stella demurely sipped her wine. She and Amal were making artistic love in the sense that they shared a great passion. But her instincts told her she shouldn't let the evening pass without addressing his other concerns.

"Amal," she said, "it's no secret how much I admire you and your body of work. I'll frankly say I've learned a tremendous amount just talking to you."

"Please, Stella, the admiration is mutual. There's no need to—"

"No, hear me out. I know your plans will all go for naught if you can't get the financing. And I want you to know that as a participant in the enterprise, I recognize I have responsibilities. I'm an actor, true, but I want to do more, to contribute in any way I can to make sure *On Distant Shores* makes it to the screen. You've been very polite not to bring up the subject, but I think we should discuss finances.''

"Sadly, art has become the indentured servant of capital.''

"That's the world we live in, all right.''

Amal's expression was the picture of lament. "If my film is meant to be made, then it will be made, my dear. I must cling to the belief.''

Stella lowered her eyes. "I wish I could tell you that I've convinced my husband to invest the seed money, but I haven't. At least, not yet. I can't make you any promises, but I still have hope. Mac moves very slowly when it comes to financial matters and I do have a dialogue going with him. I'd like to say I'm optimistic, but the truth is I'm only hopeful.''

"I appreciate your candor, Stella. I would be delighted if Mac decides to invest in our little enterprise, but I can certainly understand if he does not choose to do so.''

She could tell he was being kind, when it would have been so easy to pressure her. After all, her own desires had been on the table from the very beginning. He knew how badly she wanted this. Amal Kory was a gentleman.

"Do you have other prospects?'' she asked.

"I'm talking to people but, as you know, there's a very long courtship involved. I have one individual who's all but committed five to ten million once we raise the initial two. He wants to see things moving ahead before he jumps on board.''

"Understandable.''

Amal smiled at her somewhat sadly before sipping his wine. His eyes glistened. Stella's heart went out to him.

She said, "This aspect of the business must be so unpleasant for a creative person such as yourself.''

"The whole world must worry about money, Stella...except for a privileged few, of course. But I must confess I get very unhappy when people don't honor their commitments. Tedious, that.''

"Has something dreadful happened?"

"I'm sure you don't care to hear about it."

"Oh, but I do...if it's not confidential."

"I wouldn't want it bandied about Hollywood, but I know I can trust you," he said. "The Indian government is very particular about the export of capital. I worked out an elaborate agreement whereby I could get my own funds released and wired to me to meet my personal needs—this quite apart from the funds of the enterprise. But there's been a hitch, and now I've been told it could be several weeks before I can get my money out of the country."

"Has it caused a serious problem?"

"Some embarrassment. I suppose I shall have to find a bank that will advance me some money until the funds arrive from India."

"What about the fifty thousand?"

"Oh, I keep business and personal funds completely separate. That money your husband gave us will be used to make *On Distant Shores* and nothing else. I'm very insistent on that. But this is not a major catastrophe, just an inconvenience. I do hate going to a bank, though, and asking for money to pay the rent and buy groceries. I'm ashamed even to tell you about it, Stella. I suppose I feel free to do so because we've become so close and have spoken our hearts to one another, a rare thing between people these days."

"You're so right. And I do treasure our relationship."

"Then, let's focus on that, the good part of this business, shall we?"

"But I feel badly," she said, her heart swelling with compassion. "Are we talking about a great deal of money?"

"No, actually not. That's what's so bloody annoying.

You'd think those bureaucrats in Delhi could see their way to let me have ten or fifteen thousand of my own money, wouldn't you?''

"They won't give you that little bit?"

"Oh, they shall in due course, but because of their intransigence, I'll be forced to go to a bank with hat in hand. I'd wanted to avoid that if at all possible. People do talk, you know.''

"Amal, if it's a matter of just a few weeks, I could loan you the money.''

"No, Stella, you're a dear to offer, but I wouldn't think of it. Absolutely not.''

"But why not? We're friends. And, if you're really uncomfortable, we could make it a business deal. Once your funds arrive from India, you can invest the money in the project in my name, give me some tiny percentage for my trouble. Would you feel better if we did it that way?''

Amal stroked his chin, not looking too happy.

"To be perfectly frank,'' she said, "I was going to suggest that I put a little money in the pot to ensure this film gets made. I wasn't sure how to approach you, but now I have a good excuse. I'm only talking a modest amount, but it may help you over this hump. Would you agree to accept twenty thousand?''

"Stella, Stella, my dear. I need nowhere near that much. We're only talking a few weeks.''

"But I do want to be an investor, one of the people who were there at the beginning when your need was greatest.''

Amal Kory shook his head, his eyes shimmering so that she nearly cried herself. "How is it that fate has given me such a wonderful friend?'' he said.

"Let me get my checkbook,'' Stella said. "You'll have to give me a day to transfer funds so the check will be good.''

"I can't tell you how deeply moved I am by this. Truly."

Stella went off, feeling a deep glow of happiness. For the first time in her life, she felt genuinely part of something big. Both her husbands had kept her, each in his own way. She was never truly a partner with either of them. Amal, for all his modesty, knew how to receive as well as give, knew how to make her feel wanted and important.

When she returned, she found him standing at the fireplace, his hand resting on the mantel, the gold chain that spanned his vest gleaming. His expression was troubled.

"What's the matter?" she asked.

"I realize now I shouldn't have agreed to take your money."

"Why?"

"Because of Venita. She would see this as breach of the director-actor relationship. She's very rigid about that sort of thing. Venita and I have known each other for many years, and have worked together on countless projects, but we have never developed the kind of rapport you and I have in the short time we've known one another."

"All the more reason to accept my money, Amal. Our relationship is unique."

He shook his head with amazement. "I knew I would encounter astute businesspeople here in America, but I had no idea I'd find anyone who also had such heart."

"Please," she said. "I'm going to give you my check and I don't want to hear another word. And I won't be saying anything to Venita. This is personal business, and it's just between you and me."

Stella sat down and wrote out the check. Then she took it to him. "Friends and partners," she said.

Amal, tears running down his face, held her by the shoulders and, going up on his toes, kissed her on the cheek. "Stella, I am blessed."

* * *

West Hollywood

The radiator hose blew in Jade's car on her way home from South Central. Fortunately she was only eight or nine blocks from home when it happened. She'd phoned Mac at his office to say that she wouldn't be able to come by his place because of car trouble.

"I can drop by there on my way home," he said, "if that would be all right with you. It wouldn't be for at least an hour."

She'd agreed, even though she was bushed, emotionally wrung out. As soon as she got home she took the time for a nice long soak in the tub. Her meeting with Ricky had been emotionally charged—not so much because of the stalking business, as because of the past. But she was glad now that she'd seen him, even if it had proved embarrassing. Confronting him face-to-face had neutralized the last bits of his mystique. She saw him for the flawed and selfish human being he truly was.

"You okay?" Ruthie had asked her before she'd left.

"I'm fine."

"Really fine?"

"Absolutely."

"Seeing him with his wife was okay, then?"

"Ruthie, I saw the real Ricky Santos this afternoon. The guy I lived with was an impostor, a fraud. It still hurts a little when I think about it, but I'm in touch with reality now. I not only hate the bastard for what he did to me, but I don't care about him anymore. A guy like Mac McGowan, even with all his problems, is ten times more honorable."

"And nice."

"Oh, shut up!"

Freshly bathed, Jade put on a clean pair of jeans and

started going through her closet, looking for her favorite white cotton shirt. The possibility of dressing up a little had gone through her mind, but she put it aside. This was her uniform, it was the way she dressed. Why not be herself?

Jade came across the cocktail dress she'd worn to the ball and pulled it out for a good look, holding it up in front of the mirror to recapture the image of herself as she'd looked that night. Sure, she'd considered herself a painted hussy, but a part of her had also been fascinated by what she'd seen, enough to make her wonder what Mac would have thought had he seen her.

Not that she had any desire to be anyone other than herself for him or for anyone else—Jade was not a woman to put on airs. But getting all dolled up had made her wonder if she was more than just a pair of jeans and bicycle shorts. The other was a small part of her, maybe, but she'd discovered it was there.

Digging farther through her closet, Jade found a couple of summer dresses that had to be four or five years old. She'd worn them a couple of times when she and Ricky were together. He wasn't a party animal, but occasionally they'd gone somewhere where she couldn't wear supercasual clothes. He'd tell her she looked pretty, but never made a big deal of it. Ricky, supposedly, liked her the way she was.

Having seen Luz, Jade was a bit surprised at Ricky's indifference to her style of dress. Maybe he got all the women in teased hair and heels that he needed when he was with his wife. Jade, apparently, had been his jock-girl, his scrubbed-nose sexual athlete. There was no denying they did get it on. The bedroom after sex with Ricky often looked like the aftermath of a ten-girl slumber party. Yeah, they could get physical, all right. But sex with Ricky was the last thing she needed to think about, considering she'd unburdened herself of him forever. She resumed looking for the white blouse.

In addition to the summer dresses, Jade found a T-shirt dress on the floor in the back corner of the closet. She'd forgotten about it. During the last summer she was still with Ricky, she and Ruthie had gone to Venice Beach one Saturday, and they each bought a T-shirt dress from one of the boardwalk vendors. It had cost less than thirty bucks. Ruthie had told her the secret was wearing the dress without underwear and then telling your date halfway through the evening.

As Jade recalled, she'd only worn the dress once. She and Ricky had ended up having sex on the kitchen table. She wasn't sure why she hadn't worn it again. Maybe it was too powerful an aphrodisiac for everyday living.

Staring at the dress, Jade wondered if she'd ever have a desire to wear something like that again, just as she'd wondered if she'd ever have a desire for sex again. She was still physically healthy as best she could tell, and she still occasionally thought of sex, but only in the most general and abstract terms. Whenever a specific possibility arose—like with Art Conti—she almost got sick at the prospect. But, what about Mac?

She hadn't exactly thought of him in those terms. Mostly because he hadn't come on to her, but also because she'd been distracted by liking him. She'd told Ruthie that Mac was cuddly like a teddy bear, but that wasn't exactly a sexual thing…or was it? The man was aware of her, she knew, but whether he thought of her in that way, she didn't know. He was needy, besieged, that much was clear, but…

Jade found the shirt and hung the T-shirt dress on the hanger in its place. This was not a productive train of thought. Complications she did not need. And if she'd allowed herself to think of Mac McGowan in those terms, it was only because of what she'd been going through with

Ricky. Mac's decency made him the perfect antidote to the Ricky Santoses of the world. It was just fine to like Mac. And she'd do it in jeans and her favorite white shirt.

She'd gotten on the shirt and had just run a brush through her hair when there was a knock on the front door. That would be Mac.

It wasn't, though. When she looked out the window, who did she see standing on the porch but Ricky Santos. Alone. No Luz.

More confused than anything, she opened the door. "Ricky, what are you doing here?"

"I was thinking about our meeting, the troubles you've been having, Jade. I'm worried about you."

"You're worried about me?"

"Yeah."

"You're a married man, Ricky. You're supposed to worry about your wife." She eyed him warily. "Does Luz know you're here?"

"No."

"Why not?"

"I didn't want to upset her for no reason. She couldn't understand that you and I might still be friends."

Jade wasn't sure what he was getting at but she smelled a rat. "We're not friends, Ricky. We're not anything."

"But we were."

"Were, as in past tense. Let me be blunt. I want to forget I ever knew you. So whatever it is that brought you here, put it out of your mind."

"Honest, what brought me here is worrying about you. I thought maybe there was something I could do to help."

He said it with such innocence. But it was obvious the sonovabitch was testing the waters, to see how she'd react to him with his wife absent. The bastard. How could he be so arrogant? Did he think his pretty face entitled him? There had been moments these past several months

when it might have worked, moments when her loneliness
and unhappiness were bigger than her pride, bigger than
her self-respect. But mostly they were fleeting moments,
flashes of weakness when his arms around her, his lips on
her skin, would have been enough—if only because she
could pretend he cared.

Jade knew all too well that what truly mattered to Ricky
Santos was himself. He was still trying to play both ends
of the game. Sure he loved his wife, but he also loved
getting a little on the side. If he could console a lonely,
desperate, heartbroken woman, why not give her a crumb
of pleasure and sneak a little for himself?

Well, there were times when something wasn't better
than nothing. There were times when denying yourself was
an act of generosity to your own hungry soul. Honor
counted. As did pride. Jade knew with certainty she'd
rather do without.

"Come to think of it," she said to him, "there is something you can do."

"What?"

"Never darken my door again. Never, ever, Ricky. Stay
away. Don't even think about me, because I don't want to
think about you, let alone see you. Is that clear?"

"Would it make any difference if I tell you that I still
love you?"

"No, that's worse! I don't want to hear it, Ricky! Can't
you get that through your head?"

"But how can I help what I feel? The minute I arrived
in town, all I could think about was coming here to see
you."

She glared at him, hating him for this. "You just don't
get it, do you?"

"Jade, I have to tell you this. I confess I drove by your
house a few times. I was hoping I might get a glimpse of
you."

Her brows rose with surprise. "So, it was you, after all," she said, the color rising in her face.

"I drove by, yes."

"You tried to run down Art and you slashed my tires."

"No, no, nothing like that, Jade. All I did was drive by your house. That's all."

She searched his eyes for the truth. "Ruthie said she thought she saw you last week."

"Yes, and I saw her in front of your house. But I did nothing. My only sin is to want to see you."

"Is that true?"

"Why should I damage your car if I love you? Am I not here with love in my heart?"

"Well, you can forget it. I'm not interested, Ricky. Period. End of story."

He stood looking at her like a wounded child. But it wouldn't work. She was immune. She was too strong for him. Too wise. Too aware. Her Ricky was dead for good.

Mac pulled into a parking place a couple of doors up the street from the address on Jade's card. Spotting the house, he saw her at her door, talking to a young man. The conversation appeared to be animated, but he was too far away to see her expression. After several moments, the man turned and left. Jade went back inside, closing the door.

Mac got a good look at the guy. He was handsome, real handsome. And he wasn't a Fuller Brush salesman. He got in a car and drove off, passing Mac on his way. Mac couldn't read anything on the guy's face. There was no way to tell what had just happened. It could have been a friend who'd dropped by, a boyfriend or nobody. At least she didn't kiss him. Mac found reason in that to take heart.

As he sat there, the absurdity of the situation slowly began to sink in. What was he doing feeling jealous? Jade

Morro was not the love of his life; she was in fact just a girl he'd had a few conversations with, as much about business as anything else. Was this what his life had come to? Were things that bad that he was reduced to groundless fantasy, adolescent jealousy? He'd ended a months-long relationship with Bri Lovejoy with hardly any thought, yet here he was at Jade Morro's door, expecting what? Compassion? Love? Friendship? Help?

Mac started to get out when he spotted a car coming slowly up the street and pull into the spot where the young man's vehicle had been. The driver, a man, seemed to be checking addresses. It wasn't until the guy opened the door and got out that Mac realized it was Jaime Caldron. He couldn't have been more surprised. What was Caldron doing here? Especially at this hour?

His heart sank.

Jade sat on her bed, recalling the pain of the last time she'd sent Ricky Santos packing. His betrayal had been the deepest wound of her life. This was different. The man who'd seemed so perfect, so right, was actually rather pathetic. He had been all along, of course, but she'd been blind to it. When she stopped to think about it, it made her sad to think that a man who might have been so good was, in fact, so undeserving of her love. The lesson was obvious. Ricky had been an illusion, a creation of her imagination. The Ricky she thought she knew didn't exist.

There was another knock at the door. Mac. The prospect cheered her.

She took a quick look at her face in the bathroom mirror and went to the front room. When she looked out the window, she discovered it wasn't Mac. It was an older guy in a sport coat, fiftyish, Latino. What now?

He knocked again. Jade opened the door a crack.

"Miss Morro?"

"Yes?"

"I'm Jaime Caldron, L.A.P.D." He took his badge from his breast pocket and showed her.

Jaime Caldron. The guy who'd been investigating Mac. She opened the door wider. "What can I do for you?"

"Can we talk?"

"About what?"

"Your client, Mac McGowan."

Jade opened the door wider. "How did you know he was my client?"

"His wife is an acquaintance."

She smirked at his coyness.

"Can I come in?"

"For a few minutes. I've got things to do."

"All I need's a minute."

Caldron stepped in, glanced around as if to assess who and what he was dealing with. Jade told him to sit down. He did.

"I'm working a case involving McGowan," Caldron said. "Naturally, I'm curious what you've got going with him."

"It's confidential, Lieutenant."

He contemplated her. "There are ways to get past that."

"I work on a confidential basis unless the law says otherwise. In saying that, I'm not trying to be cute. It's my policy."

"You're telling me you aren't covering anything up."

"There's nothing to cover up."

"Is there any harm in us comparing notes?" Caldron asked.

"What's your case, Lieutenant?"

"Aubrey St. George."

"Yeah, and you suspect McGowan of...what, exactly?"

"Killing him, burying the body."

The bluntness and assurance of Caldron's words surprised her, even though she'd already been forewarned by Mac. "I can assure you my client hasn't retained me to do anything connected with a murder, which means we don't have anything to talk about."

"Am I detecting a little hostility here, or is it something else?"

"You're barking up the wrong tree, Caldron. I'm trying to save us both some time and trouble, that's all."

"So, that's it?"

"Yep, that's it."

"You're new in this business," he said with a sad but patronizing smile. "You'll learn it pays to go along to get along."

"It also pays to respect your client's privacy, otherwise you won't have any clients."

"You turning them away, Morro?"

"I'd like to keep the ones I've got."

Caldron got up. "I'll let you get back to your busy schedule. Maybe we can talk again later."

"Maybe."

He went to the door. Jade followed him. Caldron said goodbye and left.

She watched through the window as he got in his car. The detective pulled away. She followed the vehicle's departure and, in the process, noticed a Lexus parked a few doors up the street. Her neighborhood certainly wasn't a slum, but you didn't see many luxury cars parked around, either. This one looked an awful lot like Mac's. When Caldron passed by the Lexus, a guy popped up from behind the wheel, obviously having ducked out of sight so he wouldn't be spotted. It was Mac. With Caldron safely gone, he opened his door and got out of the car. As she waited, he came directly toward her, cutting diagonally across the street and across the lawn.

"Hi," he said. "Looks like you're as popular with the L.A.P.D. as I am."

"Caldron's obsessed with getting you, Mac."

"I know. What did he say?"

"He asked what I'm doing for you."

"And you said?"

"It's none of his goddamn business." She smiled. "But I was a little more polite than that. Come on in."

They stepped inside. Mac glanced around with what looked like genuine curiosity. Her decor was a mélange of cheery grandmother, budget student and practical working girl. There was not a lot of money in the place, but there was some care.

"Nice place."

"No, it's not. As you can see, I'm not a nest builder. No ribbons and bows. Minimal comfort, minimal neatness. But it suits me."

"I like it."

"After your place, that surprises me."

"Decorator. Real is better, Jade. I grew up with real. Sometimes I think I've forgotten who I am. And that, when you think about it, is a very sad thing."

She found that an interesting comment. Mac, she noticed, often said things that made a lot of sense—at least they did to her.

"Sit down," she said.

Mac dropped into her oversize love seat with a grandmotherish flower print. Jade took the faux art deco armchair she and Ricky had gotten in a secondhand shop.

"So, Caldron was paying you a get-acquainted call."

"I'd say more gentle arm-twisting, Mac. He's looking for help in making a case against you for homicide."

"He said that?"

"Basically."

"The sonovabitch."

"You guys don't like each other a whole lot."

"No."

"Well, I gave him my speech about client dealings being confidential. So, it came to nothing. I think as much as anything he's giving us a poke."

"You're pretty stoic about it," he said. "Is it your professionalism? Having seen it all before?"

"I'd like to tell you I'm not wondering, Mac, but the truth is I am. It's none of my business, in a way, but it can't help but color things."

"Nobody wants to think they're doing business with a killer."

"I wouldn't quite put it that way."

"I would," he said. "And that's why I wanted to see you. I think it's time for a little straight talk."

The soberness of his tone made her wonder whether she really wanted to hear this. "Are you sure?"

"I'm not going to lie to you, Jade. And you may not like what you hear, but we're at a point where I figure I've got to take that chance."

Mac regarded her and she held his gaze. She nervously tapped her fingertips together. He looked like he was having trouble figuring out how to say it. She decided to make it as easy for him as she could.

"St. George didn't accidentally drown in the ocean, did he?"

He drew a slow breath through his nose. "Are you asking for Caldron or for yourself?"

"For myself."

Mac nodded. "Then no, he didn't drown."

"What happened?"

He studied her as though trying to gauge the degree of trust he could afford. His hesitation made her afraid of what he might say, but she wanted to know—and not for professional reasons. For herself.

"I killed him, Jade. But it was accidental. He walked in on Stella and me making love. Naturally, he went into a rage. I can't blame him for that. But he was going to beat her and I just couldn't allow it. When I stopped him, he turned on me. I shoved him away when he came at me. He fell and hit his head. The blow killed him."

"That's it?"

"That's it."

"Mac, that could be self-defense or justifiable homicide because you were protecting her. I mean, you didn't beat him or anything, did you?"

"No, I wasn't even conscious. Aubrey hit me with a statue just as I was shoving him away. His blow knocked me out. When I came to, he was on the floor next to me, dead."

"That's not murder or even manslaughter. You should have gone to the police."

"I know. And I knew it then. But Stella was sure it would ruin our lives, and especially her career. She said the police would never believe us. I was young and stupid and I let her talk me into covering up Aubrey's death. I've been paying for it ever since. We both have, though she's never admitted it, I don't think even to herself."

"And now you've got Caldron trying to open up the case."

"Yes. And then there's the notes," Mac said. "I still don't know where they're coming from. The only explanation is either somebody made a good guess or overheard something. Now they see an opportunity to cash in probably."

"But there's still been no demand."

"No."

"The whole thing is really bizarre, Mac. It just doesn't add up. Somebody taking a shot at you and Stella. How does that fit in?"

"Beats me. That's why I hired you," he said, a smile slowly forming.

"Well, I've got a few mysteries of my own to contend with. Turns out whoever slashed my tires and tried to run down Art wasn't my former boyfriend. At least I don't think it was." She shook her head. "There seem to be a lot of random, inexplicable events. We definitely are missing pieces to the puzzle."

Mac looked at her with an awareness that was more frank than before, a questioning. She felt his intensity.

"I guess I should have asked you this first," he said, "but how does this information about Aubrey affect your position? Do you have an obligation to go to the police?"

"Well, I'm not going to."

"How do you feel about what I've said, then?"

"I'm relieved, to tell you the truth. I knew something happened. I'm glad it was this. I couldn't see you doing anything truly evil."

"Why's that?"

"Intuition."

He seemed pleased by her response. "I take that as a compliment."

"It is, I guess."

"So, where do we stand, Jade? What happens now?"

"I'm not so much in the dark. That's a plus. But we have more questions than answers. I have a feeling we won't have long to wait, though. Whoever's sending notes and taking shots isn't through. My gut instinct is all this has been a prelude."

He chuckled sadly. "You certainly know how to raise a guy's spirits."

"My job isn't to be cheerful."

"Yeah, I know. But I've got to tell you, Jade, I feel better for having had this conversation. A lot better. You're the first person in twenty years I've talked to about Aubrey. I may have enemies, and there's no question I'm in danger, but I feel like a huge weight has been lifted from my shoulders.''

"I just hope I can help."

"You've done a lot already. More than you fully appreciate, I'm sure."

The warmth of his tone, his sincerity, embarrassed her. She wasn't a superwoman, but Mac made her feel good, made her want to help him.

"I don't know about you, but I'm hungry," he said. "You eaten yet?"

She shook her head.

"How about I take you out for a bite?"

"It's late and I'm not really dressed."

"We can go someplace informal. A hamburger joint. Anything."

"Mac, I can make something. A bowl of soup, a sandwich. Of course, it'd probably have to be peanut butter and jelly. I don't keep a very well-stocked pantry."

He laughed with genuine gusto.

"So, I'm not very domestic," she said with a shrug. "What can I say?"

"No, it's not that."

"What then?"

"You probably won't believe this, but recently I've had this terrible craving for peanut butter and jelly sandwiches."

Burbank

When Manuela left the stage, her body glistening with perspiration, the drunks in the audience were standing and applauding. Blowing them a final kiss, she disappeared behind the curtain and headed for her dressing room.

"Assholes," she muttered, eliciting a smile from the next girl waiting to go on.

Of course, the bastards paid her bills.

The Bottoms Up Club was definitely jumping even though it was ten on a Monday night. Eight to eleven was prime time, when the biggest stars were on—"the front line" as Mike called his best girls. Plus, on Monday nights cover and drinks were half price, though, as Manuela recalled, tips could be half price, too. But at least the place wasn't dead. There was nothing worse than dancing to an empty house, knowing you might get a buck in tips if you were lucky.

At least Mike had put her back on the front line, much to the chagrin of some of the girl's who'd been around a while. But as Mike told her, "You got the tits, the moves and the attitude I want in my A team. If they don't like it, fuck 'em."

It had been seven years since Manuela had been a front liner for Mike O'Gill and his former partner, Jumbo Jimmy Higgins—who didn't get that name because of the size of his nose—shaking her butt in the faces of a bunch of rowdy drunks six nights a week, taking home a grand or two for her trouble. She'd forgotten how exhausting dancing could be. Of course, she'd only been twenty when she'd left Mike and Jumbo for Mule Creek as a reluctant guest of the state of California. Jumbo himself was in Quentin now, and Mike was the man. Manuela was no longer the firm twenty-year-old she'd once been, but, as Mike said, she had "a mature sexuality" that sold well. "Besides, the crowds are older these days."

Maybe all that was true, but she also knew Mike had talked to his brother, and they were definitely intrigued by the prospects of a threesome. Arnold had dropped by her dressing room Sunday night "for a closer look at her wares," as he put it, and he'd asked a couple of questions to see just how kinky she was willing to be. Seeing the delight on his face at her answers, she wondered if maybe at ten thousand she hadn't sold out too cheap. Of course, they still hadn't settled on how many times she'd have to do them for that. Hatred could only make a girl do so much.

Manuela entered her room, dumped her tips on the dressing table and mopped herself with a towel. People had no idea what hard work it was to dance under hot lights. One girl who'd done a little professional wrestling said it was a toss-up which was worse. Sitting, she began to smooth out the bills that had been thrust upon her by her adoring fans, when there was a knock on her door. "Who is it?"

"It's Arnold."

Manuela rolled her eyes. "God, not again," she muttered under her breath. "Just a second," she called.

Grabbing the little silk dressing gown lying on the chair, she slipped it on, cinching it around her waist nice and tight. Then she stashed her tip money in her drawer and opened the door. Arnold O'Gill, who the girls called "Dumbo," stood there, filling the door and half the hallway. Arnold had one of those kid haircuts, shaved on the sides and long on the top with a little blond pigtail down the back. It looked ridiculous considering two girls holding hands could barely reach around his belly. At least Mike looked like a normal fat guy.

"Hi, Arnold, what's up?"

He grinned and grabbed his crotch. "The same as always, but that's not why I'm here. There's some jerk-off at the back door asking to see you. Says he's your brother."

"Angel?"

"He didn't say his name. But the sonovabitch's got blood splattered all over the front of him. I told him to get

his ass out of here, and he got all pissy claiming there was
a family emergency. Then he told me I better ask you to
come talk to him unless I wanted my balls cut off. I was
on my way up front to call the cops, but then I thought
maybe I should check with you first, just in case.''

"Yeah, it sounds like my fucking brother, all right.
Maybe I should talk to him.''

"Okay, fine, but I don't want the sonovabitch in here.
Mike would have a shit-fit.''

"Don't worry, I'll step outside. My mother's sick, you
know.''

"She must be a fucking hemophiliac.''

Squeezing past Arnold, Manuela went down the hall and
around the corner to the stage entrance, which was basically an emergency exit accessing a closed-off parking
area where the girls left their cars. The access was on a
side street, which meant they didn't have to drive past
customers when arriving or leaving the club.

Manuela pushed the bar on the door and shoved it open.
Angel stood maybe twenty feet away, just beyond the circle of light from the lamp over the door, smoking a cigarette. She stepped out on the little concrete porch, easing
the door closed gently so that it wouldn't catch and lock
her out. Seeing her, Angel flicked the cigarette across the
asphalt parking lot and came walking toward her with his
usual swagger.

When he got close, Manuela could see the blood, but it
wasn't from a wound like last time. It looked like it had
been splattered on him.

"What happened?" she asked.

"Never mind what happened. I need some bread and I
need it fast.''

Manuela pulled the little silk wrap closed at her throat.
There was a light breeze, but it wasn't cold. The temperature was actually balmy, but Angel being close to her was

chilling, especially when he had that sound of desperation in his voice.

"Do I look like I have money on me? I'm almost naked, Angel. I'm working."

"Can you get some scratch? I need to lay low for a while."

"What did you do?"

Angel groaned, looked up at the dark sky and said, "I fucking shot a cop."

"You *what?*"

"Can't you hear? I fucking shot a cop. The stupid asshole stopped me and because I got no license he starts shoving me up against the car and all that shit. Pissed me off. So I wasted the fucker."

"With what?"

"His fucking gun, what do you think?"

"Jesus, Angel. You shoot a cop, you're dead meat."

"Don't you think I know that? That's why I need some bread. There could be witnesses. I can't go home. I gotta find a place to hang."

A siren sounded up the street, but it went on by the club. Manuela looked around, shivering. "Sounds to me like you got to get out of town."

"Right, but for that I need serious dough. When can you get that ten thousand?"

"Angel, the party's not until Friday. I can't get it before that, and maybe not even then. Me and Mike have only sort of agreed."

"Can't you do something to speed things up?"

"How am I supposed to do that?"

"Maybe they'll fuck you now instead of then."

"Jesus, Angel."

"What? I'm kind of desperate here."

"Yeah, well, aren't you forgetting something?"

"Like what?"

Manuela looked around, lowering her voice. "Like you're supposed to do Mac and his girlfriend for me. You think I'm going to fuck a couple of elephants for three months so that you can take a vacation in Mexico?"

Angel hit her with lighting quickness, the blow snapping her head to the side and knocking her against the door, causing it to slam shut. Fortunately, he hit her with an open hand, stinging her rather than breaking her jaw. She wasn't so much in pain as shock. Worst of all, she was locked out, wearing nothing but a tiny silk robe.

"Dammit, Angel, why'd you go and do that? My key's in my purse inside. Now I've got to ring the bell." Wanting to get the hell away from him, she pressed on the bell, hoping somebody would let her in quick, before her crazy brother really lost it.

"Hey, Manuela," he said, taking her arm, his voice suddenly softer. "I'm sorry. I shouldn't have done that."

"Fucking right you shouldn't have done that."

"No, really, I'm sorry. But you gotta understand. They catch me, they execute me, no question about it."

She punched the bell again. "Maybe you should have thought about that before you shot the cop."

"Please, Manuela, I'm begging you. I don't got nobody but you."

She gave him a contemptuous look. But she also knew she didn't have anybody but him, either. Not if she wanted to get Mac and the bitch cop.

The door opened then. Arnold looked out.

"What's going on?"

"Sorry, Arnold," she said. "The door accidentally closed and my key's inside."

"You all right?"

"Yeah, our mother's had an attack, but it's not too serious. I'm coming back in after a minute."

Arnold tried to see past her, but Manuela kept the door

from opening wide. Angel had moved behind it and out of Arnold's line of sight. Mike's beefy brother looked skeptical.

"You sure everything's okay?"

"Honest, nothing's wrong except my poor mother. My brother's got to buy her some medicine and I left my purse in my dressing room. Could I borrow a couple hundred from you for five minutes, Arnold? I'll pay you back as soon as I get back inside."

Arnold O'Gill struggled to get his wallet from his hip pocket. He peered inside it. "All I've got is a hundred and sixty."

"That's fine. I'll pay you back in a minute."

Arnold stuck the money out and Manuela took it. She smiled at him.

"Want to wait in my dressing room? Maybe we can talk."

The suggestion brought a grin. "Yeah, sure."

Arnold left and Manuela eased the door back so it wouldn't catch.

"Sonovabitch will probably expect a blow job." She turned to her brother. "Here."

He took the money from her. "You're a saint, Manuela."

"Yeah, well, fuck that. Listen to me, Angel. You gotta get your ass out of L.A. I know you need money to do that, so I'm going to see what I can do about getting it for you. Maybe Mike and Arnold will agree to a private party before Friday night. But I ain't doing it out of the kindness of my heart. You gotta help me if I'm going to help you."

"How?"

"Knock off the bitch cop, Jade. And don't wait for the money. Do it now to show your good faith. As soon as I get the money from Mike, you do Mac and I pay you the ten thousand. Then it's adios."

Angel looked at the money in his hand. "I guess I could do that, but I sure could use a little more scratch in the meantime."

"So take it out of the bitch's purse."

Angel shook his head. "You're a ball buster, Manuela."

"Why shouldn't I be? It don't look like I'm ever going to be somebody's wife."

With that, she went inside, letting the door slam in her brother's face.

Tuesday, August 29, 2000

Pacific Palisades

When Venita Kumar awoke, Troy Hampton was sitting up in bed next to her, reading the paper, specifically the comic strips. He was nude. "Well, if it isn't Sleeping Beauty," he said.

His admiring tone made her smile, though she hadn't exactly awakened in a cheery mood. Her dreams had been dreadful and dark. "You're up early, my little duck."

"I fell asleep early."

"Why is that?"

"I had the lay of my life."

"You say that every time."

"It's true every time."

Venita lay back on the pillow, resting her hand on his thigh. Another day, yet still no police. The whole situation was perplexing, and she'd given up trying to understand. Troy, on the other hand, had been very upbeat all evening and it seemed to carry into the morning. He'd acted as though he had millions in his checking account, even though he'd refused to elaborate on what he was up to. She wasn't quite sure whether to take what he said on faith or if she should be skeptical. Given how tenuous her future had become, she'd ended up following the course of least resistance and let things flow, focusing on Troy's libido. Sex, she'd found, was an effective distraction.

"By the way," he said, "there was something in the paper this morning that might interest you."

"What?"

Troy reached over to the pile of newspapers on the side of the bed. Pulling out the metro section, he handed it to her. "Second page, bottom right side," he said.

Venita sat up and opened the section, wondering what he could be referring to. Then, seeing a picture of Percy Gaylord, his face battered and bruised, one eye swollen shut, she just about choked. The headline read, Amnesiac Found. She read the text:

Early Monday morning a man in an amnesiac state was found wandering through an exclusive neighborhood in West Los Angeles. Police say the man, who appeared to have been beaten or fallen, was unable to give his name or say what had happened to him.

Residents of Pacific Palisades spotted the man, bleeding badly from his wounds, staggering down the middle of Northfield Street, south of Sunset Boulevard. Police and an ambulance were called. Melody Craig, spokesperson at St. John's Hospital, said the man had suffered several serious cuts and contusions, a broken arm and two broken ribs, as well as a severe concussion. His injuries are not considered life-threatening, though doctors expressed concern about the possible long-term effects of the victim's head injury.

The man, who police say carried no identification, had a camera slung over his shoulder and his clothing was badly torn. Officer Raymond Walcott of the Los Angeles Police Department said the man spoke with a "distinctive British accent," but was unable to give his name, where he lived or explain how he had received his injuries.

The victim, described as in his late thirties or early forties is dark-complected, perhaps South Asian in origin, medium height and build, wearing a gray suit when he was found. A monogrammed handkerchief with the initials "P.G.," a few coins and a map of Santa Monica were all that was found in his clothing.

Craig indicated that the attending physicians consider it likely the victim will recover his memory sometime in the next few days or weeks, indicating that amnesic episodes are not uncommon following a traumatic head injury of the type suffered by the victim. Police, using evidence found on the victim's person, hope to determine his identity and possible clues to the cause of his injuries. Anyone having information about the victim or the circumstances of his injuries are asked to call the Los Angeles Police Department at 555-3400.

"My God," Venita said, putting the paper aside. She drew her knees up to her chest and hugged them. She was facing a ticking bomb. Once Percy recovered his memory he would tell the authorities what had happened and she'd be cooked. Lord, this was worse than if he'd died. Before, they could only speculate on the cause of a death. Now there'd be an accuser.

"What are you going to do?" he asked.

She looked at him. "What do you mean?"

"If Gaylord tells the cops you shoved him, things could get pretty hairy."

Her mouth dropped open. "Troy..."

A grin slowly formed on his face. "You have no secrets from me, Venita."

"You saw," she stammered.

"Yeah, from the little room across the hall."

"Why didn't you say something?"

"Why should I?"

"But..."

"You're wondering what I think of you."

She swallowed hard. "I suppose I am."

"I don't know what the guy said, but my guess is he was threatening you in some way."

"Yes. It was about Ramda Bol, that political business in Delhi."

"That's what I figured. Gaylord's a shit disturber. You go around upsetting people's applecarts, things happen."

Venita studied him. "You seem rather placid about the whole thing."

"I assume you know what you're doing. Besides, your problems are my problems, Venita. We've both got a lot at stake."

"Troy, the fact is, he was threatening to destroy me. And he had the means. I really had no choice."

Troy stroked his chin. "So, what are you going to do now?"

"That's the problem."

"I hope you've got a solution because I was counting on you being here for me."

She took his arm, looking earnestly into his eyes. "Be assured, I'm going to make this film whatever it takes. No one is going to stop me."

He chuckled. "I guess you've proven that. At least to Gaylord."

"I'll come up with something," she said, laying her finger aside her cheek. "Percy Gaylord is a pragmatist above all else. I'll simply have to find a way to make amends."

"You do that and I'll take my hat off to you."

She somehow managed a smile. "I'm more resourceful than you might think."

"I wouldn't bet against you. But I've got work of my own. While you take care of Percy, I'll concentrate on getting the money."

She took heart, feeling profound relief. Troy, having seen what had happened, could have posed another problem. But the boy was proving more of a man than she thought.

"There's something else I've been meaning to discuss with you," he said.

She rubbed the palm of his hand with her own. "What's that, love?"

"What would you think of the idea of you and me getting married?"

"Married? Troy, are you serious?"

"Of course I am."

"But why? I mean, why now? Isn't this kind of sudden?"

"Are you saying you don't feel that way about me?"

Venita knew she had to choose her words carefully. "No, that's not what I'm saying at all. It's just...well, I hadn't expected anything so dramatic this soon."

"I think you know how I feel about you, Venita. You turn me on like...well, you know your way around the bedroom like nobody I've ever known."

"You're wonderful inspiration," she said, touching his cheek.

"Percy's not the only pragmatist. The way I see it, you and I have got a lot more in common than fucking for pleasure. We're going to be making films together. And, well, to be blunt, I need you. But you also need me. One thing is Mac's money, but another is...hell, why beat around the bush...I know some pretty damning things. And maybe you didn't know this, but in the States they can't make a husband testify against his wife. And vice versa, of course.''

"What are you saying?''

"We've got pretty damn good reasons to join forces. That's the practical side of me talking.'' He ran his hand up her leg, letting it rest on her mound. "Then, there's the amorous side.'' Grinning, he leaned over and kissed her on the corner of the mouth. "Don't mean to tell you your business, Venita, but you better get hopping with Gaylord. If that fucker wakes up and starts pointing fingers, you're in deep doo-doo.''

"You're right, of course,'' she said, swinging her legs off the bed. "It's a matter requiring urgent attention.''

She went off to have her shower, marveling. Troy had proposed marriage, all the while threatening blackmail. He'd offered her millions, while informing her the executioner's ax was about to fall. He'd completely wrested control, leaving her beholden. What unstated agendas did the boy have? she wondered.

Climbing into the shower, she resolved to take care of Troy Hampton in due course. The more pressing concern was Percy Gaylord. By surviving, he'd driven yet another stake in her heart, proving the unlikely—there were still worse fates than being a murderess.

Studio City

Mac felt like the proverbial million dollars. His step was lighter than it had been in years. He'd hummed along with the radio as he'd driven to work. Even Bev noticed a difference. When she brought him his coffee, she said, "What's with you this morning?''

"Some days a guy just feels on top of the world,'' he replied. "What can I say?''

He wasn't going to tell Bev that it was because of Jade.

He was too old for adolescent silliness. Plus, he was the boss of a major business enterprise. A guy in his shoes didn't get sappy over a young woman fourteen years his junior. But, of course, that is exactly what had happened—the part about feeling lighthearted, anyway. Beyond that, he took his euphoria with a grain of salt, knowing somebody with his problems was prone to grasping at straws. It was simple infatuation and he knew it.

Over the years he'd met women he was drawn to, he'd met women he respected and admired. He'd met smart women, attractive women, and one or two he could conceivably marry. But Jade was the first one who'd made him happy right down to his bones.

He couldn't say why, beyond the fact that she was a real person, a genuine, decent human being. Cute, yes. Sexy, yes. Crazy, eccentric and fun—yes, yes and yes. Did it mean anything? He had no idea, but he guessed that it didn't. Why? Because Mac was grown up, he was a serious person, and he knew reality was always twenty to thirty percent less than what it appeared. Always. But what the heck, he was having a good time. Without even trying. The without-even-trying part was key.

"I make you think of peanut butter and jelly sandwiches?" she'd said the previous evening. He'd confessed that as they'd eaten the snack dinner at her kitchen table.

"Yes, and don't ask me why."

"Well, is the reason good or bad?" she'd asked.

"Oh, definitely good."

"Why is it good?"

He had a hard time answering her. "I think because you make me think of happier times."

"Like your childhood?"

"Yes."

"God, that was the most miserable part of my life. I hated being a kid."

"But you like being an adult."

"Sometimes I'm not sure I do," she replied with an embarrassed grin.

After more conversation they'd decided that maybe Jade was only now coming to terms with her inner child, while Mac was lamenting the loss of his.

"We're a pathetic pair," she'd said, but Mac didn't agree at all.

He couldn't tell her what he was thinking, which was that he felt they made a pretty interesting couple—unlikely, but interesting. Jade, he could tell, was skittish and had little or no conscious interest in being anything more than friends.

Mac remained grounded enough that he wouldn't allow himself to be carried away by the fun of their friendship, though. He knew nothing of consequence was likely to come of it, though the titillation was nice. For them both, as best he could tell. But he couldn't muse about her all day. In an attempt to find some semblance of normalcy, he busied himself with routine tasks, going over the P&Ls, reviewing job lists.

It was while he was going over the list of new contracts that he noticed a familiar address in Brentwood—Stella and Aubrey's old place. Seeing it, his stomach dropped.

Mac picked up the phone and got hold of Walt Matthews, who ran the construction operation. "Where'd we pick up this job in Brentwood?" he asked.

"Let me check with sales, Mac. I'll get back to you."

Mac waited, drumming his fingers on the huge mahogany executive desk, getting up and going to the window, pacing until the phone rang. It was Bev.

"Your wife's on line three. You want to talk to her?"

He was tempted to have Bev tell Stella he'd call her back, but he didn't want her to think he was giving her the runaround. These days Stella's state of mind was as important as just about everything else he had going. "I'll take it." Mac punched the button. "What's up?"

"Mac, there's been a very serious development. We need to talk."

He considered that. "Can you give me a hint what you're talking about?"

"No, I'd like to discuss it with you face-to-face. Believe me, you'd prefer it that way, if you knew."

"Stella, if it's hand-holding you want, then—"

"It's not hand-holding," she snapped.

"Then what?"

"All right, if you must know, Jaime Caldron came by the house yesterday and we need to discuss it. Satisfied?"

Mac knew that was all he'd get. "Okay, this evening okay?"

"How about meeting for lunch?"

He took a quick look at his calendar. "I guess I can. Do you mind coming out here? I've got a full afternoon."

"Fine. Shall I come to your office?"

"Okay, we can go someplace from here."

"Noon?"

"Noon will work."

"See you then, Mac."

He hung up wondering what the hell Caldron had done. Judging by the edge to Stella's voice, and her snappishness, he'd done something.

Not thirty seconds passed before his intercom line buzzed. Bev told him it was Walt Matthews. He punched the button.

"Yeah, Walt."

"Johnny said it was a call-in. People named Kellerman. Job's scheduled to begin next week."

Mac, suspecting as much, thought for a second. "I'll want to talk to you about that before you assign a crew, Walt. Flag that one."

"Mind if I ask what's up, boss?"

"I built the existing pool. One of my early jobs in the business. I'd like a firsthand look."

"You got it, Mac."

After hanging up, Mac put his head in his hands. A week. God, how was he going to get around this? Apparently Glamour Puss felt he'd been in the ground long enough. Mac had a sudden feeling of dread. He sensed that everything was coming to a head. He'd been bobbing and weaving, but he couldn't avoid taking a few punches on the chin forever. Somebody was bound to connect, and it probably would be Jaime Caldron.

Santa Monica

Venita had decided to meet her destiny head-on. If that bloody mercenary who called himself a journalist had regained his memory and was prepared to accuse her, she might as well be there to do what she could to mitigate the damage, even if it was nothing more than buying enough time to get on the first plane out of the country.

There was no certainty she would be arrested and prosecuted, regardless of what Percy might say, because it would be her word against his. But the notoriety and hoopla would spell the end of her Hollywood venture. Troy and his supposed millions would hardly matter at that point.

Troy's newfound self-assurance had come as almost as great a surprise as Percy rising from the dead. Over a few days, the boy had discovered his manhood. Even his sexuality had changed qualitatively.

She'd been washing her hair in the shower that morning when Troy entered the stall. At first he'd caressed her breasts and nibbled at her ears, his sex rising hard against her backside. But then with a sudden desire to overwhelm her, he'd forced her to bend over and, while she supported herself with her hands on the stool, he vigorously took her from behind, ramming into her with the angry urgency of a conqueror.

That, at times, was the male way. Venita knew from experience that it could be as instinctual as it was intentional. And if a woman was in the right mood, it could be powerfully erotic. But it always made a statement. And the statement was, "I'm in charge."

Men needed to prove that the way they needed food and water, she supposed, considering how often she'd seen it. Sometimes the outburst came when a woman was at her strongest, sometimes at her weakest, but always when a man needed to feel his strength. In the case of a young man, it could be a rite of passage. But what they sometimes failed to learn was that with power came responsibility. Invariably the one who suffered most with such a failing was the woman.

The other key lesson Venita had learned was that a woman could surrender to a man's power, but she could never cede her own. Her affair with Ramda Bol was the perfect example of why that was true.

When the limousine came to a stop at the entrance of St. John's Hospital, she focused her thoughts on Percy. There was no way to know what she would find waiting for her. With any luck at all, he would be mentally deranged for the rest of his life, or at the very least, unable to recall that she'd shoved him over the wall. But obviously, she couldn't count on either outcome. No, she had to be prepared for him to recover his memory, if he hadn't already.

Inside, the receptionist told them that if they wished to see Percy, they'd have to speak with the attending physician, Dr. Yee. A guard from hospital security, a bald, potbellied man of fifty who was otherwise slim, accompanied them to the doctor's office.

Yee was Asian, short of stature, with thick glasses and unruly spikes of black hair. He received them in his office wearing a starched lab coat that was a bit too large, making him look like a child in a snowsuit. After shaking their hands, he settled into his high-back brown leather desk chair.

"So, you think you may know the identity of our patient," the doctor said.

"We saw the picture in the paper," Venita replied. "There's something of a resemblance to my cousin, Girish, though with the injuries, it was difficult to tell."

"Your cousin is missing, is he?"

"He's been living in Canada for several years. Two weeks ago he headed for the States and nobody's heard from him. We thought your patient might be Girish."

"I'll take you to see him in a minute. A few words, first. I'd like to ask you to let him react to you. If it is your cousin, you can tell me quietly. Don't embrace him unless and until he recognizes you. The face of a family member is often the trigger that brings memory flooding back. Amnesiacs are in a fragile state, for the most part. Whatever we do, we'll want to do gently. If the patient is not your cousin, you'll be simply another of the many strange faces he's seen the past few days. Do you have any questions?"

"Will I be able to speak with him?"

"We'll see how he reacts to you. Even if he is not your cousin, he may show interest because you're a countryman. We believe our patient is South Asian."

"Has he recalled anything at all, Doctor?"

"Mostly vague impressions. We know he has strong ties with England, perhaps having lived there, judging by his speech and his comments. Is that consistent with your cousin's background?''

''Yes, Girish attended university in Britain.''

''Perhaps we have our man, then.''

''I'm surprised the authorities haven't been able to make an identification if the patient is here on holiday. Presumably he obtained a visa.''

''The police, I understand, are working with Customs and Immigration, but it's been slow going. My immediate concern is the patient's health, however,'' the doctor said. ''He's obviously had a traumatic experience of some sort, something his mind is repressing. As I say, we'll go in to see him together. Is the gentleman here also a possible relative?'' Yee asked, indicating Jugnu.

''No, Mr. Singh is my employee.''

''I see. Well, perhaps you and I will see the patient alone, then. Shall we go?''

Venita and Jugnu went with the doctor. The security guard, who'd waited outside the office, went with them down the hallway. Yee asked Jugnu to wait in a small room and took Venita to the door of a patient room. The guard waited outside.

Her insides churned anxiously as Yee opened the door. She took a deep breath. Yee stepped aside to allow her to enter.

Percy lay in a hospital bed, his head and torso and arm heavily bandaged. She could only see him in profile as his head was turned toward the window.

''Hello,'' Yee said, his voice chipper. ''I've brought a visitor.''

Percy looked in their direction, only one eye appearing sufficiently open to see them well. His gaze was blank. There was no special reaction.

Venita slowly exhaled.

''What do you think?'' Yee said to her under his breath.

"No, I'm sorry, I don't believe that's Girish," she whispered.

Yee went to the bed. He put his hand on Percy's shoulder. "This lady came to say hello. Would you care to chat with her?"

"I don't mind," Percy replied.

Yee signaled for her to approach the bed. Venita moved closer. "Hello," she said cheerily. "I read in the paper you were in hospital and thought I'd pop in to see how you're doing."

"Not so well, I'm afraid. Can't recall a bloody thing. Not even my name."

"I'm sure you'll get better in due course."

Percy looked at her carefully. Venita thought she saw twinges of recognition. If so, they were deep in the recesses of his mind. She could tell by the slight frown on his face he was struggling to grasp the elusive thread of recognition. She could imagine how frustrated he must be. But at the same time she was grateful. He could just as easily have flashed on the incident in her garden, his horror growing as it all came rushing back. But there was no agitation, no cursing, only a prickle of curiosity and struggle.

"You're Indian, then," he said.

"Yes."

"Do you know who the bloody hell I am?"

"You look very much like my cousin," she said. "But you aren't Girish."

"Girish," Percy said. "No, that can't be me." He scrutinized her. "There's something about you, as well...I can't quite say what."

"Perhaps you'd enjoy talking with the lady for a while," Yee said. "Would you like that?"

"Yes," Percy said. "I rather would."

Yee addressed her. "Do you mind spending a few minutes with my patient?"

"Not at all. I'd enjoy it."

"I'll be back shortly, then," Yee said. "Give you a little time to chat." He brought a chair over for her. Smiling at them both, he left the room.

"Well, then," Venita said, "I look somewhat familiar, do I?"

"Yes, a little. What's your name?"

"Venita."

Percy pondered that, grimacing slightly.

"It could be that we do know each other," she said. "If I'm right, there's not much that can be said until you recover your memory. Your recollections may not be the most pleasant, but don't despair. The news won't be all bad." She reached into the pocket of her under blouse and removed a small envelope, which she handed to him.

"What's this?"

"A message for you, when you recover your memory. It won't mean anything to you now, but it will then. Be sure and read it before you do anything else."

He had an uncertain look.

"But no need to worry," Venita said. "Nothing urgent. Just relax. These people seem to be taking good care of you. I assure you there's no hurry."

Percy looked like he was struggling to pull a niggling thread from his memory. "You know who I am, don't you?"

"Let's just say time will answer that question. And now I must go. Rest well. And above all, don't worry."

As she got up, Dr. Yee stuck his head in the door. "How are we doing here?"

"We've had a nice little chat, Doctor," Venita said. "The only thing that might have been better is if this had been my cousin, Girish."

"I predict it won't be much longer until he regains full memory," Yee said with an approving smile.

Percy, for his part, looked perplexed, perhaps a bit bewildered. Venita was relieved. This could have been a disaster. As it was, she'd bought herself some time, maybe even gotten herself some much-needed insurance.

She shook hands with the doctor.

"Is there a way we can reach you?" he asked.

"Why don't I call you, Doctor? I'll want to check regularly to see how your patient is doing. Ta-ta!"

With that, she went off to find Jugnu.

Studio City

"A lady for you on line two, Mac," Bev said on the intercom line.

"What lady?"

"She wouldn't give her name, but said it was an urgent personal matter. Sounded young, if that means anything."

Mac couldn't imagine. "Okay, I'll take it." He pushed the button. "McGowan."

"Mr. McGowan, I know what happened to Aubrey St. George in Brentwood in his pool house twenty years ago. I'm going to tell the police and the *Los Angeles Times* unless you'd like to convince me I shouldn't."

Mac stopped breathing. What the hell was this? Stella's idea of a joke? No, she wouldn't joke about Aubrey. "Who is this?"

"It doesn't matter who it is. Are you interested in hearing how you can keep the story buried forever?"

His mind reeled. Who the hell…

"Mr. McGowan?"

"Yeah, sure. How?"

"Meet me on the upper-level observation deck at the Getty Center tomorrow at noon. The southeast corner overlooking Westwood. If you involve the police, my associates will release the story. Cooperate and the problem will go away. Do you understand, Mr. McGowan?''

''I hear what you're saying.''

''Listen very carefully. I want you to be at the railing, looking at Westwood. I'll come up next to you. Don't look at me. Keep your eyes on the view. We'll talk about solving your problem. If you look at me, it's all over. Don't fuck with me, Mr. McGowan. This is dead serious. Do you understand?''

''Yes.''

''I'll see you tomorrow at noon.''

The line went dead. Mac slipped the receiver back in the cradle. He rubbed his chin, staring out the window of his office as his heart thumped wildly. God, he decided, had a very strange sense of humor.

West Hollywood

Angel couldn't decide if the bitch was inside or not. He'd been sitting there, a couple of doors up the street from her place, for an hour, and he hadn't seen any sign of her. Maybe she'd gone before he got there, or maybe she was still inside. One thing for sure, he couldn't sit around all day waiting for her. Somebody might notice him and get suspicious.

The car he had was stolen. The Chevy he'd been driving was too hot, especially with a million cops looking for him. Angel knew he ought to be in Mexico, but there was no point in going without money to live on. He sure as hell wasn't going to spend the next ten years herding goats.

Everything now depended on Manuela and whether she could get the ten thousand out of those cocksuckers at the club. He'd called her from a pay phone, and when she answered she said, ''You done what I asked yet?''

"No, but I'm working on it."

"Do it," she said.

"I will, I will. How's it coming with the ten?"

"I don't know nothing yet. I'll know more tonight. I'll call you later." Then she hung up.

Angel wasn't feeling so good about things. His fucking sister had him by the balls, but he couldn't do anything about it but kiss her ass. Which really pissed him off. But he didn't have no other choice. He could knock over a liquor store and that might be good for two or three hundred, but what was that going to get him? A few tanks of gas, a room for a night, a broad maybe and a couple of cases of beer. Then what?

Just then the front door of the bitch's pad opened and out she came pushing a bike. A bike? She had on bike shorts, the helmet, the top, the whole number. What was this?

The next thing he knew, she out in the street and heading right toward him. Angel picked up the newspaper with the story about the cop he'd shot, hiding his face behind it as she zipped by. The bitch didn't seem to notice. She was going up the street like she really meant business.

Angel got the car started, though it took a few seconds because he was out of practice with hot wiring. By the time he got the fucker going and turned around, the bitch cop was already two blocks up the street. He hurried after her, wondering if he could just run her down with his car, or if he was better off shooting her. Of course, if he ran her down, he could always get out and pump a couple of rounds in her, just to make sure.

The bitch turned, disappearing down a side street. Angel stepped hard on the accelerator, sailing right through a stop sign. By the time he got to the corner where she turned, she'd gone another block and was turning again. Christ. Punching the gas pedal, he quickly reached the next intersection. Another stop sign. He ignored it, which proved to be a bad mistake. He was halfway across the street when a van coming the other way bashed right into his right front fender, spinning him like a top so he was sitting ass backward in the middle of the intersection.

For a moment Angel sat there in a daze. But he wasn't really hurt. Opening the car door he got out and looked over the top of the car at the driver of the van, an old fart with a gray beard and ponytail. He looked at Angel sort of cross-eyed, a little trickle of blood running down the side of his face.

Angel looked down the street in the direction Jade Morro had gone. She wasn't even in sight. Christ. He kicked the fender of his stolen car and glared over at the driver of the van. "Asshole!"

"Hey, you went right through that stop sign," the guy stammered.

"Fuck you!" Angel screamed at him.

The old guy looked bewildered. Angel reached in his car and got the gun out from under the seat. He had a notion to walk over and waste the sonovabitch, but decided against it. He didn't have any extra bullets.

Instead he crammed the gun under the band of his pants, pulled his shirt out over it and walked away. There'd be cops in a few minutes, so he couldn't fart around. As he reached the next street, a bus came along and stopped to pick up a woman with a kid. Angel jogged over and clambered onto the bus after them.

He sat down near the rear door and decided he needed a new approach. Maybe he'd go to East L.A. and find a chico with a gun, maybe some guy looking for drug money. Sometimes the best way was muscle. Break down her front door, find her and waste her. This following people around was for the birds.

Angel got off at the next stop and went looking for

another car to steal. Christ, he hoped he wasn't going to all this trouble for nothing. There was no way to be sure his fucking sister would come through.

Studio City

Stella called Mac from her car phone as she sat out front to say that she'd arrived. He imagined that she didn't want to be seen coming to his office two days running for fear she would look desperate, though he couldn't imagine how she'd care what his employees thought. The fact that she had come to see him two days in a row gave him pause for thought, though. And, as the morning wore on and he reflected on the situation, he'd grown concerned. Jaime Caldron must have put the fear of God in her.

His wife lowered the window as he came out. "Would you mind driving your own car, so I don't have to bring you back?" she asked without ceremony. "I'll want to leave directly from the restaurant."

"No problem."

"You lead the way."

Mac got in the Lexus and drove out of the lot, with Stella right behind him. He saw no reason to put on the dog when the principal objective was conversation, so he went to a large upscale coffee shop called Harvey's located over on Colfax, a place he appreciated for the apple pie, if nothing else. They got a window booth at the end with relative privacy.

Stella was surprisingly dour—he might have said petulant, except that she'd hardly said a word. Mac was beginning to get a funny feeling.

His wife was dressed in simple linen pants and top. Minimal jewelry. Understated. Somehow that also struck him as a bad sign.

The waitress was there immediately. Stella ordered a

salad, Mac the soup-and-sandwich special. They each had iced tea. Little was said until their drinks came. Stella spent a lot of time looking out the window next to them. She seemed wistful yet nervous. Mac knew something was up.

He grew impatient with her obfuscation. "So, what's with Caldron, Stella?"

"Before we get into that, I want to ask you something. What are the chances of you investing in Amal's project?"

Mac eyed her, not liking the juxtaposition of his question and hers. "Nil," he said. "I think I've made my position clear."

She grimaced. "I was afraid you'd say that."

"You couldn't have expected otherwise."

"No, you're nothing if not consistent, Mac."

"So, what's going on? Caldron putting pressure on you?"

Stella took a drink of tea, setting the glass down carefully on the paper coaster. "He made me an offer, Mac."

There was something ominous in her tone. He sensed a dramatic announcement coming. Or a threat. "What kind of offer?"

"If I testify against you, they go light on me."

Mac had a bad feeling. "And you said…"

She lowered her voice. "I told him there was nothing to testify about, that you didn't kill Aubrey."

He was relieved.

"But Caldron told me something very distressing, Mac. He said they're tearing out the pool and he plans to be there when they do. He knows."

"I already know about the pool," Mac said. "We're building the new one."

"What are we going to do?"

"I'm thinking about that. Since I'm involved, I've got some control."

She ran her finger down the side of the glass, looking very unhappy. "We're in the most danger we've been in since '78."

"Yes, I know."

"Caldron's making it very easy for me, Mac," she said.

That gave him pause. "What are you trying to say?"

"I need a good reason not to save my own neck," she said.

He stared at her, seeing clearly now what she was getting at. "Spit it out, Stella."

"I was hoping you'd want to invest with Amal for Troy's sake and for mine. Unfortunately, you've chosen not to, which is within your right, of course. But if you're going to look out for yourself, why shouldn't I, Mac?"

He hesitated for a good long time, looking her in the eye. "You're saying you want me to make it worth your while not to cooperate with Caldron. You want me to buy you off. Two million for your silence. Is that it?"

"It's asking a lot of me to stand by you, possibly go to prison for you, when you're not even willing to help Troy and me by making an investment you can easily afford."

"That's extortion, Stella."

"No, it's asking why this is a one-way street."

He flushed. "Need I remind you we're in this together and have been for twenty years? And it's not like any of this was my idea to begin with. You were the one who insisted we not go to the police. This whole thing would have been over and behind us if we'd done the right thing from the beginning."

The waitress came with their lunches. Mac and Stella sat in stony silence until she was gone.

"Aren't you forgetting something, Mac?" Stella said as soon as the waitress was beyond hearing. "Who killed Aubrey?"

"It was unintentional," he said in a low, angry tone.

"But the facts are the facts, and Jaime Caldron is giving me a very easy way to spare myself a lot of grief. All I'm asking is that you give me a damn good reason to lie for you, Mac."

"Let's call a spade a spade. You want me to buy you off."

Her eyes filled, shimmering with emotion. "I've got one last chance. I don't want to lose it."

"And you'll stop at nothing."

"I want to be in that film," she said through her teeth, resolute, determined. "And I will be, one way or another."

"I guess our marriage has been reduced to its essence, hasn't it, Stella? Two million. That's what it's come to."

"If you insist, Mac, then yes, it has."

Mac McGowan looked down at the food he hadn't touched. He not only had lost his appetite, he was disgusted to the point of nausea. Then, looking Stella in the eye, he said, "I guess I'm going to have to think about this." He slid out of the booth, took out his wallet and dropped a twenty-dollar bill on the table. "Oh, and by the way, you're not the only one after my money. I had an anonymous call from some woman this morning. She wants to blackmail me, too."

Stella looked genuinely surprised. "About Aubrey?"

"Yes, about Aubrey. Looks like you've got competition. Either that or questionable friends." With that, he turned and walked from the restaurant.

West Hollywood

Jade had ridden extra far that morning, probably double what she should have, but whenever she was anxious she tended to do that—overexercise. Some people ate, others got reclusive or slovenly or depressed. Jade just got an overwhelming urge to burn calories.

It was because of Mac McGowan. Something had happened the previous evening as they'd sat in her kitchen having a silly conversation about peanut butter and jelly sandwiches and their childhoods. Jade realized they were having a relationship. Not a big relationship in the sense of dramatic happenings. A small one, small in the sense of a feeling of togetherness, rapport.

It wasn't a date even, but they'd been together. That hadn't happened since Ricky. Some things about it were nice, but it also made her uncomfortable because she wasn't sure what it meant. She was also afraid—afraid it was somehow connected to Ricky. After all, Mac had walked in on the heels of Ricky Santos's final departure. Maybe what she was feeling toward Mac was a reaction to that. Getting involved with someone when on the rebound was always dangerous. Her mother had done that time and time again, sometimes finding the next guy before the bruises from the last guy had healed.

As Jade poked at the bowl of soup in front of her, the telephone rang. It was Mac. A twinge of nervous happiness went through her at the sound of his voice. He didn't spend long on pleasantries.

"Things seem to be coming unraveled fast," he said.

Jade listened to him describe the phone call he'd gotten from the mystery woman and his conversation with Stella over lunch. When he'd finished, she said, "Boy, you're getting it coming and going. I'm really sorry, Mac. That's got to be rough when your own wife does that to you."

"I've been thinking about it, and I'm not all that surprised. I'll give Stella one thing—her priorities have always been consistent. I guess I should consider myself fortunate that all she wants is money."

"Still…"

"So, I guess I need a plan," he said. "And frankly, you're about the only one I can turn to for advice."

"I don't think I can advise you about your wife."

"Yeah, I'll have to figure that one out, but this mystery woman, that's a whole other thing."

"I suppose you have no idea who it could be."

"I assume it's the person behind the notes. And the bad part about it is that I feel completely vulnerable, out of control. Stella and Caldron are at least known quantities. Caldron might get me yet, but I know who and what I'm dealing with. This woman, on the other hand…"

"I know what you're saying. Let me give it some thought," Jade said. "Maybe I can come up with a plan."

"We don't have the luxury of much time."

"What's your schedule like this evening? I can come by after dinner."

"How about I take you out?" he said. "Someplace nice. Seems to me I owe you. Besides, I could use a little pleasant conversation with a friend. I feel like a baby in a crib, surrounded by hungry rats."

It was a chilling metaphor, but she got his meaning. Oddly, despite her fears, the prospect of seeing Mac was not unpleasant. Maybe she even relished it. She wanted to help him, but more than that she wanted to understand him because something told her there was a key in that to understanding herself.

Santa Monica

Percy Gaylord, his head throbbing, awaited the arrival of the private investigator. Miraculously, he'd awakened from his morning nap to discover his memory had come back. It hadn't happened in a sudden flash, though. He awoke from a dream, the guy in the dream was Percy, and he was the guy. For a good ten minutes he'd lain in a sea of confusion, not altogether certain what he knew and didn't know, where dream and reality diverged, where the past and the present met.

For the longest time he struggled with the events that had gotten him where he was. Had they happened to him, or were they part of his dream? Had that been him wandering numbly through the streets? Was he the lad who'd taken the tumble off his bicycle, the young man in the auto accident with the donkey cart in Bombay, the gay blade who'd had his wallet pinched at knifepoint in Lewisham? Yes, the bits and pieces of his life were falling into place.

By the end of an hour Percy had reconstructed his trip to America and his dealings with Venita Kumar. For a while he wasn't sure if she'd come to see him in hospital or if he'd dreamed it. That was the most confounding interlude of all, even more than the murky events that had transpired in the garden of that house in the hills overlooking the ocean.

By lunch, Percy had pretty well recollected everything. And though his head ached dreadfully—the worst since he'd been in hospital—he did feel he had a grip on reality. The question was, what did he do next? Enough confusion continued to reign in his skull that he wasn't certain whether his interests were best served by consultation with the authorities or keeping his own counsel.

When the orderly had cleared away his tray, Percy again thought over the conversation he'd had with Venita, only then recalling the envelope she'd given him. Searching the drawer in the table beside his bed, he found it. Then he opened it and read her cryptic note: "Okay, you win. Spare me and I'll give you R.B.'s head on a platter." She'd simply signed it "V."

It had taken several minutes for him to sort out the full implications of the note. Venita was surrendering, she was going to give him Ramda Bol. Percy had indeed won—if Venita was to be trusted.

He realized he needed to give the meaning of that some thought. Should he proceed, it would have to be with caution. Venita Kumar was a viper. But she did hold his future in her hands and she'd offered her sword. Considering his condition, he was hardly in a position to joust with the lady. He needed a champion.

The hefty investigator, Boots Conroy, had come to mind. But Percy realized he wouldn't be able to do business with Boots without dealing first with hospital staff. And so, he'd spent the early afternoon talking to the doctors, who, as expected, immediately notified the police. A detective soon arrived to question him, but Percy had been circumspect, recalling certain things, but not others. "I'm sorry," he'd told the policeman, "the circumstances of my injury refuse to come to mind."

Eventually, they'd allowed him to rest, but he'd been permitted to ring up Boots. Now he awaited the investigator's arrival. It was time for the final, triumphal scene of this melodrama, and Boots was his man.

Holmby Hills

Soon after she arrived, Mike O'Gill had asked Manuela if she wanted some coke or a speedball or something. She'd said no, that a couple of shots of tequila was all she needed to have a good time. And so Mike got her a tumbler half full of booze.

The three of them were in the family room. Mike had a video playing on the projection TV. It was a skin flick. A black guy and a white guy were doing a Chinese girl. The sound was down low, but high enough to hear the grunting and groaning. Manuela couldn't figure out how a guy could think that seeing some chick poked and probed by two different guys at the same time would turn a woman on—unless she was into pain. Maybe one guy out of ten understood women, but probably not that many.

No, the flick was for their benefit, not hers. Arnold, seated on the sofa in a white terry robe that made him look like a polar bear, scarcely said hello when she sat down. He was busy doing a line of coke, all the while keeping one eye on the screen. Worse, he looked like he'd gained thirty pounds since yesterday. The thought was enough to make her shiver. She gulped some tequila.

"I thought maybe we could spend a little time in the spa," Mike said. "Never hurts to be relaxed."

Unconscious might even be better, Manuela thought, but she wasn't going to be snotty and say that. Mike and Arnold would have to have a good time if she was going to get the money.

Mike, not surprisingly, had driven a hard bargain. She'd have to do five threesomes with the O'Gill brothers for five thousand and the other five thousand she could pay off interest free over the course of a year. "That's not a bad deal," Mike had said. "A grand is getting up into the fancy call-girl range." What Mike didn't say and what Manuela didn't have to remind him was that there weren't many fancy call girls willing to fuck two three-hundred-pound elephants at the same time.

They'd made the date early enough in the day that Manuela could fuck the O'Gills and still get to the club for the last show, though walking would probably be a trick after doing Mike and Arnold, never mind dancing. But she'd already resolved to do it. How else, if she wanted Mac McGowan and the bitch cop dead?

"You going to tell me what you need ten G's for so urgently, Manuela?" Mike asked as he dropped down on the sofa next to her. "Or is it a secret?"

"You don't want to know, Mike."

He shrugged. "Maybe I don't."

Mike was in shorts and a flowered Hawaiian shirt. His pudgy pink feet were bare. He put one up on the coffee table, then he put his hand on her knee and glanced over at the screen, savoring the show. Manuela took another slug of tequila. Already she was starting to feel it in her head.

Now Mike was dragging his hand up the inside of her thigh as he watched the screen, sort of absently, the way somebody would pet a dog while watching a football game on TV or something.

Arnold, who was getting himself stoked, put down the little mirror he'd been using to do the line and leaned back heavily in the sofa. "So, we going to do this, or what?"

"Want to go out in the spa, then?" Mike said.

"Yeah," Manuela replied.

Mike struggled to his feet, then helped Manuela up in a gentlemanly way. Mike was at least polite. She had to say that for him. Arnold, though, looked a little crazy. He was obviously high as a kite. Mike went over to help him up, as well.

The two brothers looked at her with twin smiles. She thought, "Oh, shit," but knew it was no time to have regrets. She reminded herself how bad she wanted to get Mac McGowan, the sonovabitch who could have made her happy, but screwed her instead.

There was something a lot worse about a guy who dangled a dream in front of your nose only to jerk it away. At least the O'Gills were up front about what they were doing. She might not like fucking them, but she had to respect their honesty. Mac could learn something from them, if only not to screw around with somebody's happiness.

"You want to undress in my room or out at the spa?" Mike asked.

"In your room, if that's okay." She checked her watch. "And I'd like to make a call, if that's okay."

"Sure, no problem."

The brothers went out the slider onto the deck. Manuela grabbed her purse and headed for Mike's bedroom with its huge water bed. There was access to the deck from his room, too, so she could step out directly, without having to go back through the other rooms. Putting her purse on the bed and watching it ripple, she decided to call Angel first, before she undressed.

She got the slip of paper out of the zipper pocket in her purse and dialed the number. Angel answered on the first ring.

"Manuela?"

"Yeah, it's me. So, what happened? You do the bitch?"

"Tonight. I got everything all lined up. I'm going in her fucking door and blow her away before she knows what hit her."

"Good, Angel, that's good."

"You getting the money, then?"

"Yes, I'm getting it."

"Great."

"Don't forget, you've got to do Mac before you get it, though."

"I know. I'm going to get him first thing in the morning."

"Fine."

She looked across the room and out the slider. On the deck, but inside the protection of the privacy screen surrounding the spa, Mike and Arnold O'Gill were standing naked, Arnold testing the water with his toe. The sight of their huge bodies made her cringe.

"You want me to call and leave a message after I do the bitch?" Angel asked.

"No, I think you better not call home. Ma said the cops

have been there, so they definitely are onto you, Angel. I'll phone you at this number from the club or someplace. What's a good time?''

Outside, the O'Gills had gotten into the spa. Manuela could see that the water level was right to the top rim of the tub. She gulped more tequila, then, after taking a breath, finished off the glass. The fire in it made her shiver.

''Midnight?''

''Fine,'' Manuela said. ''I'll phone you then.''

She hung up. Then she took off her clothes, and went off to do the O'Gill brothers for a thousand dollars and the satisfaction of knowing Mac McGowan wouldn't be happy, either.

West Hollywood

With night falling, Jade found herself pacing her front room. She'd spent most of the afternoon at her kitchen table, going over the personnel files she'd gotten from Art Conti. Four of the pool maids had had prior criminal involvement with drugs, and she decided to focus her investigation there—initially, anyway. The trouble was, it had been difficult to concentrate, especially knowing that Mac's personal problem was so much more pressing. The poor guy was besieged. There were those notes, now the phone call from the mystery woman; Jaime Caldron was zeroing in on him, and his wife was threatening to turn state's evidence. And yet he was eager to take her to dinner.

''There's no guarantee I'll be able to help you, Mac,'' she'd said, concerned about the possibility of inflated expectations.

''Having dinner with me will be a big help, trust me.''

He hadn't elaborated, but the tone in his voice made her realize that his feelings for her were pretty strong. Was it simply because he was alone and under attack? The emotions of a guy in that kind of situation could be volatile. Ricky had loved her desperately, but the desperation mostly had to do with his need to share his bed. Looking back, she was able to see there wasn't much mutuality in the relationship. Instead, he'd nodded in the direction of her long-term desires in the interest of his short-term gratification. And, as Ruthie had often said, some guys just couldn't handle being alone. Was Mac one? How interested in her would he be once he was out of the woods and had his life back under control?

But what was she doing even thinking in these terms? She wasn't his girlfriend. She was his friend. Who was the needy one, anyway? The way she was obsessing, it seemed like it was more she than Mac. Jade reminded herself this was not about her so much as it was about Mac McGowan's problems and the ways she could be of help to him. Period.

After a while she started worrying about what she'd wear that evening, knowing jeans just wouldn't cut it at a nice restaurant. Probably she'd put on a good pair of pants. Or a dress. She thought of that little T-shirt dress that had turned Ricky on, wondering if she dare wear something that unsubtle with Mac. It was probably a bad idea, but the notion intrigued her enough that she decided to try it on, just to see how she looked.

Studying herself in the mirror, Jade couldn't decide if she looked sexy and feminine or like some slut trying too hard to make a statement. When the doorbell rang, she panicked, but realized it was too early for it to be Mac. She went to the front room and looked out the window, seeing Ruthie's car. Her friend, still in uniform, was on the porch, holding a little box. Jade opened the door. Ruthie looked her up and down.

"Jesus," she said. "My best friend's a transvestite."

"Very funny."

"So this is what you do when you're alone, pretend like you're a regular girl."

"Ha, ha, ha."

"Well?" Ruthie said as she entered.

"I'm going out to dinner with Mac, okay?" Jade closed the door.

"Hey, that's cool. The pool guy, right?"

"Yep."

"Well then, congratulations, girl." She handed Jade the box of chocolates in her hand.

"What's this?"

"Pampering you a little just in case you aren't pampering yourself."

"Why do I need pampering?"

"Every woman does, ditz. Hello. Anyway, you've had it rough recently, and I thought you could use a boost."

"That's really sweet of you, Ruthie."

"Besides, chocolate's an aphrodisiac, and if you've got a hot date, a few chocolates at the right moment could come in handy."

"Chocolate, an aphrodisiac?"

"That's my theory. I usually get a craving for chocolate and sex at about the same time."

"Which is most of the time, right?"

Ruthie gave her a playful tap on the jaw with her fist.

"Seriously, Jade, I'm happy for you."

"No cause for celebration. This is a working dinner."

"Maybe the man likes killing two birds with one stone. But you aren't exactly in your usual uniform, Jade. Could it be you have ulterior motives? Or do nice guys get to look at your legs just because they're nice?"

"You are a bitch, you know that?"

Ruthie threw back her head and laughed.

"But since you're the only fashion consultant I know,

tell me the truth,'' Jade said. ''Does this look all right? I mean with my face and hair. Or do I look like I forgot to change out of my nightgown or something?''

''A little makeup would help, if that's what you're asking.''

''Like just my eyes?''

''Yeah.''

''Well, I haven't bought any.''

''My drugstore's always in my purse, girlfriend, if you want to avail yourself.''

Jade considered it. Ruthie waited. Jade thought about it some more.

''I'm becoming a slut, aren't I?''

''You could say that. Want me to help you to really get down and dirty?''

''God, I feel cheap.'' She sighed. ''But what the hell, let's do it—if you don't mind.''

''Why would I mind, girl? I love seein' my friends sinkin' into the sewer.''

Jade gave her a look and they went to the bathroom where Ruthie got out all her paraphernalia.

''So, what's going on with the pool boy?''

''The poor man's besieged, even his wife's sniping at his heels.''

''She probably still loves him.''

''Isn't that sort of a strange way to show love?''

''Not unrequited love. I've never been a wife, much less an ex-wife, but I've been in love with a guy and still hated his guts. Shootin' a sonovabitch like that's possible for most women, even likely for some. But never mind the wife, how do you feel about this dude? This leadin' somewhere?''

''Ruthie, give me a break. I'm wearing a skirt for only the second time in six months. A person can bear only so much stress.''

Ruthie Gibbons began to laugh. "I love you, you know that?"

While Ruthie helped her with her eyes, they talked about Mac, though Jade was circumspect with regard to his professional problems. Ruthie respected that and didn't pry. She was a lot more interested in the personal side, anyway.

"On a scale of one to ten, how much do you like this guy?"

"That's hard to say. He's very, very…"

"Yeah, I know, nice," Ruthie said, finishing the sentence for her. "I'm trying to recall if I ever got laid by somebody whose main quality was that they were nice."

"I'm never again going to share my feelings with you as long as I live," Jade said.

"Let me ask you this. Can you picture yourself kissing the dude?"

Jade considered that. "Yes, I can."

"The idea doesn't give you a feeling like you just sucked on a lemon?"

"No."

"Well, then, maybe this will work out, after all."

"I don't know what I want to happen, to be perfectly honest. And considering all the crap he's facing, it's an impossible situation. I don't even know what I'm doing thinking in these terms."

"You're thinking that way because the guy gives you a tingle. Hey, girl, that's good enough for me. And the dude's rich! Why are you even thinking twice? I say do your hair and nails and put on the spurs."

"I'll be content to have dinner with him and talk about his case."

"When's he due?"

Jade looked at her sports watch. "In half an hour."

"Which reminds me," Ruthie said, grabbing Jade's wrist and taking off her watch.

"Hey, what are you doing?"

"It doesn't go with the dress."

"How'm I suppose to tell the time?"

"If you need to know the time, you ask the gentleman. His solid-gold Rolex should be accurate enough for your purposes."

"Honestly, Ruthie."

"Okay if I hang around to see him?"

"No. It's not that kind of thing." Jade grinned despite herself, belying her denial.

"As long as you invite me to the wedding you can say anything you want." Ruthie laughed.

Once Jade's makeup was complete, Ruthie gathered her things, dumping them back in her purse. "Well, I'll be going, maybe get over to McDonald's and have me a cheeseburger, a shake and fries before I go home. You be bad, girl."

"Thanks for the chocolates."

"Have one just before he picks you up."

They hugged. Jade thanked Ruthie for the help, then walked her to the door. Ruthie skipped out to her car, waved goodbye and drove off. It was a nice evening. Jade stood for a moment or two, enjoying the air and looking up at the trees, their leaves rustling in the light breeze.

The phone rang. She went inside to get it. "Hello?" Several moments of silence followed. She said hello again, and then she heard a dial tone.

As Mac pulled up in front of Jade's place he felt something he'd rarely felt in the past—a regret that he wasn't somebody else. Almost anybody would do. Anybody but the guy whose life was unraveling before his eyes. At the same time, he realized that but for Aubrey St. George, Stella and all they'd been through back in 1978, he wouldn't be here now. Life certainly had its little ironies.

Mac knocked on her door. Jade opened it moments later. She was in a cute little sexy dress and looked adorable. Pretty. The tan, freckled nose and lean, toned limbs were still in evidence, but so was a pert sensuality he'd only seen hints of before. Part of it was the makeup that made her big, dark eyes seem even larger, more dramatic.

"Wow. I didn't know detectives came in such pretty packages. Is this what they mean by being dressed to kill?"

She blushed. "Hey, it's either kill or be killed."

He smiled. She turned still more red.

"Seriously, you look great."

"Thanks."

"You want to head right for the restaurant?"

"Yeah," she said. "Just let me get my purse."

Jade got her shoulder bag—no little dainty purse for this girl, not considering she needed to lug her artillery and communications gear with her.

"You like California cuisine—fish, chicken and pasta?" he asked as they went out the walk.

"The healthier the better."

"I was thinking of Cambria's on Melrose. It's close by."

"I've never eaten there, but I've heard it's nice."

Mac opened the passenger door for her. She climbed in, giving him a peek at her firm, thin thighs. The inside of the car smelled good when he got in. Like gardenias. He smiled at her. Jade smiled back. Mac started the engine.

Jade said, "Tell me about the call you got from the mystery woman."

As they drove, Mac recounted the conversation in detail, adding his impressions. When he was finished, he said, "What do you think?"

She pondered his question for a while. "The caller wants to meet you in person tomorrow."

"Yeah, at the Getty."

She shook her head. "Were it not for everything else that's happened, I'd almost be inclined to think it's a practical joke. Either that or we're dealing with rank amateurs."

He was surprised. "Why's that?"

"She's taking a terrible risk, asking for a face-to-face meeting. The police could easily stake out the rendezvous site, have you wired. The second she made an extortion demand they could step in and arrest her."

"She's obviously counting on the fact that I wouldn't involve the police. And for good reason, I might add. It's the last thing I'd do."

"Even if she's confident of that, she still has balls. The voice wasn't familiar, I assume."

"Not in the least. I couldn't even hazard a guess who it was."

"You think there could be any connection with your wife?"

"Not unless Stella's teamed up with somebody and figured a two-pronged attack was more likely to succeed than simple extortion. To be frank, though, I doubt it."

"Is your wife serious about her threat to cooperate with the police?"

"Stella just might be desperate enough, Jade. She's proven she'll take risks and can be pretty audacious when she feels enough passion about something."

They arrived at Cambria's a few minutes later. A valet took the car. They followed the walk between rows of potted palms to the entrance. Mac pulled on the huge brass door handle and they went inside. The restaurant's decor was clean, modern, well lit with lots of skylights, potted plants, and waiters in white jackets. They all looked Italian, whether they officially qualified or not. Brass railings separated sections containing a few tables, each with starched white tablecloths and a slender vase containing a tropical bud. The kitchen was open, the chefs effusive. It was the sort of place where dinner for two, including wine, ran between a hundred and a hundred and fifty dollars.

The maître d' seated them. Jade seemed a little uncomfortable with the looks she was getting. It wasn't hard to see why she turned heads—a combination of her short skirt, slender tanned legs and freckled nose. She was no siren, not even a girl to lust after, the pretty eyes notwithstanding. Her allure was that of a perfectly proportioned thoroughbred—grace, strength, sleekness, a woman guys wanted to chase around a track.

Mac ordered a bottle of white Italian spring wine as an aperitif. Bri's instruction was reaping benefits he hadn't anticipated. After the wine was poured, Mac took his glass and said, "To better days for both of us."

They studied their menus until the waiter came. Jade ordered fish and vegetables. Mac had a seafood pasta dish. They each had a fish soup. While they were eating it, Jade offered a tentative plan for the next day.

"You'd have to be willing to risk the consequences of a screwup, but how about if I stake out your meeting at the Getty and follow your friend home? That way we'll know who we're dealing with."

"I don't know, Jade, sometimes I think the easiest thing would be to go in and see Caldron and make a clean breast of the whole affair."

"That's certainly an option. And I'd respect your decision to do that," she said. "But somebody's still trying to rip you off and I don't think that should be allowed to go unpunished. We're really talking about two different things."

"The policewoman in you wants to catch the crook."

"You must at least be curious."

"Yes," he said. "Believe me, I am." He put down his

soup spoon. "Meanwhile, though, I've got a proposal for you. How about if for the rest of the evening I'm not the boss and you're not the detective. Let's just be Mac and Jade. What do you say?"

She took a healthy drink of wine. "Okay."

It wasn't the most enthusiastic okay he'd ever heard, but he was willing to take it. He looked at her large but slender hand, recalling the strength of her grip. He wanted to take it, and he almost did. But he restrained himself, sensing Jade wouldn't easily countenance an unwanted advance. She struck him as hypersensitive that way. Fragile, even.

After the waiter cleared their soup bowls, she said, "I know this sounds stupid, Mac, but I'd like to know what you're thinking about us, our relationship."

"Am I making you feel uncomfortable?"

"I don't know. Maybe."

"In that case, I probably shouldn't tell you. Honesty can be a dangerous thing."

"Now I think maybe I should be worried."

"Not unless it bothers you that I think you're a great lady."

Jade looked down at her hands, her clean unpolished nails. She didn't say that it did or that it didn't. He took heart in that.

"That doesn't have to mean more than what the words say," he added. "I think it's just fine to like you and I hope you can say the same."

She peered into his eyes for several moments and said, "I can."

Mac couldn't help himself. He pulled her fingers to his lips and kissed them.

"That's in gratitude for all you've done," he murmured.

"I haven't done anything yet."

"Jade, trust me on this—you couldn't be more wrong."

* * *

Over dessert and coffee they worked out the details of what they'd do the next day at the Getty. Mac agreed to her proposal that she follow the woman after the meeting. "Even if she spots me, it's unlikely she'd go to the police or contact the media. She'd never get any money...unless she thinks she can sell her story to the tabloids," Jade said.

Mac conceded the point. Besides, he really wanted to know who the woman was and where she'd gotten her information. But he didn't want to dwell on the problem all evening. Jade, though, was reluctant to spend a lot of time on personal issues.

When they got back to her place, Mac took heart in the fact that she didn't seem eager to jump out of the car. That pleased him, perhaps more than it should, because he didn't want their evening to end just yet. He'd been around enough to know that he wouldn't and couldn't fall in love on the basis of a couple of conversations—but being enamored was within the realm of possibility. And Jade Morro absolutely fascinated him.

"I should go in," she said after several moments of silence. "Tomorrow's a big day." She seemed to say it more out of a sense of obligation than conviction.

Mac fought back the crazy impulse to ask her to come home with him. He knew it would be presumptuous on his part, but he really wanted to be with her. A lot. But at the same time, he knew she was cautious, serious and maybe skeptical, as well. He had to respect that. Nothing was to be gained by spooking her.

"I had a great time," she said, picking up her purse from the floor.

"Me, too."

"Thanks for the dinner," she said.

"Thanks for the company."

"I'll call you in the morning after I confirm that my

friend, Ruthie, is able to get us parking reservations at the Getty.''

"Wouldn't that be ironic, if we can't get in?"

"I think your lady friend would at least call and ask why you didn't show. But don't worry about it. Ruthie's a whiz. She could probably get us into a state dinner at the White House, if need be.''

Throwing caution to the winds, Mac leaned over and kissed her on the corner of the mouth, catching her by surprise. "I couldn't resist," he said. "I've been wanting to do that all evening."

She seemed at a loss for a response.

"Shall I tell you why?"

Jade shook her head. "No, I don't think it's necessary. I have a pretty good idea."

"And it upsets you?"

"Maybe it's best if we don't talk about it, Mac. We've both got a lot on our plates and don't need complications."

He took her hand and toyed with her fingers. "You're probably right, but I'm just enough of a romantic to ignore what's logical and practical."

Jade looked embarrassed. He didn't want to make her uncomfortable.

"So, I'll honor your desires," he said. "But I do hope there'll come a time when complications won't be a problem to us."

Jade gave his hand a squeeze. "You never know, Mac. You never know."

Her response gave him heart. "Maybe" was certainly more promising than "no way." Before he could express his satisfaction with the prospect, though, a car came up the street, the glare of the headlights drawing their attention. They were parked almost directly across the street from Jade's place. The vehicle slowed, stopping no more than twenty or thirty feet from them. Out of the corner of his eye, Mac saw Jade reach into her purse.

It was difficult to see into the other car, but it appeared there were two occupants. Though the vehicle was double-parked, both doors opened and two men emerged. Mac had a shock when he saw their faces were covered with dark ski masks, and they had guns. They didn't look in their direction, though. They didn't even see them. Their attention was focused on Jade's house.

"What the…" Mac muttered.

As the men ran up her walk, leaving the engine of the car running and the lights on, Jade slapped her cell phone into his hand. "Call 911, Mac. Tell them we've got an armed home invasion in progress."

As she fished her automatic out of her purse, he glanced toward the house. The two men were kicking down her front door. He couldn't believe it. Jade reached for the door handle.

"Where are you going?" Mac asked, grabbing her wrist.

"To catch some crooks." She jerked her arm free. "Make the call, Mac."

"Jade…"

But she was already out. He saw that the men were inside. He watched dumbfounded as Jade dashed across the street, her skirt riding up bare legs that flashed long and lean in the headlights of the other vehicle. She disappeared into the bushes at the front of the house. Mac dialed the emergency number and gave the dispatcher the information, along with Jade's address. Then he got out of the car.

Without a weapon he wasn't sure what to do, but he couldn't sit around and watch Jade do battle all by herself. If nothing else, he ought to be able to hamper their means of escape. Mac ran over to the car, opened the door, turned off the ignition, removed the key and heaved it up the street. Just as he straightened up, one of the men came out the front door of the house.

"Hey, get away from that car!" he shouted.

Mac ducked down behind the fender. He saw the guy coming out the walk.

"Freeze!" Jade shouted. "Drop it!"

The guy, short, slightly built, was halfway to the street. He spun, pointing the gun he held in his two extended hands. But he couldn't pick up a target in the darkness.

"I said drop it!" she screamed at him.

The guy opened fire, shooting indiscriminately in the direction of the house. Jade returned fire and appeared to hit the guy, who was spun around by the force of the blow. But he got off a couple of rounds as he staggered in the direction of the flashes coming from Jade's gun, until he was hit again and fell to the ground. Incredibly, he kept crawling toward the spot where Jade had hidden. She did not fire again.

Mac heard the wounded man cursing and coughing. He fired his gun once more, rolled onto his back and stopped moving.

It was then the second guy appeared at the door. Sticking his gun hand around the door frame, he fired three or four rounds into the bushes where Jade had hidden, then came running full tilt toward the street.

All the excitement had filled Mac's veins with adrenaline. The muzzle flashes in the dark took him back to Vietnam. It was like being in a firefight again, except he had no weapon. The guy slipped between two parked cars and came around the front of his vehicle when Mac, still hunkered behind the fender, leaped out and, lowering his head, drove his body into the guy like a linebacker taking on a running back.

The two of them crashed into one of the parked cars,

the gun flying from the guy's hand and bouncing off the hood to the ground. The gunman, who was smaller than Mac, had the wind knocked out of him, giving Mac the opportunity to spin him around and press his face into the hood. Mac leaned on him to keep him immobilized. He glanced up at the house, hoping to see Jade coming, but there was no sign of her.

"Jade!" he screamed, the realization hitting him that she might have been shot. She hadn't returned the second gunman's fire. A terrible fear rose in him. "Jade!"

She didn't respond, but Mac did hear a siren a few blocks away. Recovering, the guy began struggling. Mac kneed him in the kidneys.

"Hold still, you sonovabitch!"

Mac peered desperately at the deep shadows of the shrubbery in front of the house. He saw no sign of Jade, no movement, no sound that he could hear. He envisioned her shot and bleeding. Mac started dragging his prisoner toward the house, hoping to hang on to him until the police arrived. But halfway there, the guy really came to life. Mac tried to subdue him, but he spun free. Mac didn't chase him, He didn't really care about the bastard. It was Jade he was concerned about now.

Mac ran to the bushes and found her in the gloom. She lay on the ground next to the house, her lithe frame limp, motionless. He dropped to his knees beside her, looking for her wound. He couldn't find where she'd been shot, but he did hear her groan and see her move her head. His heart leaped with joy. He'd been sure she was dead.

"Are you all right?" he said, lifting her head and shoulders onto his lap. "Where are you hit?"

"Hit?" she said groggily.

"Didn't the guy shoot you?"

Lifting her head she peered around. "No, I clunked my head when I dived for cover. Probably on that hose bib."

At the end of the street a cop car swung around the corner, emergency lights flashing, siren wailing. Jade sat up, rubbing her head.

"Where's the guy?"

"One's lying out there on the lawn. The other one got away."

The patrol car screeched to a stop. Another came around the corner at the other end of the block. Two cops came toward the house, their service revolvers drawn. "Hold it right there!" one shouted. "Let me see your hands!"

"We're the victims, Officer," Mac called back.

Jade got to her knees. Mac helped her stand, putting his arm around her shoulders to hold her steady. The other policemen fanned out on the lawn, one going to the motionless body of the gunman.

"This is my house," she told the cops. "Two guys broke in, I think with the intention of killing me. I shot that one after he fired at me. My gun's in the bushes somewhere."

"The other ran up the street that way," Mac added. "That's their car in the street."

Jade, who was still unsteady, leaned heavily against him, groaning. She was clearly in pain. Mac kissed the top of her head and squeezed her slender waist. He could feel her skin through the thin fabric of her dress.

Two of the cops came forward, one older, a sergeant, the other a young woman. "Aren't you Jade Morro?" she said.

"Yeah."

"We met at a conference in Anaheim a couple of years ago. Dori Herrera."

"Oh, yeah, hi, Dori."

Then, to the sergeant, Herrera said, "She's L.A.P.D."

"Was," Jade corrected. "I'm a private investigator now. This is Mac McGowan, a client."

The officers reholstered their weapons. The sergeant, whose name was Meadows, asked Mac for a description of the second suspect and had one of the other cops radio an alert. Jade looked over at the body on the lawn.

"How's he?" she asked.

Meadows called to the cop attending the suspect. "Joey, what's the status over there?"

"This guy's gone," came the reply.

"Shit," Jade said. She sighed painfully. "I told him to freeze. He got off a couple of rounds before I dropped him."

"He's wearing a mask, so I don't think there's much question what happened here," Herrera said.

"I wonder who he is," Jade said, moving toward the body.

They went over in a group. There was a gory wound in the middle of the guy's chest, another in the shoulder. The officer kneeling pulled off the mask.

"Know him?" Meadows asked.

The face was Latino, but completely unfamiliar. "Never seen him before in my life," Jade said, her voice trembling slightly, betraying her assured words.

"Does he have any ID?" Meadows asked the kneeling officer.

He removed a wallet, handing it to the sergeant. Meadows opened it up. "Angel Ordoñez, Burbank. Ring any bells?"

"Jesus," Mac said.

The others looked at Mac.

"I think that could be the brother of one of my former employees," he said.

"You know him, Ms. Morro?" Meadows asked.

"No. Never even heard of him."

Meadows looked at Mac and said, "Have any idea why this guy might want to harm Miss Morro?"

"No. Me, maybe, but not Jade."

"Why you?"

"We had to let his sister go. She was upset, obviously, but I wouldn't think upset enough to want to harm anyone. Manuela and her brother both have criminal records, but why her brother would break into Jade's place, I couldn't begin to tell you."

"Maybe they knew you were taking me to dinner and came looking for you here," Jade said.

"I don't think anyone was aware I was taking you to dinner," he said. "Did you tell anyone?"

"My best friend, Ruthie Gibbons. But Ruthie only found out a short while before you arrived to pick me up. And she wouldn't have a reason to tell anyone. Besides, she's a cop herself."

"Could be they followed Mr. McGowan here and thought he was inside," Dori Herrera said.

"If so, they weren't very careful about what they were doing," Meadows said. "But we'd better get somebody over to this guy's address and see what we can find out."

Mac noticed Jade staring at the face of the dead man. When she shivered, he put his arm around her again.

"Can we go inside?" he asked the officers. "Jade got a nasty bump on the head."

"Why don't you go sit in one of the patrol cars," Meadows said. "We've got to secure the crime scene. Herrera, go with them. Have the medics check her out."

Mac and the two women made their way to the nearest patrol car. A dozen or more of Jade's neighbors had gathered in small groups to observe the excitement. Two or three of the dogs on the block were howling.

Jade put her arm around Mac's waist. "I shot a guy in the leg once, but never killed anybody."

"Ordoñez shot at you, Jade. They both did. Thank God all you got was a bump on the noggin."

"You really think this guy was after you, not me?"

"It could have been the same guy who took a shot at Stella and me a few days ago in Beverly Hills."

"And it also could have been the guy who tried to run down Art right out front."

"Manuela has reason to be upset with Art, as well as me. But I still don't understand why her brother chose your place. Why didn't he come after me, either at my home or even my office? I mean, they broke in acting like they knew exactly what they were looking for and expected to find it."

"Something is a little strange," she admitted.

"And the other guy is still on the loose. As soon as they're finished with us here, you're coming home with me," Mac said. "You don't even have a front door anymore."

"I can go to Ruthie's."

"Don't be stubborn."

"Mac..." But then she stopped arguing. Dori Herrera had a big grin on her face. Mac realized she thought they were having a lovers' spat. He liked the feel of that, even if Jade's sensibilities were a bit ruffled.

They stood next to a patrol car. Herrera opened the rear door. "You folks might as well make yourselves comfortable."

"Yeah," Jade said to Mac. "I can tell you we're going to be here for a long time." She slipped into the back seat.

Mac got in beside her. Herrera leaned over, looking in.

"Paramedics are here. What do you need?"

"A bag of ice," Jade replied.

"I'll see what I can do." She closed the door.

Mac looked over at Jade, taking her hand, interlacing his fingers in hers. "For a while there, I thought I might have lost you. My life didn't exactly flash before my eyes when I saw you lying motionless in the bushes, but almost. You scared the shit out of me.''

"Isn't that a bit of an exaggeration?''

"Nope. I just found you, Jade, and I'm not quite ready to let you go.''

She didn't say anything in reply, but she did rest her head on his shoulder.

Wednesday, August 30, 2000

Glendale

Manuela awoke to the smell of bacon, coffee and cigarette smoke. She was on Ella Vanilla's lumpy sofa. The sun coming in under the shade warmed the side of her face. Her legs ached. She was sore. She felt like a goddamn piñata. She lifted her head and peered into the other room where Ella was sitting at the table, smoking, a mug of coffee before her.

"Well, you alive?" her friend said.

"I'm not fucking sure."

"I'm glad you're awake because I gotta go to work. There's something you need to know."

"What?"

"It's bad news, Manuela."

She sat all the way up, straightening the top of the nightgown Ella had loaned her. She rubbed her face. "Okay, what?"

"Angel's dead."

Manuela's heart went bump. The words shouldn't have been a surprise because she'd known for years that one day she'd hear them—hell, by all rights, it should have happened long before now. When she'd driven home last night, the street in front of her house was full of cop cars, and she knew there was trouble. The first thing she did was turn around and get out of there. Maybe they knew about her, or maybe they didn't, but one thing was sure, she didn't want to be answering any questions. So, she'd driven to Ella's place in Glendale.

"What happened to him?" she asked.

"According to the paper he did a home invasion and got shot. And you'll never guess who did it. That detective that Art hired to check up on the maids. Jade Morro."

"Jade shot Angel?"

"According to the paper. Blew him away right out in front of her house."

Manuela's mouth sagged open. "The fucking bitch."

"Mr. McGowan was there, too."

Manuela grimaced. "Mac?"

"That's what the paper says. There was some other guy with Angel, but he got away. Cops are looking for him." Ella took a final drag on her cigarette, then stubbed out the butt on her plate. "You know anything about this, Manuela, or shouldn't I ask?"

"It don't matter," she said numbly. "Everything's so fucked up now."

Tears filled her eyes. Manuela could see that her whole life was totally messed up. As soon as the cops caught the guy with Angel, they'd know she was the one who was paying to have Jade and Mac killed. She'd go back to prison, this time for a long, long time. And while she was rotting away in the slammer, scrubbing toilets, the bitch cop would be living in Mac McGowan's big house, the beautiful house that should have been hers.

"Ella," she said, "I'm tired of getting screwed over, and I'm not putting up with it no more. I've had it. You know where I can get a gun?"

"Manuela, what are you thinking?"

"It don't matter what. In fact, better you don't know. Just tell me where I can get a gun."

"You sure?"

"Ella, do I look like I'm joking? I'm really sick of my life. Honest to God I am."

"I don't have a gun," Ella said, "but when that shithead Kenny took off, leaving me all those bills, he could have left that .22 pistol of his around here somewhere."

"Like where?" Manuela said.

Ella shrugged. "It could have been in the hall closet on the shelf, but who knows? I don't pay attention to that shit. For all I know, somebody could have already taken it."

Manuela was confused, but then she saw what Ella was getting at. She was playing dumb on purpose.

"I've got to go to the bathroom," Manuela said, getting up from the sofa.

She walked to the hall closet. She was too short to reach the shelf, but she pulled over a chair and climbed up. Sure enough, she found the gun, a nice shiny one. And it was loaded.

Manuela weighed it in her hand for a second or two. She remembered the last time she'd used a gun and the way she felt after she'd wasted that sonovabitch Donny. That time she didn't have half as good a reason as she did now. The bitch cop had shot her brother. Sure, Angel was an asshole, but he was still her brother.

But even more important than that, Mac and Jade had ruined her life. She'd never be rich, never have that house and lots of babies. Her mother would die sad and poor and it was all because of them. Well, fuck 'em. They weren't going to have it, either. She'd kill them first. With Ella Vanilla's gun.

Bel Air

Jade was vaguely aware of the aroma of coffee, but also the flowered scent of the sheets. She had a terrible headache, as well. And a lump on the side of her head like a big fat goose egg. Last night the paramedic had told her she had a slight concussion and, because she'd been unconscious for a couple of minutes, needed to be checked out by a doctor. But she didn't want to go to the hospital, even when Mac urged her to.

"All right, then," he said. "If you're going to be stubborn about not getting medical attention, I insist you come home with me."

"Why? Because you want to play doctor? I thought that syndrome usually ended around age five."

"Smart-ass. No, it's because I gave my neighbor, Dr. Chuck Benjamin, a hell of a deal on a new pool, and I've been looking for a favor he can do for me. I'll ask him to make a house call. He only has to walk across the street and up a house."

She'd liked that idea a lot better than going to the hospital, an experience that invariably bothered her because of the ordeal she'd gone through with her mother. Anyway, being with Mac had a lot of appeal. She'd feel safe and comfortable in his big house. And she trusted him.

The homicide detectives had shown up at her place about fifteen minutes after Jade got her ice bag. Their questioning had been a bit more rigorous than the beat cops. By the time she and Mac were finally allowed to leave, the second suspect hadn't been either arrested or identified. It was after eleven when they finally reached his place. She brought only a change of clothes and an overnight bag for toiletries and the few valuable possessions she had, like the emerald ring she'd inherited from her mother.

Mac's doctor-neighbor, a portly little man, was nice but hadn't looked very doctorly in a polo shirt and chinos. He concurred with the paramedic's diagnosis of a light concussion. "I am going to have Mac wake you up every couple of hours, though. Concussion can be tricky and you

were out a little longer than I'd like to see." He'd smiled
wryly. "I assume you won't mind having a male nurse."

The doc must have assumed she and Mac had something
going. She didn't bother to correct his misapprehension. It
would give the neighbors something to talk about. After
he'd left, she asked Mac if playing nurse was his fallback
position for guests who didn't want to play doctor.

"Don't get sassy. Doctor left me a big syringe with
instructions to medicate you if you start mouthing off."

"Nurse Ratchet."

"I predict you'll be sick of my face after I've awakened
you three or four times in the night."

"Mac, this may be the end of a perfectly delightful relationship."

"Go wash up and get to bed! And don't forget to scrub
behind your ears."

Jade smiled at the recollection of their repartee. Mac had
tried to put her at ease. He'd largely succeeded. Every two
hours he did come in to awaken her, but he'd been gentle,
usually tousling her hair or giving her cheek a pinch before
turning off the light and retreating to his own room. Were
it not for the dull ache in her head, she might have pro-
nounced her stay at Mac's to be a delight.

His guest room was really a guest suite with its own
bath and small sitting room. She'd taken one look at the
big four-poster bed and almost cried. First, because she'd
been dead tired, and second, because she'd never slept in
such a grand bed before. The closest had been when Ricky
had taken her to the Del Coronado in San Diego to celebrate their "engagement." How could the bastard have not
seen how cruel that would seem in retrospect?

But Mac McGowan was a different kettle of fish. He
struck her as everything Ricky Santos was not—a gentleman, a guy who didn't have to put his own interests first,
a considerate human being. And though he wasn't the pro-

totypical dreamboat, he had a quiet strength that was compelling. Mac was the kind of guy who grew on you and became more attractive the better you got to know him. Ruthie would have found his money alluring because that kind of thing impressed her. Not Jade. It wasn't that she had taken a vow of poverty or eschewed material goods—money just didn't excite her the way it did some people. She appreciated Mac for his modesty. He really was a decent person.

There was a very light rap on the door.

"Yes?" she said.

"Can I come in?" Mac's voice.

"Sure."

He stuck his head in the door. "Final wake-up call."

"I was awake."

He opened the door wider, but didn't come into the room, respecting her privacy even though three times during the night he'd come to the bed. "How do you feel?"

"Like I got hit over the head with a hose bib, but otherwise pretty good."

"Feel the pea under your mattress?"

"Sure did."

"Terrific. You know what that means, don't you?"

"What?"

"In this establishment genuine princesses get fifty percent off the rack rate."

"But that still includes breakfast, right?"

"It does indeed. Coffee's on, by the way."

"You wouldn't have tea, by any chance?"

"That's right, you're a tea drinker. I forgot. I'm sure we can accommodate you. There's also juice, muffins, oatmeal, toast, eggs any style as long as they're scrambled or boiled... That's pretty much my repertoire, I'm afraid."

"A muffin and juice would be fine."

"No extra charge for cholesterol."

She laughed. "You're a wonderful host, Mac."

"You were fortunate to come during low season."

She smiled appreciatively. "Seriously, the only place I've ever been that's ever come close to the accommodations here is the Hotel Del Coronado."

"Ah, the Del. That's where I honeymooned."

"Me, too! Well, sort of honeymooned. It was a festive weekend, let me put it that way."

Mac seemed to understand without being judgmental. It was funny how comfortable he was to be with. And how nice it was not to be afraid of being herself. Maybe that's what she disliked most about men—they seemed to force a woman to look at herself through their eyes. Mac McGowan seemed to be an exception.

"By the way," he said, "you made the paper. Actually, we both did. A brief piece in the metro section. 'P.I. Thwarts Home Invasion, Suspect Killed In Shootout,' or words to that effect. Why they threw my name in, I don't know."

"You captured one of the guys."

"And let him get away."

"Only because you were concerned about me."

"Well, none of that was in the article, so it doesn't matter. Maybe they were going for the prurient interest of me being at your place that time of night, I don't know."

"You're rich and famous," she said. "Being hounded by the media goes with the territory."

Mac laughed. "'Old Tycoon And Fetching Female Detective,' is that what you mean?"

"Not exactly," she said, blushing.

"Hopefully, that will be the end of it."

"Don't count on it."

"Well, onward and upward, I guess. I don't mean to be a stern taskmaster, but weren't you going to see if your friend was able to get us reservations at the Getty?"

"Oh, that's right! I forgot." She started to throw back the covers, until she remembered she had nothing on but panties and an oversize T-shirt, her favorite sleeping attire.

He noticed his presence was inhibiting. "I'll be down in the kitchen fixing your breakfast. You can call after you eat."

"No, I'll call first. It might take Ruthie a while to arrange things, so I need to give her a little notice. But I will avail myself of the powder room first."

"On that note, I'll leave."

Mac gave her a wink and stepped out, closing the door behind him. Jade sighed. It was a mistake to make too much of these good feelings, she told herself. In the past, happiness always seemed to transform itself into misery, raising its ugly head and biting her in the ass. To like someone too much was—in her experience—inviting trouble.

"The Getty?" Ruthie said when Jade reached her. "Why don't I get you tickets on the Concorde while I'm at it?"

"So, the blackmailer has class, what can I say?"

"Okay, I'll have two parking reservations waiting. One in your name and one in the name of..."

"Joseph McGowan."

"Right. You want me to call you back to confirm?"

"Sure, but I'm not at home. I'm at Mac's."

"You're shitting me."

"No. Spent the night...innocently, of course."

"Seein' it's you, girl, maybe I can believe that. So, you going to tell me what happened?"

"It's a long story, Ruthie, parts of which might upset you. Apparently the whole thing's in the paper. But the bottom line is, everything is copacetic now. I have to get going, though, Mac's making me breakfast."

"He's making you breakfast."

"Yeah. He really is a sweet guy."

"No, he's a smart guy. He gets sweet when he starts leaving diamonds and sapphires on your pillow."

"Bye, Ruthie."

"Hey, at least give me the damn phone number."

Jade did.

Los Angeles

The parking attendant checked Mac's name against the reservations list and waved him through. Mac drove into the covered parking structure, left the Lexus, then rode the crowded tram up to the architectural marvel perched against the side of the Santa Monica Mountains. The museum had a panoramic view of the Los Angeles Basin, which explained the observation decks and the use of glass. Mac went to the upper level, hardly noticing the paintings and statuary, though he was aware of the people. Because the facility was spacious and admission strictly controlled, the crowds were not overwhelming.

He paid special attention to younger women who appeared to be alone, watching to see if any of them might be observing him—following him, maybe. But he saw no one suspicious. To get to the observation upper deck, Mac took the escalator to the top floor, then went through the room containing the Renaissance paintings. There were some Japanese tourists out on the deck, taking pictures in the southeast corner, where the caller had told him to situate himself. Mac waited until they moved on before taking his position. Jade was around somewhere, but she'd instructed him not to look for her. They'd come separately. And she'd told him to let her worry about the woman after the meeting was over.

"Be cooperative with her," Jade suggested, "but non-committal. If you can, draw her out, get as much information as possible, and pay close attention to what she says. Nuances can be important.''

''Yes, ma'am.''

''And this time, don't try to be a hero.''

It was a jab at his attempt to take on that gunman the previous evening. When the detectives had questioned them about the man's description and actions, Mac had related their little skirmish. Jade had been duly horrified. ''You're paying me to handle the rough stuff,'' she'd said. ''No,'' he'd objected, ''I'm paying you to be the brains of the outfit. Getting into gun battles was not what I had in mind.''

Mac couldn't think of her without feeling happy. Jade could be feisty, even a little trying in her stubbornness, but he found her endearing. Now, if they could just get through the present ordeal without one or the other of them getting shot or maced or blown to pieces by an antitank weapon...

Sighing, Mac leaned on the railing and peered out at the hazy city, which broiled in the heat of the midday sun. And he waited. It was almost noon.

As he stood there, he went over the woman's instructions in his mind. He was to stand at the railing, looking at Westwood. ''I'll come up next to you,'' she'd said. ''Don't look at me. Keep your eyes on the view. We'll talk about solving your problem.'' Her tone had been threatening, but there'd been no real demand, except that he show up at the Getty to discuss Aubrey St. George.

Mac continued to wait and, by ten after, the mystery woman still hadn't showed. He started wondering if she hadn't sent him on a wild-goose chase. Maybe she regarded this as a test run to see if he had involved the police. She could be among the throng on the deck, standing off a bit maybe, watching him, looking for signs of trouble. He hoped she hadn't spotted Jade. That could be what was wrong. Once the woman had determined he wasn't alone, she may have beat a hasty retreat. Maybe he'd leave, never having seen her, only to have an angry message waiting for him at his office.

After a while Mac started getting tired of standing immobile. The instructions were not to look around, to stare at the view. But for how long? At some point he was going to flick it in. Several times someone had come and stood beside him, but no one spoke to him. They'd take a photograph or gawk at the view, then leave.

Mac kept peeking at his watch, growing more and more anxious. He wasn't enjoying the game, but he was also afraid not to play it. Then someone came up next to him again. He waited.

"Don't look at me," she said.

It was the same voice he'd heard on the phone. Mac stared down at the San Diego Freeway, looking at the mysterious figure out of the corner of his eye without turning his head. She was small; he had the impression of a wide-brimmed hat.

"Are you alone?" she asked, snapping the chewing gum in her mouth.

"Yes."

"Are you wearing a listening device?"

"No."

"Take off your jacket and put it at your feet, but do it without looking at me."

Mac did as he was told.

"I'm alone," he said, "and I'm not wired. I want this problem to go away."

"Fine, so do I."

"What are you asking for your cooperation?"

"Yeah," she said. "There's always a catch, isn't there? What I want is simple. Five million dollars."

"Five million? You're crazy."

"You can afford it. And it's enough that you'll never have to think about this again."

"How can I be sure?"

"Because this is a pain in the ass for me as much as it is for you."

"How do I know you aren't bluffing?" he said.

"About it being a pain in the ass?"

"No, about Aubrey St. George. There's been a lot of speculation about what really happened. If you're selling your silence, you'd better know something."

"You killed the sonovabitch in the pool house and buried the body under the pool you were putting in for him. Is that enough, or do you want the bloody details?"

"You seem pretty confident of your story."

"Don't fuck with me, McGowan." She snapped her gum loudly.

"All right, let's say you and I work out a mutually satisfactory figure," Mac said. "Let's say you're happy, but your good friend decides to cash in, too. What am I supposed to do then?"

"It won't happen."

"How can I be sure? I mean, if I'm going to get screwed over, anyway, why pay anything at all? Five million will buy a lot of lawyers."

"Look, I'm not here to bargain with you," she said.

"Your silence is only worth so much to me. Beyond that, I'll take my chances with the police. Let's say a million, but I'll need to know exactly how you got the information. That's a condition."

"You're fucking with me," she said angrily. Snap went her gum. "I told you not to do that."

"A deal will work only if both parties are reasonable. A million will save me a lot of trouble. Paying you more than that starts being a bigger pain than jail time."

"What about your wife and kid, McGowan? What kind of an asshole are you, anyway?"

There was something about the way she said it that gave him pause. There was angst in her voice. Was she concerned about Stella and Troy or just using that against him? If she was concerned, the question was why.

"A million is a lot for doing nothing but keeping your mouth shut," he said. From the corner of his eye he could see her fidget. He'd been in enough negotiations to know she was trying to decide if it was time to come down, or if she should still hang tough.

Snap, snap, snap. "Okay," she said after several moments. "Three million, but it's got to be in cash and I'll need to take delivery by the end of the week."

"Impossible."

"That's as far down as I'll go."

"Look, I'll pay two million. Period. But it's not going to be in cash. You'd need a moving truck. Besides, I can't raise that much cash without arousing suspicion. You need a numbered offshore account and I'll need a week to get the money together."

She was silent, the chewing and snapping having stopped. Mac knew he had her.

"Get your account set up and have instructions ready for me a week from today," he said. "But I'll need to know the source of your information. Provide those two things and you become an instant millionaire. Where do you want to meet next week?"

She remained silent. Mac restrained himself from smiling. The figure beside him shifted uneasily. Jade was right. The mystery woman was an amateur, but she was an amateur with damning information.

"I'll call and let you know where," she said, the confidence in her voice gone. "But you better be getting the money lined up."

"Okay."

"I'm going now," she said. "My associate is watching us. If he sees you turn your head, the deal's off. So stay right where you are for five minutes. Understand?"

"I understand."

Snap, snap went her gum. "I'll be in touch."

"I'll be waiting."

The brimmed hat flicked away, out of his peripheral vision. Mac did not turn his head and watch her go. He played the game her way, though he did not wait five minutes. After a couple, he picked up his jacket, put it on. Then he left the observation deck and went down to the cafeteria to buy himself a sandwich and a beer.

Jade had trouble keeping up with her. The mystery woman with the bouncing red curls under the wide-brimmed hat and sunglasses was moving smartly. If Jade were to jog along behind her, she'd be easily spotted by an accomplice.

Once they were outside the main building and in the open plaza, Jade angled off to the side rather than follow directly behind her. She kept Red in sight, but otherwise put as much distance between them as she safely could. It appeared the woman was headed back to the tram, which meant Jade could afford to lag. The only risk was Red would hop on a train just before it departed. Jade lucked out, though. A sizable crowd was waiting for the tram to take them down the hill to the parking garage. She spotted the woman waiting impatiently on the platform, checking her watch. When the tram pulled in, Jade got in the car behind the one Red boarded.

If she had a concern, it was that she'd lose her mark in the labyrinth of the parking garage. She wouldn't likely be able to follow the woman to her car, then run to get her own without losing her in the process. And so, knowing that, when she arrived at eleven-fifteen, Jade had flashed her investigator's ID and got permission from the supervisor to park in one of the official slots by the exit. That way she could pick up the woman as she came out of the garage. The question now was whether her mark would come out with short blond hair and hatless, rather than the way she'd gone in.

But Red threw Jade a curve. When the tram arrived, instead of heading for the garage, the woman made her way toward the pedestrian entrance. Outside the gate was where visitors could catch a taxi or board a bus. Of course! That was why the mystery woman didn't have to worry about a parking reservation as she and Mac had—she'd come via public transportation.

Jade realized she was in a pickle. She couldn't get her car without losing track of Red, and if she followed her to see which taxi or bus she took, she wouldn't have her car. But she couldn't risk not knowing which way Red was headed, so she followed her to the bus stop. A MTA bus pulled up just as Red got to the stop. She and half a dozen other passengers got on. Jade checked. It was a 561, northbound.

Having confirmed the line and direction the bus was headed, she dashed back to her car. On the way out of the garage, she asked the attendant the next stop of the northbound 561 after it left the Getty. The woman shrugged. "I don't know." Jade could have killed her. She couldn't blame her, but she could've killed her.

The bus was gone by the time she got there, but a southbound bus was just coming up to the stop. Pulling over, Jade jumped out of her car and ran to the bus. The driver was a little skinny guy, old enough to be her father, with a smile about as wide as the bus.

"What's the next northbound stop?" she asked breathlessly.

"Sherman Oaks, sugar pie."

"Where in Sherman Oaks?"

"Van Nuys and Moorpark."

"Via the freeway?"

"Yep. Exit Ventura."

Jade beamed. "Thanks!"

"Wish I was goin' north, sugar pie."

"Next time." She returned to her car.

In two minutes she was on the San Diego Freeway, headed north toward the valley. The climb up over the mountain was a long one, and she wondered if maybe she could catch up with the bus on the grade. As luck would have it, she did catch up with a 561 near the top of the pass. Now, if she had the right bus and Red hadn't slipped off while she wasn't looking, she'd be okay.

The bus exited the freeway and Jade followed it to Van Nuys Boulevard. But Red didn't get off. Jade was concerned. Was the mystery woman still on the bus? The bus headed north on Van Nuys with Jade in pursuit. The next stop was Victory Boulevard.

Much to Jade's relief Red came bouncing down the steps, hatless, her red curls blowing in the wind. As Jade waited, Red walked east on Victory, stopping at a parked car when she was nearly out of sight. She got in the vehicle then drove west with Jade following. At a light Jade pulled up behind her and made a note of the license number. They proceeded west, passing under the freeway. A mile or so later Red turned, pulling into an apartment complex just off Victory. Jade left her car in the street and walked into the complex. Red had left her car in a visitor's spot next to the building nearest the street. The woman knocked on the door of a ground-floor unit. Jade now had an address for her mark. It might not be Red's place, but it was an address from which she could be traced.

Jade went back to her car. She decided to hang around

a while and see what developed. She was able to see the door of the apartment where Red had gone, so she could monitor things from the comfort of her vehicle. With time to kill, she gave Ruthie a call.

"Hey, it's you, girl," Ruthie said. "Damn, if you aren't still alive. I've been checking with the morgue every hour or so."

"Alive and well."

"Why didn't you tell me this morning that you were in a shootout at the OK Corral?"

"It wasn't that big a deal."

"How many times have you done that before, even when you were wearing a badge?"

"Well…"

"Uh-huh."

"I'll tell you all about it later, but I'm chasing a bad guy at the moment and need a favor. Will you run a plate for me?"

"Sure. Don't matter if it's against regulations."

"I knew you'd be perfectly reasonable." Jade gave her the license-plate number.

"I'm expecting a nice dinner for this, by the way. And none of that tofu shit, either. Steak."

"No problem. It'll go on my expense account."

Ruthie laughed. "You're liking this millionaire business, aren't you?"

"So far so good."

"You're bad, girl. Call me back in fifteen minutes."

Jade waited, wishing she'd taken the time to go to the bathroom at the Getty before Red had shown up. Harry Naismith had once told her that the key to a successful surveillance was planning ahead. God, was he ever right.

Ten minutes later Jade phoned Ruthie back.

"Ginger Lane," Ruthie said. "She's got a Studio City address. You want it?"

"Please." Jade jotted down the address. "You're a doll."

"A doll who eats like a horse."

"Later."

Red—whose name Jade now knew to be Ginger—must be visiting someone. A coconspirator, perhaps? Or was the vehicle borrowed or stolen?

If she managed to identify Red and her accomplices, wouldn't that be a coup? Mac would be impressed—even if it turned out to be a gang who couldn't shoot straight. Stupidity, after all, could be very dangerous.

Pacific Palisades

Venita swam naked in the pool as she waited for Troy, who'd had a phone call and had gone off to the house, leaving her feeling alone and vulnerable. She still hadn't had a visit from the police, nor had she heard from Percy Gaylord. Arjay had been a bit more aloof and, she judged, somehow wary. Knowing that Percy Gaylord was after her scalp, he may have decided her days were numbered and he would be advised to search for other, less precarious endeavors.

Even Jugnu, the one steady, unfailing rock in her life, had showed signs of independence and defiance. The previous night, for the first time in all the years he'd been in her service, Jugnu had refused to pleasure her. She'd taken a strap and hit him three or four times for defying her, but he'd still refused to accommodate her, stoically taking his beating without flinching even once. Venita had been so shocked, she hadn't known what to do. Finally, she'd sent him to his room, then, distraught, fell weeping on her bed. Her entire world seemed to be conspiring against her.

Troy, though full of himself, was the one exception. He seemed so certain he would have a large sum of money soon and that together they would conquer Hollywood. He had grown more brazen, more sexually demanding, but at least he seemed to want her, still treating her like a queen, a star. Thank God she had that—if little else—to cling to.

Just then Troy came out of the house and made his way to the pool. Removing the terry robe he'd worn inside, he tossed it on a chair and dived into the water, not surfacing until he was in front of her. He took her by the shoulders and kissed her. Venita responded by twisting her body back and forth, rubbing her breasts against his chest.

He slipped his hand down between her legs. "Miss me?"

"I did indeed."

He grinned, then lay back in the water, floating. "Okay, here's the deal. I'll have two million dollars minimum in an offshore account next week. A million and a half of it will be available for *On Distant Shores,* maybe more."

Venita moved over next to his head. "Is that true?"

He regarded her from the corner of his eye. "Would I shit you?"

"How do you do it?"

"That's my thing," he said. "Yours is to get the movie made. I did hear something really freaky, though. Mac was involved in some sort of gun battle last night. It was in the morning paper."

"Truly?"

Troy stood, smoothing his wet hair back off his face. "Yeah. Happened in West Hollywood. Just think, if he'd gotten killed, we'd be talking about a whole lot more than a couple of mil."

"Yes, but we mustn't wish ill on your father."

Troy smiled sardonically. "Why not?"

Venita reached under the water, taking his member in her hand. "You're becoming quite the man, aren't you, my love?"

"Man enough."

"You've convinced me."

"Have I?"

"But of course," she said, caressing his balls.

"Would you be pissed if I called your bluff, Venita?"

"Whatever do you mean?"

"How about we go to Vegas and get married?"

"When?"

"Now," he said.

"This instant?"

"Tonight, tomorrow, whatever."

"What are you thinking?" she asked.

"I'm curious if you've got enough faith in me to take the plunge without seeing the money in my bank account."

"Oh, but aren't you the evil one."

He grinned, dripping with arrogance. "If you mean what you say, it should be a no-brainer, Venita. Am I your man, or am I not?"

"Venita! Venita!" It was Arjay, making his way toward the pool, a rather grim expression on his face. "Terribly sorry to intrude, my dear," he said, "but you have a visitor."

She couldn't imagine. "Who?"

"A gentleman named Boots Conroy, a rather prodigious chap, as it happens."

"Conroy? Never heard of him. What's it regarding, Amal?"

"He claims to be a special emissary of Percy Gaylord."

"Percy," she said, letting go of Troy Hampton's cock. She thought for a moment, realizing this meant the journalist had recovered his memory. Did that bode good or ill? she wondered. If he'd sent someone other than the police to speak for him, it could only mean his intent was to deal. Venita sighed with relief, allowing that in all probability it was a good sign. The question was, what were his terms? "Have him wait," she said. "I'll dress and be there shortly." Then to Troy, "Will you excuse me, love? I have business to tend to."

Venita went to the ladder where Jugnu stood at the edge of the pool, waiting with her robe held open. She slipped into it, then went off to see if this Mr. Conroy's tidings would bring her grief or joy. Troy claimed to have done his part in their scheme. The question to be answered now was, had she?

Van Nuys

Jade had waited until her bladder became such unpleasant company that it was either find a toilet or drown. She tried to remember if she'd seen any fast-food places on the way in—someplace nearby. If Ginger happened to leave while she was gone, it wouldn't be the end of the world. Her mission had been largely accomplished.

She had to drive a ways, but finally found a Wendy's. Thankfully the ladies' room was empty. Afterward, Jade hurried back to the apartment complex. No sooner had she gotten there when a flash of red hair in the passenger seat of a car leaving the complex caught her eye. Ginger.

It wasn't her vehicle and a guy was driving, but Jade had no doubt those red curls belonged to her mark. Jade only had a glimpse of the guy behind the wheel. The impression was darkly handsome. She followed them back to the San Diego Freeway, where they entered, southbound, headed back toward L.A. With the rush hour under way it was slow going, but she was able to keep them in sight. It wasn't until they were off the freeway, going east on Sunset Boulevard, that she got close enough to make out the plate. At a stoplight she jotted down the number, then put in another call to Ruthie.

"What's with you, girl? Do I have to escalate my demands to steak and lobster?"

"Anything your little heart desires. I'm on a roll, Ruthie," Jade said gleefully.

"You on somethin' all right, honey. Oo-ee. But never mind. Call me back in a while and I'll have a name and address."

Jade didn't try to reach her friend again until they were in Pacific Palisades.

"This one's a boy," Ruthie said. "Hernan Payro, Van Nuys, California."

Jade read her the address of the apartment complex they'd just come from. "Is that what you've got?"

"That's it, all right. My, you are on a roll."

Jade was really pleased. She wanted very badly to have positive results when she reported back to Mac. But her work for the day was far from done, it appeared. Her little coconspirators, Ginger and Hernan, were entering the high-rent district, which could well mean they were going to see yet another amigo. And if his or her living accommodations were any indication, he or she just might be the big fish in the operation. Wouldn't that be the mother of all coups?

Hernan left Sunset and drove up into the mansion-studded hills. The higher they got, the bigger and fancier the homes. Finally, they pulled into the gated drive of a modern place on the hilltop. Jade stopped down the street a bit, just close enough to keep an eye on the place. Yep, she was definitely on a roll.

Bel Air

Mac couldn't understand why Jade hadn't called. He hoped to hell she wasn't in trouble. She'd already demonstrated a willingness to slug it out with the bad guys, and he was worried she'd gotten herself into another mess. He'd told her he would be at home, and she'd agreed to contact him as soon as she had something to report.

The phone had rung twice since he'd arrived home from the Getty. Both times it was Bev with one little crisis or another. The first thing she asked him, of course, was about the shootout reported in the paper.

"Everybody here's trying to decide if the gunman was related to that little pool maid Art fired last week."

"Yes, it was her brother," Mac said. "The police confirmed it. I told them to advise Art. I hope they did. I tried calling him, but got no answer."

"Art heard about it," Bev said. "He's gone underground. I talked to him this morning. He refused to say where he is."

Mac couldn't help a chuckle. "I guess I can't blame him."

"I hope you're taking precautions," Bev said.

"I'm fine."

"They say she has a nasty violent streak, Mac. She's killed before."

"Manuela isn't going to try a home invasion, Bev. Not after what happened to her brother."

"But until she's arrested…"

"Stop worrying. The best thing you can do is cover the office for me. I'll take care of things on this end."

Bev agreed, but she wasn't happy. She'd never liked the idea of hiring ex-cons as pool maids, even though the vast majority of them had requited themselves quite well. But he wasn't going to let one or two bad apples spoil an otherwise effective program. That was not his immediate concern, however. Mac kept thinking about Jade and the mystery woman. He also thought about Stella, wondering if she was busy figuring out how to turn the screws a notch or two tighter. And then there was Jaime Caldron to consider. He'd been mysteriously quiet of late. Maybe he'd put his faith in Stella coming through for him.

Ironically, Mac couldn't say it was a bad bet. He had no idea what his wife would do, even after having been partners in crime with her for twenty years. Would she be vengeful enough to sell him down the river? All that would accomplish would be to hurt him—and Lord knew it wouldn't do a lot for her social standing, or for Troy's career, either. Still, Stella remained unpredictable. Given her seeming desperation, anything could happen.

It was rapidly becoming an untenable situation. Maybe the time had come to accept the fact he couldn't keep running from the past forever. The realization almost came as a relief. Stella and Troy had kept him going all these years, but now his wife had turned against him, and Troy seemed to have gone his own merry way. With Glamour Puss about to rise from his grave, Mac had his back to the wall and he knew it.

A drink of hard liquor before evening was a rarity for him, but he found himself craving a jolt. So, he went to the wet bar to fix himself a vodka tonic, when the phone rang again.

"Mac, I just heard. Are you all right?" It was Stella. "Why are people trying to kill you? Was it the man who took that shot at us last week?"

"I don't know, Stella, but it's quite possible."

"Do you know what it was about?"

"A problem at work, I think."

"Oh. Well, thank goodness you're safe."

"Yeah, what if I'd been killed? Who'd you blackmail then?"

"I'd like to think we're both looking out for our interests, Mac. My objective is not to hurt you, it's to get you to try to look at things from my point of view."

"That's the damnedest rationalization for extortion I've ever heard."

"Call it what you will," she said icily, "I want to know what you're going to do."

"I'm still thinking about it."

"Well, you don't have forever. Lieutenant Caldron called me this morning. He got the district attorney's office to go along with his plan. It's you they want, Mac, and I can walk, if I cooperate with them."

"It's hard to see how that'll make you a big star, Stella."

"Mac, they could put me in prison. All I want you to give me is a reason to take that risk."

"I would have thought our mutual obligation to one another was reason enough."

"Easy for you to say. You're the one who...well, you know what happened that night."

"Okay, fine, Stella, I know where you stand. What's your point? Are you giving me a deadline? Is that why you called?" There was a click on the line, indicating another call was coming through. "Hang on a second," he said. "I've got another call." He hit the flash key. "Yes?"

"Mac, it's me."

"Jade."

"Got an initial report for you."

"Hang on, let me get rid of this other call." He hit the flash key again. "Stella, I've got to go, I've got a call I have to take."

"Okay, but could you come by later so we can discuss it?"

"I'm buried at the moment, Stella. You're not the only blackmailer I have to contend with. I can only deal with one extortion attempt at a time."

"What?"

"I'll talk to you later." He hung up and went back to the call waiting.

"Jade?"

"Yo."

"Sorry. You okay?"

"Sure, why wouldn't I be?"

"I've been worried."

"Mac, you aren't supposed to worry about your investigator."

"Well, I do. And it's not a knock on your competence. It's a comment on my feelings."

There was silence on the line. Mac wondered if he'd gone too far. He didn't want to scare her.

"But that's another story," he said. "You were saying you had something to report."

"I'm about ninety percent sure who the mystery woman is. The name Ginger Lane mean anything to you?"

Mac ran it through his head. "No."

"How about Hernan Payro?"

"Hernan Payro... You know, that is vaguely familiar, but I can't tell you why."

"I'm pretty sure Ginger's the name of the woman you talked to at the Getty. I followed her to a car parked in Sherman Oaks registered to a person by that name. She drove to an apartment complex in Van Nuys and later left with a guy in a car registered to Payro. Odds are that's who the guy was. I followed them to a place in Pacific Palisades and that's where I'm staked out now. They've been inside for a while. I thought I'd hang around, see if I can find out who lives here."

"Boy, you're efficient."

"You're paying me well, I ought to be."

"When you finish up, why don't you come by?"

"For a more detailed report?"

"No, for dinner."

"Mac…"

"Yes?"

He sensed her angst even though she didn't utter a word. But then she surprised him.

"Okay. It could be a couple of hours, though."

"I'll be here."

"I have a feeling this whole thing is about to break wide open," she said.

Mac heard the joy, the elation in her voice. It was understandable; the woman was doing her job and doing it well. He was pleased, but more for her than for himself. The people who were after him no longer seemed to matter. But he knew what did.

"Jade," he said, "this may not be the best time to ask you this, but I really want to know. What do you think of me?"

"What do I think of you?"

"I mean as a person. You know my story, what I've done, the way I've lived my life. You've been a cop, you've seen a lot. Where do I fit in the picture? What kind of a human being do you see me to be?"

She was silent for a while, then she said, "That's not an easy question to answer."

"Try."

"I admire you, Mac. If for no other reason than you care. You're a decent guy."

"What about Aubrey St. George?"

"This might sound funny to you, but it doesn't fit with the Mac McGowan I know. Not that I doubt what you've told me. It's just that…I don't know, when you talk about that, it seems like you're talking about a different person."

"I see. Okay."

"I hope that doesn't hurt your feelings. If anything, I mean it as a compliment."

"No, that's fine, Jade. I understand what you're saying. I appreciate your candor."

"Honest?"

"Honest." He couldn't help smiling at the concern in her voice. "Hey, hurry home, okay?"

"Check."

Mac hung up the phone with a happier heart, but also with a sense of resolve. He'd had an insight. The noose around his neck was tighter now than it had ever been, and yet he felt almost—but not quite—free. What it boiled down to was that when he was with Jade, he was more the man he'd been before Aubrey and Stella. Innocent, maybe. Even starry-eyed. It could be he was running from the truth, kidding himself, but he liked this new Mac McGowan a lot better than the old one. This one seemed alive. This one had something to live for.

It was clear now what he had to do. It was so obvious he was surprised he hadn't latched onto it sooner. In fairness, though, something had changed. The change was Jade Morro entering his life. Not that she'd necessarily said or done anything to awaken him. But the conversation they'd just had did confirm what underneath he'd felt but hadn't been able to put his finger on. Simply stated, she'd inspired him to be the man he truly was.

Mac picked up the phone and dialed his wife. "You know, Stella," he said, "maybe you're right. Maybe we do need to talk."

"Really?" she said, sounding hopeful and delighted.

"Yes. But would you mind coming to my place?"

"I suppose I could. Are you going to give me a hint as to what you have in mind?"

"I don't want to spoil it," he said, "but I'll tell you this much, I'm going to try and accommodate you. You and Troy both. In fact, I'd like him to be here, too. Do you think you can track him down and get him to come?"

"I can certainly try."

"Please do. Tell him I'm going to do my best to make his day. That might lure him out of the bushes."

Stella hesitated. "This isn't a trick, is it?"

"Trick? No. My eyes have been opened, Stella, that's all. I'm going to do what I should have done a long time ago."

"And we'll be pleased?"

"I certainly hope so."

"What time do you want us there, Mac?"

"How about around five o'clock?"

"See you then."

Mac hung up the phone feeling great, as though a tremendous burden had been lifted from his shoulders. It was the obvious solution to his problems—giving his wife and son what they wanted, but also to take what he so desperately needed. What could make more sense than that?

Next, Mac got Jaime Caldron's business card. He dialed the number on the card, but Caldron wasn't in. Mac left a message on the detective's voice mail. "Lieutenant Caldron," he said, "this is Mac McGowan. I've had a change of heart and I'd like to talk to you about Aubrey St. George. If possible, please come to my place this afternoon at five." He hung up, feeling better by the moment. He took a big slug of the drink he'd fixed himself, grinning as he savored it. Then the doorbell rang.

Mac went to the door without thinking. Opening it, he found a small but voluptuous Hispanic woman at his door. Manuela Ordoñez. She had a gun in her hand. It was pointed directly at his midsection.

"Hi, Mr. McGowan. Remember me?"

"Manuela…"

She smiled. "Fucking A, you do remember! I thought maybe after you step on somebody, you just wipe your feet, forget they ever existed and go your merry way."

"Manuela…"

"Don't Manuela me, asshole. It's too late. Where's your girlfriend, the bitch cop?"

"If you mean Jade, she's not here."

"Fine. Then let's go inside and wait for her. That okay with you?"

"She isn't coming, Manuela."

"Oh, yeah? I bet you're lying. I seen her car here this morning. She spent the night. Don't fuck with me, Mac. I'm tired of people fucking with me."

"Look, you're making a terrible mistake."

"Yeah, well, fuck you. I didn't make the mistake. You did. Now get your ass inside."

Reaching out with her free hand, she gave him a shove in the chest, then entered the house and closed the door.

Pacific Palisades

Jade was bored. Surveillance had to be the worst job in the world, especially when all there was to do was stare at a building half hidden by a high wall. At least being near the ocean the air was milder than it had been in the valley. Even so, she was feeling rump-sprung and got out of her car to stretch her legs. As she leaned against the fender, a scrawny little man came out of the house down the street. He had a prissy white toy poodle on a leash. Man and dog made their way up the hill in her direction.

When he was nearly abreast the car, Jade said, "Excuse me, sir. Could you tell me who lives in that house there?"

He pulled on the crepey folds of skin on his neck. "Why?"

She hated questions that served no purpose except to impede. "My boyfriend's supposed to be at his grandmother's but I followed him here. I'm hoping it's not some lady friend's place."

The dog lifted its leg on the tire to Jade's car not three feet from where she stood. The man watched the little stream of pee run off the tire and trickle down the pavement. He appeared unconcerned.

"Film people," he said in answer to her question. "Foreigners. Arabs or something. To be honest, I don't give a damn, except for all the coming and going. Don't like that." He pulled gently on the leash. "Come on, Skippy." Without another word he continued on. Jade silently bid him adieu.

When the man had disappeared over the hill, Jade sat on her front bumper and stared out at the hazy gray ocean. She tried to decide how she felt about Mac's apparent desire to escalate things. Was it more male stuff, a guy on the make? Sure, he had an interest in her, but that was hardly grounds for complaint—she had an interest in him, too. But what kind of interest? That's the part that scared her. She didn't trust herself to make good choices.

About then, she heard voices coming from across the street. A heavyset guy had come out the front door of the house and said goodbye. Jade watched him waddle to a big Buick and climb in behind the wheel. She got back in her car. After maneuvering past Hernan's vehicle, the big man drove to the street. He glanced in her direction as he passed by. The face was familiar but it was the hair, the guy's big bushy head of salt-and-pepper gray hair that really rung a bell.

Who was he? Then she remembered. He was a P.I. by the name of Boots Conroy. Jade had met him while she was working with Harry Naismith. Harry hadn't thought a lot of the guy. "Boots started out as a skip-trace," she recalled Harry say. "Takes a certain mentality I don't respect hunting down bail-jumpers." Boots, who'd always been large according to Harry, had to give up skip-tracing when he got too slow afoot and the stress of the job did a number on his blood pressure. Mostly he did less demanding work now, like tracking down missing persons and finding truant husbands and wives.

The P.I.'s presence at the same hideout with Ginger and Hernan was an interesting development. On an impulse Jade decided to follow Boots, maybe ask a few questions if she could catch up with him. After all, he'd been inside the place and had to know something about the people there, including Ginger and Hernan.

She took off down the hill and had some trouble following the big guy. He was not only rotund, he had a heavy foot on the peddle. She didn't catch up with him until he'd reached the light at Sunset Boulevard. As it was, she had to run a red light so as not to lose him. It earned her a horn blast from a blonde in a Porsche. Jade would have flipped her off, but she'd long since learned to take pity on blondes.

Boots, meanwhile, had sped east on Sunset. The way he was flying, Jade wondered if he'd spotted her. She had to push the envelope to regain contact. Boots left Sunset at Allenford Avenue, a route that took him south, around the Riviera Country Club and into Santa Monica. As she followed him down Twenty-sixth Street, she had the distinct feeling Boots knew he had a tail. Considering she was cutting it a little close making traffic lights, she wondered if maybe she shouldn't just honk her horn and flash her lights to get his attention. Maybe he'd stop and talk.

At Wilshire Boots gunned the Buick through a red light and Jade knew she was cooked. Screeching to a halt she cussed the bastard, knowing he'd done it on purpose. She watched him disappearing down the street. Two blocks farther, at Santa Monica Boulevard, he made a right. When the light finally changed, Jade drove on down, turning at the same intersection herself. Naturally, there was no sign of him. She slowed, thinking he may have pulled over or into a side street. Then, reaching St. John's Hospital, who should she see in the parking lot but Boots.

He pulled into a parking space. Since there wasn't another empty slot nearby, Jade stopped behind the Buick and got out. Boots, who obviously was expecting her, lowered the window next to him. He turned his jowly face to her.

"Well, it is Harry's girl."

"Former girl," she said. "Harry and I are divorced."

Boots rubbed the first of his chins. "Maybe I did hear that. What's up, toots?"

"Thanks for making me risk life and limb to have the opportunity to tell you."

"I don't remember issuing you an invitation."

"Okay, never mind. I guess the question of the moment is are we working the same case or what?"

"I guess that depends," he said. "What case are you working?"

"I asked first."

Boots took a yellowed handkerchief from his pocket and mopped his face. His hairline was so low on his forehead that there couldn't be much more than two inches between the gray forest of hair atop his head and his eyebrows. Dissecting his brow was a furrow that was so deep it collected perspiration like a rain gutter. Boots made another swipe at it. "I asked second."

"I'm interested in the couple that arrived half an hour before you left that house up in Pacific Palisades, Boots. Ginger and Hernan."

"Actually, they don't interest me and I can't tell you a thing about them."

"How about the folks who live there?"

"Now, that's another story."

"Who's your client?" she asked.

"Who's yours?"

Jade decided it was worth risking the truth. "A guy named Mac McGowan."

"Yeah?"

"Well, you going to reciprocate?" she said.

"Nope. I respect my clients' privacy, honey."

"If your client lives in the place, I can find out who he is easy enough."

"I'll save you the trouble. He don't." A drop of sweat formed on Boots's nose, he dabbed it off, then swabbed the rivulet on his brow again. "So, how about we end this conversation? It's goddamn hot in this tin can."

"What are you doing here, anyway?"

"Visiting a sick friend, all right? And I'm going inside."

She could see Boots was beginning to lose patience.

"I'll walk you in, if you don't mind."

"Do I look like I need a nursemaid, for crissakes?"

He rolled up the window, opened the door and struggled to get out. Jade thought of offering him a hand, but was afraid it would wound his pride. After Boots locked his car door, they slowly walked toward the entrance to the hospital.

"Look, toots," he said, "I can guarantee you that you aren't interested in what I'm doing. I'm sort of mediating a pissing match between a bunch of foreigners. Those kids you asked about aren't involved. They're just friends of the Hampton kid."

"Hampton kid?"

"Oh, shit." Boots said it like he'd just stepped in doggie-do.

"Boots, you mean Troy Hampton?"

He groaned.

"I have a feeling our cases overlap, even if they are different," Jade said.

"Fine, so let's leave it at that."

They walked for a while without talking, then Jade decided to try another ploy. "Your job a big one or a little one?"

"What do you care?"

"Mine's a big one. Lots of dough involved. My client, Mr. McGowan, spends liberally. I'm sure he'd pay handsomely just to know who all was in that house and what they're up to."

The suggestion got his attention. "What kind of figure are we talking?"

"A grand."

Boots scoffed. "That'd barely cover my bar bill."

She knew he was faking disdain. Boots, according to Harry, was small potatoes in every respect save mass. "All I need is names and a capsule summary of what's going on. How many drinks will that cost me?"

"Two grand."

"Twelve hundred."

"Eighteen."

"Boots, we're headed for fifteen, so let's just do it. Will you take my personal check?"

"Okay, but satisfy my curiosity. What's the inside scoop on you and Harry?"

"That's none of your fucking business."

"All right already. I was just wondering, okay?"

They'd come to the hospital entrance. Boots was puffing, but the air-conditioning inside was obviously a great relief. They sat in the lobby. The big guy searched for his inner chin again. "Let's see now, where should I begin?"

Jade waited patiently for the tale to begin, watching poor Boots's rivulet rise to flood stage.

Pacific Palisades

With Jugnu standing behind her, Venita sat at the umbrella table watching Troy dancing with his friends to the music from the "boom box." He had an open bottle of champagne in his hand, which the three of them had been passing back and forth. They were children basically and, much to Venita's amazement and dismay, they held her professional life in their hands. That's what it had come down to.

The detective, Boots Conroy, had described the state of her affairs pretty succinctly when he'd said, "Mr. Gaylord will give you Hollywood if you give him Ramda Bol." And that was the bargain she'd made. She would disclose the entire Ramda Bol story, and in the process make herself a persona non grata in her own country. That meant Hollywood would be her life now—Hollywood with its unpredictability, its vicissitudes, its pretense and its deceptions. But also its glory. The question was, would Hollywood have her?

Venita understood the answer depended on the moxie and balls of a twenty-year-old boy-man, who, coincidentally, was lobbying to become her husband. Venita could only imagine what her father and her husband, Ranjit Govind, would think of that. And yet, here she was, hanging on by a thread. The queen, though very nearly having lost her head, was not yet dead.

Arjay came out of the house just then, joining her at the table. He observed the trio for several moments. "My, my," he said over the blare of the music. "Bacchanalia, American style."

"Yes," she replied. "Children at play."

He leaned toward her and, in a confidential tone, said, "But they're so good at making money, these Americans. This experience has convinced me, Venita, that I should like to have my own little company of spielers, as they say Down Under. I suspect I should do quite well as Fagin with a merry little band of ruffians such as these."

"You're gainfully employed at present, Arjay, lest you forget."

"Indeed. Fear not, my dear, I'm perfectly aware of my obligations." He watched Hernan in particular. "Oh, by the way, there was news from India on the telly just now that should be of considerable interest."

"Oh?"

"There's been a drastic shake-up in the Congress Party. The old guard is out and a group led by Gian Mohindra has taken power."

"Mohindra?" She pondered the news, her excitement growing. "He hated Ramda. They were sworn enemies. Ramda always told me if Mohindra were to take power he would probably leave the country."

"I should think Mohindra would gladly see him to the airport."

"Interesting," Venita said, a lilt in her voice as she contemplated the possibilities.

If Ramda was no longer a factor in Indian politics, she was no longer a threat to him. It could mean that in a blink of the eye she'd gone from persona non grata to martyred heroine and was free to return to India and her adoring fans. How delicious to think she could retake her place in the firmament of Indian stardom. Of course, her heart's desire was to direct in Hollywood—a fading beauty had only so many years to look forward to, but a brilliant director could go on and on. Could she somehow manage both?

To some degree her hand was being forced by Percy Gaylord, but at least her options were multiplying. Ah, but the gods were being good to her. Only hours ago she stood in jeopardy of becoming a condemned murderess, and now she once more had the opportunity to become a goddess on two continents! What joy!

"What will you do?" Arjay asked.

"I shall see if my young lover is the man he pretends to be."

At that moment Cala came trotting out from the house and whispered something in her ear. Venita sent the woman away and told Jugnu to turn down the music.

"Troy," Venita said, "your mother has rung you up. It sounds as though it may be urgent."

"Thank heavens," Stella said. "I've been trying to reach you everywhere. I thought perhaps Amal would know where you were."

"Yeah, Mom, I'm visiting him and Venita. So, what's up?"

"You've heard about Mac..."

"The shootout? Yeah, I heard."

"I don't know if that brought it about or what, but I think I've convinced him to support our efforts."

"Huh?"

"Mac's given in, Troy."

"He's going to invest in the film?"

"I think so. He wants us both at his house at five. He said he's got good news that will make your day."

Troy was incredulous. "He said he was going to give us the money?"

"Not in so many words, but—"

"Ma, you're jumping to conclusions, then."

"No, Troy, I don't believe so. Mac and I have been in an extended negotiation for several days. He knows what I want and he's told me he'll accommodate me. And he specifically said he wants you there."

"I smell a rat."

"Believe me, he has every reason to capitulate."

"Is that all he said? He didn't mention anything else?"

"Mac has his problems, but this is what he's focused

on. Don't you see, Troy? This is what we've been dreaming about."

Troy didn't know what to think. Mac had made his deal with Ginger and now he'd agreed to give him and Stella money, too? Surely he wasn't planning to pay off everybody. Somebody was mistaken. Or was Mac setting them all up?

"Troy, aren't you pleased?"

"Yeah, Mom, that's great. I'm having trouble believing it's actually happening."

"I think Mac wanted to do it all along, dear," she said. "He just needed to be nudged."

"That I can believe."

"Five o'clock, Mac's place," his mother said. "And, Troy, please don't do anything to provoke him. He's under tremendous pressure. Trust me, this hasn't been easy for him. And for God's sake, don't forget, the man still believes he's your father."

Troy groaned inwardly at that. "I can't tell you how that gets me...really makes me sick."

"Well, it will all be over soon, dear. Once we're busy making movies and Mac sees our success, he'll lighten up."

"Do you think the sonovabitch is really going to leave me his money? I hate the thought of kissing his butt for years only to find out he disinherited me."

"Don't borrow trouble. But I can't talk now, I've got to run. I'll see you at Mac's at five."

Troy hung up the phone, but sat there a moment longer, pondering his mother's news. Something was wrong, though he couldn't say what. Surely Ginger hadn't misread the situation. Or had Mac simply outfoxed them? Maybe his mother had been duped, as well.

But what could the bastard do? He'd killed Aubrey St. George. There was no way he could change that.

Troy returned to his friends. Taking Venita aside, he walked with her out toward the pavilion.

"Is everything all right?" she asked.

"There's a meeting at Mac's at five," he said. "I'd like you and Amal to go with me."

"What's the meeting regarding?"

"According to my mother, we're going to get the money."

"For the film."

"Supposedly."

She studied him. "You aren't sure?"

"I'm being cautious. We'll get it eventually, Venita. Whether it's today or not remains to be seen."

"Five o'clock?"

"Five o'clock."

Bel Air

Mac watched her pacing. At the rate she was going, she'd wear out his carpet. Manuela had to be deranged. She was completely irrational. Chances were she was high on something, too, which didn't help matters. There was no doubt about her hatred. He just couldn't understand it, especially not her bitterness toward Jade.

Every time he tried to engage her in conversation, she'd cut him off. "I don't want to hear you," she screamed at him. "I listened to you last time and look what happened!"

"But, Manuela—"

She shoved the gun so hard into his throat that he was certain she was about to blow his head off. "Didn't you hear me? Shut the fuck up!"

Mostly she'd muttered to herself, alternately cursing and crying. She blamed him for her misery. Her brother was dead, her mother was dying, she was going to spend the rest of her life in prison.

"There's only one thing left that will make me happy," she told him. "That's seeing your face when I shoot her."

"Manuela, Jade's never done anything to you. She doesn't even know you."

Spinning, her eyes round as saucers, Manuela pointed the gun at him and fired. The bullet smashed into the chair next to his head. Mac was stunned. Manuela began to laugh until she cried. Then for some inexplicable reason she went over to the ostrich egg on the table, pointed the gun at it and fired, shattering the egg, the stand and the top of the table.

After another fifteen minutes of pacing, Manuela abruptly stopped and glared at him. "So, where the fuck is she?"

"I don't know. There's no guarantee she's coming here."

"She will."

Mac could see the woman was obsessed. He wasn't going to stand idly by and let her kill Jade, but he had to pick his spot. He'd only get one chance, and so far she hadn't given him an opportunity, keeping her distance from him as she paced.

He didn't know how she'd gotten here, but he could only hope she'd been foolish enough to leave her vehicle where Jade could see it. Barring that, if he could cause something else to be amiss, something that would put Jade on the alert.... Anything. But what?

It was then he heard a vehicle in the drive. His heart sank at the thought it might be Jade. Manuela went to the window, but not without keeping one eye on him.

"Well, guess who?" Manuela said, her joy demonic.

Mac knew he had only seconds. Once Jade was at the door, it could be too late. There was a small bronze figure of an owl on the end table next to the sofa across from him. He'd been eyeing it, trying to figure out how he could use it as a weapon. He could fling it at her, but if he missed, or didn't manage a telling blow, it would do no good. But then it occurred to him that by throwing it through the window Jade would know there was trouble.

It was his best shot, but he didn't have time to reflect. He had to do it now!

Manuela gave him a quick glance, and the second her head was turned Mac leaped up, dashed to the table and flung the owl through the bay window, practically in one motion. Manuela, enraged, started to fire at him, but didn't, probably realizing the gunshot would send Jade running, if the shattering glass didn't.

"Sonovabitch!" she snarled. It was above a stage whisper, but less than a shout.

"Mac?" It was Jade, outside.

"Run, Jade!" he screamed, and dived onto the floor.

Manuela lost it. She fired at him. The bullet grazed his arm and went into the couch. The next thing he heard was her running to the front door, which she threw open. She fired another shot.

As Mac got to his knees, grasping his bleeding arm, Manuela came running back into the sitting room and leaped onto the sofa. Mac was certain she was going to shoot him, but she didn't. "Get up, you sonovabitch!" she shouted.

Mac stood and Manuela moved around behind him, ignoring his wound. She pressed the muzzle of her gun against the base of his skull.

"Get going," she said, giving him a shove in the back.

They went to the French doors accessing the patio. Mac realized Jade had escaped, probably having run around the house. Manuela was going to use him as a shield and maybe for bait. They went out onto the patio.

"Here's your boyfriend!" she shouted. "Unless you want to see me kill him right now, come out of the bushes."

Mac hoped Jade had the sense to get the hell away. The last thing he wanted was for her to play hero. But she'd already shown herself to be a warrior. Manuela pushed him up the slope toward the pool, probably to get a better perspective of the grounds.

Though his arm stung, Mac realized he'd only been grazed, the bullet barely having torn his skin.

"Come out, you cunt!" Manuela screamed at Jade. "You afraid?"

They reached the deck of the pool. Manuela pressed the muzzle of her gun hard against the base of his skull.

"I'm giving you thirty seconds," she called.

Mac knew she was crazy enough to shoot him dead. But if she did, she'd have no bargaining chip, nobody to hide behind. Was she smart enough to realize that? The woman was obviously over the edge.

"Fifteen seconds!"

Mac prepared himself. He wasn't going to let fate decide, in any case. When the countdown got to zero, he'd go for the gun.

"Five seconds!"

"All right!" Jade yelled from the shrubs at the far side of the yard. "You win, I'm coming out."

"No!" he roared.

Manuela brought the butt of the pistol down sharply on his shoulder. Mac's knees buckled, but he managed to keep his feet. Then to his horror, Jade emerged from the bushes.

"What do you want, Manuela?" she called.

"I want you up here."

"Fine, but why don't you explain the problem."

"The problem is, if it wasn't for your candy ass and

this jerk-off, I'd be happy instead of doing this shit. Come on up here.''

Mac groaned when he saw Jade slowly moving in their direction. She had come four or five steps when there was a cacophony of chirping and cawing in the trees. Dogs up and down the canyon began barking. Then a sudden rumble welled up out of the bowels of the earth and the ground began shaking.

''What the fuck?'' Manuela said.

The ground rolled under them and they swayed like drunken sailors. The water in the pool sloshed and the rumble grew louder and louder, as though a giant train were racing up the canyon.

''Jesus Christ.''

Mac, realizing Manuela was momentarily distracted, spun around violently. His elbow hit her gun hand, causing her to fire the pistol errantly into the air. He then gave her a shove. Manuela screamed as she went flying into the pool.

The ground still shaking under him, Mac turned and loped down the slope toward Jade, who'd come several steps in his direction. Grabbing her hand, he pulled her back toward the shrubs. When they were well into the vegetation, he stopped.

''What in the hell were you doing?'' he said angrily. ''Don't you know she was going to shoot you?'' He glanced up toward the pool to see if Manuela had emerged, but she hadn't.

The ground had stopped shaking, but the birds and dogs weren't yet finished. Jade put her hands on her hips. ''I was trying to save your butt, McGowan,'' she said indignantly.

''Well, I was trying to save yours. You're the one she wanted to shoot.''

''That's not the way it sounded from where I was sitting." Then she noticed his arm. "Mac, you've been wounded."

"Just a nick."

She pulled back the frayed cloth of his shirt. "You sure?"

"Mostly blood."

They both glanced up toward the pool, but there was still no sign of Manuela, though they heard a feeble, choking cry.

"Do you suppose she can't swim?" he asked.

"She could be faking it. I'll go check."

"No, I'll go check."

They both started briskly up the slope. By the time they got to the pool, Manuela was floating facedown in the water.

"Jesus," Mac said.

He took his wallet out of his pocket, handed it to Jade and dived into the water. Coming up behind the drowning woman, he flopped her over and pulled her to the side of the pool. Jade took her arms. By the time he'd climbed out of the water, Jade pretty much had her on the deck. Manuela appeared to be unconscious.

"Is she breathing?" he asked.

"No."

Jade, on her knees, opened Manuela's jaw, scooped, pinched her nose shut and blew into her mouth. After a couple of breaths, Manuela coughed. A few seconds later, she came to.

Blinking, she looked at them, a confused expression on her face, then coughed some more. Once she was breathing halfway normally, she said, "What happened?"

"The people you were trying to kill saved your life," Mac told her.

Manuela's chin dropped to her chest. "Shit."

"Yeah," he grumbled under his breath. "I couldn't agree more."

Mac sat on his bed in his sweats and pulled on his socks. His arm was bandaged, but the wound was superficial. He'd showered carefully so as not to get his bandage wet, but hadn't bothered drying his hair. There was a knock on his door. "Yes?"

"It's me," Jade said.

"Come in."

She opened the door, then stood in the doorway, her hands on her hips, her expression official, stern. He had an overwhelming desire to take her in his arms. But since she was on duty, being professional, he restrained himself. Cuteness was not supposed to matter in circumstances such as these.

"They've taken Manuela away," she said. "Jaime Caldron is out by the pool, talking to the other detectives. And guess who's out front?"

"Stella?"

"Yes. And your son, too. Plus, the Indian movie star and her entourage."

"The whole gang, huh?"

She laughed. "Mac, I need to brief you on what I found out before I got here. There are some things you need to know."

"Am I going to like it?"

"I don't think so."

He ran his fingers back through his damp hair. "Lay it on me, then. No, wait. First, come over here." He indicated the bed beside him.

Jade made her way over, looking a bit uncomfortable. Mac put an arm around her shoulders, even knowing she probably didn't appreciate the familiarity at a crime scene, not with everybody still full of adrenaline. But he wanted to have his say.

"Before we get to official business, can I just thank you for what you did out there today? You risked your life for me, and I want you to know I'm really touched."

"I'd have done it for anybody."

"No, don't say that. I want you to have done it for me because I'm such a special guy."

"You are special," she said with a grin. "You're paying me double my usual rate."

He cuffed her chin playfully. "Let me ask you something. How would you feel about me if tomorrow I filed for bankruptcy?"

"I'd think you're still a nice guy. Just poorer."

He liked that. Then Mac did what he'd wanted to do for several days. He leaned over and kissed her on the lips. It was an affectionate kiss. His mouth lingered near hers. As they pulled apart, she slowly opened her eyes.

"That wasn't fair."

"I know, but how many guys get to kiss a star detective?"

She poked her tongue in her cheek and colored.

"Okay," Mac said with feigned sternness. "Let's have your report."

Jade cleared her throat. He could tell she was flustered and he loved it. She cleared her throat again and somehow managed to look grim.

"Ginger, the five-million-dollar girl, and Hernan, are your son's pals, Mac."

"Troy's?"

"Right. Hernan is his roommate."

He was stunned. He had to make an effort to close his mouth. "You're saying my kid's behind the extortion plot?"

"I'm not a hundred percent certain, but circumstantial

evidence points to that. The big house in Pacific Palisades
I followed Ginger and Hernan to is occupied by the Indian
movie folks. Your son and the woman...let's see what's
her name?...Venus...no..."

"Venita Kumar."

"Yes, Venita and Troy are having...well, an affair."

He shook his head, feeling like somebody who'd been
asleep for several months. "And she's in on the blackmail-
extortion thing?"

"That I don't know."

"Well, she's been trying to raise several million bucks
for her movie deal," he said. "If she isn't involved, she
was going to benefit, that's certain. But my son's the one
shaking me down. Christ. How'd he find out about Aubrey? From Stella?"

"I don't know. I haven't talked to them," she replied.
"This is coming from third parties."

"Knowing the people I'm dealing with, it all makes
sense. I should have figured it had to do with that goddamn
movie deal."

"There's more, I'm afraid. Apparently, Venita's director
friend, Arjay, is not quite the real thing."

"You said Arjay. You mean Amal."

"No, the real Amal Kory is at a retreat in India or Nepal
or someplace. This guy's name is Arjay Pantel and he's a
grifter, basically."

"The movie mogul my wife wanted me to invest millions with is a con man, is that what you're telling me?"

"Essentially."

"Good thing I'm a tight sonovabitch. If I'd given them
the two million, I wonder where they'd be now?"

Jade shrugged.

"What about Stella? Is she in on this?"

"Again, I don't know. She might be. Her threats to go
to the police could have been insurance in case this deal

didn't work out. All I can tell you for sure is they're all here and seem like a happy little group."

"Drooling at the prospect of getting my money. Obviously they aren't aware you're onto them."

"I doubt it. I got my information from a detective working for a guy who's blackmailing Venita, an Indian journalist by the name of Percy Gaylord."

"He's blackmailing her?"

"Forcing her to reveal the inside scoop about a political scandal back in India."

"Sounds like I'm not the only one on the rack."

"Nope."

"Lord," he said, shaking his head.

"It's a complicated situation, Mac. I figure I may have sorted out about forty percent of it. Enough to know we're in a spider's nest."

She proceeded to tell him the rest. Mac listened gravely. After she'd finished, he rubbed his chin, trying to figure out what to do with the information, when the phone rang. He gave Jade an "excuse me" pat on the knee, scooted to the head of the bed and picked up the receiver. "Yes?"

"Mac, it's Bev."

"Don't tell me, the office is lying in ruins."

"No, only minor damage here. How's your house?"

"Still standing, which is more than you can say for me." He lay back against the headboard, giving Jade a wink.

"You okay?" Bev asked.

"Yes, just a figure of speech. What's up? Everybody curious if the guy who signs their paychecks is still among the living?"

"People here have been calling home to check on their families and so forth," she said.

"Send everybody home, if that's the question."

"No, that's not why I called."

He could tell by her tone he wasn't going to like this, either.

"Some reports have also been coming in from the field. One in particular I thought you ought to know about. I understand you asked Walt to keep an eye on a job in Brentwood where you'd put in the original pool..."

Mac's blood went cold. "Yes? What about it?"

"One of the engineers was at the site when the quake hit."

"And?"

"Apparently, the hillside gave way and part of the pool went sliding down into the canyon."

Mac closed his eyes, pressing the bridge of his nose with his fingers.

"Since we hadn't broken ground," Bev went on, "Walt said we don't have any exposure, but something very troubling turned up, Mac."

He knew what she was going to say.

"It seems there was a body under the pool. Our guy looks down and see's this skeleton hanging right there at the precipice sticking out from broken chunks of concrete. He called the police."

Mac drew a long, slow breath. The irony struck him. Twenty years and Glamour Puss chose today. Somehow, though, it seemed fitting.

"Mac?"

"Okay, I hear you. Thanks for the report, Bev." He hung up the phone and looked at Jade. "The earthquake sheared the hillside behind that house in Brentwood, exposing Aubrey St. George's remains."

"What are you going to do?"

"This doesn't change anything. I decided what I was going to do earlier. All this does is make it easier. But in light of what you've told me about Troy and the Indians, I'll have to reconsider how I'm going to do this."

She looked perplexed.

"You'll see what I mean." He glanced at the bedstand clock. "Jade, would you mind assembling the suspects and Lieutenant Caldron in the drawing room? I'll be down in a few minutes."

She moved up next to him, taking his hand. "You're a good person," she said. "What you did twenty years ago doesn't matter…at least, not to me. I want you to know that."

He reached out, taking her chin in his hand. "Thanks."

"Would you kiss me again?" she asked.

"Are detectives allowed to fraternize with confessed felons?"

"I don't see how a kiss can hurt."

Mac took her into his arms and kissed her deeply. He wished he could just hold her, forget the world, but that clearly wasn't to be. The pretense, the long wait for justice, was finally over.

"If and when I'm finally through this, would you consider going away someplace with me?"

"Like where?"

"Hawaii would be nice."

She stroked his hand. "Let's get this behind us first."

Jade kissed him on the cheek and left the room. Mac watched her leave, staring at the door after she'd closed it. In the course of just a few minutes, he'd lived through the best and worst of times. The moment he'd always known at some level would come was in fact upon him. He was glad. But because of Jade, he also felt hope—hope about the future, murky though it was. Mostly, though, he felt hope for himself. He'd been traveling a long and difficult road. He wanted the journey over. He wanted the future to be different.

Mac put on his shoes, ran his fingers through his hair and looked to see if his checkbook was on his dresser.

* * *

As Mac walked in, a hush came over the room. "Good afternoon, everyone," he said. "Thank you all for coming." He glanced around, making eye contact with each person in turn.

Stella and Arjay Pantel were seated on the larger sofa and Troy and Venita were on the love seat, holding hands. Stella eyed them, not looking at all pleased. A large bearded man in a turban stood behind Venita. Lieutenant Jaime Caldron sat alone in an armchair. Jade was standing off to the side.

"I don't know if you've all been formally introduced. Mr. Kory and Miss Kumar, the lady standing over there is the private investigator working for me, Ms. Morro, and this gentleman is Lieutenant Jaime Caldron of the L.A.P.D. He's here because of certain events that occurred twenty years ago. I intend to discuss that at length, Lieutenant, but if you'll bear with me I'd like to deal with some family matters first. I have an announcement I'd like to make, as well."

Mac studied the faces staring back at him, seeing a little of everything, ranging from confusion to distress to amusement. It was Jade's expression he liked best. He saw understanding and, though he hadn't told her his intentions, he suspected she had a pretty good idea what was coming.

"Let me get right to the point," he said. "Stella and Troy, I know you're both intent on being in Mr. Kory's film and that you want me to invest in it. I've resisted because I don't think it's good business, but also because I'm reluctant to get involved with strangers. I've always believed you can't know a person too well if you're going to get in bed with them...figuratively and literally both."

Mac noted Stella's uneasiness, though it was difficult to decide whether she was more troubled by his comments, or the way Troy was behaving toward Venita. Only one person's reaction was certain—Troy's. The kid loathed him. His feelings were unmistakable.

"Troy, you've never taken advice from me," Mac said, moving a bit closer to him and Venita, "but you seem especially annoyed today. Have I offended you...any more than usual, that is?"

"I'm beginning to wonder if you brought us here to jerk our chains."

"Troy!" Stella said.

"It's a fair comment," Mac said. "But the answer is no. My intent is to communicate. I want to know how you both feel and I'd like to express my views, too."

"Well, I've got an announcement myself," Troy said. "I know this is coming as a surprise, but you might as well know. Venita and I are engaged."

Stella blanched. "What? You can't be serious!"

Venita scooted forward in her seat to speak, directing her comments mostly to Stella. "I know this comes unexpectedly," she said, adjusting the portion of her lavender sari that lay across her shoulder. "Perhaps you're concerned about the differences in our ages, perhaps you have doubts because of differences in Troy's and my background, but I assure you that my feelings for your son are profound. I didn't expect anything like this to happen. I didn't seek it. But we do love each other. If we can't have your blessing, I hope you at least understand."

Stella appeared ready to cry, but was incapable of speech.

"I think congratulations are in order," Mac said. "I can't speak for Stella, but I personally wish you both the best." He cleared his throat. "But your personal lives and the film deal are two separate issues as far as I'm concerned."

Troy did not look pleased about that. Mac turned to his wife.

"You've made your commitment to this movie very clear to me, Stella. It wouldn't be a reach to say nothing is more important to you."

She colored, but lifted her chin. "It's Troy's and my dream, that's true, but it's also a wonderful opportunity for you, Mac."

He couldn't help smiling at the innocence of her tone. It was especially ironic considering she had been trying to extort millions from him. But that was Stella.

"Never mind me," he said. "This is about you and Troy. I've made my decision. I plan to give you each a million dollars to invest in Mr. Kory's film."

Venita and Arjay brightened right along with Stella and Troy.

"You are serious, Mac," his wife said.

"Of course. You can be very persuasive, Stella, when you put your mind to it."

She seemed uncertain whether to be offended or not. He reached into his pocket and took out two checks, holding them up. "Here's a million dollars each. But there is a catch," he said. "You only get the money if you invest it in *On Distant Shores* with Amal and Venita."

"Mac," Stella said, "that's our intention. How can it be a catch?"

"I'm afraid you based your decision on incomplete information."

"What are you talking about?"

Mac glanced at Jade, who smiled at him. "Stella," he said, "before donating this much money to a project and people I couldn't vouch for, I thought the responsible thing to do was check things out, ask a few questions. Would you care to hear what I've learned?"

Venita Kumar drew herself up. Arjay Pantel's composure began showing signs of cracking. He shifted uncomfortably. Mac stared at him, then at Venita, who was staring daggers back at him in anticipation of what she surely knew was coming. Stella seemed confused.

"Let me be direct," Mac said. "Mr. Kory is an acclaimed film director, no doubt about that. And yes, you'd be lucky if he took you under his wing. The problem is, I learned that Mr. Kory is a reclusive guy. In fact, for a number of months he's been in a retreat in a remote part of India."

Arjay Pantel squirmed. Stella looked at him.

"Mac, what are you talking about?"

"There's a journalist in St. John's Hospital in Santa Monica, a guy named Percy Gaylord, who can give you all the details," he replied. "The short version is this. The gentleman seated next to you is actually Arjay Pantel. If you asked Lieutenant Caldron how best to describe Mr. Pantel's profession, the term he'd probably use is con artist."

"What?" Stella said indignantly.

"I'm afraid it's true. This guy is an impostor."

Venita moved to the edge of her seat. Troy got to his feet. "What kind of bullshit is this? You didn't bring us here to give us money for the project. You want to dump on our friends."

"Ask Mr. Pantel about his criminal record, Troy."

Arjay rose. "This is most amusing, Mr. McGowan. But I see no reason to sit here and endure your baseless accusations."

"Do you deny that what I just said is true?"

"I shan't dignify that with a response. Good day." With that, he headed for the door.

"Mac McGowan," Stella fumed, "this is a disgrace!"

Now Venita was on her feet. "You are a brutal man, sir," she said, her eyes flashing.

"Is the guy who just walked out the door the same one who directed you in the films you did with Amal Kory,

Miss Kumar, or did you develop amnesia, like your friend Percy Gaylord?''

''I am a reputable film star, the widow of the late and most assuredly great director, Ranjit Govind.''

''Then perhaps you'd like to explain why you hired a con artist to play the role of Kory to dupe my wife and son.''

Venita shook with rage. ''You mean to destroy me. You feel threatened. That's what this is about!''

''You don't have to prove your acting credentials, Miss Kumar. Your performance speaks for itself. But I understand you were run out of your own country on a rail. I don't know the details, and I'm sure as hell not going to judge whether it was justified or not. But I do know this, you're a fraud.''

''You're a bloody liar!'' she screamed.

Her servant came around the love seat and took her by the arm. He tried to pull her away. Venita resisted.

''I won't be insulted this way. I won't, I tell you. I refuse!''

''The game's over, Miss Kumar,'' Mac said.

''You don't want me to marry your son. That's why you're doing this.''

''Wait a minute,'' Troy said, confusion replacing his anger. ''That stuff about Amal is bullshit, isn't it, Venita? I mean, that is Amal.''

She glared at Mac before turning to his son. ''Troy,'' she said with unexpected gentleness, ''sometimes an actor must improvise. Amal Kory adores me. He adores my work. He truly does. But he's on a spiritual quest and couldn't come to America at the moment. My reputation is as an actress, not a director. I knew that American cinema would never accept me in front of the camera—not as a leading lady, a star—but I'm absolutely certain I can make it behind the camera, given the opportunity. The

trouble is, I don't have directing credentials. I needed a
name to work with. My goal was to take control in my
own right by the second or third project. This is all true.
Every word of it, I swear to you. And it will work. I'm
certain.''

"Then that guy who left is a phony."

"Don't you see that doesn't matter? I'm the talent, Troy.
I will handle the direction. Nothing's changed really. All
we need to do is drop the pretense. Take your father's
check. Let's marry like we've planned." She took him by
the arm. "Please, Troy, don't let this minor detail get in
the way of a truly great opportunity for us both."

"Venita, do you know how hard it is for an established
director to get a film in this town? They'll laugh at you,
whether I give you a million dollars or not."

"No, Troy, when people see what I can do, investors
will flock to us. You must trust me, my darling."

Stella, who'd been quiet, began sobbing mournfully.
Everyone fell silent, turning in her direction.

"Dear God," she said, "I gave that man twenty thousand dollars."

"Pantel?" Mac said.

"Yes…I thought…I thought he adored me, my work…I
thought we were going to do fabulous things together…
I thought he had money coming from India…he…he
said…"

Venita looked aghast. "You gave Arjay twenty thousand?"

Stella nodded, sobbing.

"The thief!" Venita exclaimed. "The bloody fucking
thief!"

Stella wiped her eyes. "He told me his funds would be
coming within a few weeks. I offered…oh, good Lord.
Twenty thousand dollars. And it's your fault, Venita. You
brought a swindler into my home. You vouched for him."

She turned to Caldron. "You're a policeman! That man who just left stole my money!"

"You want to make out a complaint? Is that what you're saying?"

Stella looked at Mac desperately, pleadingly.

"Trickery is one way to take a person's money, Stella," he said. "Extortion's another. Mr. Pantel set his sights a little lower, that's all."

She sank back on the sofa, weeping. Troy looked practically as bewildered as his mother. He dropped back into the chair. Venita Kumar turned first one way, then the other, looking for a compassionate face.

"This is insane," she exclaimed. "Am I the only one who sees it? I'm a star. Millions adore me. What's wrong with you bloody people?"

Troy sat with his head in his hands. Tears ran down Stella's cheeks. Venita, seeing what was happening around her, got in Mac's face.

"This is all because of your villainy!" she railed. "If it wasn't for you, none of this would have happened."

She lunged at him then, striking him with her fists. Jaime Caldron got to his feet, but before he could say or do anything, Venita's servant quickly grabbed her by the arm and jerked her away.

"That's enough!" he shouted hoarsely. "Enough!"

"Don't you dare speak to me that way...you... you...donkey!" she cried.

Jugnu jerked her back, ignoring her. "I am sorry for this, sir," he said to Mac, his voice a low rumble. "She has lost her reason. Allow me to take her from this country. There is no need to punish her. She can make no more trouble for your family."

"Do whatever you want," Mac said.

Jugnu began dragging Venita toward the door.

"No!" she wailed. "A chance! That's all I'm asking. A chance! Troy..."

Moments later they were gone and the room was in silence except for Stella's sobbing. Troy looked at Mac. He seethed with hatred.

"You couldn't just tell us, you had to make a big show of it."

"Maybe I was a little heavy-handed, but you know what? You and your mother haven't exactly been gentle with me. I won't be going into the details now, not in front of Lieutenant Caldron, but I know what you and your friends Ginger and Hernan are up to and, frankly, Troy, I'm appalled that you'd stoop to that. So you don't have much cause to be indignant."

Troy stared at him with contempt. Mac, the checks in his hand, said, "Am I right that you don't wish to share this with Miss Kumar and Mr. Pantel?"

"Okay, fine, you made your point," Troy said. "Why don't you just tell us what you want. A signed confession?"

"Remorse is too much to expect, I suppose, but I wouldn't mind a little consideration. It's no secret you don't like me, Troy. But the irony is, I don't know why. Sure, I haven't embraced your Hollywood dream, and maybe I've been less tolerant than I should have been, but have I been that bad a father?"

Troy shook his head. "You haven't a clue. You really don't."

"Troy," Stella interjected. "Be quiet!"

"Why? Do you think after this he's going to—"

"Troy, shut up!"

"No, I'm not going to shut up!" he shouted, standing again, his face red. "I'm sick and tired of this father-son bullshit, Mom. Maybe you can spend your life pretending but I can't. Not anymore." He glared at Mac. "You can't understand why I hate you. Well, how would *you* feel about the man who killed your father, your real father? I'm not your son, you sorry sonovabitch.''

Mac looked at his wife. Her face was buried in her hands. She cried softly.

''Stella?''

She continued to sob.

''Stella?''

Finally she looked up at him, her eyes red. In a small voice she said, ''I didn't know for sure until after Troy was born. The doctor confirmed he was Aubrey's with a blood test.''

''And you didn't tell me?'' Mac felt as though he'd been kicked in the stomach.

''I was afraid you'd...well, I knew how you felt about Aubrey. How could I ask you to raise his son?''

''So, instead you told him and let him hate me.''

''I didn't intend for him to know. He guessed.''

''But did you have to tell him what happened that night, Stella?''

''I didn't,'' she said, shaking her head. ''I swear.'' She looked at her son. ''How did you find out?''

''I overheard the two of you arguing one day,'' Troy replied. ''You didn't know I was in the house.''

''No wonder you hate me,'' Mac said, flabbergasted. He glanced at Jaime Caldron, who had listened quietly as their family drama played out. Then at Jade, who seemed as distraught as he felt.

''Well, I almost got my revenge,'' Troy said. ''But what goes around comes around. You've got bigger problems than me, Mac. Seeing you twist in the wind is almost as good as having your money.'' He shook his head, looking wistful. ''Well, unless somebody would like to put me in handcuffs, I'm going to split.'' He hesitated a moment and, when nobody said anything, he said, "In that case, I'm going to call a cab. See you around, Mom."

He started to leave when Stella said, "Take my car, Troy. Here." She dug in her purse and fished out her car keys and tossed them to him.

"What about you?"

"I'll find transportation. But I'll want to talk to you later. It's very important."

"Okay. Call me. Nice party, Mac."

He left the house. Nobody said a word until he'd started the car and driven away. Mac sat down on the love seat across from Caldron. The detective waited.

"This was the point where I was going to make a big, dramatic confession, Lieutenant, but my son…uh…I guess that's Stella's son…stole my thunder."

"I knew why you invited me here, Mr. McGowan. You get points for that."

Mac glanced at Jade, who then came over and sat next to him. She took his hand.

"Points," Mac said, staring off. "Twenty years I've lived with this, now I get points." He shook his head. "Maybe I deserved it. God knows, I didn't rush to set things right."

"You weren't being selfish," Stella said, wiping her eyes. "You were trying to protect us, Troy and me. I never doubted that."

"Thanks, Stella, but what have I accomplished?"

"You kept us from giving a fortune to those dreadful people. Had it not been for them, none of this would have happened. Lieutenant Caldron would not be here now."

"No, Stella," Mac said. "The whole thing was going to come out. None of you are aware of this, but this afternoon the pool over at Aubrey's place crumbled away in the earthquake. Aubrey's body was found."

Jade squeezed his hand. He was so emotionally wrung out, he didn't feel as relieved as he'd expected.

"To your credit, you invited me here before the quake," Caldron said.

"More points?" Mac said ironically.

"Murder is no small thing. You need all the consideration you can get, Mr. McGowan."

"I know this will sound self-serving coming twenty years after the fact, but I didn't murder Aubrey, Lieutenant. I killed him accidentally. I didn't even intend to hurt him. I was trying to stop him from beating Stella. We were having an affair and he walked in on us. During the scuffle he fell and hit his head."

"It was justifiable homicide," Jade interjected. "He was defending Stella."

Caldron looked back and forth between Mac and Stella. "Why didn't you come forward with your story at the time?"

"We were afraid to," Mac said. "That's what it amounted to."

"So, instead you buried the body. That's not the act of an innocent man, Mr. McGowan. In my humble opinion the prosecutor's got a clear case for murder, manslaughter minimum. Especially if the forensics back it up. The science and tech guys can do some pretty amazing things these days—not to rain on your parade or anything, Mr. McGowan." He turned to Stella. "But an eyewitness can make or break any case. Your son says he heard you and Mr. McGowan arguing and he heard reference to the fact that Mr. McGowan killed Aubrey St. George. I don't know what your story is now, ma'am, but your only real option at this point is to tell the truth."

Stella sat with her head bowed.

"You could be an accessory," Caldron went on. "You could have compounded a felony, aided and abetted. No question you were involved in the cover-up. And I'm wondering what your role was in disposing of the body. What I'm saying is, you've got a lot to lose. As far as I'm concerned, the offer to help us make the case against your husband is still open.''

Caldron stared intensely at Stella when she glanced up. So did Mac and Jade.

Stella clasped her hands, looking down at them prayerfully. Mac's heart pounded hard. He had no idea what to expect. Stella had been shaken to the core and had just watched her family disintegrate before her eyes. Her dreams had been dashed. She could be bitter, vengeful. He could only hope she cared about her dignity and her self-respect enough to back him up. He silently pleaded for the truth.

Stella drew a deep breath and gazed heavenward with shimmering eyes. ''Mac didn't kill Aubrey, Lieutenant.'' She paused dramatically, her eyes shimmering. ''I did.''

''You?''

''Yes, Mac struggled with Aubrey and yes, he was trying to keep Aubrey from beating me, but he didn't kill him. He was unconscious.''

Mac was astounded. ''Stella, what are you saying?''

''Aubrey knocked you out with the statue. When you awoke, I told you that he'd fallen and hit his head after you shoved him. But that isn't what happened. Aubrey fell all right. Then he got up. He was about to hit you again, kill you, I imagine. I picked up the Chinese cheop and I struck him, crushed his skull. I didn't set out to kill him, but before it was over, I wanted him dead.''

''Stella,'' Mac said, ''there's no need to go into it, not without an attorney. It's enough that you saved my life. That's justifiable homicide. Leave it at that.''

''Fine, whatever. The point is, I killed him because I

didn't want you to die and him to live. He was a mean bastard, he truly was.''

Mac glanced at Jade. He could tell she was thinking the same thing he was. Stella had made a damning admission, one that couldn't have been lost on Caldron, who was listening attentively, now leaning forward in his chair.

"But you told Mr. McGowan he killed St. George thinking that way he'd be less likely to report the death?'' he said.

"Yes, and I wanted Mac beholden to me for keeping his secret. I did what I thought was necessary to keep my life and my career from falling apart.''

"And so for twenty years you let me believe I killed a man...''

"I know that seems cruel, Mac, but if it weren't for me, you'd very likely be dead. Aubrey was in a terrible rage and you were completely vulnerable. I didn't have to make this admission. Nobody knew what happened but Aubrey and me. And he's dead.''

"Why did you, then?'' Mac asked. "Lieutenant Caldron was prepared to hang me.''

She again looked up toward the ceiling, blinking back tears that threatened. She bit her lip. She touched her hair. "Why?'' She leveled her gaze on him as another tear slid down her cheek. "I won't insult you by saying I did it for you, Mac. I did it for me, of course.'' She gave him a bittersweet smile. "I've always done what I've done for me. Ever since I was Judy Miller.

"I guess when Amal—or whatever his name is—walked out not only with my twenty thousand dollars, but also with my dreams, it struck me that everything was lost, it was over. And don't think these past twenty years have been easy for me, Mac. This has been eating at me, too. Yes, I was obsessed with my career and with Troy, but I've had to live with myself and it hasn't been easy. I'm a much better actor than you give me credit for.'' She wiped her eyes with a tissue. "The point is, I decided enough's enough.''

"Stella, I contributed plenty to this mess. You weren't the only one making mistakes.''

"Oh, Mac, you have no idea. I was willing to do anything, use you any way I could. I not only tried to extort money from you, I was the one who sent you those anonymous notes.''

"You did?''

"Yes, I had my gardener deliver them. The first time I was in Palm Springs just so you wouldn't think it was me. I knew there was no other likely candidate. You had to wonder.''

"I suppose it crossed my mind, but I couldn't imagine why you'd do it.''

"I was desperate. I thought it would bring us back together. I even thought we might reconcile.''

"But not because you cared about me.''

"No,'' she said, lowering her eyes. "Because I was hoping you'd invest in that film and make me a star.''

Mac could see Jade looked relieved, happy for him. He was still stunned. Stella had just played the most dramatic scene of her life and he, ironically, was the beneficiary.

"Well, there you have it, Lieutenant Caldron,'' Stella said with a sigh. "My confession. Do you arrest me now?''

"We may as well get a formal statement and take it from there.''

"Stella, let me call Maury,'' Mac said. "You should have a lawyer with you.''

"I'll call my own attorney,'' she said.

"I'll want a statement from you, too, Mr. McGowan,'' Caldron said to Mac. "What happens from here on out will be up to the D.A.''

"Dear Lord, what a day," Stella said. "Lieutenant, shall we go? I need to get this over with and I want to talk to my son." She got to her feet. Mac, Caldron and Jade did as well. Stella offered Mac her hand. "I'm truly sorry, Mac. I hope you can forgive me."

"Stella, I'm happy to be alive and I guess I have you to thank for that."

"Only fair to warn you, I'll ask my lawyers to try to make me as comfortable as I can be in my old age. As far as money is concerned, I won't make it easy on you."

"I wouldn't expect less."

She smiled at Jade. "Goodbye, Miss Morro. I won't presume to offer you any advice, except to say this. His stubbornness can be infuriating. But he does have a soft heart." Then to Caldron. "Shall we go?"

Stella headed for the door. Caldron handed Mac another of his cards.

"Statement tomorrow?"

"Sure."

"Call me to set up a time."

The detective followed Stella out the door. When they'd gone, Mac turned to Jade.

"What's there to say after that? Even with all the surprises I've had in the last few days, if anyone had told me that Stella would essentially confess to having murdered Aubrey…"

"She backed off some," Jade said, "but maybe she understood that with Aubrey's body found, forensics would show repeated blows. What I don't understand is why she didn't let you take the fall. It would have been your word against hers."

"Maybe she was telling the truth about being tired of living the lie," he said. "After all, her dreams have been dashed."

"Or there could be a little deviousness left in the woman," Jade said.

"What do you mean?"

"Honestly?"

"Yeah."

"Book deal," Jade said. "And if she works it right, she could play herself in the movie."

Mac threw back his head and laughed. "You know, you just could be right."

"This is going to be the talk of Hollywood for months," Jade said. "The story will be all over the country. Stella's going to get the fame she's always craved, just not the way she'd hoped. And who knows, they may not convict her. There are some self-defense and justifiable-homicide arguments to be made."

"Plus, she was an abused wife. Aubrey did beat her."

"She could get a break from the prosecutors or, if it gets to that, sympathy from the jury. My guess is the worst she's facing is a manslaughter conviction."

"I hope for her sake it's not too gruesome. Stella's not truly evil, though she is selfish."

"Well, she certainly took advantage of you. Look what she put you through all those years. And recently the notes, the blackmail. Then she came here expecting you to give her a couple of million dollars."

"At least she ended up telling the truth. I can be thankful for that."

Jade put her arm around him and leaned her head on his shoulder. "Mac, I'm really happy for you."

"I'm not completely off the hook, but I've gotta tell you, I feel like a tremendous burden has been lifted," he said, caressing Jade's fingers. "The sad thing is that I wasted all these years. If I'd been tougher and smarter I'd have saved myself and some others a lot of grief."

"You know," Jade said, "I was complaining to my

friend, Ruthie, once about all the stuff I've gone through with my mother, Ricky and everything. You know what she said?''

"What?"

"She said, 'Hey, girlfriend, don't knock it. All that shit got you here, didn't it? Think about it. Isn't this where you want to be?'''

New York Times Bestselling Author

REBECCA BRANDEWYNE

DESTINY'S DAUGHTER

Determined to track down her father's killers, Bryony St. Blaze travels to England to find Hamish Neville, the one man who knows about her father's research of a secret order known as the Abbey of the Divine.

But after an attempt is made on Bryony's life, the two are forced to go into hiding, dependent on one another for their very survival. Piece by piece, they assemble the puzzle to locate the lost book her father was murdered for. But time is running out. Can they unlock the secrets of the hidden treasure before the mysterious and deadly order catches up with them?

> "I have been reading and enjoying Rebecca Brandewyne for years. She is a wonderful writer."
> —Jude Deveraux

On sale January 2001 wherever paperbacks are sold!

New York Times **Bestselling Author**

JAYNE ANN KRENTZ

Man with a PAST

Cole Stockton had a will of steel and a raw determination
to go after what he wanted—including Kelsey Murdock.
He invaded her life, assaulting her with his sensuality.
Kelsey sensed something dangerous about the man—in
the secrets he refused to share, the past that haunted
him. Involvement with Cole meant too many questions
and no answers. But when a business trip turns into a
perilous survival game, Kelsey must trust Cole's secrets
to keep them both alive.

"A master of the genre... Nobody does it better!"
—*Romantic Times Magazine*

Available December 2000
wherever paperbacks are sold!

R.J. KAISER

66625	FRUITCAKE	___ $5.99 U.S.	___ $6.99 CAN.
66510	JANE DOE	___ $5.99 U.S.	___ $6.99 CAN.
66460	PAYBACK	___ $5.99 U.S.	___ $6.99 CAN.

(limited quantities available)

TOTAL AMOUNT	$_____
POSTAGE & HANDLING	$_____
($1.00 for one book; 50¢ for each additional)	
APPLICABLE TAXES*	$_____
TOTAL PAYABLE	$_____

(check or money order—please do not send cash)

To order, complete this form and send it, along with a check or money order for the total above, payable to MIRA Books®, to: **In the U.S.:** 3010 Walden Avenue, P.O. Box 9077, Buffalo, NY 14269-9077; **In Canada:** P.O. Box 636, Fort Erie, Ontario, L2A 5X3.

Name:_____
Address:_____ City:_____
State/Prov.:_____ Zip/Postal Code:_____
Account Number (if applicable):_____
075 CSAS

*New York residents remit applicable sales taxes.
Canadian residents remit applicable GST and provincial taxes.